THE MARBLE FAUN

OR

𝕿𝖍𝖊 𝕽𝖔𝖒𝖆𝖓𝖈𝖊 𝖔𝖋 𝕸𝖔𝖓𝖙𝖊 𝕭𝖊𝖓𝖎

BY

NATHANIEL HAWTHORNE

WITH SIXTEEN FULL-PAGE
ILLUSTRATIONS

BOSTON AND NEW YORK
HOUGHTON, MIFFLIN AND COMPANY
𝕿𝖍𝖊 𝕽𝖎𝖛𝖊𝖗𝖘𝖎𝖉𝖊 𝕻𝖗𝖊𝖘𝖘, 𝕮𝖆𝖒𝖇𝖗𝖎𝖉𝖌𝖊
MDCCCC

CONTENTS.

LIST OF ILLUSTRATIONS.

INTRODUCTORY NOTE.

THE MARBLE FAUN.

THE last of Hawthorne's completed romances was
also thought by its author to be his best. "The
Marble Faun" certainly was the outcome of copious
observation and mature deliberation; and it was produced after he had rested from composition for the
space of five years. He began the book in the winter
of 1859, at Rome, while harassed by illness in his
family, and to some extent distracted by the number
of interests appealing to him on all sides — "interruptions," as he expressed it, "from things to see and
things to suffer."

He wrote to Mr. Fields at this time: "I take great
credit to myself for having sternly shut myself up for
an hour or two almost every day, and come to close
grips with a romance which I have been trying to
tear out of my mind. As for my success, I can't say
much. . . . I only know that I have produced what
seems to be a larger amount of scribble than either
of my former romances, and that portions of it interested me a good deal while I was writing them."

He had already begun to sketch the romance during the previous summer while at Florence, where
he wrote, in his journal, with reference to this new
scheme: "It leaves me little heart for journalizing

and describing new things ; and six months of unin-
terrupted monotony would be more valuable to me just
now, than the most brilliant succession of novelties."
Soon after this he removed from his quarters in the
city to the villa of Montauto on the hill called Bello-
sguardo, about a mile from Florence. This is a lovely
spot, and the view from it over the valley of the Arno
has since been described by a sympathetic traveller,
himself a poet, as suggesting an outlook upon some
" glade of heaven." The villa itself, which remains
standing, and is occasionally occupied by American
tenants, is a capacious, old-fashioned building, with a
tower, and served as the model for Donatello's ancestral home, Monte Beni. At the time of Hawthorne's
residence there, it was invested with a sort of tradition not likely to lessen its desirability for him — that
of being haunted. A murder was said to have been
committed at some epoch conveniently remote, in a
small oratory, in the tower ; and from time to time
semi-unaccountable sounds — the rustling of unseen
robes, stealthy steps, and groans from the oratory, —
were heard, which passed as evidence that the tragedy
was reënacting by the murderer and the victim. Here
Hawthorne continued, no doubt, to dream over his new
story, perhaps putting an occasional touch to it. On
the journey thence to Siena, in October, he left the
manuscript in a bag, under one of the seats in the
railway carriage ; but, as he notes down, on going to
search for his luggage, " At last the whole of our ten
trunks and tin bandbox were produced, and finally
my leather bag, in which was my journal and a manuscript book containing my sketch of a romance. It
gladdened my very heart to see it."

While in Rome, Hawthorne went on laboring and

meditating upon "The Marble Faun," the general theme and scope of which he occasionally descanted upon to his friend John Lothrop Motley, during the rambles which they took together; though the romancer never gave the historian any clew to the whole problem of his still unfinished work. Partly because of the interruptions already mentioned, and partly for other reasons, the book did not progress beyond the stage of an elaborate sketch until Hawthorne quitted the Continent. "I find this Italian air," he had said in a letter from Florence, "not favorable to the close toil of composition, although it is a very good air to dream in. I must breathe the fogs of old England, or the east-winds of Massachusetts, in order to put me into working trim." Finally, on getting to England, he systematically set about concluding his task, as Mrs. Hawthorne has explained.

"More than four months were now taken up in writing 'The Marble Faun,' in great part at the seaside town of Redcar, Yorkshire, Mr. Hawthorne having concluded to remain another year in England, chiefly to accomplish that romance. In Redcar, where he remained till September or October, he wrote no journal, but only the book. He then went to Leamington, where he finished 'The Marble Faun,' in March [1860]." [1]

"The long, hairy ears of Midas," in the "Virtuoso's Collection," have already been spoken of as furnishing a slight intimation of Hawthorne's interest in such a phenomenon,[2] long before he went to Italy. But the first positive trace of the conception, which

[1] *French and Italian Note-Books,* June 22, 1859.
[2] See the prefatory note to *Mosses from an Old Manse,* in this edition.

was to ripen into "The Marble Faun," appears in the
"French and Italian Note-Books," under the date of
April 22, 1858. Setting down a brief account of his
visit to the Capitol, Hawthorne says : —

"We afterwards went into the sculpture gallery,
where I looked at the Faun of Praxiteles, and was
sensible of a peculiar charm in it; a sylvan beauty and
homeliness, friendly and wild at once. The lengthened but not preposterous ears, and the little tail
which we infer, have an exquisite effect, and make the
spectator smile in his very heart. This race of fauns
was the most delightful of all that antiquity imagined.
It seems to me that a story, with all sorts of fun and
pathos in it, might be contrived on the idea of their
species having become intermingled with the human
race . . . the pretty hairy ears should occasionally
reappear in members of the family; and the moral
instincts and intellectual characteristics of the faun
might be most picturesquely brought out, without det-
riment to the human interest of the story. Fancy
this combination in the person of a young lady ! "

It is believed by a member of the author's family
that one of the Counts of Montauto, whose personal
appearance and grace were known to have made an
impression on Hawthorne, furnished him with suggestions which established a connection between the Faun
of Praxiteles and the Montauto villa as it afterward
appeared, under the guise of Monte Beni. This living
figure may also perhaps have assisted him in giving
reality to his conception of Donatello. The young
Italian of the romance, whose resemblance to the
statue is made an important point, receives appropri-
ately the name of a famous Italian sculptor; a name
of which the associations form a link between the mar-

ble and the man. The assertion has often been put forth in private, and it may be in print also, that Hawthorne made studies for other personages in the story from people of his acquaintance, and even from members of his own family or household. It is perhaps advisable to state here that there is no authority whatever for such an assertion, excepting the unaided fancy of those who, having known something of his connections, chose to trace purely imaginary resemblances. With the problem of Donatello's development into a being with a conscience was interwoven the mystery of Miriam's situation, concerning which no more need be said in this place than that it was evidently inspired by the author's reflections upon the story of Beatrice Cenci.[1] Of the original of Hilda's tower in the Via Portoghese, at Rome, a description is given in the "Note-Books" (May 15, 1858), together with the legend accounting for the perpetual light at the Virgin's shrine on the tower. (Among Italians, this story has imparted to the building the name of *Torre del Simio*.)

Several names were proposed for the romance, and among them "The Transformation of the Faun." This the English publishers shortened to "Transformation," while in America the work was brought out with the better known title, preferred by Hawthorne himself, "The Marble Faun: a Romance of Monte Beni." Among the many tokens of success which its publication brought to Hawthorne was a letter from Motley, with an extract from which this note may close : —

"Everything that you have ever written, I believe,

---

[1] Should the reader care to see a discussion of this matter, the ninth chapter of *A Study of Hawthorne* may be consulted.

I have read many times. . . . But the ' Romance of
Monte Beni,' has the additional charm for me that it
is the first book of yours that I have read since I had
the pleasure of making your personal acquaintance.
My memory goes back at once to those walks (alas,
not too frequent) we used to take along the Tiber, or
in the Campagna ; . . . and it is delightful to get
hold of the book now, and know that it is impossible
for you any longer, after waving your wand as you
occasionally did then, indicating where the treasure
was hidden, to sink it again beyond plummet's sound.
. . . With regard to the story, which has been somewhat criticised, I can only say that to me it is quite
satisfactory. I like those shadowy, weird, fantastic,
Hawthornesque shapes flitting through the golden
gloom which is the atmosphere of the book. I like
the misty way in which the story is indicated rather
than revealed ; the outlines are quite definite enough
from the beginning to the end, to those who have imagination enough to follow you in your airy flights ;
and to those who complain, I suppose that nothing less
than an illustrated edition, with a large gallows on the
last page, with Donatello in the most pensile of attitudes — his ears revealed through a white night-cap —
would be satisfactory."

In replying to this, Hawthorne wrote : " You work
out my imperfect efforts and half make the book with
your warm imagination ; and see what I myself saw,
but could only hint at. Well, the romance is a success, even if it never finds another reader."

G. P. L.

PREFACE.

—————◆—————

It is now seven or eight years (so many, at all events, that I cannot precisely remember the epoch) since the author of this romance last appeared before the Public. It had grown to be a custom with him to introduce each of his humble publications with a familiar kind of preface, addressed nominally to the Public at large, but really to a character with whom he felt entitled to use far greater freedom. He meant it for that one congenial friend, — more comprehensive of his purposes, more appreciative of his success, more indulgent of his shortcomings, and, in all respects, closer and kinder than a brother, — that all-sympathizing critic, in short, whom an author never actually meets, but to whom he implicitly makes his appeal whenever he is conscious of having done his best.

The antique fashion of Prefaces recognized this genial personage as the " Kind Reader," the " Gentle Reader," the " Beloved," the " Indulgent," or, at coldest, the " Honored Reader," to whom the prim old author was wont to make his preliminary explanations and apologies, with the certainty that they would be favorably received. I never personally encountered, nor corresponded through the post with this representative essence of all delightful and desirable qualities which a reader can possess. But, fortunately for myself, I never therefore concluded him to be merely a mythic

character. I had always a sturdy faith in his actual
existence, and wrote for him year after year, during
which the great eye of the Public (as well it might)
almost utterly overlooked my small productions.

Unquestionably, this gentle, kind, benevolent, indulgent, and most beloved and honored Reader did once
exist for me, and (in spite of the infinite chances
against a letter's reaching its destination without a
definite address) duly received the scrolls which I
flung upon whatever wind was blowing, in the faith
that they would find him out. But, is he extant now ?
In these many years, since he last heard from me, may
he not have deemed his earthly task accomplished, and
have withdrawn to the paradise of gentle readers,
wherever it may be, to the enjoyments of which his
kindly charity on my behalf must surely have entitled
him ? I have a sad foreboding that this may be the
truth. The "Gentle Reader," in the case of any individual author, is apt to be extremely short-lived; he
seldom outlasts a literary fashion, and, except in very
rare instances, closes his weary eyes before the writer
has half done with him. If I find him at all, it will
probably be under some mossy gravestone, inscribed
with a half-obliterated name which I shall never recognize.

Therefore, I have little heart or confidence (especially, writing as I do, in a foreign land, and after
a long, long absence from my own) to presume upon
the existence of that friend of friends, that unseen
brother of the soul, whose apprehensive sympathy has
so often encouraged me to be egotistical in my prefaces, careless though unkindly eyes should skim over
what was never meant for them. I stand upon ceremony now ; and, after stating a few particulars about

the work which is here offered to the Public, must make my most reverential bow, and retire behind the curtain.

This Romance was sketched out during a residence of considerable length in Italy, and has been rewritten and prepared for the press in England. The author proposed to himself merely to write a fanciful story, evolving a thoughtful moral, and did not purpose attempting a portraiture of Italian manners and character. He has lived too long abroad not to be aware that a foreigner seldom acquires that knowledge of a country at once flexible and profound, which may justify him in endeavoring to idealize its traits.

Italy, as the site of his Romance, was chiefly valuable to him as affording a sort of poetic or fairy precinct, where actualities would not be so terribly insisted upon as they are, and must needs be, in America. No author, without a trial, can conceive of the difficulty of writing a romance about a country where there is no shadow, no antiquity, no mystery, no picturesque and gloomy wrong, nor anything but a commonplace prosperity, in broad and simple daylight, as is happily the case with my dear native land. It will be very long, I trust, before romance-writers may find congenial and easily handled themes, either in the annals of our stalwart republic, or in any characteristic and probable events of our individual lives. Romance and poetry, ivy, lichens, and wall-flowers, need ruin to make them grow.

In rewriting these volumes, the author was somewhat surprised to see the extent to which he had introduced descriptions of various Italian objects, antique, pictorial, and statuesque. Yet these things fill the mind everywhere in Italy, and especially in Rome, and cannot easily be kept from flowing out upon the page when one writes freely, and with self-enjoyment. And, again, while reproducing the book, on the broad and dreary sands of Redcar, with the gray German Ocean tumbling in upon me, and the northern blast always howling in my ears, the complete change of scene made these Italian reminiscences shine out so vividly that I could not find it in my heart to cancel them.

An act of justice remains to be performed towards two men of genius with whose productions the author has allowed himself to use a quite unwarrantable freedom. Having imagined a sculptor in this Romance, it was necessary to provide him with such works in marble as should be in keeping with the artistic ability which he was supposed to possess. With this view, the author laid felonious hands upon a certain bust of Milton, and a statue of a pearl-diver, which he found in the studio of Mr. PAUL AKERS, and secretly conveyed them to the premises of his imaginary friend, in the Via Frezza. Not content even with these spoils, he committed a further robbery upon a magnificent statue of Cleopatra, the production of Mr. WILLIAM W. STORY, an artist whom his country and the world will not long fail to appreciate. He had thoughts of appropriating, likewise, a certain door of bronze by Mr. RANDOLPH ROGERS, representing the history of Columbus in a series of admirable bas-reliefs, but was deterred by an unwillingness to meddle with public property. Were he capable of stealing from a lady, he would certainly have made free with Miss HOSMER's admirable statue of Zenobia.

He now wishes to restore the above-mentioned beautiful pieces of sculpture to their proper owners, with many thanks, and the avowal of his sincere admiration. What he has said of them in the Romance does not partake of the fiction in which they are imbedded, but expresses his genuine opinion, which, he has little doubt, will be found in accordance with that of the Public. It is, perhaps, unnecessary to say, that, while stealing their designs, the Author has not taken a similar liberty with the personal characters of either of these gifted sculptors; his own man of marble being entirely imaginary.

LEAMINGTON, *December* 15, 1859.

many thanks, and the avowal of his sincere admiration. What he has said of them in the Romance does
not partake of the fiction in which they are imbedded,
but expresses his genuine opinion, which, he has little
doubt, will be found in accordance with that of the
Public. It is, perhaps, unnecessary to say, that, with
a similar liberty with the personal characters of either
of these gifted sculptors, his own, than of marble
being entirely imaginary.

LANKATON, December 19, 1852.

THE

ROMANCE OF MONTE BENI.

CHAPTER I.

MIRIAM, HILDA, KENYON, DONATELLO.

FOUR individuals, in whose fortunes we should be glad to interest the reader, happened to be standing in one of the saloons of the sculpture gallery in the Capitol at Rome. It was that room (the first, after ascending the staircase) in the centre of which reclines the noble and most pathetic figure of the Dying Gladiator, just sinking into his death-swoon. Around the walls stand the Antinous, the Amazon, the Lycian Apollo, the Juno ; all famous productions of antique sculpture, and still shining in the undiminished majesty and beauty of their ideal life, although the marble that embodies them is yellow with time, and perhaps corroded by the damp earth in which they lay buried for centuries. Here, likewise, is seen a symbol (as apt at this moment as it was two thousand years ago) of the Human Soul, with its choice of Innocence or Evil close at hand, in the pretty figure of a child, clasping a dove to her bosom, but assaulted by a snake.

From one of the windows of this saloon, we may see a flight of broad stone steps, descending along·

side the antique and massive foundation of the Capitol, towards the battered triumphal arch of Septimius
Severus, right below. Farther on, the eye skirts along
the edge of the desolate Forum (where Roman washerwomen hang out their linen to the sun), passing over
a shapeless confusion of modern edifices, piled rudely
up with ancient brick and stone, and over the domes
of Christian churches, built on the old pavements of
heathen temples, and supported by the very pillars
that once upheld them. At a distance beyond — yet
but a little way, considering how much history is
heaped into the intervening space — rises the great
sweep of the Coliseum, with the blue sky brightening
through its upper tier of arches. Far off, the view
is shut in by the Alban Mountains, looking just the
same, amid all this decay and change, as when Rom-
ulus gazed thitherward over his half-finished wall.

We glance hastily at these things, — at this bright
sky, and those blue distant mountains, and at the
ruins, Etruscan, Roman, Christian, venerable with a
threefold antiquity, and at the company of world-famous statues in the saloon, — in the hope of putting
the reader into that state of feeling which is experienced oftenest at Rome. It is a vague sense of ponderous remembrances; a perception of such weight
and density in a by-gone life, of which this spot was
the centre, that the present moment is pressed down
or crowded out, and our individual affairs and interests are but half as real here as elsewhere. Viewed
through this medium, our narrative — into which are
woven some airy and unsubstantial threads, intermixed with others, twisted out of the commonest stuff
of human existence — may seem not widely different
from the texture of all our lives.

Side by side with the massiveness of the Roman Past, all matters that we handle or dream of nowadays look evanescent and visionary alike.

It might be that the four persons whom we are seeking to introduce were conscious of this dreamy character of the present, as compared with the square blocks of granite wherewith the Romans built their lives. Perhaps it even contributed to the fanciful merriment which was just now their mood. When we find ourselves fading into shadows and unrealities, it seems hardly worth while to be sad, but rather to laugh as gayly as we may, and ask little reason wherefore.

Of these four friends of ours, three were artists, or connected with art; and, at this moment, they had been simultaneously struck by a resemblance between one of the antique statues, a well-known masterpiece of Grecian sculpture, and a young Italian, the fourth member of their party.

"You must needs confess, Kenyon," said a dark-eyed young woman, whom her friends called Miriam, "that you never chiselled out of marble, nor wrought in clay, a more vivid likeness than this, cunning a bust-maker as you think yourself. The portraiture is perfect in character, sentiment, and feature. If it were a picture, the resemblance might be half illusive and imaginary; but here, in this Pentelic marble, it is a substantial fact, and may be tested by absolute touch and measurement. Our friend Donatello is the very Faun of Praxiteles. Is it not true, Hilda?"

"Not quite — almost — yes, I really think so," replied Hilda, a slender, brown-haired, New England girl, whose perceptions of form and expression were wonderfully clear and delicate. "If there is any difference between the two faces, the reason may be, I suppose, that the Faun dwelt in woods and fields, and consorted with his like; whereas, Donatello has known cities a little, and such people as ourselves. But the resemblance is very close, and very strange."

"Not so strange," whispered Miriam, mischievously; "for no Faun in Arcadia was ever a greater simpleton than Donatello. He has hardly a man's share of wit, small as that may be. It is a pity there are no longer any of this congenial race of rustic creatures for our friend to consort with!"

"Hush, naughty one!" returned Hilda. "You are very ungrateful, for you well know he has wit enough to worship you, at all events."

"Then the greater fool he!" said Miriam, so bitterly that Hilda's quiet eyes were somewhat startled.

"Donatello, my dear friend," said Kenyon, in Italian, "pray gratify us all by taking the exact attitude of this statue."

The young man laughed, and threw himself into the position in which the statue has been standing for two or three thousand years. In truth, allowing for the difference of costume, and if a lion's skin could have been substituted for his modern talma, and a rustic pipe for his stick, Donatello might have figured perfectly as the marble Faun, miraculously softened into flesh and blood.

"Yes; the resemblance is wonderful," observed Kenyon, after examining the marble and the man with the accuracy of a sculptor's eye. "There is one point, however, or, rather, two points, in respect to which our friend Donatello's abundant curls will not permit us to say whether the likeness is carried into minute detail."

And the sculptor directed the attention of the party to the ears of the beautiful statue which they were contemplating.

But we must do more than merely refer to this exquisite work of art; it must be described, however inadequate may be the effort to express its magic peculiarity in words.

The Faun is the marble image of a young man, leaning his right arm on the trunk or stump of a tree, one hand hangs carelessly by his side; in the other he holds the fragment of a pipe, or some such sylvan instrument of music. His only garment — a lion's skin, with the claws upon his shoulder — falls half - way down his back, leaving the limbs and entire front of the figure nude. The form, thus displayed, is marvellously graceful, but has a fuller and more rounded outline, more flesh, and less of heroic muscle, than the old sculptors were wont to assign to their types of masculine beauty. The character of the face corresponds with the figure; it is most agreeable in outline and feature, but rounded and somewhat voluptuously developed, especially about the throat and chin; the nose is almost straight, but very slightly curves inward, thereby acquiring an indescribable charm of geniality and humor. The mouth, with its full yet delicate lips, seems so nearly to smile outright, that it calls forth a responsive smile. The whole statue — unlike anything else that ever was wrought in that severe material of marble — conveys the idea of an amiable and sensual creature, easy, mirthful, apt for jollity, yet not incapable of being touched by pathos. It is impossible to gaze long at this stone image without conceiving a kindly sentiment towards it, as if its substance were warm to the touch, and imbued with

actual life. It comes very close to some of our pleas‑
antest sympathies.

Perhaps it is the very lack of moral severity, of any
high and heroic ingredient in the character of the
Faun, that makes it so delightful an object to the hu‑
man eye and to the frailty of the human heart. The
being here represented is endowed with no principle
of virtue, and would be incapable of comprehending
such ; but he would be true and honest by dint of his
simplicity. We should expect from him no sacrifice
or effort for an abstract cause ; there is not an atom
of martyr's stuff in all that softened marble ; but he
has a capacity for strong and warm attachment, and
might act devotedly through its impulse, and even die
for it at need. It is possible, too, that the Faun might
be educated through the medium of his emotions, so
that the coarser animal portion of his nature might
eventually be thrown into the background, though
never utterly expelled.

The animal nature, indeed, is a most essential part
of the Faun's composition ; for the characteristics of
the brute creation meet and combine with those of hu‑
manity in this strange yet true and natural conception
of antique poetry and art. Praxiteles has subtly dif‑
fused throughout his work that mute mystery which
so hopelessly perplexes us whenever we attempt to
gain an intellectual or sympathetic knowledge of the
lower orders of creation. The riddle is indicated,
however, only by two definite signs ; these are the two
ears of the Faun, which are leaf-shaped, terminating
in little peaks, like those of some species of animals.
Though not so seen in the marble, they are probably
to be considered as clothed in fine, downy fur. In
the coarser representations of this class of mytholog

ical creatures, there is another token of brute kindred, — a certain caudal appendage; which, if the Faun of Praxiteles must be supposed to possess it at all, is hidden by the lion's skin that forms his garment. The pointed and furry ears, therefore, are the sole indications of his wild, forest nature.

Only a sculptor of the finest imagination, the most delicate taste, the sweetest feeling, and the rarest artistic skill — in a word, a sculptor and a poet too — could have first dreamed of a Faun in this guise, and then have succeeded in imprisoning the sportive and frisky thing in marble. Neither man nor animal, and yet no monster, but a being in whom both races meet on friendly ground. The idea grows coarse as we handle it, and hardens in our grasp. But, if the spectator broods long over the statue, he will be conscious of its spell; all the pleasantness of sylvan life, all the genial and happy characteristics of creatures that dwell in woods and fields, will seem to be mingled and kneaded into one substance, along with the kindred qualities in the human soul. Trees, grass, flowers, woodland streamlets, cattle, deer, and unsophisticated man. The essence of all these was compressed long ago, and still exists, within that discolored marble surface of the Faun of Praxiteles.

And, after all, the idea may have been no dream, but rather a poet's reminiscence of a period when man's affinity with nature was more strict, and his fellowship with every living thing more intimate and dear.

CHAPTER II.

THE FAUN.

"DONATELLO," playfully cried Miriam, "do not leave us in this perplexity! Shake aside those brown curls, my friend, and let us see whether this marvellous resemblance extends to the very tips of the ears. If so, we shall like you all the better!"

" No, no, dearest signorina," answered Donatello, laughing, but with a certain earnestness. "I entreat you to take the tips of my ears for granted." As he spoke, the young Italian made a skip and jump, light enough for a veritable faun; so as to place himself quite beyond the reach of the fair hand that was out-stretched, as if to settle the matter by actual examination. " I shall be like a wolf of the Apennines," he continued, taking his stand on the other side of the Dying Gladiator, " if you touch my ears ever so softly. None of my race could endure it. It has always been a tender point with my forefathers and me."

He spoke in Italian, with the Tuscan rusticity of accent, and an unshaped sort of utterance, betokening that he must heretofore have been chiefly conversant with rural people.

" Well, well," said Miriam, "your tender point — your two tender points, if you have them — shall be safe, so far as I am concerned. But how strange this likeness is, after all! and how delightful, if it really includes the pointed ears! Oh, it is impossible, of course," she continued, in English, "with a real and commonplace young man like Donatello; but you see how this peculiarity defines the position of the Faun; and, while putting him where he cannot exactly assert his brotherhood, still disposes us kindly towards the kindred creature. He is not supernatural, but just on the verge of nature, and yet within it. What is the nameless charm of this idea, Hilda? You can feel it more delicately than I."

"It perplexes me," said Hilda, thoughtfully, and shrinking a little; "neither do I quite like to think about it."

"But, surely," said Kenyon, "you agree with Miriam and me that there is something very touching and impressive in this statue of the Faun. In some long-past age, he must really have existed. Nature needed, and still needs, this beautiful creature; standing betwixt man and animal, sympathizing with each, comprehending the speech of either race, and interpreting the whole existence of one to the other. What a pity that he has forever vanished from the hard and dusty paths of life, — unless," added the sculptor, in a sportive whisper, "Donatello be actually he!"

"You cannot conceive how this fantasy takes hold of me," responded Miriam, between jest and earnest. "Imagine, now, a real being, similar to this mythic Faun; how happy, how genial, how satisfactory would be his life, enjoying the warm, sensuous, earthy side of nature; revelling in the merriment of woods and streams; living as our four-footed kindred do, — as mankind did in its innocent childhood; before sin, sorrow or morality itself had ever been thought of! Ah! Kenyon, if Hilda and you and I — if I, at least — had pointed ears! For I suppose the Faun had no conscience, no remorse, no burden on the heart, no troublesome recollections of any sort; no dark future either."

"What a tragic tone was that last, Miriam!" said the sculptor; and, looking into her face, he was startled to behold it pale and tear-stained. "How suddenly this mood has come over you!"

"Let it go as it came," said Miriam, "like a thunder-shower in this Roman sky. All is sunshine again, you see!"

Donatello's refractoriness as regarded his ears had evidently cost him something, and he now came close to Miriam's side, gazing at her with an appealing air, as if to solicit forgiveness. His mute, helpless gesture of entreaty had something pathetic in it, and yet might well enough excite a laugh, so like it was to what you may see in the aspect of a hound when he thinks himself in fault or disgrace. It was difficult to make out the character of this young man. So full of animal life as he was, so joyous in his deportment, so handsome, so physically well-developed, he made no impression of incompleteness, of maimed or stinted nature. And yet, in social intercourse, these familiar friends of his habitually and instinctively allowed for him, as for a child or some other lawless thing, exacting no strict obedience to conventional rules, and hardly noticing his eccentricities enough to pardon them. There was an indefinable characteristic about Donatello that set him outside of rules.

He caught Miriam's hand, kissed it, and gazed into her eyes without saying a word. She smiled, and bestowed on him a little careless caress, singularly like what one would give to a pet dog when he puts himself in the way to receive it. Not that it was so decided a caress either, but only the merest touch, somewhere between a pat and a tap of the finger ; it might be a mark of fondness, or perhaps a playful pretence of punishment. At all events, it appeared to afford Donatello exquisite pleasure ; insomuch that he danced quite round the wooden railing that fences in the Dying Gladiator.

"It is the very step of the Dancing Faun," said Miriam, apart, to Hilda. "What a child, or what a simpleton, he is! I continually find myself treating Donatello as if he were the merest unfledged chicken ; and yet he can claim no such privileges in the right of his tender age, for he is at least — how old should you think him, Hilda?"

"Twenty years, perhaps," replied Hilda, glancing at Donatello ; "but, indeed, I cannot tell ; hardly so old, on second thoughts, or possibly older. He has nothing to do with time, but has a look of eternal youth in his face."

"All underwitted people have that look," said Miriam, scornfully.

"Donatello has certainly the gift of eternal youth, as Hilda suggests," observed Kenyon, laughing; "for, judging by the date of this statue, which, I am more and more convinced, Praxiteles carved on purpose for him, he must be at least twenty-five centuries old, and he still looks as young as ever."

"What age have you, Donatello?" asked Miriam.

"Signorina, I do not know," he answered ; "no great age, however ; for I have only lived since I met you."

"Now, what old man of society could have turned a silly compliment more smartly than that!" exclaimed Miriam. "Nature and art are just at one sometimes.

But what a happy ignorance is this of our friend Donatello! Not to know his own age! It is equivalent to being immortal on earth. If I could only forget mine!"

"It is too soon to wish that," observed the sculptor; "you are scarcely older than Donatello looks."

"I shall be content, then," rejoined Miriam, "if I could only forget one day of all my life." Then she seemed to repent of this allusion, and hastily added, "A woman's days are so tedious that it is a boon to leave even one of them out of the account."

The foregoing conversation had been carried on in a mood in which all imaginative people, whether artists or poets, love to indulge. In this frame of mind, they sometimes find their profoundest truths side by side with the idlest jest, and utter one or the other, apparently without distinguishing which is the most valuable, or assigning any considerable value to either. The resemblance between the marble Faun and their living companion had made a deep, half-serious, half-mirthful impression on these three friends, and had taken them into a certain airy region, lifting up, as it is so pleasant to feel them lifted, their heavy earthly feet from the actual soil of life. The world had been set afloat, as it were, for a moment, and relieved them, for just so long, of all customary responsibility for what they thought and said.

It might be under this influence — or, perhaps, because sculptors always abuse one another's works — that Kenyon threw in a criticism upon the Dying Gladiator.

"I used to admire this statue exceedingly," he remarked, "but, latterly, I find myself getting weary and annoyed that the man should be such a length of

time leaning on his arm in the very act of death. If
he is so terribly hurt, why does he not sink down and
die without further ado? Flitting moments, imminent emergencies, imperceptible intervals between two
breaths, ought not to be incrusted with the eternal repose of marble; in any sculptural subject, there should
be a moral stand-still, since there must of necessity be
a physical one. Otherwise, it is like flinging a block
of marble up into the air, and, by some trick of enchantment, causing it to stick there. You feel that it
ought to come down, and are dissatisfied that it does
not obey the natural law."

"I see," said Miriam, mischievously, "you think
that sculpture should be a sort of fossilizing process.
But, in truth, your frozen art has nothing like the
scope and freedom of Hilda's and mine. In painting
there is no similar objection to the representation of
brief snatches of time; perhaps, because a story can
be so much more fully told in picture, and buttressed
about with circumstances that give it an epoch. For
instance, a painter never would have sent down yonder Faun out of his far antiquity, lonely and desolate,
with no companion to keep his simple heart warm."

"Ah, the Faun!" cried Hilda, with a little gesture
of impatience; "I have been looking at him too long;
and now, instead of a beautiful statue, immortally
young, I see only a corroded and discolored stone.
This change is very apt to occur in statues."

"And a similar one in pictures, surely," retorted
the sculptor. "It is the spectator's mood that trans-
figures the Transfiguration itself. I defy any painter
to move and elevate me without my own consent and
assistance."

"Then you are deficient of a sense," said Miriam.

The party now strayed onward from hall to hall of
that rich gallery, pausing here and there, to look at
the multitude of noble and lovely shapes, which have
been dug up out of the deep grave in which old Rome
lies buried. And still, the realization of the antique
Faun, in the person of Donatello, gave a more vivid
character to all these marble ghosts. Why should not
each statue grow warm with life! Antinous might
lift his brow, and tell us why he is forever sad. The
Lycian Apollo might strike his lyre; and, at the first
vibration, that other Faun in red marble, who keeps
up a motionless dance, should frisk gayly forth, leading yonder Satyrs, with shaggy goat-shanks, to clatter
their little hoofs upon the floor, and all join hands
with Donatello! Bacchus, too, a rosy flush diffusing
itself over his time-stained surface, could come down
from his pedestal, and offer a cluster of purple grapes
to Donatello's lips; because the god recognizes him
as the woodland elf who so often shared his revels.
And here, in this sarcophagus, the exquisitely carved
figures might assume life, and chase one another
round its verge with that wild merriment which is
so strangely represented on those old burial coffers:
though still with some subtile allusion to death, carefully veiled, but forever peeping forth amid emblems
of mirth and riot.

As the four friends descended the stairs, however,
their play of fancy subsided into a much more sombre mood; a result apt to follow upon such exhilaration as that which had so recently taken possession of
them.

" Do you know," said Miriam, confidentially to
Hilda, " I doubt the reality of this likeness of Donatello to the Faun, which we have been talking so much

about ? To say the truth, it never struck me so forcibly as it did Kenyon and yourself, though I gave in to whatever you were pleased to fancy, for the sake of a moment's mirth and wonder."

" I was certainly in earnest, and you seemed equally so," replied Hilda, glancing back at Donatello, as if to reassure herself of the resemblance. " But faces change so much, from hour to hour, that the same set of features has often no keeping with itself ; to an eye, at least, which looks at expression more than outline. How sad and sombre he has grown all of a sudden ! "

" Angry too, methinks ! nay, it is anger much more than sadness," said Miriam. " I have seen Donatello in this mood once or twice before. If you consider him well, you will observe an odd mixture of the bull-dog, or some other equally fierce brute, in our friend's composition ; a trait of savageness hardly to be expected in such a gentle creature as he usually is. Donatello is a very strange young man. I wish he would not haunt my footsteps so continually."

" You have bewitched the poor lad," said the sculptor, laughing. " You have a faculty of bewitching people, and it is providing you with a singular train of followers. I see another of them behind yonder pillar ; and it is his presence that has aroused Donatello's wrath."

They had now emerged from the gateway of the palace ; and partly concealed by one of the pillars of the portico stood a figure such as may often be encountered in the streets and piazzas of Rome, and nowhere else. He looked as if he might just have stepped out of a picture, and, in truth, was likely enough to find his way into a dozen pictures ; being no other than one of those living models, dark, bushy-bearded, wild of aspect and attire, whom artists convert into saints or assassins, according as their pictorial purposes demand.

" Miriam," whispered Hilda, a little startled, " it is your model ! "

CHAPTER III.

SUBTERRANEAN REMINISCENCES.

MIRIAM'S model has so important a connection with our story, that it is essential to describe the singular mode of his first appearance, and how he subsequently became a self-appointed follower of the young female artist. In the first place, however, we must devote a page or two to certain peculiarities in the position of Miriam herself.

There was an ambiguity about this young lady, which, though it did not necessarily imply anything wrong, would have operated unfavorably as regarded her reception in society, anywhere but in Rome. The truth was, that nobody knew anything about Miriam, either for good or evil. She had made her appearance without introduction, had taken a studio, put her card upon the door, and showed very considerable talent as a painter in oils. Her fellow-professors of the brush, it is true, showered abundant criticisms upon her pictures, allowing them to be well enough for the idle half-efforts of an amateur, but lacking both the trained skill and the practice that distinguish the works of a true artist.

Nevertheless, be their faults what they might, Miriam's pictures met with good acceptance among the patrons of modern art. Whatever technical merit they lacked, its absence was more than supplied by a warmth and passionateness, which she had the faculty of putting into her productions, and which all the world could feel. Her nature had a great deal of color, and, in accordance with it, so likewise had her pictures.

Miriam had great apparent freedom of intercourse; her manners were so far from evincing shyness, that it seemed easy to become acquainted with her, and not difficult to develop a casual acquaintance into intimacy. Such, at least, was the impression which she made, upon brief contact, but not such the ultimate conclusion of those who really sought to know her. So airy, free, and affable was Miriam's deportment towards all who came within her sphere, that possibly they might never be conscious of the fact; but so it was, that they did not get on, and were seldom any further advanced into her good graces to-day than yesterday. By some subtile quality, she kept people at a distance, without so much as letting them know that they were excluded from her inner circle. She resembled one of those images of light, which conjurers evoke and cause to shine before us, in apparent tangibility, only an arm's-length beyond our grasp: we make a step in advance, expecting to seize the illusion, but find it still precisely so far out of our reach. Finally, society began to recognize the impossibility of getting nearer to Miriam, and gruffly acquiesced.

There were two persons, however, whom she appeared to acknowledge as friends in the closer and truer sense of the word; and both of these more favored individuals did credit to Miriam's selection. One was a young American sculptor, of high promise and rapidly increasing celebrity; the other, a girl of the same country, a painter like Miriam herself, but in a widely different sphere of art. Her heart flowed out towards these two ; she requited herself by their society and friendship (and especially by Hilda's) for all the loneliness with which, as regarded the rest of the world, she chose to be surrounded. Her two friends were conscious of the strong, yearning grasp which Miriam laid upon them, and gave her their affection in full measure ; Hilda, indeed, responding with the fervency of a girl's first friendship, and Kenyon with a manly regard, in which there was nothing akin to what is distinctively called love.

A sort of intimacy subsequently grew up between these three friends and a fourth individual; it was a young Italian, who, casually visiting Rome, had been attracted by the beauty which Miriam possessed in a remarkable degree. He had sought her, followed her, and insisted, with simple perseverance, upon being admitted at least to her acquaintance ; a boon which had been granted, when a more artful character, seeking it by a more subtle mode of pursuit, would probably have failed to obtain it. This young man, though anything but intellectually brilliant, had many agreeable characteristics which won him the kindly and half-contemptuous regard of Miriam and her two friends. It was he whom they called Donatello, and whose wonderful resemblance to the Faun of Praxiteles forms the keynote of our narrative.

Such was the position in which we find Miriam some few months after her establishment at Rome. It must be added, however, that the world did not permit her to hide her antecedents without making her the subject of a good deal of conjecture ; as was natural enough, considering the abundance of her personal charms, and the degree of notice that she attracted as an artist. There were many stories about

Miriam's origin and previous life, some of which had a very probable air, while others were evidently wild and romantic fables. We cite a few, leaving the reader to designate them either under the probable or the romantic head.

It was said, for example. that Miriam was the daughter and heiress of a great Jewish banker (an idea perhaps suggested by a certain rich Oriental character in her face), and had fled from her paternal home to escape a union with a cousin, the heir of another of that golden brotherhood; the object being, to retain their vast accumulation of wealth within the family. Another story hinted that she was a German princess, whom, for reasons of state, it was proposed to give in marriage either to a decrepit sovereign, or a prince still in his cradle. According to a third statement, she was the offspring of a Southern American planter, who had given her an elaborate education and endowed her with his wealth; but the one burning drop of African blood in her veins so affected her with a sense of ignominy, that she relinquished all and fled her country. By still another account she was the lady of an English nobleman; and, out of mere love and honor of art, had thrown aside the splendor of her rank, and come to seek a subsistence by her pencil in a Roman studio.

In all the above cases, the fable seemed to be instigated by the large and bounteous impression which Miriam invariably made, as if necessity and she could have nothing to do with one another. Whatever deprivations she underwent must needs be voluntary. But there were other surmises, taking such a commonplace view as that Miriam was the daughter of a merchant or financier, who had been ruined in a great commercial crisis ; and, possessing a taste for art, she had attempted to support herself by the pencil, in preference to the alternative of going out as governess.

Be these things how they might, Miriam, fair as she looked, was plucked up out of a mystery, and had its roots still clinging to her. She was a beautiful and attractive woman, but based, as it were, upon a cloud, and all surrounded with misty substance; so that the result was to render her sprite-like in her most ordinary manifestations. This was the case even in respect to Kenyon and Hilda, her especial friends. But such was the effect of Miriam's natural language, her generosity, kindliness, and native truth of character, that these two received her as a dear friend into their hearts, taking her good qualities as evident and genuine, and never imagining that what was hidden must be therefore evil.

We now proceed with our narrative.

The same party of friends, whom we have seen at the sculpture gallery of the Capitol, chanced to have gone together, some months before, to the catacomb of St. Calixtus. They went joyously down into that vast tomb, and wandered by torchlight through a sort of dream, in which reminiscences of church - aisles and grimy cellars — and chiefly the latter — seemed to be broken into fragments, and hopelessly intermingled. The intricate passages along which they followed their guide had been hewn, in some forgotten age, out of a dark-red, crumbly stone. On either side were horizontal niches, where, if they held their torches closely, the shape of a human body was discernible in white ashes, into which the entire mortality of a man or woman had resolved itself. Among all this extinct dust, there might perchance be a thigh-bone, which crumbled at a touch ; or possibly a skull, grinning at its own wretched plight, as is the ugly and empty habit of the thing.

Sometimes their gloomy pathway tended upward, so that, through a crevice, a little daylight glimmered down upon them, or even a streak of sunshine peeped into a burial niche ; then again, they went downward by gradual descent, or by abrupt, rudely hewn steps, into deeper and deeper recesses of the earth. Here and there the narrow and tortuous passages widened somewhat, developing themselves into small chapels; which once, no doubt, had been adorned with marble-work and lighted with ever-burning lamps and tapers. All such illumination and ornament, however, had long since been extinguished and stript away ; except, indeed, that the low roofs of a few of these ancient sites of worship were covered with dingy stucco, and frescoed with scriptural scenes and subjects, in the dreariest stage of ruin.

In one such chapel, the guide showed them a low arch, beneath which the body of St. Cecilia had been buried after her martyrdom, and where it lay till a sculptor saw it, and rendered it forever beautiful in marble.

In a similar spot they found two sarcophagi, one containing a skeleton, and the other a shrivelled body, which still wore the garments of its former lifetime.

" How dismal all this is ! " said Hilda, shuddering. " I do not know why we came here, nor why we should stay a moment longer."

" I hate it all ! " cried Donatello, with peculiar energy. " Dear friends, let us hasten back into the blessed daylight ! "

From the first, Donatello had shown little fancy for

SAINT CECILIA

the expedition ; for, like most Italians, and in especial
accordance with the law of his own simple and physically happy nature, this young man had an infinite repugnance to graves and skulls, and to all that ghast-
liness which the Gothic mind loves to associate with
the idea of death. He shuddered, and looked fearfully round, drawing nearer to Miriam, whose attractive influence alone had enticed him into that gloomy
region.

"What a child you are, poor Donatello!" she observed, with the freedom which she always used towards him. "You are afraid of ghosts!"

"Yes, signorina; terribly afraid!" said the truthful
Donatello.

"I also believe in ghosts," answered Miriam, "and
could tremble at them, in a suitable place. But these
sepulchres are so old, and these skulls and white ashes
so very dry, that methinks they have ceased to be
haunted. The most awful idea connected with the
catacombs is their interminable extent, and the possibility of going astray into this labyrinth of darkness,
which broods around the little glimmer of our tapers."

"Has any one ever been lost here?" asked Kenyon
of the guide.

"Surely, signor; one, no longer ago than my father's time," said the guide ; and he added, with the
air of a man who believed what he was telling, "but
the first that went astray here was a pagan of old
Rome, who hid himself in order to spy out and betray
the blessed saints, who then dwelt and worshipped in
these dismal places. You have heard the story, sign-
or? A miracle was wrought upon the accursed one;
and, ever since (for fifteen centuries at least), he has

been groping in the darkness, seeking his way out of the catacomb."

"Has he ever been seen?" asked Hilda, who had great and tremulous faith in marvels of this kind.

"These eyes of mine never beheld him, signorina; the saints forbid!" answered the guide. "But it is well known that he watches near parties that come into the catacomb, especially if they be heretics, hoping to lead some straggler astray. What this lost wretch pines for, almost as much as for the blessed sunshine, is a companion to be miserable with him."

"Such an intense desire for sympathy indicates something amiable in the poor fellow, at all events," observed Kenyon.

They had now reached a larger chapel than those heretofore seen; it was of a circular shape, and, though hewn out of the solid mass of red sandstone, had pillars, and a carved roof, and other tokens of a regular architectural design. Nevertheless, considered as a church, it was exceedingly minute, being scarcely twice a man's stature in height, and only two or three paces from wall to wall; and while their collected torches illuminated this one small, consecrated spot, the great darkness spread all round it, like that immenser mystery which envelops our little life, and into which friends vanish from us, one by one.

"Why, where is Miriam?" cried Hilda.

The party gazed hurriedly from face to face, and became aware that one of their party had vanished into the great darkness, even while they were shuddering at the remote possibility of such a misfortune.

CHAPTER IV.

THE SPECTRE OF THE CATACOMB.

"SURELY, she cannot be lost!" exclaimed Kenyon. "It is but a moment since she was speaking."

"No, no!" said Hilda, in great alarm. "She was behind us all; and it is a long while since we have heard her voice!"

"Torches! torches!" cried Donatello, desperately. "I will seek her, be the darkness ever so dismal!"

But the guide held him back, and assured them all that there was no possibility of assisting their lost companion, unless by shouting at the very top of their voices. As the sound would go very far along these close and narrow passages, there was a fair probability that Miriam might hear the call, and be able to re-trace her steps.

Accordingly, they all — Kenyon with his bass voice; Donatello with his tenor; the guide with that high and hard Italian cry, which makes the streets of Rome so resonant; and Hilda with her slender scream, piercing farther than the united uproar of the rest — began to shriek, halloo, and bellow, with the utmost force of their lungs. And, not to prolong the reader's suspense (for we do not particularly seek to interest him in this scene, telling it only on account of the trouble and strange entanglement which followed), they soon heard a responsive call, in a female voice.

"It was the signorina!" cried Donatello, joyfully.

"Yes; it was certainly dear Miriam's voice," said Hilda. "And here she comes! Thank Heaven! Thank Heaven!"

The figure of their friend was now discernible by her own torchlight, approaching out of one of the cavernous passages. Miriam came forward, but not with the eagerness and tremulous joy of a fearful girl, just rescued from a labyrinth of gloomy mystery. She made no immediate response to their inquiries and tumultuous congratulations; and, as they afterwards remembered, there was something absorbed, thoughtful, and self-concentrated in her deportment. She looked pale, as well she might, and held her torch with a nervous grasp, the tremor of which was seen in the irregular twinkling of the flame. This last was the chief perceptible sign of any recent agitation or alarm.

"Dearest, dearest Miriam," exclaimed Hilda, throwing her arms about her friend, "where have you been straying from us? Blessed be Providence, which has rescued you out of that miserable darkness!"

"Hush, dear Hilda!" whispered Miriam, with a strange little laugh. "Are you quite sure that it was Heaven's guidance which brought me back. If so, it was by an odd messenger, as you will confess. See; there he stands."

Startled at Miriam's words and manner, Hilda gazed into the duskiness whither she pointed, and there beheld a figure standing just on the doubtful limit of obscurity, at the threshold of the small, illuminated chapel. Kenyon discerned him at the same instant, and drew nearer with his torch; although the guide attempted to dissuade him, averring that, once beyond the consecrated precincts of the chapel, the apparition would have power to tear him limb from limb. It struck the sculptor, however, when he afterwards recurred to these circumstances, that the guide manifested no such apprehension on his own account as he professed on behalf of others; for he kept pace with Kenyon as the latter approached the figure, though still endeavoring to restrain him.

In fine, they both drew near enough to get as good a view of the spectre as the smoky light of their torches, struggling with the massive gloom, could supply.

The stranger was of exceedingly picturesque, and even melodramatic aspect. He was clad in a voluminous cloak, that seemed to be made of a buffalo's hide, and a pair of those goat-skin breeches, with the hair outward, which are still commonly worn by the peasants of the Roman Campagna. In this garb, they look like antique Satyrs; and, in truth, the Spectre of the Catacomb might have represented the last survivor of that vanished race, hiding himself in sepulchral gloom, and mourning over his lost life of woods and streams.

Furthermore, he had on a broad-brimmed, conical hat, beneath the shadow of which a wild visage was indistinctly seen, floating away, as it were, into a dusky wilderness of mustache and beard. His eyes winked, and turned uneasily from the torches, like a creature to whom midnight would be more congenial than noonday.

On the whole, the spectre might have made a considerable impression on the sculptor's nerves, only that he was in the habit of observing similar figures, almost every day, reclining on the Spanish steps, and waiting for some artist to invite them within the magic

realm of picture. Nor, even thus familiarized with
the stranger's peculiarities of appearance, could Kenyon help wondering to see such a personage, shaping
himself so suddenly out of the void darkness of the
catacomb.

"What are you?" said the sculptor, advancing his
torch nearer. "And how long have you been wandering here?"

"A thousand and five hundred years!" muttered
the guide, loud enough to be heard by all the party.
"It is the old pagan phantom that I told you of, who
sought to betray the blessed saints!"

"Yes; it is a phantom!" cried Donatello, with a
shudder. "Ah, dearest signorina, what a fearful thing
has beset you in those dark corridors!"

"Nonsense, Donatello," said the sculptor. "The
man is no more a phantom than yourself. The only
marvel is, how he comes to be hiding himself in the
catacomb. Possibly, our guide might solve the riddle."

The spectre himself here settled the point of his
tangibility, at all events, and physical substance, by
approaching a step nearer, and laying his hand on
Kenyon's arm.

"Inquire not what I am, nor wherefore I abide in
the darkness," said he, in a hoarse, harsh voice, as if
a great deal of damp were clustering in his throat.
"Henceforth, I am nothing but a shadow behind her
footsteps. She came to me when I sought her not.
She has called me forth, and must abide the consequences of my reappearance in the world."

"Holy Virgin! I wish the signorina joy of her
prize," said the guide, half to himself. "And in any
case, the catacomb is well rid of him."

We need follow the scene no further. So much is essential to the subsequent narrative, that, during the short period while astray in those tortuous passages, Miriam had encountered an unknown man, and led him forth with her, or was guided back by him, first into the torchlight, thence into the sunshine.

It was the further singularity of this affair, that the connection, thus briefly and casually formed, did not terminate with the incident that gave it birth. As if her service to him, or his service to her, whichever it might be, had given him an indefeasible claim on Miriam's regard and protection, the Spectre of the Catacomb never long allowed her to lose sight of him, from that day forward. He haunted her footsteps with more than the customary persistency of Italian mendicants, when once they have recognized a bene-factor. For days together, it is true, he occasionally vanished, but always reappeared, gliding after her through the narrow streets, or climbing the hundred steps of her staircase and sitting at her threshold.

Being often admitted to her studio, he left his fea-tures, or some shadow or reminiscence of them, in many of her sketches and pictures. The moral at-mosphere of these productions was thereby so influ-enced, that rival painters pronounced it a case of hopeless mannerism, which would destroy all Miriam's prospects of true excellence in art.

The story of this adventure spread abroad, and made its way beyond the usual gossip of the Fores-tieri, even into Italian circles, where, enhanced by a still potent spirit of superstition, it grew far more wonderful than as above recounted. Thence, it came back among the Anglo-Saxons, and was communi-cated to the German artists, who so richly supplied it with romantic ornaments and excrescences, after their fashion, that it became a fantasy worthy of Tieck or Hoffmann. For nobody has any conscience about adding to the improbabilities of a marvellous tale.

The most reasonable version of the incident, that could anywise be rendered acceptable to the auditors, was substantially the one suggested by the guide of the catacomb, in his allusion to the legend of Memmius. This man, or demon, or man-demon, was a spy during the persecutions of the early Christians, probably under the Emperor Diocletian, and penetrated into the catacomb of St. Calixtus, with the malignant purpose of tracing out the hiding-places of the refugees. But, while he stole craftily through those dark corridors, he chanced to come upon a little chapel, where tapers were burning before an altar and a crucifix, and a priest was in the performance of his sacred office. By divine indulgence, there was a single moment's grace allowed to Memmius, during which, had he been capable of Christian faith and love, he might have knelt before the cross, and received the holy light into his soul, and so have been blest forever. But he resisted the sacred impulse. As soon, therefore, as that one moment had glided by, the light of the consecrated tapers, which represent all truth, bewildered the wretched man with everlasting error, and the blessed cross itself was stamped as a seal upon his heart, so that it should never open to receive conviction.

Thenceforth, this heathen Memmius has haunted the wide and dreary precincts of the catacomb, seeking, as some say, to beguile new victims into his own misery; but, according to other statements, endeavoring to prevail on any unwary visitor to take him by the hand, and guide him out into the daylight. Should his wiles and entreaties take effect, however, the man-demon would remain only a little while above ground. He would gratify his fiendish malignity by perpetrating signal mischief on his benefactor, and perhaps bringing some old pestilence or other forgotten and long-buried evil on society; or, possibly, teaching the modern world some decayed and dusty kind of crime, which the antique Romans knew; and then would hasten back to the catacomb, which, after so long haunting it, has grown his most congenial home.

Miriam herself, with her chosen friends, the sculptor and the gentle Hilda, often laughed at the monstrous fictions that had gone abroad in reference to her adventure. Her two confidants (for such they were, on all ordinary subjects) had not failed to ask an explanation of the mystery, since undeniably a mystery there was, and one sufficiently perplexing in itself, without any help from the imaginative faculty. And, sometimes responding to their inquiries with a melancholy sort of playfulness, Miriam let her fancy run off into wilder fables than any which German ingenuity or Italian superstition had contrived.

For example, with a strange air of seriousness over all her face, only belied by a laughing gleam in her dark eyes, she would aver that the spectre (who had been an artist in his mortal lifetime) had promised to teach her a long lost, but invaluable secret of old Roman fresco-painting. The knowledge of this process would place Miriam at the head of modern art; the sole condition being agreed upon, that she should return with him into his sightless gloom, after enriching a certain extent of stuccoed wall with the most brilliant and lovely designs. And what true votary of art would not purchase unrivalled excellence, even **at** so vast a sacrifice!

Or, if her friends still solicited a soberer account, Miriam replied, that, meeting the old infidel in one of the dismal passages of the catacomb, she had entered into controversy with him, hoping to achieve the glory and satisfaction of converting him to the Christian faith. For the sake of so excellent a result, she had even staked her own salvation against his, binding herself to accompany him back into his penal gloom, if, within a twelve-month's space, she should not have convinced him of the errors through which he had so long groped and stumbled. But, alas! up to the present time, the controversy had gone direfully in favor of the man-demon; and Miriam (as she whispered in Hilda's ear) had awful forebodings, that, in a few more months, she must take an eternal farewell of the sun!

It was somewhat remarkable that all her romantic fantasies arrived at this self-same dreary termination; it appeared impossible for her even to imagine any other than a disastrous result from her connection with her ill-omened attendant.

This singularity might have meant nothing, however, had it not suggested a despondent state of mind, which was likewise indicated by many other tokens. Miriam's friends had no difficulty in perceiving that, in one way or another, her happiness was very seriously compromised. Her spirits were often depressed into deep melancholy. If ever she was gay, it was seldom with a healthy cheerfulness. She grew moody, moreover, and subject to fits of passionate ill-temper; which usually wreaked itself on the heads of those who loved her best. Not that Miriam's indifferent acquaintances were safe from similar outbreaks of her displeasure, especially if they ventured upon any allusion to the model. In such cases, they were left with little disposition to renew the subject, but inclined, on the other hand, to interpret the whole matter as much to her discredit as the least favorable coloring of the facts would allow.

It may occur to the reader, that there was really no demand for so much rumor and speculation in regard to an incident, which might well enough have been explained without going many steps beyond the limits of probability. The spectre might have been merely a Roman beggar, whose fraternity often harbor in stranger shelters than the catacombs; or one of those pilgrims, who still journey from remote countries to kneel and worship at the holy sites, among which these haunts of the early Christians are esteemed especially sacred. Or, as was perhaps a more plausible theory, he might be a thief of the city, a robber of the Campagna, a political offender, or an assassin, with blood upon his hand; whom the negligence or connivance of the police allowed to take refuge in those subterranean fastnesses, where such outlaws have been accustomed to hide themselves from a far antiquity downward. Or he might have been a lunatic, fleeing instinctively from man, and making it his dark pleasure to dwell among the tombs, like him whose awful cry echoes afar to us from Scripture times.

And, as for the stranger's attaching himself so devotedly to Miriam, her personal magnetism might be allowed a certain weight in the explanation. For what remains, his pertinacity need not seem so very singular to those who consider how slight a link serves to connect these vagabonds of idle Italy with any person that may have the ill-hap to bestow charity, or be otherwise serviceable to them, or betray the slightest interest in their fortunes.

Thus little would remain to be accounted for, except the deportment of Miriam herself; her reserve, her brooding melancholy, her petulance, and moody passion. If generously interpreted, even these morbid symptoms might have sufficient cause in the stimulating and exhaustive influences of imaginative art, exercised by a delicate young woman, in the nervous and unwholesome atmosphere of Rome. Such, at least, was the view of the case which Hilda and Kenyon endeavored to impress on their own minds, and impart to those whom their opinions might influence.

One of Miriam's friends took the matter sadly to heart. This was the young Italian. Donatello, as we have seen, had been an eye-witness of the stranger's first appearance, and had ever since nourished a singular prejudice against the mysterious, dusky, death-scented apparition. It resembled not so much a human dislike or hatred, as one of those instinctive, unreasoning antipathies which the lower animals sometimes display, and which generally prove more trustworthy than the acutest insight into character. The shadow of the model, always flung into the light which Miriam diffused around her, caused no slight trouble to Donatello. Yet he was of a nature so remarkably genial and joyous, so simply happy, that he might well afford to have something subtracted from his comfort, and make tolerable shift to live upon what remained.

CHAPTER V.

THE court-yard and staircase of a palace built three
hundred years ago are a peculiar feature of modern
Rome, and interest the stranger more than many
things of which he has heard loftier descriptions.
You pass through the grand breadth and height of a
squalid entrance - way, and perhaps see a range of
dusky pillars, forming a sort of cloister round the
court, and in the intervals, from pillar to pillar, are
strewn fragments of antique statues, headless and leg-
less torsos, and busts that have invariably lost — what
it might be well if living men could lay aside in that
unfragrant atmosphere — the nose. Bas - reliefs, the
spoil of some far older palace, are set in the surrounding walls, every stone of which has been ravished
from the Coliseum, or any other imperial ruin which
earlier barbarism had not already levelled with the
earth. Between two of the pillars, moreover, stands
an old sarcophagus without its lid, and with all its
more prominently projecting sculptures broken off ;
perhaps it once held famous dust, and the bony framework of some historic man, although now only a re-
ceptacle for the rubbish of the court-yard, and a half-
worn broom.

In the centre of the court, under the blue Italian
sky, and with the hundred windows of the vast palace
gazing down upon it, from four sides, appears a foun-

tain.   It brims over from one stone basin to another,
or gushes from a Naiad's urn, or spurts its many little jets from the mouths of nameless monsters, which
were merely grotesque and artificial when Bernini, or
whoever was their unnatural father, first produced
them ; but now the patches of moss, the tufts of grass,
the trailing maiden - hair, and all sorts of verdant
weeds that thrive in the cracks and crevices of moist
marble, tell us that Nature takes the fountain back
into her great heart, and cherishes it as kindly as if
it were a woodland spring.   And, hark, the pleasant
murmur, the gurgle, the plash !   You might hear just
those tinkling sounds from any tiny waterfall in the
forest, though here they gain a delicious pathos from
the stately echoes that reverberate their natural language.   So the fountain is not altogether glad, after
all its three centuries at play !

In one of the angles of the court-yard, a pillared
door - way gives access to the staircase, with its spacious breadth of low, marble steps, up which, in
former times, have gone the princes and cardinals of
the great Roman family who built this palace.   Or
they have come down, with still grander and loftier
mien, on their way to the Vatican or the Quirinal,
there to put off their scarlet hats in exchange for the
triple crown.   But, in fine, all these illustrious personages have gone down their hereditary staircase for
the last time, leaving it to be the thoroughfare of ambassadors, English noblemen, American millionnaires,
artists, tradesmen, washerwomen, and people of every
degree ; all of whom find such gilded and marble-
panelled saloons as their pomp and luxury demand, or
such homely garrets as their necessity can pay for,
within this one multifarious abode.   Only, in not a

single nook of the palace (built for splendor, and the accommodation of a vast retinue, but with no vision of a happy fireside or any mode of domestic enjoyment) does the humblest or the haughtiest occupant find comfort.

Up such a staircase, on the morning after the scene at the sculpture gallery, sprang the light foot of Donatello. He ascended from story to story, passing lofty door-ways, set within rich frames of sculptured marble, and climbing unweariedly upward, until the glories of the first piano and the elegance of the middle height were exchanged for a sort of Alpine region, cold and naked in its aspect. Steps of rough stone, rude wooden balustrades, a brick pavement in the passages, a dingy whitewash on the walls; these were here the palatial features. Finally, he paused before an oaken door, on which was pinned a card, bearing the name of Miriam Schaefer, artist in oils. Here Donatello knocked, and the door immediately fell somewhat ajar; its latch having been pulled up by means of a string on the inside. Passing through a little anteroom, he found himself in Miriam's presence.

"Come in, wild Faun," she said, "and tell me the latest news from Arcady!"

The artist was not just then at her easel, but was busied with the feminine task of mending a pair of gloves.

There is something extremely pleasant, and even touching, — at least, of very sweet, soft, and winning effect, — in this peculiarity of needlework, distinguishing women from men. Our own sex is incapable of any such by-play aside from the main business of life; but women — be they of what earthly rank they may, however gifted with intellect or genius, or endowed

with awful beauty — have always some little handiwork ready to fill the tiny gap of every vacant moment.   A needle is familiar to the fingers of them all.
A queen, no doubt, plies it on occasion ; the woman
poet can use it as adroitly as her pen ; the woman's
eye, that has discovered a new star, turns from its
glory to send the polished little instrument gleaming
along the hem of her kerchief, or to darn a casual
fray in her dress.   And they have greatly the advantage of us in this respect.   The slender thread of silk
or cotton keeps them united with the small, familiar,
gentle interests of life, the continually operating influences of which do so much for the health of the
character, and carry off what would otherwise be a
dangerous accumulation of morbid sensibility.   A vast
deal of human sympathy runs along this electric line,
stretching from the throne to the wicker chair of the
humblest seamstress, and keeping high and low in a
species of communion with their kindred beings.   Methinks it is a token of healthy and gentle characteristics, when women of high thoughts and accomplish-
ments love to sew ; especially as they are never more
at home with their own hearts than while so occupied.

And when the work falls in a woman's lap, of its
own accord, and the needle involuntarily ceases to fly,
it is a sign of trouble, quite as trustworthy as the
throb of the heart itself.   This was what happened to
Miriam.   Even while Donatello stood gazing at her,
she seemed to have forgotten his presence, allowing
him to drop out of her thoughts, and the torn glove
to fall from her idle fingers.   Simple as he was, the
young man knew by his sympathies that something
was amiss.

"Dear lady, you are sad," said he, drawing close to
her.

" It is nothing, Donatello," she replied, resuming her work; " yes; a little sad, perhaps; but that is not strange for us people of the ordinary world, especially for women. You are of a cheerfuller race, my friend, and know nothing of this disease of sadness. But why do you come into this shadowy room of mine?"

" Why do you make it so shadowy?" asked he.

" We artists purposely exclude sunshine, and all but a partial light," said Miriam, " because we think it necessary to put ourselves at odds with Nature before trying to imitate her. That strikes you very strangely, does it not? But we make very pretty pictures sometimes with our artfully arranged lights and shadows. Amuse yourself with some of mine, Donatello, and by and by I shall be in the mood to begin the portrait we were talking about."

The room had the customary aspect of a painter's studio; one of those delightful spots that hardly seem to belong to the actual world, but rather to be the outward type of a poet's haunted imagination, where there are glimpses, sketches, and half-developed hints of beings and objects grander and more beautiful than we can anywhere find in reality. The windows were closed with shutters, or deeply curtained, except one, which was partly open to a sunless portion of the sky, admitting only from high upward that partial light which, with its strongly marked contrast of shadow, is the first requisite towards seeing objects pictorially. Pencil-drawings were pinned against the wall or scattered on the tables. Unframed canvases turned their backs on the spectator, presenting only a blank to the eye, and churlishly concealing whatever riches of scenery or human beauty Miriam's skill had depicted on the other side.

In the obscurest part of the room Donatello was half startled at perceiving duskily a woman with long dark hair, who threw up her arms with a wild gesture of tragic despair, and appeared to beckon him into the darkness along with her.

"Do not be afraid, Donatello," said Miriam, smiling to see him peering doubtfully into the mysterious dusk. "She means you no mischief, nor could perpetrate any if she wished it ever so much. It is a lady of exceedingly pliable disposition; now a heroine of romance, and now a rustic maid; yet all for show; being created, indeed, on purpose to wear rich shawls and other garments in a becoming fashion. This is the true end of her being, although she pretends to assume the most varied duties and perform many parts in life, while really the poor puppet has nothing on earth to do. Upon my word, I am satirical unawares, and seem to be describing nine women out of ten in the person of my lay-figure. For most purposes she has the advantage of the sisterhood. Would I were like her!"

"How it changes her aspect," exclaimed Donatello, "to know that she is but a jointed figure! When my eyes first fell upon her, I thought her arms moved, as if beckoning me to help her in some direful peril."

"Are you often troubled with such sinister freaks of fancy?" asked Miriam. "I should not have supposed it."

"To tell you the truth, dearest signorina," answered the young Italian, "I am apt to be fearful in old, gloomy houses, and in the dark. I love no dark or dusky corners, except it be in a grotto, or among the thick green leaves of an arbor, or in some nook of the woods, such as I know many in the neighborhood of my home. Even there, if a stray sunbeam steal in, the shadow is all the better for its cheerful glimmer"

"Yes; you are a Faun, you know," said the fair artist, laughing at the remembrance of the scene of the day before. "But the world is sadly changed nowadays; grievously changed, poor Donatello, since those happy times when your race used to dwell in the Arcadian woods, playing hide-and-seek with the nymphs in grottos and nooks of shrubbery. You have reappeared on earth some centuries too late."

"I do not understand you now," answered Donatello, looking perplexed; "only signorina, I am glad to have my lifetime while you live; and where you are, be it in cities or fields, I would fain be there too."

"I wonder whether I ought to allow you to speak in this way," said Miriam, looking thoughtfully at him. "Many young women would think it behoved them to be offended. Hilda would never let you speak so, I dare say. But he is a mere boy," she added, aside, "a simple boy, putting his boyish heart to the proof on the first woman whom he chances to meet. If yonder lay-figure had had the luck to meet him first, she would have smitten him as deeply as I."

"Are you angry with me?" asked Donatello, dolorously.

"Not in the least," answered Miriam, frankly giving him her hand. "Pray look over some of these sketches till I have leisure to chat with you a little. I hardly think I am in spirits enough to begin your portrait to-day."

Donatello was as gentle and docile as a pet spaniel; as playful, too, in his general disposition, or saddening with his mistress's variable mood like that or any other kindly animal which has the faculty of bestowing its sympathies more completely than men or women can ever do. Accordingly, as Miriam bade him, he tried to turn his attention to a great pile and confusion of pen-and-ink sketches and pencil-drawings which lay tossed together on a table. As it chanced, however, they gave the poor youth little delight.

The first that he took up was a very impressive sketch, in which the artist had jotted down her rough ideas for a picture of Jael driving the nail through the temples of Sisera. It was dashed off with remarkable power, and showed a touch or two that were actually life-like and death-like, as if Miriam had been standing by when Jael gave the first stroke of her murderous hammer, or as if she herself were Jael, and felt irresistibly impelled to make her bloody confession in this guise.

Her first conception of the stern Jewess had evidently been that of perfect womanhood, a lovely form, and a high, heroic face of lofty beauty; but, dissatisfied either with her own work or the terrible story itself, Miriam had added a certain wayward quirk of her pencil, which at once converted the heroine into a vulgar murderess. It was evident that a Jael like this would be sure to search Sisera's pockets as soon as the breath was out of his body.

In another sketch she had attempted the story of Judith, which we see represented by the old masters so often, and in such various styles. Here, too, beginning with a passionate and fiery conception of the subject in all earnestness, she had given the last touches in utter scorn, as it were, of the feelings which at first took such powerful possession of her hand. The head of Holofernes (which by the by had a pair of twisted mustaches, like those of a certain potentate of the day) being fairly cut off, was screwing its eyes upward and twirling its features into a diabolical grin

of triumphant malice, which it flung right in Judith's
face. On her part, she had the startled aspect that
might be conceived of a cook if a calf's head should
sneer at her when about to be popped into the dinner-
pot.

Over and over again, there was the idea of woman,
acting the part of a revengeful mischief towards man.
It was, indeed, very singular to see how the artist's
imagination seemed to run on these stories of bloodshed, in which woman's hand was crimsoned by the
stain; and how, too, — in one form or another, grotesque or sternly sad, — she failed not to bring out
the moral, that woman must strike through her own
heart to reach a human life, whatever were the motive
that impelled her.

One of the sketches represented the daughter of
Herodias receiving the head of John the Baptist in a
charger. The general conception appeared to be taken
from Bernardo Luini's picture, in the Uffizzi Gallery
at Florence; but Miriam had imparted to the saint's
face a look of gentle and heavenly reproach, with sad
and blessed eyes fixed upward at the maiden; by the
force of which miraculous glance, her whole womanhood was at once awakened to love and endless remorse.

These sketches had a most disagreeable effect on
Donatello's peculiar temperament. He gave a shudder; his face assumed a look of trouble, fear, and
disgust; he snatched up one sketch after another, as
if about to tear it in pieces. Finally, shoving away
the pile of drawings, he shrank back from the table
and clasped his hands over his eyes.

"What is the matter, Donatello?" asked Miriam,
looking up from a letter which she was now writing.

"Ah! I did not mean you to see those drawings. They are ugly phantoms that stole out of my mind; not things that I created, but things that haunt me. See! here are some trifles that perhaps will please you better."

She gave him a portfolio, the sketches in which indicated a happier mood of mind, and one, it is to be hoped, more truly characteristic of the artist. Supposing neither of these classes of subject to show anything of her own individuality, Miriam had evidently a great scope of fancy, and a singular faculty of putting what looked like heart into her productions. The latter sketches were domestic and common scenes, so finely and subtilely idealized that they seemed such as we may see at any moment, and everywhere; while still there was the indefinable something added, or taken away, which makes all the difference between sordid life and an earthly paradise. The feeling and sympathy in all of them were deep and true. There was the scene, that comes once in every life, of the lover winning the soft and pure avowal of bashful affection from the maiden whose slender form half leans towards his arm, half shrinks from it, we know not which. There was wedded affection in its successive stages, represented in a series of delicately conceived designs, touched with a holy fire, that burned from youth to age in those two hearts, and gave one identical beauty to the faces throughout all the changes of feature.

There was a drawing of an infant's shoe, half worn out, with the airy print of the blessed foot within; a thing that would make a mother smile or weep out of the very depths of her heart; and yet an actual mother would not have been likely to appreciate the

poetry of the little shoe, until Miriam revealed it to
her. It was wonderful, the depth and force with
which the above, and other kindred subjects, were depicted, and the profound significance which they often
acquired. The artist, still in her fresh youth, could
not probably have drawn any of these dear and rich
experiences from her own life; unless, perchance, that
first sketch of all, the avowal of maiden affection, were
a remembered incident, and not a prophecy. But it is
more delightful to believe that, from first to last, they
were the productions of a beautiful imagination, dealing with the warm and pure suggestions of a woman's
heart, and thus idealizing a truer and lovelier picture
of the life that belongs to woman, than an actual acquaintance with some of its hard and dusty facts could
have inspired. So considered, the sketches intimated
such a force and variety of imaginative sympathies as
would enable Miriam to fill her life richly with the
bliss and suffering of womanhood, however barren it
might individually be.

There was one observable point, indeed, betokening
that the artist relinquished, for her personal self, the
happiness which she could so profoundly appreciate
for others. In all those sketches of common life, and
the affections that spiritualize it, a figure was por-
trayed apart; now it peeped between the branches of
a shrubbery, amid which two lovers sat; now it was
looking through a frosted window, from the outside,
while a young wedded pair sat at their new fireside
within; and once it leaned from a chariot, which six
horses were whirling onward in pomp and pride, and
gazed at a scene of humble enjoyment by a cottage-
door. Always it was the same figure, and always depicted with an expression of deep sadness; and in

every instance, slightly as they were brought out, the face and form had the traits of Miriam's own.

"Do you like these sketches better, Donatello?" asked Miriam.

"Yes," said Donatello, rather doubtfully.

"Not much, I fear," responded she, laughing. "And what should a boy like you — a Faun, too — know about the joys and sorrows, the intertwining light and shadow, of human life? I forgot that you were a Faun. You cannot suffer deeply; therefore you can but half enjoy. Here, now, is a subject which you can better appreciate."

The sketch represented merely a rustic dance, but with such extravagance of fun as was delightful to behold; and here there was no drawback, except that strange sigh and sadness which always come when we are merriest.

"I am going to paint the picture in oils," said the artist; "and I want you, Donatello, for the wildest dancer of them all. Will you sit for me, some day? — or, rather, dance for me?"

"Oh, most gladly, signorina!" exclaimed Donatello. "See; it shall be like this."

And forthwith he began to dance, and flit about the studio, like an incarnate sprite of jollity, pausing at last on the extremity of one toe, as if that were the only portion of himself whereby his frisky nature could come in contact with the earth. The effect in that shadowy chamber, whence the artist had so carefully excluded the sunshine, was as enlivening as if one bright ray had contrived to shimmer in and frolic around the walls, and finally rest just in the centre of the floor.

"That was admirable!" said Miriam, with an ap-

proving smile. "If I can catch you on my canvas, it
will be a glorious picture; only I am afraid you will
dance out of it, by the very truth of the representation, just when I shall have given it the last touch.
We will try it one of these days. And now, to reward
you for that jolly exhibition, you shall see what has
been shown to no one else."

She went to her easel, on which was placed a picture with its back turned towards the spectator. Re-
versing the position, there appeared the portrait of a
beautiful woman, such as one sees only two or three,
if even so many times, in all a lifetime; so beautiful,
that she seemed to get into your consciousness and
memory, and could never afterwards be shut out, but
haunted your dreams, for pleasure or for pain; holding your inner realm as a conquered territory, though
without deigning to make herself at home there.

She was very youthful, and had what was usually
thought to be a Jewish aspect; a complexion in which
there was no roseate bloom, yet neither was it pale;
dark eyes, into which you might look as deeply as your
glance would go, and still be conscious of a depth that
you had not sounded, though it lay open to the day.
She had black, abundant hair, with none of the vulgar
glossiness of other women's sable locks; if she were
really of Jewish blood, then this was Jewish hair, and
a dark glory such as crowns no Christian maiden's
head. Gazing at this portrait, you saw what Rachel
might have been, when Jacob deemed her worth the
wooing seven years, and seven more; or perchance she
might ripen to be what Judith was, when she van-
quished Holofernes with her beauty, and slew him for
too much adoring it.

Miriam watched Donatello's contemplation of the

picture, and seeing his simple rapture, a smile of pleasure brightened on her face, mixed with a little scorn;
at least, her lips curled, and her eyes gleamed, as if
she disdained either his admiration or her own enjoyment of it.

"Then you like the picture, Donatello?" she asked.

"Oh, beyond what I can tell!" he answered. "So
beautiful! — so beautiful!"

"And do you recognize the likeness?"

"Signorina," exclaimed Donatello, turning from the
picture to the artist, in astonishment that she should
ask the question, "the resemblance is as little to be
mistaken as if you had bent over the smooth surface
of a fountain, and possessed the witchcraft to call forth
the image that you made there! It is yourself!"

Donatello said the truth; and we forbore to speak
descriptively of Miriam's beauty earlier in our narrative, because we foresaw this occasion to bring it perhaps more forcibly before the reader.

We know not whether the portrait were a flattered
likeness; probably not, regarding it merely as the delineation of a lovely face; although Miriam, like all
self-painters, may have endowed herself with certain
graces which other eyes might not discern. Artists
are fond of painting their own portraits; and, in Florence, there is a gallery of hundreds of them, including
the most illustrious, in all of which there are autobi-
ographical characteristics, so to speak; traits, expressions, loftinesses, and amenities, which would have been
invisible, had they not been painted from within. Yet
their reality and truth are none the less. Miriam, in
like manner, had doubtless conveyed some of the intimate results of her heart-knowledge into her own portrait, and perhaps wished to try whether they would

be perceptible to so simple and natural an observer as Donatello.

"Does the expression please you?" she asked.

"Yes," said Donatello, hesitatingly; "if it would only smile so like the sunshine as you sometimes do. No, it is sadder than I thought at first. Cannot you make yourself smile a little, signorina?"

"A forced smile is uglier than a frown," said Miriam, a bright, natural smile breaking out over her face even as she spoke.

"Oh, catch it now!" cried Donatello, clapping his hands. "Let it shine upon the picture! There! it has vanished already! And you are sad again, very sad; and the picture gazes sadly forth at me, as if some evil had befallen it in the little time since I looked last."

"How perplexed you seem, my friend!" answered Miriam. "I really half believe you are a Faun, there is such a mystery and terror for you in these dark moods, which are just as natural as daylight to us people of ordinary mould. I advise you, at all events, to look at other faces with those innocent and happy eyes, and never more to gaze at mine!"

"You speak in vain," replied the young man, with a deeper emphasis than she had ever before heard in his voice; "shroud yourself in what gloom you will, I must needs follow you."

"Well, well, well," said Miriam, impatiently; "but leave me now; for to speak plainly, my good friend, you grow a little wearisome. I walk this afternoon in the Borghese grounds. Meet me there, if it suits your pleasure."

CHAPTER VI.

AFTER Donatello had left the studio, Miriam herself came forth, and taking her way through some of the intricacies of the city, entered what might be called either a widening of a street, or a small piazza. The neighborhood comprised a baker's oven, emitting the usual fragrance of sour bread; a shoe-shop; a linen-draper's shop; a pipe and cigar shop; a lottery office; a station for French soldiers, with a sentinel pacing in front; and a fruit-stand, at which a Roman matron was selling the dried kernels of chestnuts, wretched little figs, and some bouquets of yesterday. A church, of course, was near at hand, the façade of which ascended into lofty pinnacles, whereon were perched two or three winged figures of stone, either angelic or allegorical, blowing stone trumpets in close vicinity to the upper windows of an old and shabby palace. This palace was distinguished by a feature not very common in the architecture of Roman edifices; that is to say, a mediæval tower, square, massive, lofty, and battlemented and machicolated at the summit.

At one of the angles of the battlements stood a shrine of the Virgin, such as we see everywhere at the street-corners of Rome, but seldom or never, except in this solitary instance, at a height above the ordinary level of men's views and aspirations. Connected

with this old tower and its lofty shrine, there is a
legend which we cannot here pause to tell; but for
centuries a lamp has been burning before the Virgin's
image, at noon, at midnight, and at all hours of the
twenty - four, and must be kept burning forever, as
long as the tower shall stand; or else the tower itself, the palace, and whatever estate belongs to it,
shall pass from its hereditary possessor, in accordance
with an ancient vow, and become the property of the
Church.

As Miriam approached, she looked upward, and
saw, — not, indeed, the flame of the never-dying lamp,
which was swallowed up in the broad sunlight that
brightened the shrine, but a flock of white doves,
skimming, fluttering, and wheeling about the topmost
height of the tower, their silver wings flashing in the
pure transparency of the air. Several of them sat on
the ledge of the upper window, pushing one another
off by their eager struggle for this favorite station,
and all tapping their beaks and flapping their wings
tumultuously against the panes; some had alighted in
the street, far below, but flew hastily upward, at the
sound of the window being thrust ajar, and opening in
the middle, on rusty hinges, as Roman windows do.

A fair young girl, dressed in white, showed herself
at the aperture for a single instant, and threw forth
as much as her two small hands could hold of some
kind of food, for the flock of eleemosynary doves. It
seemed greatly to the taste of the feathered people;
for they tried to snatch beakfuls of it from her grasp,
caught it in the air, and rushed downward after it
upon the pavement.

"What a pretty scene this is," thought Miriam, with
a kindly smile, "and how like a dove she is herself,

the fair, pure creature! The other doves know her for a sister, I am sure."

Miriam passed beneath the deep portal of the palace, and turning to the left, began to mount flight after flight of a staircase, which, for the loftiness of its aspiration, was worthy to be Jacob's ladder, or, at all events, the staircase of the Tower of Babel. The city bustle, which is heard even in Rome, the rumble of wheels over the uncomfortable paving-stones, the hard harsh cries reëchoing in the high and narrow streets, grew faint and died away; as the turmoil of the world will always die, if we set our faces to climb heavenward. Higher, and higher still; and now, glancing through the successive windows that threw in their narrow light upon the stairs, her view stretched across the roofs of the city, unimpeded even by the stateliest palaces. Only the domes of churches ascend into this airy region, and hold up their golden crosses on a level with her eye; except, that, out of the very heart of Rome, the column of Antoninus thrusts itself upward, with St. Paul upon its summit, the sole human form that seems to have kept her company.

Finally, the staircase came to an end; save that, on one side of the little entry where it terminated, a flight of a dozen steps gave access to the roof of the tower and the legendary shrine. On the other side was a door, at which Miriam knocked, but rather as a friendly announcement of her presence than with any doubt of hospitable welcome; for, awaiting no response, she lifted the latch and entered.

"What a hermitage you have found for yourself, dear Hilda!" she exclaimed. "You breathe sweet air, above all the evil scents of Rome; and even so, in your maiden elevation, you dwell above our vanities and passions, our moral dust and mud, with the doves and the angels for your nearest neighbors. I should not wonder if the Catholics were to make a saint of you, like your namesake of old; especially as you have almost avowed yourself of their religion, by undertaking to keep the lamp alight before the Virgin's shrine."

"No, no, Miriam!" said Hilda, who had come joyfully forward to greet her friend. "You must not call me a Catholic. A Christian girl — even a daughter of the Puritans — may surely pay honor to the idea of divine Womanhood, without giving up the faith of her forefathers. But how kind you are to climb into my dove-cote!"

"It is no trifling proof of friendship, indeed," answered Miriam; "I should think there were three hundred stairs at least."

"But it will do you good," continued Hilda. "A height of some fifty feet above the roofs of Rome gives me all the advantages that I could get from fifty miles of distance. The air so exhilarates my spirits, that sometimes I feel half inclined to attempt a flight from the top of my tower, in the faith that I should float upward."

"Oh, pray don't try it!" said Miriam, laughing. "If it should turn out that you are less than an angel, you would find the stones of the Roman pavement very hard; and if an angel, indeed, I am afraid you would never come down among us again."

This young American girl was an example of the freedom of life which it is possible for a female artist to enjoy at Rome. She dwelt in her tower, as free to descend into the corrupted atmosphere of the city be-

neath, as one of her companion doves to fly **downward**
into the street ; — all alone, perfectly independent, under her own sole guardianship, unless watched over by
the Virgin, whose shrine she tended ; doing what she
liked without a suspicion or a shadow upon the snowy
whiteness of her fame.   The customs of artist life
bestow such liberty upon the sex, which is elsewhere
restricted within so much narrower limits ; and it is
perhaps an indication that, whenever we admit women
to a wider scope of pursuits and professions, we must
also remove the shackles of our present conventional
rules, which would then become an insufferable restraint on either maid or wife.   The system seems to
work unexceptionably in Rome ; and in many other
cases, as in Hilda's, purity of heart and life are allowed to assert themselves, and to be their own proof
and security, to a degree unknown in the society of
other cities.

Hilda, in her native land, had early shown what was
pronounced by connoisseurs a decided genius for the
pictorial art.   Even in her school-days — still not so
very distant — she had produced sketches that were
seized upon by men of taste, and hoarded as among
the choicest treasures of their portfolios ; scenes delicately imagined, lacking, perhaps, the reality which
comes only from a close acquaintance with life, but so
softly touched with feeling and fancy, that you seemed
to be looking at humanity with angels' eyes.   With
years and experience she might be expected to attain
a darker and more forcible touch, which would impart
to her designs the relief they needed.   Had Hilda remained in her own country, it is not improbable that
she might have produced original works worthy to
hang in that gallery of native art which, we hope, is

destined to extend its rich length through many future centuries. An orphan, however, without near relatives, and possessed of a little property, she had found it within her possibilities to come to Italy; that central clime, whither the eyes and the heart of every artist turn, as if pictures could not be made to glow in any other atmosphere, as if statues could not assume grace and expression, save in that land of whitest marble.

Hilda's gentle courage had brought her safely over land and sea; her mild, unflagging perseverance had made a place for her in the famous city, even like a flower that finds a chink for itself, and a little earth to grow in, on whatever ancient wall its slender roots may fasten. Here she dwelt, in her tower, possessing a friend or two in Rome, but no home companion except the flock of doves, whose cote was in a ruinous chamber contiguous to her own. They soon became as familiar with the fair-haired Saxon girl as if she were a born sister of their brood; and her customary white robe bore such an analogy to their snowy plumage that the confraternity of artists called Hilda the Dove, and recognized her aerial apartment as the Dove-cote. And while the other doves flew far and wide in quest of what was good for them, Hilda likewise spread her wings, and sought such ethereal and imaginative sustenance as God ordains for creatures of her kind.

We know not whether the result of her Italian studies, so far as it could yet be seen, will be accepted as a good or desirable one. Certain it is, that since her arrival in the pictorial land, Hilda seemed to have entirely lost the impulse of original design, which brought her thither. No doubt the girl's early dreams had been of sending forms and hues of beauty into the visible world out of her own mind ; of compelling scenes of poetry and history to live before men's eyes, through conceptions and by methods individual to herself. But more and more, as she grew familiar with the miracles of art that enrich so many galleries in Rome, Hilda had ceased to consider herself as an original artist. No wonder that this change should have befallen her. She was endowed with a deep and sensitive faculty of appreciation ; she had the gift of discerning and worshipping excellence in a most unusual measure. No other person, it is probable, recognized so adequately, and enjoyed with such deep delight, the pictorial wonders that were here displayed. She saw — no, not saw, but felt — through and through a picture ; she bestowed upon it all the warmth and richness of a woman's sympathy ; not by any intellectual effort, but by this strength of heart, and this guiding light of sympathy, she went straight to the central point, in which the master had conceived his work. Thus, she viewed it, as it were, with his own eyes, and hence her comprehension of any picture that interested her was perfect.

This power and depth of appreciation depended partly upon Hilda's physical organization, which was at once healthful and exquisitely delicate ; and, connected with this advantage, she had a command of hand, a nicety and force of touch, which is an endowment separate from pictorial genius, though indispensable to its exercise.

It has probably happened in many other instances, as it did in Hilda's case, that she ceased to aim at original achievement in consequence of the very gifts which so exquisitely fitted her to profit by familiarity

with the works of the mighty old masters. Reverenc-
ing these wonderful men so deeply, she was too grateful for all they bestowed upon her, too loyal, too humble, in their awful presence, to think of enrolling
herself in their society. Beholding the miracles of
beauty which they had achieved, the world seemed already rich enough in original designs, and nothing
more was so desirable as to diffuse those self - same
beauties more widely among mankind. All the youthful hopes and ambitions, the fanciful ideas which she
had brought from home, of great pictures to be conceived in her feminine mind, were flung aside, and, so
far as those most intimate with her could discern, relinquished without a sigh. All that she would henceforth attempt — and that most reverently, not to say
religiously — was to catch and reflect some of the
glory which had been shed upon canvas from the immortal pencils of old.

So Hilda became a copyist : in the Pinacotheca of
the Vatican, in the galleries of the Pamfili-Doria palace, the Borghese, the Corsini, the Sciarra, her easel
was set up before many a famous picture by Guido,
Domenichino, Raphael, and the devout painters of
earlier schools than these. Other artists and visitors
from foreign lands beheld the slender, girlish figure
in front of some world-known work, absorbed, unconscious of everything around her, seeming to live only
in what she sought to do. They smiled, no doubt, at
the audacity which led her to dream of copying those
mighty achievements. But, if they paused to look
over her shoulder, and had sensibility enough to understand what was before their eyes, they soon felt
inclined to believe that the spirits of the old masters
were hovering over Hilda, and guiding her delicate

white hand. In truth, from whatever realm of bliss
and many-colored beauty those spirits might descend,
it would have been no unworthy errand to help so
gentle and pure a worshipper of their genius in giving
the last divine touch to her repetitions of their works.

Her copies were indeed marvellous. Accuracy was
not the phrase for them ; a Chinese copy is accurate.
Hilda's had that evanescent and ethereal life — that
flitting fragrance, as it were, of the originals — which
it is as difficult to catch and retain as it would be for
a sculptor to get the very movement and varying color
of a living man into his marble bust. Only by watching the efforts of the most skilful copyists — men who
spend a lifetime, as some of them do, in multiplying
copies of a single picture — and observing how invariably they leave out just the indefinable charm that in-
volves the last, inestimable value, can we understand
the difficulties of the task which they undertake.

It was not Hilda's general practice to attempt reproducing the whole of a great picture, but to select some
high, noble, and delicate portion of it, in which the
spirit and essence of the picture culminated : the Virgin's celestial sorrow, for example, or a hovering angel, imbued with immortal light, or a saint with the
glow of heaven in his dying face, — and these would
be rendered with her whole soul. If a picture had
darkened into an indistinct shadow through time and
neglect, or had been injured by cleaning, or retouched
by some profane hand, she seemed to possess the
faculty of seeing it in its pristine glory. The copy
would come from her hands with what the beholder
felt must be the light which the old master had left
upon the original in bestowing his final and most
ethereal touch. In some instances even (at least, so

those believed who best appreciated Hilda's power and
sensibility) she had been enabled to execute what the
great master had conceived in his imagination, but had
not so perfectly succeeded in putting upon canvas ; a
result surely not impossible when such depth of sympathy as she possessed was assisted by the delicate skill
and accuracy of her slender hand. In such cases the
girl was but a finer instrument, a more exquisitely effective piece of mechanism, by the help of which the
spirit of some great departed painter now first achieved
his ideal, centuries after his own earthly hand, that
other tool, had turned to dust.

Not to describe her as too much a wonder, however,
Hilda, or the Dove, as her well-wishers half laughingly
delighted to call her, had been pronounced by good
judges incomparably the best copyist in Rome.   After
minute examination of her works, the most skilful
artists declared that she had been led to her results
by following precisely the same process step by step
through which the original painter had trodden to the
development of his idea.   Other copyists — if such
they are worthy to be called — attempt only a super-
ficial imitation.   Copies of the old masters in this
sense are produced by thousands ; there are artists, as
we have said, who spend their lives in painting the
works, or perhaps one single work, of one illustrious
painter over and over again : thus they convert themselves into Guido machines, or Raphaelic machines.
Their performances, it is true, are often wonderfully
deceptive to a careless eye ; but working entirely from
the outside, and seeking only to reproduce the surface,
these men are sure to leave out that indefinable nothing, that inestimable something, that constitutes the
life and soul through which the picture gets its im-

mortality. Hilda was no such machine as this; she wrought religiously, and therefore wrought a miracle.

It strikes us that there is something far higher and nobler in all this, in her thus sacrificing herself to the devout recognition of the highest excellence in art, than there would have been in cultivating her not inconsiderable share of talent for the production of works from her own ideas. She might have set up for herself, and won no ignoble name; she might have helped to fill the already crowded and cumbered world with pictures, not destitute of merit, but falling short, if by ever so little, of the best that has been done; she might thus have gratified some tastes that were incapable of appreciating Raphael. But this could be done only by lowering the standard of art to the comprehension of the spectator. She chose the better and loftier and more unselfish part, laying her individual hopes, her fame, her prospects of enduring remembrance, at the feet of those great departed ones, whom she so loved and venerated; and therefore the world was the richer for this feeble girl.

Since the beauty and glory of a great picture are confined within itself, she won out that glory by patient faith and self-devotion, and multiplied it for mankind. From the dark, chill corner of a gallery, — from some curtained chapel in a church, where the light came seldom and aslant, — from the prince's carefully guarded cabinet, where not one eye in thousands was permitted to behold it, — she brought the wondrous picture into daylight, and gave all its magic splendor for the enjoyment of the world. Hilda's faculty of genuine admiration is one of the rarest to be found in human nature; and let us try to recompense her in kind by admiring her generous self-surrender, and her brave, humble magnanimity in choosing to be the handmaid of those old magicians, instead of a minor enchantress within a circle of her own.

The handmaid of Raphael, whom she loved with a virgin's love! Would it have been worth Hilda's while to relinquish this office for the sake of giving the world a picture or two which it would call original; pretty fancies of snow and moonlight; the counterpart in picture of so many feminine achievements in literature!

CHAPTER VII.

BEATRICE.

MIRIAM was glad to find the Dove in her turret-home ; for being endowed with an infinite activity, and taking exquisite delight in the sweet labor of which her life was full, it was Hilda's practice to flee abroad betimes, and haunt the galleries till dusk. Happy were those (but they were very few) whom she ever chose to be the companions of her day; they saw the art-treasures of Rome, under her guidance, as they had never seen them before. Not that Hilda could dissertate, or talk learnedly about pictures; she would probably have been puzzled by the technical terms of her own art. Not that she had much to say about what she most profoundly admired; but even her silent sympathy was so powerful that it drew your own along with it, endowing you with a second-sight that enabled you to see excellences with almost the depth and delicacy of her own perceptions.

All the Anglo-Saxon denizens of Rome, by this time, knew Hilda by sight. Unconsciously, the poor child had become one of the spectacles of the Eternal City, and was often pointed out to strangers, sitting at her easel among the wild-bearded young men, the white-haired old ones, and the shabbily dressed, painfully plain women, who make up the throng of copyists. The old custodes knew her well, and watched over her as their own child. Sometimes a young artist, instead of going on with a copy of the picture before which he had placed his easel, would enrich his canvas with an original portrait of Hilda at her work. A lovelier subject could not have been selected, nor one which required nicer skill and insight in doing it anything like justice. She was pretty at all times, in our native New England style, with her light-brown ringlets, her delicately tinged, but healthful cheek, her sensitive, intelligent, yet most feminine and kindly face. But, every few moments, this pretty and girlish face grew beautiful and striking, as some inward thought and feeling brightened, rose to the surface, and then, as it were, passed out of sight again; so that, taking into view this constantly recurring change, it really seemed as if Hilda were only visible by the sunshine of her soul.

In other respects, she was a good subject for a portrait, being distinguished by a gentle picturesqueness, which was perhaps unconsciously bestowed by some minute peculiarity of dress, such as artists seldom fail to assume. The effect was to make her appear like an inhabitant of picture-land, a partly ideal creature, not to be handled, nor even approached too closely. In her feminine self, Hilda was natural, and of pleasant deportment, endowed with a mild cheerfulness of temper, not overflowing with animal spirits, but never long despondent. There was a certain simplicity that made every one her friend, but it was combined with a subtile attribute of reserve, that insensibly kept those at a distance who were not suited to her sphere.

Miriam was the dearest friend whom she had ever known. Being a year or two the elder, of longer acquaintance with Italy, and better fitted to deal with its crafty and selfish inhabitants, she had helped Hilda to arrange her way of life, and had encouraged her through those first weeks, when Rome is so dreary to every new-comer.

"But how luckily that you are at home to-day," said Miriam, continuing the conversation which was begun, many pages back. "I hardly hoped to find you, though I had a favor to ask, — a commission to put into your charge. But what picture is this?"

"See!" said Hilda, taking her friend's hand, and leading her in front of the easel. "I wanted your opinion of it."

"If you have really succeeded," observed Miriam, recognizing the picture at the first glance, "it will be the greatest miracle you have yet achieved."

The picture represented simply a female head; a very youthful, girlish, perfectly beautiful face, enveloped in white drapery, from beneath which strayed a lock or two of what seemed a rich, though hidden luxuriance of auburn hair. The eyes were large and brown, and met those of the spectator, but evidently with a strange, ineffectual effort to escape. There was a little redness about the eyes, very slightly indicated, so that you would question whether or no the girl had been weeping. The whole face was quiet; there was no distortion or disturbance of any single feature; nor was it easy to see why the expression was not cheerful, or why a single touch of the artist's pencil should not brighten it into joyousness. But, in fact, it was the very saddest picture ever painted or conceived; it involved an unfathomable depth of sorrow, the sense of which came to the observer by a sort of intuition. It was a sorrow that removed this beautiful girl out of the sphere of humanity, and set her in a far-off region, the remoteness of which—

while yet her face is so close before us — makes us shiver as at a spectre.

"Yes, Hilda," said her friend, after closely examining the picture, "you have done nothing else so wonderful as this. But by what unheard-of solicitations or secret interest have you obtained leave to copy Guido's Beatrice Cenci? It is an unexampled favor; and the impossibility of getting a genuine copy has filled the Roman picture-shops with Beatrices, gay, grievous, or coquettish, but never a true one among them."

"There has been one exquisite copy, I have heard," said Hilda, "by an artist capable of appreciating the spirit of the picture. It was Thompson, who brought it away piecemeal, being forbidden (like the rest of us) to set up his easel before it. As for me, I knew the Prince Barberini would be deaf to all entreaties; so I had no resource but to sit down before the picture, day after day, and let it sink into my heart. I do believe it is now photographed there. It is a sad face to keep so close to one's heart; only, what is so very beautiful can never be quite a pain. Well; after studying it in this way, I know not how many times, I came home, and have done my best to transfer the image to canvas."

"Here it is then," said Miriam, contemplating Hilda's work with great interest and delight, mixed with the painful sympathy that the picture excited. "Everywhere we see oil-paintings, crayon-sketches, cameos, engravings, lithographs, pretending to be Beatrice, and representing the poor girl with blubbered eyes, a leer of coquetry, a merry look as if she were dancing, a piteous look as if she were beaten, and twenty other modes of fantastic mistake. But here is Guido's very Beatrice; she that slept in the dungeon, and awoke, betimes, to ascend the scaffold. And now that you have done it, Hilda, can you interpret what the feeling is, that gives this picture such a mysterious force? For my part, though deeply sensible of its influence, I cannot seize it."

"Nor can I, in words," replied her friend. "But while I was painting her, I felt all the time as if she were trying to escape from my gaze. She knows that her sorrow is so strange and so immense, that she ought to be solitary forever, both for the world's sake and her own; and this is the reason we feel such a distance between Beatrice and ourselves, even when our eyes meet hers. It is infinitely heart-breaking to meet her glance, and to feel that nothing can be done to help or comfort her; neither does she ask help or comfort, knowing the hopelessness of her case better than we do. She is a fallen angel, — fallen, and yet sinless; and it is only this depth of sorrow, with its weight and darkness, that keeps her down upon earth, and brings her within our view even while it sets her beyond our reach."

"You deem her sinless?" asked Miriam; "that is not so plain to me. If I can pretend to see at all into that dim region, whence she gazes so strangely and sadly at us, Beatrice's own conscience does not acquit her of something evil, and never to be forgiven!"

"Sorrow so black as hers oppresses her very nearly as sin would," said Hilda.

"Then," inquired Miriam, "do you think that there was no sin in the deed for which she suffered?"

"Ah!" replied Hilda, shuddering, "I really had quite forgotten Beatrice's history, and was thinking of her only as the picture seems to reveal her character. Yes, yes; it was terrible guilt, an inexpiable crime,

GUIDO'S BEATRICE CENCI

and she feels it to be so. Therefore it is that the forlorn creature so longs to elude our eyes, and forever vanish away into nothingness! Her doom is just!"

"O Hilda, your innocence is like a sharp steel sword!" exclaimed her friend. "Your judgments are often terribly severe, though you seem all made up of gentleness and mercy. Beatrice's sin may not have been so great: perhaps it was no sin at all, but the best virtue possible in the circumstances. If she viewed it as a sin, it may have been because her nature was too feeble for the fate imposed upon her. Ah!" continued Miriam, passionately, "if I could only get within her consciousness! — if I could but clasp Beatrice Cenci's ghost, and draw it into myself! I would give my life to know whether she thought herself innocent, or the one great criminal since time began."

As Miriam gave utterance to these words, Hilda looked from the picture into her face, and was startled to observe that her friend's expression had become almost exactly that of the portrait; as if her passionate wish and struggle to penetrate poor Beatrice's mystery had been successful.

"Oh, for Heaven's sake, Miriam, do not look so!" she cried. "What an actress you are! And I never guessed it before. Ah! now you are yourself again!" she added, kissing her. "Leave Beatrice to me in future."

"Cover up your magical picture, then," replied her friend, "else I never can look away from it. It is strange, dear Hilda, how an innocent, delicate, white soul like yours has been able to seize the subtle mystery of this portrait; as you surely must, in order to reproduce it so perfectly. Well; we will not talk of it any more. Do you know, I have come to you this morning on a small matter of business. Will you undertake it for me?"

"Oh, certainly," said Hilda, laughing; "if you choose to trust me with business."

"Nay, it is not a matter of any difficulty," answered Miriam; "merely to take charge of this packet, and keep it for me awhile."

"But why not keep it yourself?" asked Hilda.

"Partly because it will be safer in your charge," said her friend. "I am a careless sort of person in ordinary things; while you, for all you dwell so high above the world, have certain little housewifely ways of accuracy and order. The packet is of some slight importance; and yet, it may be, I shall not ask you for it again. In a week or two, you know, I am leaving Rome. You, setting at defiance the malarial fever, mean to stay here and haunt your beloved galleries through the summer. Now, four months hence, unless you hear more from me, I would have you deliver the packet according to its address."

Hilda read the direction; it was to Signore Luca Barboni, at the Palazzo Cenci, third piano.

"I will deliver it with my own hand," said she, "precisely four months from to-day, unless you bid me to the contrary. Perhaps I shall meet the ghost of Beatrice in that grim old palace of her forefathers."

"In that case," rejoined Miriam, "do not fail to speak to her, and try to win her confidence. Poor thing! she would be all the better for pouring her heart out freely, and would be glad to do it, if she were sure of sympathy. It irks my brain and heart to think of her, all shut up within herself." She withdrew the cloth that Hilda had drawn over the picture, and took another long look at it, — "Poor sister Beatrice! for she was still a woman, Hilda, still a sister, be her sin or sorrow what they might. How well you have done it, Hilda! I know not whether Guido will thank you, or be jealous of your rivalship."

"Jealous, indeed!" exclaimed Hilda. "If Guido had not wrought through me, my pains would have been thrown away."

"After all," resumed Miriam, "if a woman had painted the original picture, there might have been something in it which we miss now. I have a great mind to undertake a copy myself, and try to give it what it lacks. Well; good-by. But, stay! I am going for a little airing to the grounds of the Villa Borghese this afternoon. You will think it very foolish, but I always feel the safer in your company, Hilda, slender little maiden as you are. Will you come?"

"Ah, not to-day, dearest Miriam," she replied; "I have set my heart on giving another touch or two to this picture, and shall not stir abroad till nearly sunset."

"Farewell, then," said her visitor. "I leave you in your dove-cote. What a sweet, strange life you lead here; conversing with the souls of the old masters, feeding and fondling your sister-doves, and trimming the Virgin's lamp! Hilda, do you ever pray to the Virgin while you tend her shrine?"

"Sometimes I have been moved to do so," replied the Dove, blushing, and lowering her eyes; "she was a woman once. Do you think it would be wrong?"

"Nay, that is for you to judge," said Miriam; "but when you pray next, dear friend, remember me!"

She went down the long descent of the lower staircase, and just as she reached the street the flock of doves again took their hurried flight from the pavement to the topmost window. She threw her eyes upward and beheld them hovering about Hilda's head; for, after her friend's departure, the girl had been more impressed than before by something very sad and troubled in her manner. She was, therefore, leaning forth from her airy abode, and flinging down a kind, maidenly kiss, and a gesture of farewell, in the hope that these might alight upon Miriam's heart, and comfort its unknown sorrow a little. Kenyon the sculptor, who chanced to be passing the head of the street, took note of that ethereal kiss, and wished that he could have caught it in the air and got Hilda's leave to keep it.

CHAPTER VIII.

THE SUBURBAN VILLA.

Donatello, while it was still a doubtful question betwixt afternoon and morning, set forth to keep the appointment which Miriam had carelessly tendered him in the grounds of the Villa Borghese.

The entrance to these grounds (as all my readers know, for everybody nowadays has been in Rome) is just outside of the Porta del Popolo. Passing beneath that not very impressive specimen of Michael Angelo's architecture, a minute's walk will transport the visitor from the small, uneasy, lava stones of the Roman pavement into broad, gravelled carriage-drives, whence a little farther stroll brings him to the soft turf of a beautiful seclusion. A seclusion, but seldom a solitude; for priest, noble, and populace, stranger and native, all who breathe Roman air, find free admission, and come hither to taste the languid enjoyment of the day-dream that they call life.

But Donatello's enjoyment was of a livelier kind. He soon began to draw long and delightful breaths among those shadowy walks. Judging by the pleasure which the sylvan character of the scene excited in him, it might be no merely fanciful theory to set him down as the kinsman, not far remote, of that wild, sweet, playful, rustic creature, to whose marble image he bore so striking a resemblance. How mirthful a discovery would it be (and yet with a touch of pathos

in it), if the breeze which sported fondly with his
clustering locks were to waft them suddenly aside,
and show a pair of leaf-shaped, furry ears! What an
honest strain of wildness would it indicate! and into
what regions of rich mystery would it extend Donatello's sympathies, to be thus linked (and by no monstrous chain) with what we call the inferior tribes of
being, whose simplicity, mingled with his human intelligence, might partly restore what man has lost of
the divine!

The scenery amid which the youth now strayed was
such as arrays itself in the imagination when we read
the beautiful old myths, and fancy a brighter sky, a
softer turf, a more picturesque arrangement of venerable trees, than we find in the rude and untrained
landscapes of the Western world. The ilex-trees, so
ancient and time-honored were they, seemed to have
lived for ages undisturbed, and to feel no dread of
profanation by the axe any more than overthrow by
the thunder-stroke. It had already passed out of
their dreamy old memories that only a few years ago
they were grievously imperilled by the Gaul's last assault upon the walls of Rome. As if confident in the
long peace of their lifetime, they assumed attitudes of
indolent repose. They leaned over the green turf in
ponderous grace, throwing abroad their great branches
without danger of interfering with other trees, though
other majestic trees grew near enough for dignified
society, but too distant for constraint. Never was
there a more venerable quietude than that which slept
among their sheltering boughs; never a sweeter sunshine than that now gladdening the gentle gloom
which these leafy patriarchs strove to diffuse over the
swelling and subsiding lawns.

In other portions of the grounds the stone-pines lifted their dense clump of branches upon a slender length of stem, so high that they looked like green islands in the air, flinging down a shadow upon the turf so far off that you hardly knew which tree had made it. Again, there were avenues of cypress, resembling dark flames of huge funeral candles, which spread dusk and twilight round about them instead of cheerful radiance. The more open spots were all a-bloom, even so early in the season, with anemones of wondrous size, both white and rose-colored, and violets that betrayed themselves by their rich fragrance, even if their blue eyes failed to meet your own. Daisies, too, were abundant, but larger than the modest little English flower, and therefore of small account.

These wooded and flowery lawns are more beautiful than the finest of English park-scenery, more touching, more impressive, through the neglect that leaves Nature so much to her own ways and methods. Since man seldom interferes with her, she sets to work in her quiet way and makes herself at home. There is enough of human care, it is true, bestowed, long ago and still bestowed, to prevent wildness from growing into deformity; and the result is an ideal landscape, a woodland scene that seems to have been projected out of the poet's mind. If the ancient Faun were other than a mere creation of old poetry, and could have reappeared anywhere, it must have been in such a scene as this.

In the openings of the wood there are fountains plashing into marble basins, the depths of which are shaggy with water-weeds; or they tumble like natural cascades from rock to rock, sending their murmur

afar, to make the quiet and silence more appreciable.
Scattered here and there with careless artifice, stand
old altars bearing Roman inscriptions. Statues, gray
with the long corrosion of even that soft atmosphere,
half hide and half reveal themselves, high on pedestals,
or perhaps fallen and broken on the turf. Terminal
figures, columns of marble or granite porticos, arches,
are seen in the vistas of the wood-paths, either veritable relics of antiquity, or with so exquisite a touch of
artful ruin on them that they are better than if really
antique. At all events, grass grows on the tops of the
shattered pillars, and weeds and flowers root themselves in the chinks of the massive arches and fronts
of temples, and clamber at large over their pediments,
as if this were the thousandth summer since their
winged seeds alighted there.

What a strange idea — what a needless labor — to
construct artificial ruins in Rome, the native soil of
ruin ! But even these sportive imitations, wrought by
man in emulation of what time has done to temples
and palaces, are perhaps centuries old, and, beginning
as illusions, have grown to be venerable in sober earnest. The result of all is a scene, pensive, lovely,
dream-like, enjoyable and sad, such as is to be found
nowhere save in these princely villa-residences in the
neighborhood of Rome ; a scene that must have required generations and ages, during which growth,
decay, and man's intelligence wrought kindly together,
to render it so gently wild as we behold it now.

The final charm is bestowed by the malaria. There
is a piercing, thrilling, delicious kind of regret in the
idea of so much beauty thrown away, or only enjoyable at its half-development, in winter and early spring,
and never to be dwelt amongst, as the home-scenery

of any human being. For if you come hither in summer, and stray through these glades in the golden sunset, fever walks arm in arm with you, and death awaits you at the end of the dim vista. Thus the scene is like Eden in its loveliness; like Eden, too, in the fatal spell that removes it beyond the scope of man's actual possessions. But Donatello felt nothing of this dream-like melancholy that haunts the spot. As he passed among the sunny shadows, his spirit seemed to acquire new elasticity. The flicker of the sunshine, the sparkle of the fountain's gush, the dance of the leaf upon the bough, the woodland fragrance, the green freshness, the old sylvan peace and freedom, were all intermingled in those long breaths which he drew.

The ancient dust, the mouldiness of Rome, the dead atmosphere in which he had wasted so many months, the hard pavements, the smell of ruin and decaying generations, the chill palaces, the convent-bells, the heavy incense of altars, the life that he had led in those dark, narrow streets, among priests, soldiers, nobles, artists, and women, — all the sense of these things rose from the young man's consciousness like a cloud which had darkened over him without his knowing how densely.

He drank in the natural influences of the scene, and was intoxicated as by an exhilarating wine. He ran races with himself along the gleam and shadow of the wood-paths. He leapt up to catch the overhanging bough of an ilex, and swinging himself by it alighted far onward, as if he had flown thither through the air. In a sudden rapture he embraced the trunk of a sturdy tree, and seemed to imagine it a creature worthy of affection and capable of a tender response; he clasped it closely in his arms, as a Faun might have clasped the warm feminine grace of the nymph, whom antiquity supposed to dwell within that rough, encircling rind. Then, in order to bring himself closer to the genial earth, with which his kindred instincts linked him so strongly, he threw himself at full length on the turf, and pressed down his lips, kissing the violets and daisies, which kissed him back again, though shyly, in their maiden fashion.

While he lay there, it was pleasant to see how the green and blue lizards, who had been basking on some rock or on a fallen pillar that absorbed the warmth of the sun, scrupled not to scramble over him with their small feet; and how the birds alighted on the nearest twigs and sang their little roundelays unbroken by any chirrup of alarm; they recognized him, it may be, as something akin to themselves, or else they fancied that he was rooted and grew there; for these wild pets of nature dreaded him no more in his buoyant life than if a mound of soil and grass and flowers had long since covered his dead body, converting it back to the sympathies from which human existence had estranged it.

All of us, after a long abode in cities, have felt the blood gush more joyously through our veins with the first breath of rural air; few could feel it so much as Donatello, a creature of simple elements, bred in the sweet sylvan life of Tuscany, and for months back dwelling amid the mouldy gloom and dim splendor of old Rome. Nature has been shut out for numberless centuries from those stony-hearted streets, to which he had latterly grown accustomed; there is no trace of her, except for what blades of grass spring out of the pavements of the less trodden piazzas, or what weeds cluster and tuft themselves on the cornices of ruins. Therefore his joy was like that of a child that had gone astray from home, and finds him suddenly in his mother's arms again.

At last, deeming it full time for Miriam to keep her tryst, he climbed to the tiptop of the tallest tree, and thence looked about him, swaying to and fro in the gentle breeze, which was like the respiration of that great leafy, living thing. Donatello saw beneath him the whole circuit of the enchanted ground; the statues and columns pointing upward from among the shrubbery, the fountains flashing in the sunlight, the paths winding hither and thither, and continually finding out some nook of new and ancient pleasantness. He saw the villa, too, with its marble front incrusted all over with bas-reliefs, and statues in its many niches. It was as beautiful as a fairy palace, and seemed an abode in which the lord and lady of this fair domain might fitly dwell, and come forth each morning to enjoy as sweet a life as their happiest dreams of the past night could have depicted. All this he saw, but his first glance had taken in too wide a sweep, and it was not till his eyes fell almost directly beneath him, that Donatello beheld Miriam just turning into the path that led across the roots of his very tree.

He descended among the foliage, waiting for her to come close to the trunk, and then suddenly dropped from an impending bough, and alighted at her side. It was as if the swaying of the branches had let a ray of sunlight through. The same ray likewise glimmered among the gloomy meditations that encompassed Miriam, and lit up the pale, dark beauty of her face, while it responded pleasantly to Donatello's glance.

"I hardly know," said she, smiling, "whether you have sprouted out of the earth, or fallen from the clouds. In either case you are welcome."

And they walked onward together.

CHAPTER IX.

THE FAUN AND NYMPH.

MIRIAM'S sadder mood, it might be, had at first an effect on Donatello's spirits. It checked the joyous ebullition into which they would otherwise have effervesced when he found himself in her society, not, as heretofore, in the old gloom of Rome, but under that bright soft sky and in those Arcadian woods. He was silent for a while; it being, indeed, seldom Donatello's impulse to express himself copiously in words. His usual modes of demonstration were by the natural language of gesture, the instinctive movement of his agile frame, and the unconscious play of his features, which, within a limited range of thought and emotion, would speak volumes in a moment.

By and by, his own mood seemed to brighten Miriam's, and was reflected back upon himself. He began inevitably, as it were, to dance along the wood-path, flinging himself into attitudes of strange comic grace. Often, too, he ran a little way in advance of his companion, and then stood to watch her as she approached along the shadowy and sun-fleckered path. With every step she took, he expressed his joy at her nearer and nearer presence by what might be thought an extravagance of gesticulation, but which doubtless was the language of the natural man, though laid aside and forgotten by other men, now that words have been feebly substituted in the place of signs and symbols.

He gave Miriam the idea of a being not precisely man, nor yet a child, but, in a high and beautiful sense, an animal, — a creature in a state of development less than what mankind has attained, yet the more perfect within itself for that very deficiency. This idea filled her mobile imagination with agreeable fantasies, which, after smiling at them herself, she tried to convey to the young man.

"What are you, my friend?" she exclaimed, always keeping in mind his singular resemblance to the Faun of the Capitol. "If you are, in good truth, that wild and pleasant creature whose face you wear, pray make me known to your kindred. They will be found here-abouts, if anywhere. Knock at the rough rind of this ilex - tree, and summon forth the Dryad! Ask the water-nymph to rise dripping from yonder fountain, and exchange a moist pressure of the hand with me! Do not fear that I shall shrink, even if one of your rough cousins, a hairy Satyr, should come capering on his goat-legs out of the haunts of far antiquity, and propose to dance with me among these lawns! And will not Bacchus, — with whom you consorted so familiarly of old, and who loved you so well,— will he not meet us here, and squeeze rich grapes into his cup for you and me?"

Donatello smiled; he laughed heartily, indeed, in sympathy with the mirth that gleamed out of Miriam's deep, dark eyes. But he did not seem quite to understand her mirthful talk, nor to be disposed to explain what kind of creature he was, or to inquire with what divine or poetic kindred his companion feigned to link him. He appeared only to know that Miriam was beautiful, and that she smiled graciously upon him; that the present moment was very sweet, and himself most happy, with the sunshine, the sylvan scenery, and woman's kindly charm, which it enclosed within its small circumference. It was delightful to see the trust which he reposed in Miriam, and his pure joy in her propinquity; he asked nothing, sought nothing, save to be near the beloved object, and brimmed over with ecstasy at that simple boon. A creature of the happy tribes below us sometimes shows the capacity of this enjoyment; a man, seldom or never.

"Donatello," said Miriam, looking at him thoughtfully, but amused, yet not without a shade of sorrow, "you seem very happy; what makes you so?"

"Because I love you!" answered Donatello.

He made this momentous confession as if it were the most natural thing in the world; and on her part, — such was the contagion of his simplicity, — Miriam heard it without anger or disturbance, though with no responding emotion. It was as if they had strayed across the limits of Arcadia, and come under a civil polity where young men might avow their passion with as little restraint as a bird pipes its note to a similar purpose.

"Why should you love me, foolish boy?" said she. "We have no points of sympathy at all. There are not two creatures more unlike, in this wide world, than you and I!"

"You are yourself, and I am Donatello," replied he. "Therefore I love you! There needs no other reason."

Certainly, there was no better or more explicable reason. It might have been imagined that Donatello's unsophisticated heart would be more readily attracted to a feminine nature of clear simplicity like his own, than to one already turbid with grief or wrong, as

Miriam's seemed to be. Perhaps, on the other hand, his character needed the dark element, which it found in her. The force and energy of will, that sometimes flashed through her eyes, may have taken him captive; or, not improbably, the varying lights and shadows of her temper, now so mirthful, and anon so sad with mysterious gloom, had bewitched the youth. Analyze the matter as we may, the reason assigned by Donatello himself was as satisfactory as we are likely to attain.

Miriam could not think seriously of the avowal that had passed. He held out his love so freely, in his open palm, that she felt it could be nothing but a toy, which she might play with for an instant, and give back again. And yet Donatello's heart was so fresh a fountain, that, had Miriam been more world-worn than she was, she might have found it exquisite to slake her thirst with the feelings that welled up and brimmed over from it. She was far, very far, from the dusty mediæval epoch, when some women have a taste for such refreshment. Even for her, however, there was an inexpressible charm in the simplicity that prompted Donatello's words and deeds; though, unless she caught them in precisely the true light, they seemed but folly, the offspring of a maimed or imperfectly developed intellect. Alternately, she almost admired, or wholly scorned him, and knew not which estimate resulted from the deeper appreciation. But it could not, she decided for herself, be other than an innocent pastime, if they two — sure to be separated by their different paths in life, to-morrow — were to gather up some of the little pleasures that chanced to grow about their feet, like the violets and wood-anemones, to-day.

Yet an impulse of rectitude impelled Miriam to give him what she still held to be a needless warning against an imaginary peril.

"If you were wiser, Donatello, you would think me a dangerous person," said she. "If you follow my footsteps, they will lead you to no good. You ought to be afraid of me."

"I would as soon think of fearing the air we breathe," he replied.

"And well you may, for it is full of malaria," said Miriam ; she went on, hinting at an intangible confession, such as persons with overburdened hearts often make to children or dumb animals, or to holes in the earth, where they think their secrets may be at once revealed and buried. "Those who come too near me are in danger of great mischiefs, I do assure you. Take warning, therefore! It is a sad fatality that has brought you from your home among the Apennines, — some rusty old castle, I suppose, with a village at its foot, and an Arcadian environment of vineyards, fig-trees, and olive-orchards, — a sad mischance, I say, that has transported you to my side. You have had a happy life hitherto, — have you not, Donatello?"

"Oh, yes," answered the young man ; and, though not of a retrospective turn, he made the best effort he could to send his mind back into the past. "I remember thinking it happiness to dance with the contadinas at a village feast; to taste the new, sweet wine at vintage-time, and the old, ripened wine, which our podere is famous for, in the cold winter evenings; and to devour great, luscious figs, and apricots, peaches, cherries, and melons. I was often happy in the woods, too, with hounds and horses, and very happy in watching all sorts of creatures and birds that haunt the leafy solitudes. But never half so happy as now!"

"In these delightful groves?" she asked.

"Here, and with you," answered Donatello. "Just as we are now."

"What a fulness of content in him! How silly, and how delightful!" said Miriam to herself. Then addressing him again: "But, Donatello, how long will this happiness last?"

"How long!" he exclaimed; for it perplexed him even more to think of the future than to remember the past. "Why should it have any end? How long! Forever! forever! forever!"

"The child! the simpleton!" said Miriam, with sudden laughter, and checking it as suddenly. "But is he a simpleton indeed? Here, in those few natural words, he has expressed that deep sense, that profound conviction of its own immortality, which genuine love never fails to bring. He perplexes me, — yes, and bewitches me, — wild, gentle, beautiful creature that he is! It is like playing with a young greyhound!"

Her eyes filled with tears, at the same time that a smile shone out of them. Then first she became sensible of a delight and grief at once, in feeling this zephyr of a new affection, with its untainted freshness, blow over her weary, stifled heart, which had no right to be revived by it. The very exquisiteness of the enjoyment made her know that it ought to be a forbidden one.

"Donatello," she hastily exclaimed, "for your own sake, leave me! It is not such a happy thing as you imagine it, to wander in these woods with me, a girl from another land, burdened with a doom that she tells to none. I might make you dread me, — per haps hate me, — if I chose ; and I must choose, if I find you loving me too well ! "

" I fear nothing ! " said Donatello, looking into her unfathomable eyes with perfect trust. " I love always ! "

" I speak in vain," thought Miriam within herself.

" Well, then, for this one hour, let me be such as he imagines me. To-morrow will be time enough to come back to my reality. My reality ! what is it ? Is the past so indestructible ? the future so immitigable ? Is the dark dream, in which I walk, of such solid, stony substance, that there can be no escape out of its dungeon ? Be it so ! There is, at least, that ethereal quality in my spirit, that it can make me as gay as Donatello himself, — for this one hour ? "

And immediately she brightened up, as if an inward flame, heretofore stifled, were now permitted to fill her with its happy lustre, glowing through her cheeks and dancing in her eye-beams.

Donatello, brisk and cheerful as he seemed before, showed a sensibility to Miriam's gladdened mood by breaking into still wilder and ever - varying activity. He frisked around her, bubbling over with joy, which clothed itself in words that had little individual meaning, and in snatches of song that seemed as natural as bird - notes. Then they both laughed together, and heard their own laughter returning in the echoes, and laughed again at the response, so that the ancient and solemn grove became full of merriment for these two blithe spirits. A bird happening to sing cheerily, Donatello gave a peculiar call, and the little feathered creature came fluttering about his head, as if it had known him through many summers.

" How close he stands to nature ! " said Miriam, ob

serving this pleasant familiarity between her companion and the bird. " He shall make me as natural as
himself for this one hour."

As they strayed through that sweet wilderness, she
felt more and more the influence of his elastic temperament. Miriam was an impressible and impulsive
creature, as unlike herself, in different moods, as if a
melancholy maiden and a glad one were both bound
within the girdle about her waist, and kept in magic
thraldom by the brooch that clasped it. Naturally, it
is true, she was the more inclined to melancholy, yet
fully capable of that high frolic of the spirits which
richly compensates for many gloomy hours ; if her
soul was apt to lurk in the darkness of a cavern, she
could sport madly in the sunshine before the cavern's
mouth. Except the freshest mirth of animal spirits,
like Donatello's, there is no merriment, no wild exhilaration, comparable to that of melancholy people
escaping from the dark region in which it is their custom to keep themselves imprisoned.

So the shadowy Miriam almost outdid Donatello on
his own ground. They ran races with each other, side
by side, with shouts and laughter ; they pelted one
another with early flowers, and gathering them up
twined them with green leaves into garlands for both
their heads. They played together like children, or
creatures of immortal youth. So much had they flung
aside the sombre habitudes of daily life, that they
seemed born to be sportive forever, and endowed with
eternal mirthfulness instead of any deeper joy. It
was a glimpse far backward into Arcadian life, or,
further still, into the Golden Age, before mankind
was burdened with sin and sorrow, and before pleasure had been darkened with those shadows that bring
it into high relief, and make it happiness.

"Hark!" cried Donatello, stopping short, as he was about to bind Miriam's fair hands with flowers, and lead her along in triumph, "there is music somewhere in the grove!"

"It is your kinsman, Pan, most likely," said Miriam, "playing on his pipe. Let us go seek him, and make him puff out his rough cheeks and pipe his merriest air! Come; the strain of music will guide us onward like a gayly colored thread of silk."

"Or like a chain of flowers," responded Donatello, drawing her along by that which he had twined. "This way!—Come!"

CHAPTER X.

As the music came fresher on their ears, they danced to its cadence, extemporizing new steps and attitudes. Each varying movement had a grace which might have been worth putting into marble, for the long delight of days to come, but vanished with the movement that gave it birth, and was effaced from memory by another. In Miriam's motion, freely as she flung herself into the frolic of the hour, there was still an artful beauty; in Donatello's, there was a charm of indescribable grotesqueness hand in hand with grace; sweet, bewitching, most provocative of laughter, and yet akin to pathos, so deeply did it touch the heart. This was the ultimate peculiarity, the final touch, distinguishing between the sylvan creature and the beautiful companion at his side. Setting apart only this, Miriam resembled a Nymph, as much as Donatello did a Faun.

There were flitting moments, indeed, when she played the sylvan character as perfectly as he. Catching glimpses of her, then, you would have fancied that an oak had sundered its rough bark to let her dance freely forth, endowed with the same spirit in her human form as that which rustles in the leaves; or that she had emerged through the pebbly bottom of a fountain, a water-nymph, to play and sparkle in the sun-

shine, flinging a quivering light around her, and suddenly disappearing in a shower of rainbow drops.

As the fountain sometimes subsides into its basin,
so in Miriam there were symptoms that the frolic of
her spirits would at last tire itself out.

" Ah ! Donatello," cried she, laughing, as she
stopped to take breath ; " you have an unfair advantage over me ! I am no true creature of the woods ;
while you are a real Faun, I do believe. When your
curls shook just now, methought I had a peep at the
pointed ears."

Donatello snapped his fingers above his head, as
fauns and satyrs taught us first to do, and seemed to
radiate jollity out of his whole nimble person. Nevertheless, there was a kind of dim apprehension in his
face, as if he dreaded that a moment's pause might
break the spell, and snatch away the sportive companion whom he had waited for through so many dreary
months.

" Dance ! dance !" cried he, joyously. " If we
take breath, we shall be as we were yesterday. There,
now, is the music, just beyond this clump of trees.
Dance, Miriam, dance ! "

They had now reached an open, grassy glade (of
which there are many in that artfully constructed wilderness), set round with stone seats, on which the
aged moss had kindly essayed to spread itself instead
of cushions. On one of the stone benches sat the
musicians, whose strains had enticed our wild couple
thitherward. They proved to be a vagrant band, such
as Rome, and all Italy, abounds with ; comprising a
harp, a flute, and a violin, which, though greatly the
worse for wear, the performers had skill enough to pro-
voke and modulate into tolerable harmony. It chanced

to be a feast-day; and, instead of playing in the sun-scorched piazzas of the city, or beneath the windows of some unresponsive palace, they had bethought themselves to try the echoes of these woods; for, on the festas of the Church, Rome scatters its merry-makers all abroad, ripe for the dance or any other pastime.

As Miriam and Donatello emerged from among the trees, the musicians scraped, tinkled, or blew, each according to his various kind of instrument, more inspiringly than ever. A dark-cheeked little girl, with bright black eyes, stood by, shaking a tambourine set round with tinkling bells, and thumping it on its parchment head. Without interrupting his brisk, though measured movement, Donatello snatched away this unmelodious contrivance, and flourishing it above his head, produced music of indescribable potency, still dancing with frisky step, and striking the tambourine, and ringing its little bells, all in one jovial act.

It might be that there was magic in the sound, or contagion, at least, in the spirit which had got possession of Miriam and himself, for very soon a number of festal people were drawn to the spot, and struck into the dance, singly, or in pairs, as if they were all gone mad with jollity. Among them were some of the plebeian damsels whom we meet bareheaded in the Roman streets, with silver stilettos thrust through their glossy hair; the contadinas, too, from the Campagna and the villages, with their rich and picturesque costumes of scarlet and all bright hues, such as fairer maidens might not venture to put on. Then came the modern Roman from Trastevere, perchance, with his old cloak drawn about him like a toga, which anon, as his active motion heated him, he flung aside. Three

French soldiers capered freely into the throng, in wide scarlet trousers, their short swords dangling at their sides; and three German artists in gray flaccid hats and flaunting beards; and one of the Pope's Swiss guardsmen in the strange motley garb which Michael Angelo contrived for them. Two young English tourists (one of them a lord) took contadine partners and dashed in, as did also a shaggy man in goat-skin breeches, who looked like rustic Pan in person, and footed it as merrily as he. Besides the above there was a herdsman or two from the Campagna, and a few peasants in sky-blue jackets, and small-clothes tied with ribbons at the knees; haggard and sallow were these last, poor serfs, having little to eat and nothing but the malaria to breathe; but still they plucked up a momentary spirit and joined hands in Donatello's dance.

Here, as it seemed, had the Golden Age come back again within the precincts of this sunny glade, thawing mankind out of their cold formalities, releasing them from irksome restraint, mingling them together in such childlike gayety that new flowers (of which the old bosom of the earth is full) sprang up beneath their footsteps. The sole exception to the geniality of the moment, as we have understood, was seen in a countryman of our own, who sneered at the spectacle, and declined to compromise his dignity by making part of it.

The harper thrummed with rapid fingers; the violin-player flashed his bow back and forth across the strings; the flautist poured his breath in quick puffs of jollity, while Donatello shook the tambourine above his head, and led the merry throng with unweariable steps. As they followed one another in a wild ring of mirth, it seemed the realization of one of those bas-reliefs where a dance of nymphs, satyrs, or bacchanals is twined around the circle of an antique vase ; or it was like the sculptured scene on the front and sides of a sarcophagus, where, as often as any other device, a festive procession mocks the ashes and white bones that are treasured up within. You might take it for a marriage-pageant ; but after a while, if you look at these merry-makers, following them from end to end of the marble coffin, you doubt whether their gay movement is leading them to a happy close. A youth has suddenly fallen in the dance ; a chariot is over-turned and broken, flinging the charioteer headlong to the ground ; a maiden seems to have grown faint or weary and is drooping on the bosom of a friend. Always some tragic incident is shadowed forth or thrust sidelong into the spectacle ; and when once it has caught your eye you can look no more at the fes-tal portions of the scene, except with reference to this one slightly suggested doom and sorrow.

As in its mirth, so in the darker characteristic here alluded to, there was an analogy between the sculp-tured scene on the sarcophagus and the wild dance which we have been describing. In the midst of its madness and riot Miriam found herself suddenly con-fronted by a strange figure that shook its fantastic garments in the air, and pranced before her on its tip-toes, almost vying with the agility of Donatello him-self.   It was the model.

A moment afterwards Donatello was aware that she had retired from the dance. He hastened towards her, and flung himself on the grass beside the stone bench on which Miriam was sitting. But a strange distance and unapproachableness had all at once en-

veloped her ; and though he saw her within reach of
his arm, yet the light of her eyes seemed as far off as
that of a star, nor was there any warmth in the melancholy smile with which she regarded him.

" Come back ! " cried he. " Why should this happy
hour end so soon ? "

" It must end here, Donatello," said she, in answer
to his words and outstretched hand ; " and such hours,
I believe, do not often repeat themselves in a lifetime.
Let me go, my friend ; let me vanish from you quietly
among the shadows of these trees. See, the companions of our pastime are vanishing already ! "

Whether it was that the harp-strings were broken,
the violin out of tune, or the flautist out of breath, so
it chanced that the music had ceased, and the dancers
come abruptly to a pause. All that motley throng of
rioters was dissolved as suddenly as it had been drawn
together. In Miriam's remembrance the scene had a
character of fantasy. It was as if a company of satyrs,
fauns, and nymphs, with Pan in the midst of them,
had been disporting themselves in these venerable
woods only a moment ago ; and now in another moment, because some profane eye had looked at them
too closely, or some intruder had cast a shadow on
their mirth, the sylvan pageant had utterly disappeared. If a few of the merry-makers lingered among
the trees, they had hidden their racy peculiarities under the garb and aspect of ordinary people, and sheltered themselves in the weary commonplace of daily
life. Just an instant before it was Arcadia and the
Golden Age. The spell being broken, it was now
only that old tract of pleasure-ground, close by the
people's gate of Rome, — a tract where the crimes
and calamities of ages, the many battles, blood reck-

lessly poured out, and deaths of myriads, have corrupted all the soil, creating an influence that makes
the air deadly to human lungs.

"You must leave me," said Miriam to Donatello,
more imperatively than before; "have I not said it?
Go; and look not behind you."

"Miriam," whispered Donatello, grasping her hand
forcibly, "who is it that stands in the shadow yonder,
beckoning you to follow him?"

"Hush; leave me!" repeated Miriam. "Your
hour is past; his hour has come."

Donatello still gazed in the direction which he had
indicated, and the expression of his face was fearfully
changed, being so disordered, perhaps with terror, —
at all events with anger and invincible repugnance, —
that Miriam hardly knew him. His lips were drawn
apart so as to disclose his set teeth, thus giving him
a look of animal rage, which we seldom see except in
persons of the simplest and rudest natures. A shudder
seemed to pass through his very bones.

"I hate him!" muttered he.

"Be satisfied; I hate him too!" said Miriam.

She had no thought of making this avowal, but was
irresistibly drawn to it by the sympathy of the dark
emotion in her own breast with that so strongly expressed by Donatello. Two drops of water or of blood
do not more naturally flow into each other than did
her hatred into his.

"Shall I clutch him by the throat?" whispered
Donatello, with a savage scowl. "Bid me do so, and
we are rid of him forever."

"In Heaven's name, no violence!" exclaimed Miriam, affrighted out of the scornful control which she
had hitherto held over her companion, by the fierce

ness that he so suddenly developed. "Oh, have pity on me, Donatello, if for nothing else, yet because in the midst of my wretchedness I let myself be your playmate for this one wild hour! Follow me no farther. Henceforth, leave me to my doom. Dear friend, — kind, simple, loving friend, — make me not more wretched by the remembrance of having thrown fierce hates or loves into the wellspring of your happy life!"

"Not follow you!" repeated Donatello, soothed from anger into sorrow, less by the purport of what she said, than by the melancholy sweetness of her voice, — "not follow you! What other path have I?"

"We will talk of it once again," said Miriam, still soothingly; "soon — to-morrow — when you will; only leave me now."

CHAPTER XI.

In the Borghese Grove, so recently uproarious with merriment and music, there remained only Miriam and her strange follower.

A solitude had suddenly spread itself around them. It perhaps symbolized a peculiar character in the relation of these two, insulating them, and building up an insuperable barrier between their life-streams and other currents, which might seem to flow in close vicinity. For it is one of the chief earthly incommodities of some species of misfortune, or of a great crime, that it makes the actor in the one, or the sufferer of the other, an alien in the world, by interposing a wholly unsympathetic medium betwixt himself and those whom he yearns to meet.

Owing, it may be, to this moral estrangement, — this chill remoteness of their position, — there have come to us but a few vague whisperings of what passed in Miriam's interview that afternoon with the sinister personage who had dogged her footsteps ever since the visit to the catacomb. In weaving these mystic utterances into a continuous scene, we undertake a task resembling in its perplexity that of gathering up and piecing together the fragments of a letter which has been torn and scattered to the winds. Many words of deep significance, many entire sentences, and those possibly the most important ones, have flown too far on the winged breeze to be recovered. If we insert our own conjectural amendments, we perhaps give a purport utterly at variance with the true one. Yet unless we attempt something in this way, there must remain an unsightly gap, and a lack of continuousness and dependence in our narrative; so that it would arrive at certain inevitable catastrophes without due warning of their imminence.

Of so much we are sure, that there seemed to be a sadly mysterious fascination in the influence of this ill-omened person over Miriam; it was such as beasts and reptiles of subtle and evil nature sometimes exercise upon their victims. Marvellous it was to see the hopelessness with which — being naturally of so courageous a spirit — she resigned herself to the thraldom in which he held her. That iron chain, of which some of the massive links were round her feminine waist, and the others in his ruthless hand, — or which, perhaps, bound the pair together by a bond equally torturing to each, — must have been forged in some such unhallowed furnace as is only kindled by evil passions and fed by evil deeds.

Yet, let us trust, there may have been no crime in Miriam, but only one of those fatalities which are among the most insoluble riddles propounded to mortal comprehension; the fatal decree by which every crime is made to be the agony of many innocent persons, as well as of the single guilty one.

It was, at any rate, but a feeble and despairing kind of remonstrance which she had now the energy to oppose against his persecution.

"You follow me too closely," she said, in low, faltering accents; "you allow me too scanty room to draw my breath. Do you know what will be the end of this?"

"I know well what must be the end," he replied.

"Tell me, then," said Miriam, "that I may compare your foreboding with my own. Mine is a very dark one."

"There can be but one result, and that soon," answered the model. "You must throw off your present mask and assume another. You must vanish out of the scene: quit Rome with me, and leave no trace whereby to follow you. It is in my power, as you well know, to compel your acquiescence in my bidding. You are aware of the penalty of a refusal."

"Not that penalty with which you would terrify me," said Miriam; "another there may be, but not so grievous."

"What is that other?" he inquired.

"Death! simply death!" she answered.

"Death," said her persecutor, "is not so simple and opportune a thing as you imagine. You are strong and warm with life. Sensitive and irritable as your spirit is, these many months of trouble, this latter thraldom in which I hold you, have scarcely made your cheek paler than I saw it in your girlhood. Miriam, — for I forbear to speak another name, at which these leaves would shiver above our heads, — Miriam, you cannot die!"

"Might not a dagger find my heart?" said she, for the first time meeting his eyes. "Would not poison make an end of me? Will not the Tiber drown me?"

"It might," he answered; "for I allow that you are mortal. But, Miriam, believe me, it is not your fate to die while there remains so much to be sinned and suffered in the world. We have a destiny which we must needs fulfil together. I, too, have struggled to escape it. I was as anxious as yourself to break the tie between us, — to bury the past in a fathomless grave, — to make it impossible that we should ever meet, until you confront me at the bar of Judgment! You little can imagine what steps I took to render all this secure; and what was the result? Our strange interview in the bowels of the earth convinced me of the futility of my design."

"Ah, fatal chance!" cried Miriam, covering her face with her hands.

"Yes, your heart trembled with horror when you recognized me," rejoined he; "but you did not guess that there was an equal horror in my own!"

"Why would not the weight of earth above our heads have crumbled down upon us both, forcing us apart, but burying us equally?" cried Miriam, in a burst of vehement passion. "Oh, that we could have wandered in those dismal passages till we both perished, taking opposite paths in the darkness, so that when we lay down to die our last breaths might not mingle!"

"It were vain to wish it," said the model. "In all that labyrinth of midnight paths, we should have found one another out to live or die together. Our fates cross and are entangled. The threads are twisted into a strong cord, which is dragging us to an evil doom. Could the knots be severed, we might escape. But neither can your slender fingers untie these knots, nor my masculine force break them. We must submit!"

"Pray for rescue, as I have," exclaimed Miriam. "Pray for deliverance from me, since I am your evil genius, as you mine. Dark as your life has been, I have known you to pray in times past!"

At these words of Miriam, a tremor and horror appeared to seize upon her persecutor, insomuch that he shook and grew ashy pale before her eyes. In this man's memory, there was something that made it awful for him to think of prayer; nor would any torture be more intolerable than to be reminded of such divine comfort and succor as await pious souls merely for the asking. This torment was perhaps the token of a native temperament deeply susceptible of religious impressions, but which had been wronged, violated, and debased, until, at length, it was capable only of terror from the sources that were intended for our purest and loftiest consolation. He looked so fearfully at her, and with such intense pain struggling in his eyes, that Miriam felt pity.

And, now, all at once, it struck her that he might be mad. It was an idea that had never before seriously occurred to her mind, although, as soon as suggested, it fitted marvellously into many circumstances that lay within her knowledge. But, alas! such was her evil fortune, that, whether mad or no, his power over her remained the same, and was likely to be used only the more tyrannously, if exercised by a lunatic.

"I would not give you pain," she said, soothingly; "your faith allows you the consolations of penance and absolution. Try what help there may be in these, and leave me to myself."

"Do not think it, Miriam," said he; "we are bound together, and can never part again."

"Why should it seem so impossible?" she rejoined. "Think how I had escaped from all the past! I had made for myself a new sphere, and found new friends, new occupations, new hopes and enjoyments. My heart, methinks, was almost as unburdened as if there had been no miserable life behind me. The human spirit does not perish of a single wound, nor exhaust itself in a single trial of life. Let us but keep asunder, and all may go well for both."

"We fancied ourselves forever sundered," he replied. "Yet we met once, in the bowels of the earth; and, were we to part now, our fates would fling us together again in a desert, on a mountain-top, or in whatever spot seemed safest. You speak in vain, therefore."

"You mistake your own will for an iron necessity," said Miriam; "otherwise, you might have suffered me to glide past you like a ghost, when we met among those ghosts of ancient days. Even now you might bid me pass as freely."

"Never!" said he, with unmitigable will; "your reappearance has destroyed the work of years. You know the power that I have over you. Obey my bidding; or, within a short time, it shall be exercised: nor will I cease to haunt you till the moment comes."

"Then," said Miriam, more calmly, "I foresee the end, and have already warned you of it. It will be death!"

"Your own death, Miriam, — or mine?" he asked, looking fixedly at her.

"Do you imagine me a murderess?" said she, shuddering; "you, at least, have no right to think me so!"

"Yet," rejoined he, with a glance of dark meaning, "men have said that this white hand had once a crimson stain." He took her hand as he spoke, and held it in his own, in spite of the repugnance, amounting to nothing short of agony, with which she struggled to regain it. Holding it up to the fading light (for there was already dimness among the trees), he appeared to examine it closely, as if to discover the imaginary blood-stain with which he taunted her.   He smiled as he let it go.   " It looks very white," said he ; " but I have known hands as white, which all the water in the ocean would not have washed clean."

" It had no stain," retorted Miriam, bitterly, " until you grasped it in your own."

The wind has blown away whatever else they may have spoken.

They went together towards the town, and, on their way, continued to make reference, no doubt, to some strange and dreadful history of their former life, belonging equally to this dark man and to the fair and youthful woman whom he persecuted.   In their words, or in the breath that uttered them, there seemed to be an odor of guilt, and a scent of blood.   Yet, how can we imagine that a stain of ensanguined crime should attach to Miriam!   Or how, on the other hand, should spotless innocence be subjected to a thraldom like that which she endured from the spectre, whom she herself had evoked out of the darkness!   Be this as it might, Miriam, we have reason to believe, still continued to beseech him, humbly, passionately, wildly, only to go his way, and leave her free to follow her own sad path.

Thus they strayed onward through the green wilderness of the Borghese grounds, and soon came near the city wall, where, had Miriam raised her eyes, she might have seen Hilda and the sculptor leaning on the parapet.   But she walked in a mist of trouble, and could distinguish little beyond its limits.   As they came within public observation, her persecutor fell behind, throwing off the imperious manner which he had assumed during their solitary interview.   The Porta del Popolo swarmed with life.   The merry-makers, who had spent the feast-day outside the walls, were now thronging in; a party of horsemen were entering beneath the arch; a travelling-carriage had been drawn up just within the verge, and was passing through the villanous ordeal of the papal custom-house. In the broad piazza, too, there was a motley crowd.

But the stream of Miriam's trouble kept its way through this flood of human life, and neither mingled with it nor was turned aside. With a sad kind of feminine ingenuity, she found a way to kneel before her tyrant undetected, though in full sight of all the people, still beseeching him for freedom, and in vain.

CHAPTER XII.

HILDA, after giving the last touches to the picture of Beatrice Cenci, had flown down from her dove-cote, late in the afternoon, and gone to the Pincian Hill, in the hope of hearing a strain or two of exhilarating music. There, as it happened, she met the sculptor; for, to say the truth, Kenyon had well noted the fair artist's ordinary way of life, and was accustomed to shape his own movements, so as to bring him often within her sphere.

The Pincian Hill is the favorite promenade of the Roman aristocracy. At the present day, however, like most other Roman possessions, it belongs less to the native inhabitants than to the barbarians from Gaul, Great Britain, and beyond the sea, who have established a peaceful usurpation over whatever is enjoyable or memorable in the Eternal City. These foreign guests are indeed ungrateful, if they do not breathe a prayer for Pope Clement, or whatever Holy Father it may have been, who levelled the summit of the mount so skilfully, and bounded it with the parapet of the city wall; who laid out those broad walks and drives, and overhung them with the deepening shade of many kinds of tree; who scattered the flowers of all seasons, and of every clime, abundantly over those green, central lawns; who scooped out hollows, in fit places, and, setting great basins of marble in them, caused

ever-gushing fountains to fill them to the brim ; who
reared up the immemorial obelisk out of the soil that
had long hidden it ; who placed pedestals along the
borders of the avenues, and crowned them with busts
of that multitude of worthies — statesmen, heroes, artists, men of letters and of song — whom the whole
world claims as its chief ornaments, though Italy produced them all. In a word, the Pincian garden is
one of the things that reconcile the stranger (since he
fully appreciates the enjoyment, and feels nothing of
the cost) to the rule of an irresponsible dynasty of
Holy Fathers, who seem to have aimed at making life
as agreeable an affair as it can well be.

In this pleasant spot, the red-trousered French soldiers are always to be seen ; bearded and grizzled vet-
erans, perhaps with medals of Algiers or the Crimea
on their breasts. To them is assigned the peaceful
duty of seeing that children do not trample on the
flower-beds, nor any youthful lover rifle them of their
fragrant blossoms to stick in the beloved one's hair.
Here sits (drooping upon some marble bench, in the
treacherous sunshine) the consumptive girl, whose
friends have brought her, for cure, to a climate that
instils poison into its very purest breath. Here, all
day, come nursery-maids, burdened with rosy English
babies, or guiding the footsteps of little travellers from
the far Western world. Here, in the sunny afternoons, roll and rumble all kinds of equipages, from the
cardinal's old-fashioned and gorgeous purple carriage
to the gay barouche of modern date. Here horsemen
gallop on thoroughbred steeds. Here, in short, all the
transitory population of Rome, the world's great wa-
tering-place, rides, drives, or promenades ! Here are
beautiful sunsets ; and here, whichever way you turn

your eyes, are scenes as well worth gazing at, both in
themselves and for their historic interest, as any that
the sun ever rose and set upon.   Here, too, on certain
afternoons of the week, a French military band flings
out rich music over the poor old city, floating her with
strains as loud as those of her own echoless triumphs.

Hilda and the sculptor (by the contrivance of the
latter, who loved best to be alone with his young
country-woman) had wandered beyond the throng of
promenaders, whom they left in a dense cluster around
the music.   They strayed, indeed, to the farthest
point of the Pincian Hill, and leaned over the parapet, looking down upon the Muro Torto, a massive
fragment of the oldest Roman wall, which juts over,
as if ready to tumble down by its own weight, yet
seems still the most indestructible piece of work that
men's hands ever piled together.   In the blue distance
rose Soracte, and other heights, which have gleamed
afar, to our imaginations, but look scarcely real to our
bodily eyes, because, being dreamed about so much,
they have taken the aerial tints which belong only to
a dream.   These, nevertheless, are the solid framework of hills that shut in Rome, and its wide surrounding Campagna; no land of dreams, but the
broadest page of history, crowded so full with memorable events that one obliterates another; as if Time
had crossed and recrossed his own records till they
grew illegible.

But, not to meddle with history, — with which our
narrative is no otherwise concerned, than that the
very dust of Rome is historic, and inevitably settles
on our page and mingles with our ink, — we will return to our two friends, who were still leaning over
the wall.   Beneath them lay the broad sweep of the

Borghese grounds, covered with trees, amid which appeared the white gleam of pillars and statues, and
the flash of an upspringing fountain, all to be overshadowed at a later period of the year by the thicker
growth of foliage.

The advance of vegetation, in this softer climate, is
less abrupt than the inhabitant of the cold North is
accustomed to observe. Beginning earlier, — even in
February, — Spring is not compelled to burst into
Summer with such headlong haste; there is time to
dwell upon each opening beauty, and to enjoy the
budding leaf, the tender green, the sweet youth and
freshness of the year; it gives us its maiden charm,
before settling into the married Summer, which, again,
does not so soon sober itself into matronly Autumn.
In our own country, the virgin Spring hastens to its
bridal too abruptly. But, here, after a month or two
of kindly growth, the leaves of the young trees, which
cover that portion of the Borghese grounds nearest
the city wall, were still in their tender half-development.

In the remoter depths, among the old groves of ilex-
trees, Hilda and Kenyon heard the faint sound of
music, laughter, and mingling voices. It was probably the uproar — spreading even so far as the walls
of Rome, and growing faded and melancholy in its
passage — of that wild sylvan merriment, which we
have already attempted to describe. By and by, it
ceased; although the two listeners still tried to distinguish it between the bursts of nearer music from
the military band. But there was no renewal of that
distant mirth. Soon afterwards, they saw a solitary
figure advancing along one of the paths that lead from
the obscurer part of the ground towards the gateway.

"Look! is it not Donatello?" said Hilda.

"He it is, beyond a doubt," replied the sculptor. "But how gravely he walks, and with what long looks behind him! He seems either very weary, or very sad. I should not hesitate to call it sadness, if Donatello were a creature capable of the sin and folly of low spirits. In all these hundred paces, while we have been watching him, he has not made one of those little caprioles in the air which are characteristic of his natural gait. I begin to doubt whether he is a veritable Faun."

"Then," said Hilda, with perfect simplicity, "you have thought him — and do think him — one of that strange, wild, happy race of creatures, that used to laugh and sport in the woods, in the old, old times? So do I, indeed! But I never quite believed, till now, that fauns existed anywhere but in poetry."

The sculptor at first merely smiled. Then, as the idea took further possession of his mind, he laughed outright, and wished from the bottom of his heart (being in love with Hilda, though he had never told her so) that he could have rewarded or punished her for its pretty absurdity with a kiss.

"O Hilda, what a treasure of sweet faith and pure imagination you hide under that little straw hat!" cried he, at length. "A Faun! a Faun! Great Pan is not dead, then, after all! The whole tribe of mythical creatures yet live in the moonlit seclusion of a young girl's fancy, and find it a lovelier abode and play-place, I doubt not, than their Arcadian haunts of yore. What bliss, if a man of marble, like myself, could stray thither, too!"

"Why do you laugh so?" asked Hilda, reddening; for she was a little disturbed at Kenyon's ridicule, however kindly expressed. " What can I have said, that you think so very foolish ? "

" Well, not foolish, then," rejoined the sculptor, " but wiser, it may be, than I can fathom. Really, however, the idea does strike one as delightfully fresh, when we consider Donatello's position and external environment. Why, my dear Hilda, he is a Tuscan born, of an old noble race in that part of Italy; and he has a moss-grown tower among the Apennines, where he and his forefathers have dwelt, under their own vines and fig-trees, from an unknown antiquity. His boyish passion for Miriam has introduced him familiarly to our little circle; and our republican and artistic simplicity of intercourse has included this young Italian, on the same terms as one of ourselves. But, if we paid due respect to rank and title, we should bend reverentially to Donatello, and salute him as his Excellency the Count di Monte Beni."

" That is a droll idea, — much droller than his being a Faun ! " said Hilda, laughing in her turn. " This does not quite satisfy me, however, especially as you yourself recognized and acknowledged his wonderful resemblance to the statue."

" Except as regards the pointed ears," said Kenyon ; adding, aside, " and one other little peculiarity, generally observable in the statues of fauns."

" As for his Excellency the Count di Monte Beni's ears," replied Hilda, smiling again at the dignity with which this title invested their playful friend, " you know we could never see their shape, on account of his clustering curls. Nay, I remember, he once started back, as shyly as a wild deer, when Miriam made a pretense of examining them. How do you explain that ? "

"Oh, I certainly shall not contend against such a weight of evidence; the fact of his faunship being otherwise so probable," answered the sculptor, still hardly retaining his gravity. "Faun or not, Donatello — or the Count di Monte Beni — is a singularly wild creature, and, as I have remarked on other occasions, though very gentle, does not love to be touched. Speaking in no harsh sense, there is a great deal of animal nature in him, as if he had been born in the woods, and had run wild all his childhood, and were as yet but imperfectly domesticated. Life, even in our day, is very simple and unsophisticated in some of the shaggy nooks of the Apennines."

"It annoys me very much," said Hilda, "this inclination, which most people have, to explain away the wonder and the mystery out of everything. Why could not you allow me — and yourself, too — the satisfaction of thinking him a Faun?"

"Pray keep your belief, dear Hilda, if it makes you any happier," said the sculptor; "and I shall do my best to become a convert. Donatello has asked me to spend the summer with him, in his ancestral tower, where I purpose investigating the pedigree of these sylvan counts, his forefathers; and if their shadows beckon me into dreamland, I shall willingly follow. By the by, speaking of Donatello, there is a point on which I should like to be enlightened."

"Can I help you, then?" said Hilda, in answer to his look.

"Is there the slightest chance of his winning Miriam's affections?" suggested Kenyon.

"Miriam! she, so accomplished and gifted!" exclaimed Hilda; "and he, a rude, uncultivated boy! No, no, no!"

" It would seem impossible," said the sculptor. "But, on the other hand, a gifted woman flings away her affections so unaccountably, sometimes! Miriam, of late, has been very morbid and miserable, as we both know. Young as she is, the morning light seems already to have faded out of her life ; and now comes Donatello, with natural sunshine enough for himself and her, and offers her the opportunity of making her heart and life all new and cheery again. People of high intellectual endowments do not require similar ones in those they love. They are just the persons to appreciate the wholesome gush of natural feeling, the honest affection, the simple joy, the fulness of contentment with what he loves, which Miriam sees in Donatello. True ; she may call him a simpleton. It is a necessity of the case ; for a man loses the capacity for this kind of affection, in proportion as he cultivates and refines himself."

" Dear me ! " said Hilda, drawing imperceptibly away from her companion. " Is this the penalty of refinement ? Pardon me ; I do not believe it. It is because you are a sculptor, that you think nothing can be finely wrought except it be cold and hard, like the marble in which your ideas take shape. I am a painter, and know that the most delicate beauty may be softened and warmed throughout."

" I said a foolish thing, indeed," answered the sculptor. " It surprises me, for I might have drawn a wiser knowledge out of my own experience. It is the surest test of genuine love, that it brings back our early simplicity to the worldliest of us."

Thus talking, they loitered slowly along beside the parapet which borders the level summit of the Pincian with its irregular sweep. At intervals they looked through the lattice-work of their thoughts at the varied prospects that lay before and beneath them.

From the terrace where they now stood there is an abrupt descent towards the Piazza del Popolo; and looking down into its broad space they beheld the tall palatial edifices, the church-domes, and the ornamented gateway, which grew and were consolidated out of the thought of Michael Angelo. They saw, too, the red granite obelisk, oldest of things, even in Rome, which rises in the centre of the piazza, with a fourfold fountain at its base. All Roman works and ruins (whether of the empire, the far-off republic, or the still more distant kings) assume a transient, visionary, and impalpable character when we think that this indestructible monument supplied one of the recollections which Moses and the Israelites bore from Egypt into the desert. Perchance, on beholding the cloudy pillar and the fiery column, they whispered awe-stricken to one another, "In its shape it is like that old obelisk which we and our fathers have so often seen on the borders of the Nile." And now that very obelisk, with hardly a trace of decay upon it, is the first thing that the modern traveller sees after entering the Flaminian Gate!

Lifting their eyes, Hilda and her companion gazed westward, and saw beyond the invisible Tiber the Castle of St. Angelo; that immense tomb of a pagan emperor, with the archangel at its summit.

Still farther off appeared a mighty pile of buildings, surmounted by the vast dome, which all of us have shaped and swelled outward, like a huge bubble, to the utmost scope of our imaginations, long before we see it floating over the worship of the city. It may be most worthily seen from precisely the point where

our two friends were now standing. At any nearer
view the grandeur of St. Peter's hides itself behind
the immensity of its separate parts, so that we see
only the front, only the sides, only the pillared length
and loftiness of the portico, and not the mighty whole.
But at this distance the entire outline of the world's
cathedral, as well as that of the palace of the world's
chief priest, is taken in at once. In such remoteness,
moreover, the imagination is not debarred from lend-
ing its assistance, even while we have the reality before our eyes, and helping the weakness of human
sense to do justice to so grand an object. It requires
both faith and fancy to enable us to feel, what is nevertheless so true, that yonder, in front of the purple
outline of hills, is the grandest edifice ever built by
man, painted against God's loveliest sky.

After contemplating a little while a scene which
their long residence in Rome had made familiar to
them, Kenyon and Hilda again let their glances fall
into the piazza at their feet. They there beheld Miriam, who had just entered the Porta del Popolo, and
was standing by the obelisk and fountain. With a
gesture that impressed Kenyon as at once suppliant
and imperious, she seemed to intimate to a figure
which had attended her thus far, that it was now her
desire to be left alone. The pertinacious model, however, remained immovable.

And the sculptor here noted a circumstance, which,
according to the interpretation he might put upon it,
was either too trivial to be mentioned, or else so mysteriously significant that he found it difficult to believe his eyes. Miriam knelt down on the steps of the
fountain; so far there could be no question of the fact.
To other observers, if any there were, she probably

appeared to take this attitude merely for the convenience of dipping her fingers into the gush of water
from the mouth of one of the stone lions.   But as she
clasped her hands together after thus bathing them,
and glanced upward at the model, an idea took strong
possession of Kenyon's mind that Miriam was kneeling to this dark follower there in the world's face!

"Do you see it?" he said to Hilda.

"See what?" asked she, surprised at the emotion
of his tone.   "I see Miriam, who has just bathed her
hands in that delightfully cool water.   I often dip my
fingers into a Roman fountain, and think of the brook
that used to be one of my playmates in my New England village."

"I fancied I saw something else," said Kenyon;
"but it was doubtless a mistake."

But, allowing that he had caught a true glimpse
into the hidden significance of Miriam's gesture, what
a terrible thraldom did it suggest!   Free as she seemed
to be, — beggar as he looked, — the nameless vagrant
must then be dragging the beautiful Miriam through
the streets of Rome, fettered and shackled more cruelly
than any captive queen of yore following in an emperor's triumph.   And was it conceivable that she
would have been thus enthralled unless some great
error — how great Kenyon dared not think — or some
fatal weakness had given this dark adversary a van-
tage-ground?

"Hilda," said he, abruptly, "who and what is Miriam?   Pardon me; but are you sure of her?"

"Sure of her!" repeated Hilda, with an angry
blush, for her friend's sake.   "I am sure that she is
kind, good, and generous; a true and faithful friend,
whom I love dearly, and who loves me as well!   What
more than this need I be sure of?"

"And your delicate instincts say all this in her favor? — nothing against her?" continued the sculptor, without heeding the irritation of Hilda's tone. "These are my own impressions, too. But she is such a mystery! We do not even know whether she is a countrywoman of ours, or an Englishwoman, or a German. There is Anglo-Saxon blood in her veins, one would say, and a right English accent on her tongue, but much that is not English breeding, nor American. Nowhere else but in Rome, and as an artist, could she hold a place in society without giving some clew to her past life."

"I love her dearly," said Hilda, still with displeasure in her tone, "and trust her most entirely."

"My heart trusts her at least, whatever my head may do," replied Kenyon; "and Rome is not like one of our New England villages, where we need the permission of each individual neighbor for every act that we do, every word that we utter, and every friend that we make or keep. In these particulars the papal despotism allows us freer breath than our native air; and if we like to take generous views of our associates, we can do so, to a reasonable extent, without ruining ourselves."

"The music has ceased," said Hilda; "I am going now."

There are three streets that, beginning close beside each other, diverge from the Piazza del Popolo towards the heart of Rome: on the left, the Via del Babuino; on the right, the Via della Ripetta; and between these two that world-famous avenue, the Corso. It appeared that Miriam and her strange companion were passing up the first-mentioned of these three, and were soon hidden from Hilda and the sculptor.

The two latter left the Pincian by the broad and stately walk that skirts along its brow. Beneath them, from the base of the abrupt descent, the city spread wide away in a close contiguity of red-earthen roofs, above which rose eminent the domes of a hundred churches, beside here and there a tower, and the upper windows of some taller or higher situated palace, looking down on a multitude of palatial abodes. At a distance, ascending out of the central mass of edifices, they could see the top of the Antonine column, and near it the circular roof of the Pantheon looking heavenward with its ever-open eye.

Except these two objects, almost everything that they beheld was mediæval, though built, indeed, of the massive old stones and indestructible bricks of imperial Rome ; for the ruins of the Coliseum, the Golden House, and innumerable temples of Roman gods, and mansions of Cæsars and senators, had supplied the material for all those gigantic hovels, and their walls were cemented with mortar of inestimable cost, being made of precious antique statues, burnt long ago for this petty purpose.

Rome, as it now exists, has grown up under the Popes, and seems like nothing but a heap of broken rubbish, thrown into the great chasm between our own days and the Empire, merely to fill it up ; and, for the better part of two thousand years, its annals of obscure policies, and wars, and continually recurring misfortunes, seem also but broken rubbish, as compared with its classic history.

If we consider the present city as at all connected with the famous one of old, it is only because we find it built over its grave. A depth of thirty feet of soil has covered up the Rome of ancient days, so that it

lies like the dead corpse of a giant, decaying for centuries, with no survivor mighty enough even to bury
it, until the dust of all those years has gathered slowly
over its recumbent form and made a casual sepulchre.

We know not how to characterize, in any accordant
and compatible terms, the Rome that lies before us;
its sunless alleys, and streets of palaces; its churches,
lined with the gorgeous marbles that were originally
polished for the adornment of pagan temples; its
thousands of evil smells, mixed up with fragrance of
rich incense, diffused from as many censers; its little
life, deriving feeble nutriment from what has long
been dead. Everywhere, some fragment of ruin suggesting the magnificence of a former epoch; everywhere, moreover, a Cross, — and nastiness at the foot
of it. As the sum of all, there are recollections that
kindle the soul, and a gloom and languor that depress
it beyond any depth of melancholic sentiment that can
be elsewhere known.

Yet how is it possible to say an unkind or irreveren-
tial word of Rome? The city of all time, and of all
the world! The spot for which man's great life and
deeds have done so much, and for which decay has
done whatever glory and dominion could not do! At
this moment, the evening sunshine is flinging its
golden mantle over it, making all that we thought
mean magnificent; the bells of all the churches suddenly ring out, as if it were a peal of triumph because
Rome is still imperial.

"I sometimes fancy," said Hilda, on whose susceptibility the scene always made a strong impression,
"that Rome — mere Rome — will crowd everything
else out of my heart."

"Heaven forbid!" ejaculated the sculptor.

They had now reached the grand stairs that ascend from the Piazza di Spagna to the hither brow of the Pincian Hill. Old Beppo, the millionnaire of his ragged fraternity, — it is a wonder that no artist paints him as the cripple whom St. Peter heals at the Beautiful Gate of the Temple, — was just mounting his donkey to depart, laden with the rich spoil of the day's beggary.

Up the stairs, drawing his tattered cloak about his face, came the model, at whom Beppo looked askance, jealous of an encroacher on his rightful domain. The figure passed away, however, up the Via Sistina. In the piazza below, near the foot of the magnificent steps, stood Miriam, with her eyes bent on the ground, as if she were counting those little, square, uncomfortable paving-stones, that make it a penitential pilgrimage to walk in Rome. She kept this attitude for several minutes, and when, at last, the importunities of a beggar disturbed her from it, she seemed bewildered and pressed her hand upon her brow.

"She has been in some sad dream or other, poor thing!" said Kenyon, sympathizingly; "and even now, she is imprisoned there in a kind of cage, the iron bars of which are made of her own thoughts."

"I fear she is not well," said Hilda. "I am going down the stairs, and will join Miriam."

"Farewell, then," said the sculptor. "Dear Hilda, this is a perplexed and troubled world! It soothes me inexpressibly to think of you in your tower, with white doves and white thoughts for your companions, so high above us all, and with the Virgin for your household friend. You know not how far it throws its light, that lamp which you keep burning at her shrine! I passed beneath the tower last night, and the ray cheered me, — because you lighted it."

"It has for me a religious significance," replied Hilda, quietly, "and yet I am no Catholic."

They parted, and Kenyon made haste along the Via Sistina, in the hope of overtaking the model, whose haunts and character he was anxious to investigate, for Miriam's sake. He fancied that he saw him a long way in advance, but before he reached the Fountain of the Triton, the dusky figure had vanished.

CHAPTER XIII.

A SCULPTOR'S STUDIO.

ABOUT this period, Miriam seems to have been goaded by a weary restlessness that drove her abroad on any errand or none. She went one morning to visit Kenyon in his studio, whither he had invited her to see a new statue, on which he had staked many hopes, and which was now almost completed in the clay. Next to Hilda, the person for whom Miriam felt most affection and confidence was Kenyon; and in all the difficulties that beset her life, it was her impulse to draw near Hilda for feminine sympathy, and the sculptor for brotherly counsel.

Yet it was to little purpose that she approached the edge of the voiceless gulf between herself and them. Standing on the utmost verge of that dark chasm, she might stretch out her hand, and never clasp a hand of theirs; she might strive to call out, " Help, friends! help!" but, as with dreamers when they shout, her voice would perish inaudibly in the remoteness that seemed such a little way. This perception of an in-finite, shivering solitude, amid which we cannot come close enough to human beings to be warmed by them, and where they turn to cold, chilly shapes of mist, is one of the most forlorn results of any accident, misfor-tune, crime, or peculiarity of character, that puts an individual ajar with the world. Very often, as in Miriam's case, there is an insatiable instinct that demands friendship, love, and intimate communion, but is forced to pine in empty forms ; a hunger of the heart, which finds only shadows to feed upon.

Kenyon's studio was in a cross-street, or, rather, an ugly and dirty little lane, between the Corso and the Via della Ripetta; and though chill, narrow, gloomy, and bordered with tall and shabby structures, the lane was not a whit more disagreeable than nine tenths of the Roman streets. Over the door of one of the houses was a marble tablet, bearing an inscription, to the purport that the sculpture-rooms within had formerly been occupied by the illustrious artist Canova. In these precincts (which Canova's genius was not quite of a character to render sacred, though it certainly made them interesting) the young American sculptor had now established himself.

The studio of a sculptor is generally but a rough and dreary-looking place, with a good deal the aspect, indeed, of a stone-mason's workshop. Bare floors of brick or plank, and plastered walls; an old chair or two, or perhaps only a block of marble (containing, however, the possibility of ideal grace within it) to sit down upon; some hastily scrawled sketches of nude figures on the whitewash of the wall. These last are probably the sculptor's earliest glimpses of ideas that may hereafter be solidified into imperishable stone, or perhaps may remain as impalpable as a dream. Next there are a few very roughly modelled little figures in clay or plaster, exhibiting the second stage of the idea as it advances towards a marble immortality; and then is seen the exquisitely designed shape of clay, more interesting than even the final marble, as being the intimate production of the sculptor himself, moulded throughout with his loving hands, and nearest to his imagination and heart. In the plaster-cast, from this clay model, the beauty of the statue strangely disappears, to shine forth again with pure white radiance, in the precious marble of Carrara. Works in all these stages of advancement, and some with the final touch upon them, might be found in Kenyon's studio.

Here might be witnessed the process of actually chiselling the marble, with which (as it is not quite satisfactory to think) a sculptor in these days has very little to do. In Italy, there is a class of men whose merely mechanical skill is perhaps more exquisite than was possessed by the ancient artificers, who wrought out the designs of Praxiteles ; or, very possibly, by Praxiteles himself. Whatever of illusive representation can be effected in marble, they are capable of achieving, if the object be before their eyes. The sculptor has but to present these men with a plaster-cast of his design, and a sufficient block of marble, and tell them that the figure is imbedded in the stone, and must be freed from its encumbering superfluities ; and, in due time, without the necessity of his touching the work with his own finger, he will see before him the statue that is to make him renowned. His creative power has wrought it with a word.

In no other art, surely, does genius find such effective instruments, and so happily relieve itself of the drudgery of actual performance ; doing wonderfully nice things by the hands of other people, when it may be suspected they could not always be done by the sculptor's own. And how much of the admiration which our artists get for their buttons and button-holes, their shoe-ties, their neck-cloths, — and these, at our present epoch of taste, make a large share of the renown, — would be abated, if we were generally aware that the sculptor can claim no credit for such pretty performances, as immortalized in marble! They are not his work, but that of some nameless machine in human shape.

Miriam stopped an instant in an antechamber, to look at a half-finished bust, the features of which seemed to be struggling out of the stone; and, as it were, scattering and dissolving its hard substance by the glow of feeling and intelligence. As the skilful workman gave stroke after stroke of the chisel with apparent carelessness, but sure effect, it was impossible not to think that the outer marble was merely an extraneous environment; the human countenance within its embrace must have existed there since the limestone ledges of Carrara were first made. Another bust was nearly completed, though still one of Kenyon's most trustworthy assistants was at work, giving delicate touches, shaving off an impalpable something, and leaving little heaps of marble-dust to attest it.

" As these busts in the block of marble," thought Miriam, " so does our individual fate exist in the limestone of time. We fancy that we carve it out; but its ultimate shape is prior to all our action."

Kenyon was in the inner room, but, hearing a step in the antechamber, he threw a veil over what he was at work upon, and came out to receive his visitor. He was dressed in a gray blouse, with a little cap on the top of his head; a costume which became him better than the formal garments which he wore, whenever he passed out of his own domains. The sculptor had a face which, when time had done a little more for it, would offer a worthy subject for as good an artist as himself: features finely cut, as if already marble; an ideal forehead, deeply set eyes, and a mouth much hidden in a light-brown beard, but apparently sensitive and delicate.

"I will not offer you my hand," said he ; "it is grimy with Cleopatra's clay."

"No ; I will not touch clay ; it is earthy and human," answered Miriam. "I have come to try whether there is any calm and coolness among your marbles. My own art is too nervous, too passionate, too full of agitation, for me to work at it whole days together, without intervals of repose. So, what have you to show me ? "

"Pray look at everything here," said Kenyon. "I love to have painters see my work. Their judgment is unprejudiced, and more valuable than that of the world generally, from the light which their own art throws on mine. More valuable, too, than that of my brother sculptors, who never judge me fairly, — nor I them, perhaps."

To gratify him, Miriam looked round at the specimens in marble or plaster, of which there were several in the room, comprising originals or casts of most of the designs that Kenyon had thus far produced. He was still too young to have accumulated a large gallery of such things. What he had to show were chiefly the attempts and experiments, in various directions, of a beginner in art, acting as a stern tutor to himself, and profiting more by his failures than by any successes of which he was yet capable. Some of them, however, had great merit ; and in the pure, fine glow of the new marble, it may be, they dazzled the judgment into awarding them higher praise than they deserved. Miriam admired the statue of a beautiful youth, a pearl-fisher, who had got entangled in the weeds at the bottom of the sea, and lay dead among the pearl-oysters, the rich shells, and the sea-weeds, all of like value to him now.

"The poor young man has perished among the prizes that he sought," remarked she. "But what a strange efficacy there is in death! If we cannot all win pearls, it causes an empty shell to satisfy us just as well. I like this statue, though it is too cold and stern in its moral lesson; and, physically, the form has not settled itself into sufficient repose."

In another style, there was a grand, calm head of Milton, not copied from any one bust or picture, yet more authentic than any of them, because all known representations of the poet had been profoundly studied, and solved in the artist's mind. The bust over the tomb in Grey Friars Church, the original miniatures and pictures, wherever to be found, had mingled each its special truth in this one work; wherein, likewise, by long perusal and deep love of the "Paradise Lost," the "Comus," the "Lycidas," and "L'Allegro," the sculptor had succeeded, even better than he knew, in spiritualizing his marble with the poet's mighty genius. And this was a great thing to have achieved, such a length of time after the dry bones and dust of Milton were like those of any other dead man.

There were also several portrait-busts, comprising those of two or three of the illustrious men of our own country, whom Kenyon, before he left America, had asked permission to model. He had done so, because he sincerely believed that, whether he wrought the busts in marble or bronze, the one would corrode and the other crumble in the long lapse of time, beneath these great men's immortality. Possibly, however, the young artist may have under-estimated the durability of his material. Other faces there were, too, of men who (if the brevity of their remembrance, after death, can be augured from their little value in life) should have been represented in snow rather than marble. Posterity will be puzzled what to do with busts like these, the concretions and petrifactions of a vain self-estimate; but will find, no doubt, that they serve to build into stone-walls, or burn into quick-lime, as well as if the marble had never been blocked into the guise of human heads.

But it is an awful thing, indeed, this endless endurance, this almost indestructibility, of a marble bust! Whether in our own case, or that of other men, it bids us sadly measure the little, little time during which our lineaments are likely to be of interest to any human being. It is especially singular that Americans should care about perpetuating themselves in this mode. The brief duration of our families, as a hereditary household, renders it next to a certainty that the great-grandchildren will not know their father's grandfather, and that half a century hence at furthest, the hammer of the auctioneer will thump its knock-down blow against his blockhead, sold at so much for the pound of stone! And it ought to make us shiver, the idea of leaving our features to be a dusty-white ghost among strangers of another generation, who will take our nose between their thumb and fingers (as we have seen men do by Cæsar's), and infallibly break it off if they can do so without detection!

"Yes," said Miriam, who had been revolving some such thoughts as the above, "it is a good state of mind for mortal man, when he is content to leave no more definite memorial than the grass, which will sprout kindly and speedily over his grave, if we do not make the spot barren with marble. Methinks, too, it will be a fresher and better world, when it flings off this great burden of stony memories, which the ages have deemed it a piety to heap upon its back."

"What you say," remarked Kenyon, "goes against my whole art. Sculpture, and the delight which men naturally take in it, appear to me a proof that it is good to work with all time before our view."

"Well, well," answered Miriam, "I must not quarrel with you for flinging your heavy stones at poor Posterity; and, to say the truth, I think you are as likely to hit the mark as anybody. These busts, now. much as I seem to scorn them, make me feel as if you were a magician. You turn feverish men into cool, quiet marble. What a blessed change for them! Would you could do as much for me!"

"Oh, gladly!" cried Kenyon, who had long wished to model that beautiful and most expressive face. "When will you begin to sit?"

"Poh! that was not what I meant," said Miriam. "Come, show me something else."

"Do you recognize this?" asked the sculptor.

He took out of his desk a little old-fashioned ivory coffer, yellow with age; it was richly carved with antique figures and foliage; and had Kenyon thought fit to say that Benvenuto Cellini wrought this precious box, the skill and elaborate fancy of the work would by no means have discredited his word, nor the old artist's fame. At least, it was evidently a production of Benvenuto's school and century, and might once have been the jewel-case of some grand lady at the court of the De' Medici.

Lifting the lid, however, no blaze of diamonds was

disclosed, but only, lapped in fleecy cotton, a small, beautifully shaped hand, most delicately sculptured in marble. Such loving care and nicest art had been lavished here, that the palm really seemed to have a tenderness in its very substance. Touching those lovely fingers, — had the jealous sculptor allowed you to touch, — you could hardly believe that a virgin warmth would not steal from them into your heart.

"Ah, this is very beautiful!" exclaimed Miriam, with a genial smile. "It is as good in its way as Loulie's hand with its baby-dimples, which Powers showed me at Florence, evidently valuing it as much as if he had wrought it out of a piece of his great heart. As good as Harriet Hosmer's clasped hands of Browning and his wife, symbolizing the individuality and heroic union of two high, poetic lives! Nay, I do not question that it is better than either of those, because you must have wrought it passionately, in spite of its maiden palm and dainty finger-tips."

"Then you do recognize it?" asked Kenyon.

"There is but one right hand on earth that could have supplied the model," answered Miriam; "so small and slender, so perfectly symmetrical, and yet with a character of delicate energy. I have watched it a hundred times at its work; but I did not dream that you had won Hilda so far! How have you persuaded that shy maiden to let you take her hand in marble?"

"Never! She never knew it!" hastily replied Kenyon, anxious to vindicate his mistress's maidenly reserve. "I stole it from her. The hand is a reminiscence. After gazing at it so often, and even holding it once for an instant, when Hilda was not thinking of me, I should be a bungler indeed, if I could not now reproduce it to something like the life."

"May you win the original one day!" said Miriam, kindly.

"I have little ground to hope it," answered the sculptor, despondingly; "Hilda does not dwell in our mortal atmosphere; and gentle and soft as she appears, it will be as difficult to win her heart as to entice down a white bird from its sunny freedom in the sky. It is strange, with all her delicacy and fragility, the impression she makes of being utterly sufficient to herself. No; I shall never win her. She is abundantly capable of sympathy, and delights to receive it, but she has no need of love."

"I partly agree with you," said Miriam. "It is a mistaken idea, which men generally entertain, that nature has made women especially prone to throw their whole being into what is technically called love. We have, to say the least, no more necessity for it than yourselves; only we have nothing else to do with our hearts. When women have other objects in life, they are not apt to fall in love. I can think of many women distinguished in art, literature, and science, — and multitudes whose hearts and minds find good employment in less ostentatious ways, — who lead high, lonely lives, and are conscious of no sacrifice so far as your sex is concerned."

"And Hilda will be one of these!" said Kenyon, sadly; "the thought makes me shiver for myself, and — and for her, too."

"Well," said Miriam, smiling, "perhaps she may sprain the delicate wrist which you have sculptured to such perfection. In that case you may hope. These old masters to whom she has vowed herself, and whom her slender hand and woman's heart serve so faithfully, are your only rivals."

The sculptor sighed as he put away the treasure of Hilda's marble hand into the ivory coffer, and thought how slight was the possibility that he should ever feel responsive to his own the tender clasp of the original. He dared not even kiss the image that he himself had made : it had assumed its share of Hilda's remote and shy divinity.

" And now," said Miriam, " show me the new statue which you asked me hither to see."

CHAPTER XIV.

CLEOPATRA.

"My new statue!" said Kenyon, who had positively forgotten it in the thought of Hilda; "here it is, under this veil."

"Not a nude figure, I hope," observed Miriam. "Every young sculptor seems to think that he must give the world some specimen of indecorous womanhood, and call it Eve, Venus, a Nymph, or any name that may apologize for a lack of decent clothing. I am weary, even more than I am ashamed, of seeing such things. Nowadays people are as good as born in their clothes, and there is practically not a nude human being in existence. An artist, therefore, as you must candidly confess, cannot sculpture nudity with a pure heart, if only because he is compelled to steal guilty glimpses at hired models. The marble inevitably loses its chastity under such circumstances. An old Greek sculptor, no doubt, found his models in the open sunshine, and among pure and princely maidens, and thus the nude statues of antiquity are as modest as violets, and sufficiently draped in their own beauty. But as for Mr. Gibson's colored Venuses (stained, I believe, with tobacco-juice), and all other nudities of to-day, I really do not understand what they have to say to this generation, and would be glad to see as many heaps of quicklime in their stead."

"You are severe upon the professors of my art,"

said Kenyon, half smiling, half seriously; " not that you are wholly wrong, either. We are bound to accept drapery of some kind, and make the best of it. But what are we to do ? Must we adopt the costume of to-day, and carve, for example, a Venus in a hoop-petticoat ? "

" That would be a bowlder, indeed ! " rejoined Miriam, laughing. " But the difficulty goes to confirm me in my belief that, except for portrait-busts, sculpture has no longer a right to claim any place among living arts. It has wrought itself out, and come fairly to an end. There is never a new group nowadays ; never even so much as a new attitude. Greenough (I take my examples among men of merit) imagined nothing new ; nor Crawford either, except in the tailoring line. There are not, as you will own, more than half a dozen positively original statues or groups in the world, and these few are of immemorial antiquity. A person familiar with the Vatican, the Uffizzi Gallery, the Naples Gallery, and the Louvre, will at once refer any modern production to its antique prototype ; which, moreover, had begun to get out of fashion, even in old Roman days."

" Pray stop, Miriam," cried Kenyon, " or I shall fling away the chisel forever ! "

" Fairly own to me, then, my friend," rejoined Miriam, whose disturbed mind found a certain relief in this declamation, " that you sculptors are, of necessity, the greatest plagiarists in the world."

" I do not own it," said Kenyon, " yet cannot utterly contradict you, as regards the actual state of the art. But as long as the Carrara quarries still yield pure blocks, and while my own country has marble mountains, probably as fine in quality, I shall steadfastly believe that future sculptors will revive this noblest of the beautiful arts, and people the world with new shapes of delicate grace and massive grandeur. Perhaps," he added, smiling, "mankind will consent to wear a more manageable costume; or, at worst, we sculptors shall get the skill to make broadcloth transparent, and render a majestic human character visible through the coats and trousers of the present day."

"Be it so!" said Miriam; "you are past my counsel. Show me the veiled figure, which I am afraid, I have criticised beforehand. To make amends, I am in the mood to praise it now."

But, as Kenyon was about to take the cloth off the clay model, she laid her hand on his arm.

"Tell me first what is the subject," said she, "for I have sometimes incurred great displeasure from members of your brotherhood by being too obtuse to puzzle out the purport of their productions. It is so difficult, you know, to compress and define a character or story, and make it patent at a glance, within the narrow scope attainable by sculpture! Indeed I fancy it is still the ordinary habit with sculptors, first to finish their group of statuary, — in such development as the particular block of marble will allow, — and then to choose the subject; as John of Bologna did with his ' Rape of the Sabines.' Have you followed that good example?"

"No; my statue is intended for Cleopatra," replied Kenyon, a little disturbed by Miriam's raillery. "The special epoch of her history you must make out for yourself."

He drew away the cloth that had served to keep the moisture of the clay model from being exhaled. The sitting figure of a woman was seen. She was draped

from head to foot in a costume minutely and scrupulously studied from that of ancient Egypt, as revealed
by the strange sculpture of that country, its coins, drawings, painted mummy-cases, and whatever other tokens
have been dug out of its pyramids, graves, and catacombs.   Even the stiff Egyptian head-dress was ad-
hered to, but had been softened into a rich feminine
adornment, without losing a particle of its truth.   Difficulties that might well have seemed insurmountable
had been courageously encountered and made flexible
to purposes of grace and dignity; so that Cleopatra
sat attired in a garb proper to her historic and queenly
state, as a daughter of the Ptolemies, and yet such
as the beautiful woman would have put on as best
adapted to heighten the magnificence of her charms,
and kindle a tropic fire in the cold eyes of Octavius.

A marvellous repose — that rare merit in statuary,
except it be the lumpish repose native to the block
of stone — was diffused throughout the figure.   The
spectator felt that Cleopatra had sunk down out of
the fever and turmoil of her life, and for one instant
— as it were, between two pulse-throbs — had relinquished all activity, and was resting throughout every
vein and muscle.   It was the repose of despair, indeed;
for Octavius had seen her, and remained insensible to
her enchantments.   But still there was a great smoul-
dering furnace deep down in the woman's heart.   The
repose, no doubt, was as complete as if she were never
to stir hand or foot again; and yet, such was the creature's latent energy and fierceness, she might spring
upon you like a tigress, and stop the very breath that
you were now drawing midway in your throat.

The face was a miraculous success.   The sculptor
had not shunned to give the full Nubian lips, and other

characteristics of the Egyptian physiognomy. His courage and integrity had been abundantly rewarded; for Cleopatra's beauty shone out richer, warmer, more triumphantly beyond comparison, than if, shrinking timidly from the truth, he had chosen the tame Grecian type. The expression was of profound, gloomy, heavily revolving thought; a glance into her past life and present emergencies, while her spirit gathered itself up for some new struggle, or was getting sternly reconciled to impending doom. In one view, there was a certain softness and tenderness, — how breathed into the statue, among so many strong and passionate elements, it is impossible to say. Catching another glimpse, you beheld her as implacable as a stone and cruel as fire.

In a word, all Cleopatra — fierce, voluptuous, passionate, tender, wicked, terrible, and full of poisonous and rapturous enchantment — was kneaded into what, only a week or two before, had been a lump of wet clay from the Tiber. Soon, apotheosized in an indestructible material, she would be one of the images that men keep forever, finding a heat in them which does not cool down, throughout the centuries.

"What a woman is this!" exclaimed Miriam, after a long pause. "Tell me, did she ever try, even while you were creating her, to overcome you with her fury or her love? Were you not afraid to touch her, as she grew more and more towards hot life beneath your hand? My dear friend, it is a great work! How have you learned to do it?"

"It is the concretion of a good deal of thought, emotion, and toil of brain and hand," said Kenyon, not without a perception that his work was good; "but I know not how it came about at last. I kindled a great fire within my mind, and threw in the material, — as Aaron threw the gold of the Israelites into the furnace, — and in the midmost heat uprose Cleopatra, as you see her."

"What I most marvel at," said Miriam, "is the womanhood that you have so thoroughly mixed up with all those seemingly discordant elements. Where did you get that secret? You never found it in your gentle Hilda, yet I recognize its truth."

"No, surely, it was not in Hilda," said Kenyon. "Her womanhood is of the ethereal type, and incompatible with any shadow of darkness or evil."

"You are right," rejoined Miriam; "there are women of that ethereal type as you term it, and Hilda is one of them. She would die of her first wrong-doing, — supposing for a moment that she could be capable of doing wrong. Of sorrow, slender as she seems, Hilda might bear a great burden; of sin, not a feather's weight. Methinks now, were it my doom, I could bear either, or both at once; but my conscience is still as white as Hilda's. Do you question it?"

"Heaven forbid, Miriam!" exclaimed the sculptor.

He was startled at the strange turn which she had so suddenly given to the conversation. Her voice, too, — so much emotion was stifled rather than expressed in it, — sounded unnatural.

"Oh, my friend," cried she, with sudden passion, "will you be my friend indeed? I am lonely, lonely, lonely! There is a secret in my heart that burns me, — that tortures me! Sometimes I fear to go mad of it; sometimes I hope to die of it; but neither of the two happens. Ah, if I could but whisper it to only one human soul! And you — you see far into womanhood; you receive it widely into your large view

Perhaps — perhaps, but Heaven only knows, you might understand me! Oh, let me speak!"

"Miriam, dear friend," replied the sculptor, "if I can help you, speak freely, as to a brother."

"Help me? No!" said Miriam.

Kenyon's response had been perfectly frank and kind; and yet the subtlety of Miriam's emotion detected a certain reserve and alarm in his warmly expressed readiness to hear her story. In his secret soul, to say the truth, the sculptor doubted whether it were well for this poor, suffering girl to speak what she so yearned to say, or for him to listen. If there were any active duty of friendship to be performed, then, indeed, he would joyfully have come forward to do his best. But if it were only a pent-up heart that sought an outlet? in that case it was by no means so certain that a confession would do good. The more her secret struggled and fought to be told, the more certain would it be to change all former relations that had subsisted between herself and the friend to whom she might reveal it. Unless he could give her all the sympathy, and just the kind of sympathy that the occasion required, Miriam would hate him by and by, and herself still more, if he let her speak.

This was what Kenyon said to himself; but his reluctance, after all, and whether he were conscious of it or no, resulted from a suspicion that had crept into his heart and lay there in a dark corner. Obscure as it was, when Miriam looked into his eyes, she detected it at once.

"Ah, I shall hate you!" cried she, echoing the thought which he had not spoken; she was half choked with the gush of passion that was thus turned back upon her. "You are as cold and pitiless as your own marble."

"No; but full of sympathy, God knows!" replied he.

In truth his suspicions, however warranted by the mystery in which Miriam was enveloped, had vanished in the earnestness of his kindly and sorrowful emotion. He was now ready to receive her trust.

"Keep your sympathy, then, for sorrows that admit of such solace," said she, making a strong effort to compose herself. "As for my griefs, I know how to manage them. It was all a mistake: you can do nothing for me, unless you petrify me into a marble companion for your Cleopatra there; and I am not of her sisterhood, I do assure you. Forget this foolish scene, my friend, and never let me see a reference to it in your eyes when they meet mine hereafter."

"Since you desire it, all shall be forgotten," answered the sculptor, pressing her hand as she departed; "or, if ever I can serve you, let my readiness to do so be remembered. Meanwhile, dear Miriam, let us meet in the same clear, friendly light as heretofore."

"You are less sincere than I thought you," said Miriam, "if you try to make me think that there will be no change."

As he attended her through the antechamber, she pointed to the statue of the pearl-diver.

"My secret is not a pearl," said she; "yet a man might drown himself in plunging after it."

After Kenyon had closed the door, she went wearily down the staircase, but paused midway, as if debating with herself whether to return.

"The mischief was done," thought she; "and I might as well have had the solace that ought to come with it. I have lost, — by staggering a little way beyond the mark, in the blindness of my distress, — I have lost, as we shall hereafter find, the genuine friendship of this clear-minded, honorable, true-hearted young man, and all for nothing. What if I should go back this moment and compel him to listen?"

She ascended two or three of the stairs, but again paused, murmured to herself, and shook her head.

"No, no, no," she thought; "and I wonder how I ever came to dream of it. Unless I had his heart for my own, — and that is Hilda's, nor would I steal it from her, — it should never be the treasure-place of my secret. It is no precious pearl, as I just now told him; but my dark-red carbuncle — red as blood — is too rich a gem to put into a stranger's casket."

She went down the stairs, and found her Shadow waiting for her in the street.

CHAPTER XV.

AN ÆSTHETIC COMPANY.

ON the evening after Miriam's visit to Kenyon's studio, there was an assemblage composed almost entirely of Anglo-Saxons, and chiefly of American artists, with a sprinkling of their English brethren; and some few of the tourists who still lingered in Rome, now that Holy Week was past. Miriam, Hilda, and the sculptor were all three present, and, with them, Donatello, whose life was so far turned from its natural bent, that, like a pet spaniel, he followed his beloved mistress wherever he could gain admittance.

The place of meeting was in the palatial, but somewhat faded and gloomy apartment of an eminent member of the æsthetic body. It was no more formal an occasion than one of those weekly receptions, common among the foreign residents of Rome, at which pleasant people — or disagreeable ones, as the case may be — encounter one another with little ceremony.

If anywise interested in art, a man must be difficult to please who cannot find fit companionship among a crowd of persons, whose ideas and pursuits all tend towards the general purpose of enlarging the world's stock of beautiful productions.

One of the chief causes that make Rome the favorite residence of artists — their ideal home which they sigh for in advance, and are so loath to migrate from, after once breathing its enchanted air — is, doubtless, that they there find themselves in force, and are numerous enough to create a congenial atmosphere. In every other clime they are isolated strangers; in this land of art, they are free citizens.

Not that, individually, or in the mass, there appears to be any large stock of mutual affection among the brethren of the chisel and the pencil. On the contrary, it will impress the shrewd observer that the jealousies and petty animosities, which the poets of our day have flung aside, still irritate and gnaw into the hearts of this kindred class of imaginative men. It is not difficult to suggest reasons why this should be the fact. The public, in whose good graces lie the sculptor's or the painter's prospects of success, is infinitely smaller than the public to which literary men make their appeal. It is composed of a very limited body of wealthy patrons; and these, as the artist well knows, are but blind judges in matters that require the utmost delicacy of perception. Thus, success in art is apt to become partly an affair of intrigue; and it is almost inevitable that even a gifted artist should look askance at his gifted brother's fame, and be chary of the good word that might help him to sell still another statue or picture. You seldom hear a painter heap generous praise on anything in his special line of art; a sculptor never has a favorable eye for any marble but his own.

Nevertheless, in spite of all these professional grudges, artists are conscious of a social warmth from each other's presence and contiguity. They shiver at the remembrance of their lonely studios in the unsympathizing cities of their native land. For the sake of such brotherhood as they can find, more than for any good that they get from galleries, they linger year after year in Italy, while their originality dies out of them, or is polished away as a barbarism.

The company this evening included several men and women whom the world has heard of, and many others, beyond all question, whom it ought to know. It would be a pleasure to introduce them upon our humble pages, name by name, and — had we confidence enough in our own taste — to crown each well-deserving brow according to its deserts. The opportunity is tempting, but not easily manageable, and far too perilous, both in respect to those individuals whom we might bring forward, and the far greater number that must needs be left in the shade. Ink, moreover, is apt to have a corrosive quality, and might chance to raise a blister, instead of any more agreeable titillation, on skins so sensitive as those of artists. We must therefore forego the delight of illuminating this chapter with personal allusions to men whose renown glows richly on canvas, or gleams in the white moonlight of marble.

Otherwise we might point to an artist who has studied Nature with such tender love that she takes him to her intimacy, enabling him to reproduce her in landscapes that seem the reality of a better earth, and yet are but the truth of the very scenes around us, observed by the painter's insight and interpreted for us by his skill. By his magic, the moon throws her light far out of the picture, and the crimson of the summer night absolutely glimmers on the beholder's face. Or we might indicate a poet-painter, whose song has the vividness of picture, and whose canvas is peopled with angels, fairies, and water-sprites, done to the ethereal life, because he saw them face to face in his poetic mood. Or we might bow before an artist, who has wrought too sincerely, too religiously, with too earnest a feeling, and too delicate a touch, for the world at once to recognize how much toil and thought are compressed into the stately brow of Prospero, and Miranda's maiden loveliness ; or from what a depth within this painter's heart the Angel is leading forth St. Peter.

Thus it would be easy to go on, perpetrating a score of little epigrammatical allusions, like the above, all kindly meant, but none of them quite hitting the mark, and often striking where they were not aimed. It may be allowable to say, however, that American art is much better represented at Rome in the pictorial than in the sculpturesque department. Yet the men of marble appear to have more weight with the public than the men of canvas ; perhaps on account of the greater density and solid substance of the material in which they work, and the sort of physical advantage which their labors thus acquire over the illusive unreality of color. To be a sculptor seems a distinction in itself; whereas a painter is nothing, unless individually eminent.

One sculptor there was, an Englishman, endowed with a beautiful fancy, and possessing at his fingers' ends the capability of doing beautiful things. He was a quiet, simple, elderly personage, with eyes brown and bright, under a slightly impending brow, and a Grecian profile, such as he might have cut with his own chisel. He had spent his life, for forty years, in making Venuses, Cupids, Bacchuses, and a vast deal of other marble progeny of dream-work, or rather frost-work : it was all a vapory exhalation out of the Grecian mythology, crystallizing on the dull window-panes of to-day. Gifted with a more delicate power than any

other man alive, he had foregone to be a Christian reality, and perverted himself into a Pagan idealist, whose
business or efficacy, in our present world, it would be
exceedingly difficult to define.   And, loving and rever-
encing the pure material in which he wrought, as surely
this admirable sculptor did, he had nevertheless robbed
the marble of its chastity, by giving it an artificial
warmth of hue.   Thus it became a sin and shame to
look at his nude goddesses.   They had revealed themselves to his imagination, no doubt, with all their deity
about them ; but, bedaubed with buff-color, they stood
forth to the eyes of the profane in the guise of naked
women.   But, whatever criticism may be ventured on
his style, it was good to meet a man so modest and
yet imbued with such thorough and simple conviction
of his own right principles and practice, and so quietly
satisfied that his kind of antique achievement was all
that sculpture could effect for modern life.

This eminent person's weight and authority among
his artistic brethren were very evident ; for beginning
unobtrusively to utter himself on a topic of art, he
was soon the centre of a little crowd of younger sculptors.   They drank in his wisdom, as if it would serve
all the purposes of original inspiration ; he, meanwhile, discoursing with gentle calmness, as if there
could possibly be no other side, and often ratifying,
as it were, his own conclusions by a mildly emphatic
" Yes."

The veteran sculptor's unsought audience was composed mostly of our own countrymen.   It is fair to
say, that they were a body of very dexterous and
capable artists, each of whom had probably given
the delighted public a nude statue, or had won credit
for even higher skill by the nice carving of button-

holes, shoe-ties, coat-seams, shirt-bosoms, and other such
graceful peculiarities of modern costume.   Smart,
practical men they doubtless were, and some of them
far more than this, but, still, not precisely what an un-
initiated person looks for in a sculptor.   A sculptor,
indeed, to meet the demands which our preconceptions
make upon him, should be even more indispensably
a poet than those who deal in measured verse and
rhyme.   His material, or instrument, which serves
him in the stead of shifting and transitory language,
is a pure, white, undecaying substance.   It insures
immortality to whatever is wrought in it, and therefore makes it a religious obligation to commit no idea
to its mighty guardianship, save such as may repay
the marble for its faithful care, its incorruptible fidel-
ity, by warming it with an ethereal life.   Under this
aspect, marble assumes a sacred character; and no
man should dare to touch it unless he feels within
himself a certain consecration and a priesthood, the
only evidence of which, for the public eye, will be the
high treatment of heroic subjects, or the delicate evo-
lution of spiritual, through material beauty.

No ideas such as the foregoing — no misgivings suggested by them — probably troubled the self-compla-
cency of most of these clever sculptors.   Marble, in
their view, had no such sanctity as we impute to it.
It was merely a sort of white limestone from Carrara,
cut into convenient blocks, and worth, in that state,
about two or three dollars per pound; and it was susceptible of being wrought into certain shapes (by their
own mechanical ingenuity, or that of artisans in their
employment) which would enable them to sell it again
at a much higher figure.   Such men, on the strength
of some small knack in handling clay, which might

have been fitly employed in making wax-work, are
bold to call themselves sculptors. How terrible should
be the thought, that the nude woman whom the modern artist patches together, bit by bit, from a dozen
heterogeneous models, meaning nothing by her, shall
last as long as the Venus of the Capitol! — that his
group of — no matter what, since it has no moral or
intellectual existence — will not physically crumble
any sooner than the immortal agony of the Laocoön!

Yet we love the artists, in every kind; even these,
whose merits we are not quite able to appreciate.
Sculptors, painters, crayon-sketchers, or whatever
branch of æsthetics they adopted, were certainly pleas-
anter people, as we saw them that evening, than the
average whom we meet in ordinary society. They
were not wholly confined within the sordid compass of
practical life; they had a pursuit which, if followed
faithfully out, would lead them to the beautiful, and
always had a tendency thitherward, even if they lingered to gather up golden dross by the wayside. Their
actual business (though they talked about it very
much as other men talk of cotton, politics, flour-bar-
rels, and sugar) necessarily illuminated their conversation with something akin to the ideal. So, when
the guests collected themselves in little groups, here
and there, in the wide saloon, a cheerful and airy gossip began to be heard. The atmosphere ceased to be
precisely that of common life; a faint, mellow tinge,
such as we see in pictures, mingled itself with the
lamplight.

This good effect was assisted by many curious little treasures of art, which the host had taken care to
strew upon his tables. They were principally such
bits of antiquity as the soil of Rome and its neighbor-

hood are still rich in; seals, gems, small figures of
bronze, mediæval carvings in ivory ; things which had
been obtained at little cost, yet might have borne no
inconsiderable value in the museum of a virtuoso.

As interesting as any of these relics was a large
portfolio of old drawings, some of which, in the opinion of their possessor, bore evidence on their faces of
the touch of master-hands.   Very ragged and ill-con-
ditioned they mostly were, yellow with time, and tattered with rough usage ; and, in their best estate, the
designs had been scratched rudely with pen and ink,
on coarse paper, or, if drawn with charcoal or a pencil, were now half rubbed out.   You would not anywhere see rougher and homelier things than these.
But this hasty rudeness made the sketches only the
more valuable ; because the artist seemed to have bestirred himself at the pinch of the moment, snatching
up whatever material was nearest, so as to seize the
first glimpse of an idea that might vanish in the
twinkling of an eye.   Thus, by the spell of a creased,
soiled, and discolored scrap of paper, you were enabled to steal close to an old master, and watch him in
the very effervescence of his genius.

According to the judgment of several connoisseurs,
Raphael's own hand had communicated its magnetism
to one of these sketches ; and, if genuine, it was evidently his first conception of a favorite Madonna, now
hanging in the private apartment of the Grand Duke,
at Florence.   Another drawing was attributed to Leonardo da Vinci, and appeared to be a somewhat varied
design for his picture of Modesty and Vanity, in the
Sciarra Palace.   There were at least half a dozen
others, to which the owner assigned as high an origin.
It was delightful to believe in their authenticity, at

all events ; for these things make the spectator more vividly sensible of a great painter's power, than the final glow and perfected art of the most consummate picture that may have been elaborated from them. There is an effluence of divinity in the first sketch ; and there, if anywhere, you find the pure light of inspiration, which the subsequent toil of the artist serves to bring out in stronger lustre, indeed, but likewise adulterates it with what belongs to an inferior mood. The aroma and fragrance of new thought were perceptible in these designs, after three centuries of wear and tear. The charm lay partly in their very imperfection ; for this is suggestive, and sets the imagination at work ; whereas, the finished picture, if a good one, leaves the spectator nothing to do, and, if bad, confuses, stupefies, disenchants, and disheartens him.

Hilda was greatly interested in this rich portfolio. She lingered so long over one particular sketch, that Miriam asked her what discovery she had made.

" Look at it carefully," replied Hilda, putting the sketch into her hands. " If you take pains to disentangle the design from those pencil-marks that seem to have been scrawled over it, I think you will see something very curious."

" It is a hopeless affair, I am afraid," said Miriam. " I have neither your faith, dear Hilda, nor your perceptive faculty. Fie ! what a blurred scrawl it is indeed ! "

The drawing had originally been very slight, and had suffered more from time and hard usage than almost any other in the collection ; it appeared, too, that there had been an attempt (perhaps by the very hand that drew it) to obliterate the design. By Hilda's help, however, Miriam pretty distinctly made out a winged figure with a drawn sword, and a dragon, or a demon, prostrate at his feet.

"I am convinced," said Hilda, in a low, reverential tone, "that Guido's own touches are on that ancient scrap of paper! If so, it must be his original sketch for the picture of the Archangel Michael setting his foot upon the demon, in the Church of the Cappuccini. The composition and general arrangement of the sketch are the same with those of the picture; the only difference being, that the demon has a more upturned face, and scowls vindictively at the Archangel, who turns away his eyes in painful disgust."

"No wonder!" responded Miriam. "The expression suits the daintiness of Michael's character, as Guido represents him. He never could have looked the demon in the face!"

"Miriam!" exclaimed her friend, reproachfully, "you grieve me, and you know it, by pretending to speak contemptuously of the most beautiful and the divinest figure that mortal painter ever drew."

"Forgive me, Hilda!" said Miriam. "You take these matters more religiously than I can, for my life. Guido's Archangel is a fine picture, of course, but it never impressed me as it does you."

"Well; we will not talk of that," answered Hilda. "What I wanted you to notice, in this sketch, is the face of the demon. It is entirely unlike the demon of the finished picture. Guido, you know, always affirmed that the resemblance to Cardinal Pamfili was either casual or imaginary. Now, here is the face as he first conceived it."

"And a more energetic demon, altogether, than that of the finished picture," said Kenyon, taking the sketch into his hand. "What a spirit is conveyed into the ugliness of this strong, writhing, squirming dragon, under the Archangel's foot! Neither is the face an impossible one. Upon my word, I have seen it some-where, and on the shoulders of a living man!"

"And so have I," said Hilda. "It was what struck me from the first."

"Donatello, look at this face!" cried Kenyon.

The young Italian, as may be supposed, took little interest in matters of art, and seldom or never ven-tured an opinion respecting them. After holding the sketch a single instant in his hand, he flung it from him with a shudder of disgust and repugnance, and a frown that had all the bitterness of hatred.

"I know the face well!" whispered he. "It is Miriam's model!"

It was acknowledged both by Kenyon and Hilda that they had detected, or fancied, the resemblance which Donatello so strongly affirmed; and it added not a little to the grotesque and weird character which, half playfully, half seriously, they assigned to Mir-iam's attendant, to think of him as personating the demon's part in a picture of more than two centuries ago. Had Guido, in his effort to imagine the utmost of sin and misery, which his pencil could represent, hit ideally upon just this face? Or was it an actual portrait of somebody, that haunted the old master, as Miriam was haunted now? Did the ominous shadow follow him through all the sunshine of his earlier ca-reer, and into the gloom that gathered about its close? And when Guido died, did the spectre betake himself to those ancient sepulchres, there awaiting a new vic-tim, till it was Miriam's ill-hap to encounter him?

"I do not acknowledge the resemblance at all," said Miriam, looking narrowly at the sketch; "and, as

I have drawn the face twenty times, I think you will own that I am the best judge."

A discussion here arose, in reference to Guido's Archangel, and it was agreed that these four friends should visit the Church of the Cappuccini the next morning, and critically examine the picture in question ; the similarity between it and the sketch being, at all events, a very curious circumstance.

It was now a little past ten o'clock, when some of the company, who had been standing in a balcony, declared the moonlight to be resplendent. They proposed a ramble through the streets, taking in their way some of those scenes of ruin which produced their best effects under the splendor of the Italian moon.

CHAPTER XVI.

THE proposal for a moonlight ramble was received with acclamation by all the younger portion of the company. They immediately set forth and descended from story to story, dimly lighting their way by waxen tapers, which are a necessary equipment to those whose thoroughfare, in the night - time, lies up and down a Roman staircase. Emerging from the court-yard of the edifice, they looked upward and saw the sky full of light, which seemed to have a delicate purple or crimson lustre, or, at least, some richer tinge than the cold, white moonshine of other skies. It gleamed over the front of the opposite palace, showing the architectural ornaments of its cornice and pillared portal, as well as the iron-barred basement-windows, that gave such a prison-like aspect to the structure, and the shabbiness and squalor that lay along its base. A cobbler was just shutting up his little shop, in the basement of the palace; a cigar-vender's lantern flared in the blast that came through the archway; a French sentinel paced to and fro before the portal; a homeless dog, that haunted thereabouts, barked as obstreperously at the party as if he were the domestic guardian of the precincts.

The air was quietly full of the noise of falling water, the cause of which was nowhere visible, though apparently near at hand. This pleasant, natural sound, not unlike that of a distant cascade in the forest, may be heard in many of the Roman streets and piazzas, when the tumult of the city is hushed ; for consuls, emperors, and popes, the great men of every age, have found no better way of immortalizing their memories, than by the shifting, indestructible, ever new, yet unchanging, upgush and downfall of water. They have written their names in that unstable element, and proved it a more durable record than brass or marble.

"Donatello, you had better take one of those gay, boyish artists for your companion," said Miriam, when she found the Italian youth at her side. " I am not now in a merry mood, as when we set all the world a-dancing the other afternoon, in the Borghese grounds."

" I never wish to dance any more," answered Donatello.

"What a melancholy was in that tone ! " exclaimed Miriam. "You are getting spoilt in this dreary Rome, and will be as wise and as wretched as all the rest of mankind, unless you go back soon to your Tuscan vineyards. Well; give me your arm then ! But take care that no friskiness comes over you. We must walk evenly and heavily to-night! "

The party arranged itself according to its natural affinities or casual likings ; a sculptor generally choosing a painter, and a painter a sculptor, for his companion, in preference to brethren of their own art. Kenyon would gladly have taken Hilda to himself, and have drawn her a little aside from the throng of merry wayfarers. But she kept near Miriam, and seemed, in her gentle and quiet way, to decline a separate alliance either with him or any other of her acquaintances.

So they set forth, and had gone but a little way,
when the narrow street emerged into a piazza, on one
side of which glistening, and dimpling in the moonlight, was the most famous fountain in Rome.   Its
murmur — not to say its uproar — had been in the
ears of the company, ever since they came into the
open air.   It was the Fountain of Trevi, which draws
its precious water from a source far beyond the walls,
whence it flows hitherward through old subterranean
aqueducts, and sparkles forth as pure as the virgin
who first led Agrippa to its well-spring, by her father's
door.

"I shall sip as much of this water as the hollow
of my hand will hold," said Miriam.   "I am leaving
Rome in a few days ; and the tradition goes, that a
parting draught at the Fountain of Trevi insures the
traveller's return, whatever obstacles and improbabilities may seem to beset him.   Will you drink, Donatello ?"

"Signorina, what you drink, I drink," said the
youth.

They and the rest of the party descended some steps
to the water's brim, and, after a sip or two, stood gazing at the absurd design of the fountain, where some
sculptor of Bernini's school had gone absolutely mad
in marble.   It was a great palace-front, with niches
and many bas-reliefs, out of which looked Agrippa's
legendary virgin, and several of the allegoric sisterhood ; while, at the base, appeared Neptune, with his
floundering steeds, and Tritons blowing their horns
about him, and twenty other artificial fantasies, which
the calm moonlight soothed into better taste than was
native to them.

And, after all, it was as magnificent a piece of work

FOUNTAIN OF TREVI

as ever human skill contrived. At the foot of the palatial façade was strown, with careful art and ordered
irregularity, a broad and broken heap of massive rock,
looking as if it might have lain there since the deluge.
Over a central precipice fell the water, in a semicircu-
lar cascade; and from a hundred crevices, on all sides,
snowy jets gushed up, and streams spouted out of the
mouths and nostrils of stone monsters, and fell in glistening drops; while other rivulets, that had run wild,
came leaping from one rude step to another, over
stones that were mossy, slimy, and green with sedge,
because, in a century of their wild play, Nature had
adopted the Fountain of Trevi, with all its elaborate
devices, for her own. Finally, the water, tumbling,
sparkling, and dashing, with joyous haste and never-
ceasing murmur, poured itself into a great marble-
brimmed reservoir, and filled it with a quivering tide;
on which was seen, continually, a snowy semicircle of
momentary foam from the principal cascade, as well
as a multitude of snow-points from smaller jets. The
basin occupied the whole breadth of the piazza, whence
flights of steps descended to its border. A boat might
float, and make voyages from one shore to another in
this mimic lake.

In the daytime, there is hardly a livelier scene in
Rome than the neighborhood of the Fountain of Trevi;
for the piazza is then filled with the stalls of vegetable
and fruit-dealers, chestnut-roasters, cigar-venders, and
other people, whose petty and wandering traffic is
transacted in the open air. It is likewise thronged
with idlers, lounging over the iron railing, and with
Forestieri, who came hither to see the famous fountain. Here, also, are seen men with buckets, urchins
with cans, and maidens (a picture as old as the patri-

archal times) bearing their pitchers upon their heads. For the water of Trevi is in request, far and wide, as the most refreshing draught for feverish lips, the pleasantest to mingle with wine, and the wholesomest to drink, in its native purity, that can anywhere be found. But now, at early midnight, the piazza was a solitude; and it was a delight to behold this untamable water, sporting by itself in the moonshine, and compelling all the elaborate trivialities of art to assume a natural aspect, in accordance with its own powerful simplicity.

"What would be done with this water-power," suggested an artist, "if we had it in one of our American cities? Would they employ it to turn the machinery of a cotton-mill, I wonder?"

"The good people would pull down those rampant marble deities," said Kenyon, "and, possibly, they would give me a commission to carve the one-and-thirty (is that the number?) sister States, each pouring a silver stream from a separate can into one vast basin, which should represent the grand reservoir of national prosperity."

"Or, if they wanted a bit of satire," remarked an English artist, "you could set those same one-and-thirty States to cleansing the national flag of any stains that it may have incurred. The Roman washerwomen at the lavatory yonder, plying their labor in the open air, would serve admirably as models."

"I have often intended to visit this fountain by moonlight," said Miriam, "because it was here that the interview took place between Corinne and Lord Neville, after their separation and temporary estrangement. Pray come behind me, one of you, and let me try whether the face can be recognized in the water."

Leaning over the stone brim of the basin, she heard footsteps stealing behind her, and knew that somebody was looking over her shoulder. The moonshine fell directly behind Miriam, illuminating the palace-front and the whole scene of statues and rocks, and filling the basin, as it were, with tremulous and palpable light. Corinne, it will be remembered, knew Lord Neville by the reflection of his face in the water. In Miriam's case, however (owing to the agitation of the water, its transparency, and the angle at which she was compelled to lean over), no reflected image appeared; nor, from the same causes, would it have been possible for the recognition between Corinne and her lover to take place. The moon, indeed, flung Miriam's shadow at the bottom of the basin, as well as two more shadows of persons who had followed her, on either side.

"Three shadows!" exclaimed Miriam. "Three separate shadows, all so black and heavy that they sink in the water! There they lie on the bottom, as if all three were drowned together. This shadow on my right is Donatello; I know him by his curls, and the turn of his head. My left-hand companion puzzles me; a shapeless mass, as indistinct as the premonition of calamity! Which of you can it be? Ah!"

She had turned round, while speaking, and saw beside her the strange creature, whose attendance on her was already familiar, as a marvel and a jest, to the whole company of artists. A general burst of laughter followed the recognition; while the model leaned towards Miriam, as she shrank from him, and muttered something that was inaudible to those who witnessed the scene. By his gestures, however, they concluded that he was inviting her to bathe her hands.

" He cannot be an Italian ; at least not a Roman," observed an artist. " I never knew one of them to care about ablution. See him now ! It is as if he were trying to wash off the time-stains and earthly soil of a thousand years ! "

Dipping his hands into the capacious washbowl before him, the model rubbed them together with the utmost vehemence. Ever and anon, too, he peeped into the water, as if expecting to see the whole Fountain of Trevi turbid with the results of his ablution. Miriam looked at him, some little time, with an aspect of real terror, and even imitated him by leaning over to peep into the basin. Recovering herself, she took up some of the water in the hollow of her hand, and practised an old form of exorcism by flinging it in her persecutor's face.

" In the name of all the Saints," cried she, " vanish, Demon, and let me be free of you now and forever ! "

" It will not suffice," said some of the mirthful party, " unless the Fountain of Trevi gushes with holy water."

In fact, the exorcism was quite ineffectual upon the pertinacious demon, or whatever the apparition might be. Still he washed his brown, bony talons ; still he peered into the vast basin, as if all the water of that great drinking-cup of Rome must needs be stained black or sanguine ; and still he gesticulated to Miriam to follow his example. The spectators laughed loudly, but yet with a kind of constraint; for the creature's aspect was strangely repulsive and hideous.

Miriam felt her arm seized violently by Donatello. She looked at him, and beheld a tiger-like fury gleaming from his wild eyes.

"Bid me drown him!" whispered he, shuddering between rage and horrible disgust. "You shall hear his death-gurgle in another instant!"

"Peace, peace, Donatello!" said Miriam, soothingly, for this naturally gentle and sportive being seemed all aflame with animal rage. "Do him no mischief! He is mad; and we are as mad as he, if we suffer ourselves to be disquieted by his antics. Let us leave him to bathe his hands till the fountain run dry, if he find solace and pastime in it. What is it to you or me, Donatello? There, there! Be quiet, foolish boy!"

Her tone and gesture were such as she might have used in taming down the wrath of a faithful hound, that had taken upon himself to avenge some supposed affront to his mistress. She smoothed the young man's curls (for his fierce and sudden fury seemed to bristle among his hair), and touched his cheek with her soft palm, till his angry mood was a little assuaged.

"Signorina, do I look as when you first knew me?" asked he, with a heavy, tremulous sigh, as they went onward, somewhat apart from their companions. "Methinks there has been a change upon me, these many months; and more and more, these last few days. The joy is gone out of my life; all gone! all gone! Feel my hand! Is it not very hot? Ah; and my heart burns hotter still!"

"My poor Donatello, you are ill!" said Miriam, with deep sympathy and pity. "This melancholy and sickly Rome is stealing away the rich, joyous life that belongs to you. Go back, my dear friend, to your home among the hills, where (as I gather from what you have told me) your days were filled with simple and blameless delights.　Have you found aught in the world that is worth what you there enjoyed?　Tell me truly, Donatello!"

"Yes!" replied the young man.

"And what, in Heaven's name?" asked she.

"This burning pain in my heart," said Donatello; "for you are in the midst of it."

By this time, they had left the Fountain of Trevi considerably behind them.　Little further allusion was made to the scene at its margin; for the party regarded Miriam's persecutor as diseased in his wits, and were hardly to be surprised by any eccentricity in his deportment.

Threading several narrow streets, they passed through the Piazza of the Holy Apostles, and soon came to Trajan's Forum.　All over the surface of what once was Rome, it seems to be the effort of Time to bury up the ancient city, as if it were a corpse, and he the sexton; so that, in eighteen centuries, the soil over its grave has grown very deep, by the slow scattering of dust, and the accumulation of more modern decay upon older ruin.

This was the fate, also, of Trajan's Forum, until some papal antiquary, a few hundred years ago, began to hollow it out again, and disclosed the full height of the gigantic column wreathed round with bas-reliefs of the old emperor's warlike deeds.　In the area before it stands a grove of stone, consisting of the broken and unequal shafts of a vanished temple, still keeping a majestic order, and apparently incapable of further demolition.　The modern edifices of the piazza (wholly built, no doubt, out of the spoil of its old magnificence) look down into the hollow space whence these pillars rise.

One of the immense gray granite shafts lay in the piazza, on the verge of the area. It was a great, solid fact of the Past, making old Rome actually sensible to the touch and eye; and no study of history, nor force of thought, nor magic of song, could so vitally assure us that Rome once existed, as this sturdy specimen of what its rulers and people wrought.

"And see!" said Kenyon, laying his hand upon it, "there is still a polish remaining on the hard substance of the pillar; and even now, late as it is, I can feel very sensibly the warmth of the noonday sun, which did its best to heat it through. This shaft will endure forever. The polish of eighteen centuries ago, as yet but half rubbed off, and the heat of to-day's sunshine, lingering into the night, seem almost equally ephemeral in relation to it."

"There is comfort to be found in the pillar," remarked Miriam, "hard and heavy as it is. Lying here forever, as it will, it makes all human trouble appear but a momentary annoyance."

"And human happiness as evanescent too," observed Hilda, sighing; "and beautiful art hardly less so! I do not love to think that this dull stone, merely by its massiveness, will last infinitely longer than any picture, in spite of the spiritual life that ought to give it immortality!"

"My poor little Hilda," said Miriam, kissing her compassionately, "would you sacrifice this greatest mortal consolation, which we derive from the transitoriness of all things, — from the right of saying, in every conjecture, 'This, too, will pass away,' — would you give up this unspeakable boon, for the sake of making a picture eternal?"

Their moralizing strain was interrupted by a demonstration from the rest of the party, who, after talking and laughing together, suddenly joined their voices, and shouted at full pitch, —

" Trajan !   Trajan ! "

" Why do you deafen us with such an uproar ? " inquired Miriam.

In truth, the whole piazza had been filled with their idle vociferation ; the echoes from the surrounding houses reverberating the cry of " Trajan," on all sides ; as if there was a great search for that imperial personage, and not so much as a handful of his ashes to be found.

" Why, it was a good opportunity to air our voices in this resounding piazza," replied one of the artists. " Besides, we had really some hopes of summoning Trajan to look at his column, which, you know, he never saw in his lifetime.   Here is your model (who, they say, lived and sinned before Trajan's death) still wandering about Rome ; and why not the Emperor Trajan ? "

" Dead emperors have very little delight in their columns, I am afraid," observed Kenyon.   " All that rich sculpture of Trajan's bloody warfare, twining from the base of the pillar to its capital, may be but an ugly spectacle for his ghostly eyes, if he considers that this huge, storied shaft must be laid before the judgment-seat, as a piece of the evidence of what he did in the flesh.   If ever I am employed to sculpture a hero's monument, I shall think of this, as I put in the bas-reliefs of the pedestal ! "

" There are sermons in stones," said Hilda, thoughtfully, smiling at Kenyon's morality ; " and especially in the stones of Rome."

The party moved on, but deviated a little from the straight way, in order to glance at the ponderous remains of the temple of Mars Ultor, within which a convent of nuns is now established, — a dove-cote, in the war-god's mansion. At only a little distance, they passed the portico of a Temple of Minerva, most rich and beautiful in architecture, but wofully gnawed by time and shattered by violence, besides being buried midway in the accumulation of soil, that rises over dead Rome like a flood-tide. Within this edifice of antique sanctity, a baker's shop was now established, with an entrance on one side; for, everywhere, the remnants of old grandeur and divinity have been made available for the meanest necessities of to-day.

"The baker is just drawing his loaves out of the oven," remarked Kenyon. "Do you smell how sour they are? I should fancy that Minerva (in revenge for the desecration of her temple) had slyly poured vinegar into the batch, if I did not know that the modern Romans prefer their bread in the acetous fermentation."

They turned into the Via Alessandria, and thus gained the rear of the Temple of Peace, and, passing beneath its great arches, pursued their way along a hedge-bordered lane. In all probability, a stately Roman street lay buried beneath that rustic-looking pathway; for they had now emerged from the close and narrow avenues of the modern city, and were treading on a soil where the seeds of antique grandeur had not yet produced the squalid crop that elsewhere sprouts from them. Grassy as the lane was, it skirted along heaps of shapeless ruin, and the bare site of the vast temple that Hadrian planned and built. It terminated on the edge of a somewhat abrupt descent, at the foot of which, with a muddy ditch between, rose, in the bright moonlight, the great curving wall and multitudinous arches of the Coliseum.

CHAPTER XVII.

MIRIAM'S TROUBLE.

As usual of a moonlight evening, several carriages stood at the entrance of this famous ruin, and the precincts and interior were anything but a solitude. The French sentinel on duty beneath the principal archway eyed our party curiously, but offered no obstacle to their admission. Within, the moonlight filled and flooded the great empty space; it glowed upon tier above tier of ruined, grass-grown arches, and made them even too distinctly visible. The splendor of the revelation took away that inestimable effect of dimness and mystery by which the imagination might be assisted to build a grander structure than the Coliseum, and to shatter it with a more picturesque decay. Byron's celebrated description is better than the reality. He beheld the scene in his mind's eye, through the witchery of many intervening years, and faintly illuminated it as if with starlight instead of this broad glow of moonshine.

The party of our friends sat down, three or four of them on a prostrate column, another on a shapeless lump of marble, once a Roman altar; others on the steps of one of the Christian shrines. Goths and barbarians though they were, they chatted as gayly together as if they belonged to the gentle and pleasant race of people who now inhabit Italy. There was much pastime and gayety just then in the area of the

THE COLISEUM

Coliseum, where so many gladiators and wild beasts
had fought and died, and where so much blood of
Christian martyrs had been lapped up by that fiercest
of wild beasts, the Roman populace of yore. Some
youths and maidens were running merry races across
the open space, and playing at hide-and-seek a little
way within the duskiness of the ground-tier of arches,
whence now and then you could hear the half-shriek,
half-laugh of a frolicsome girl, whom the shadow had
betrayed into a young man's arms. Elder groups were
seated on the fragments of pillars and blocks of marble
that lay round the verge of the arena, talking in the
quick, short ripple of the Italian tongue. On the steps
of the great black cross in the centre of the Coliseum
sat a party singing scraps of songs, with much laughter
and merriment between the stanzas.

It was a strange place for song and mirth. That
black cross marks one of the special blood-spots of the
earth where, thousands of times over, the dying gladiator fell, and more of human agony has been endured
for the mere pastime of the multitude than on the
breadth of many battle-fields. From all this crime
and suffering, however, the spot has derived a more
than common sanctity. An inscription promises seven
years' indulgence, seven years of remission from the
pains of purgatory, and earlier enjoyment of heavenly
bliss, for each separate kiss imprinted on the black
cross. What better use could be made of life, after
middle-age, when the accumulated sins are many and
the remaining temptations few, than to spend it all in
kissing the black cross of the Coliseum!

Besides its central consecration, the whole area has
been made sacred by a range of shrines, which are
erected round the circle, each commemorating some

scene or circumstance of the Saviour's passion and suffering.   In accordance with an ordinary custom a pilgrim was making his progress from shrine to shrine upon his knees, and saying a penitential prayer at each.   Light-footed girls ran across the path along which he crept, or sported with their friends close by the shrines where he was kneeling.   The pilgrim took no heed, and the girls meant no irreverence; for in Italy religion jostles along side by side with business and sport, after a fashion of its own, and people are accustomed to kneel down and pray, or see others praying, between two fits of merriment, or between two sins.

To make an end of our description, a red twinkle of light was visible amid the breadth of shadow that fell across the upper part of the Coliseum.   Now it glimmered through a line of arches, or threw a broader gleam as it rose out of some profound abyss of ruin; now it was muffled by a heap of shrubbery which had adventurously clambered to that dizzy height; and so the red light kept ascending to loftier and loftier ranges of the structure, until it stood like a star where the blue sky rested against the Coliseum's topmost wall.   It indicated a party of English or Americans paying the inevitable visit by moonlight, and exalting themselves with raptures that were Byron's, not their own.

Our company of artists sat on the fallen column, the pagan altar, and the steps of the Christian shrine, enjoying the moonlight and shadow, the present gayety and the gloomy reminiscences of the scene, in almost equal share.   Artists, indeed, are lifted by the ideality of their pursuits a little way off the earth, and are therefore able to catch the evanescent fragrance that floats in the atmosphere of life above the heads of the ordinary crowd. Even if they seem endowed with little imagination individually, yet there is a property, a gift, a talisman, common to their class, entitling them to partake somewhat more bountifully than other people in the thin delights of moonshine and romance.

"How delightful this is!" said Hilda; and she sighed for very pleasure.

"Yes," said Kenyon, who sat on the column, at her side. "The Coliseum is far more delightful, as we enjoy it now, than when eighty thousand persons sat squeezed together, row above row, to see their fellow-creatures torn by lions and tigers limb from limb. What a strange thought that the Coliseum was really built for us, and has not come to its best uses till almost two thousand years after it was finished!"

"The Emperor Vespasian scarcely had us in his mind," said Hilda, smiling; "but I thank him none the less for building it."

"He gets small thanks, I fear, from the people whose bloody instincts he pampered," rejoined Kenyon. "Fancy a nightly assemblage of eighty thousand melancholy and remorseful ghosts, looking down from those tiers of broken arches, striving to repent of the savage pleasures which they once enjoyed, but still longing to enjoy them over again."

"You bring a Gothic horror into this peaceful moonlight scene," said Hilda.

"Nay, I have good authority for peopling the Coliseum with phantoms," replied the sculptor. "Do you remember that veritable scene in Benvenuto Cellini's autobiography, in which a necromancer of his acquaintance draws a magic circle — just where the black cross

stands now, I suppose — and raises myriads of de-
mons? Benvenuto saw them with his own eyes, —
giants, pygmies, and other creatures of frightful aspect, — capering and dancing on yonder walls. Those
spectres must have been Romans, in their lifetime, and
frequenters of this bloody amphitheatre."

"I see a spectre, now!" said Hilda, with a little
thrill of uneasiness. "Have you watched that pilgrim, who is going round the whole circle of shrines,
on his knees, and praying with such fervency at every
one? Now that he has revolved so far in his orbit,
and has the moonshine on his face as he turns towards
us, methinks I recognize him!"

"And so do I," said Kenyon. "Poor Miriam! Do
you think she sees him?"

They looked round, and perceived that Miriam had
risen from the steps of the shrine and disappeared.
She had shrunk back, in fact, into the deep obscurity
of an arch that opened just behind them.

Donatello, whose faithful watch was no more to be
eluded than that of a hound, had stolen after her,
and became the innocent witness of a spectacle that
had its own kind of horror. Unaware of his presence, and fancying herself wholly unseen, the beautiful
Miriam began to gesticulate extravagantly, gnashing
her teeth, flinging her arms wildly abroad, stamping
with her foot. It was as if she had stepped aside for
an instant, solely to snatch the relief of a brief fit of
madness. Persons in acute trouble, or laboring under
strong excitement, with a necessity for concealing it,
are prone to relieve their nerves in this wild way;
although, when practicable, they find a more effectual
solace in shrieking aloud.

Thus, as soon as she threw off her self-control, under

the dusky arches of the Coliseum, we may consider Miriam as a mad woman, concentrating the elements of a long insanity into that instant.

"Signorina! signorina! have pity on me!" cried Donatello, approaching her; "this is too terrible!"

"How dare you look at me!" exclaimed Miriam, with a start; then, whispering below her breath, "men have been struck dead for a less offence!"

"If you desire it, or need it," said Donatello, humbly, "I shall not be loath to die."

"Donatello," said Miriam, coming close to the young man, and speaking low, but still the almost insanity of the moment vibrating in her voice, "if you love yourself; if you desire those earthly blessings, such as you, of all men, were made for; if you would come to a good old age among your olive-orchards and your Tuscan vines, as your forefathers did; if you would leave children to enjoy the same peaceful, happy, innocent life, then flee from me. Look not behind you! Get you gone without another word." He gazed sadly at her, but did not stir. "I tell you," Miriam went on, "there is a great evil hanging over me! I know it; I see it in the sky; I feel it in the air! It will overwhelm me as utterly as if this arch should crumble down upon our heads! It will crush you, too, if you stand at my side! Depart, then; and make the sign of the cross, as your faith bids you, when an evil spirit is nigh. Cast me off, or you are lost forever."

A higher sentiment brightened upon Donatello's face than had hitherto seemed to belong to its simple expression and sensuous beauty.

"I will never quit you," he said; "you cannot drive me from you."

"Poor Donatello!" said Miriam, in a changed tone,

and rather to herself than him. "Is there no other that seeks me out, — follows me, — is obstinate to share my affliction and my doom, — but only you! They call me beautiful; and I used to fancy that, at my need, I could bring the whole world to my feet. And lo! here is my utmost need; and my beauty and my gifts have brought me only this poor, simple boy. Half-witted, they call him; and surely fit for nothing but to be happy. And I accept his aid! To-morrow, to-morrow, I will tell him all! Ah! what a sin to stain his joyous nature with the blackness of a woe like mine!"

She held out her hand to him, and smiled sadly as Donatello pressed it to his lips. They were now about to emerge from the depth of the arch; but, just then, the kneeling pilgrim, in his revolution round the orbit of the shrines, had reached the one on the steps of which Miriam had been sitting. There, as at the other shrines, he prayed, or seemed to pray. It struck Kenyon, however, — who sat close by, and saw his face distinctly, — that the suppliant was merely performing an enjoined penance, and without the penitence that ought to have given it effectual life. Even as he knelt, his eyes wandered, and Miriam soon felt that he had detected her, half hidden as she was within the obscurity of the arch.

"He is evidently a good Catholic, however," whispered one of the party. "After all, I fear we cannot identify him with the ancient pagan who haunts the catacombs."

"The doctors of the Propaganda may have converted him," said another; "they have had fifteen hundred years to perform the task."

The company now deemed it time to continue their

ramble. Emerging from a side entrance of the Coliseum, they had on their left the Arch of Constantine,
and, above it, the shapeless ruins of the Palace of the
Cæsars ; portions of which have taken shape anew, in
mediæval convents and modern villas. They turned
their faces cityward, and, treading over the broad
flagstones of the old Roman pavement, passed through
the Arch of Titus. The moon shone brightly enough
within it, to show the seven-branched Jewish candlestick, cut in the marble of the interior. The original
of that awful trophy lies buried, at this moment, in
the yellow mud of the Tiber ; and, could its gold of
Ophir again be brought to light, it would be the most
precious relic of past ages, in the estimation of both
Jew and Gentile.

Standing amid so much ancient dust, it is difficult
to spare the reader the commonplaces of enthusiasm,
on which hundreds of tourists have already insisted.
Over this half-worn pavement, and beneath this Arch
of Titus, the Roman armies had trodden in their outward march, to fight battles, a world's width away.
Returning victorious, with royal captives and inestimable spoil, a Roman triumph, that most gorgeous pageant of earthly pride, had streamed and flaunted in
hundred-fold succession over these same flagstones, and
through this yet stalwart archway. It is politic, however, to make few allusions to such a past ; nor, if we
would create an interest in the characters of our story,
is it wise to suggest how Cicero's foot may have stepped
on yonder stone, or how Horace was wont to stroll near
by, making his footsteps chime with the measure of the
ode that was ringing in his mind. The very ghosts of
that massive and stately epoch have so much density
that the actual people of to-day seem the thinner of the

two, and stand more ghostlike by the arches and columns, letting the rich sculpture be discerned through their ill-compacted substance.

The party kept onward, often meeting pairs and groups of midnight strollers like themselves. On such a moonlight night as this, Rome keeps itself awake and stirring, and is full of song and pastime, the noise of which mingles with your dreams, if you have gone betimes to bed. But it is better to be abroad, and take our own share of the enjoyable time; for the languor that weighs so heavily in the Roman atmosphere by day is lightened beneath the moon and stars.

They had now reached the precincts of the Forum.

CHAPTER XVIII.

ON THE EDGE OF A PRECIPICE.

"LET us settle it," said Kenyon, stamping his foot firmly down, "that this is precisely the spot where the chasm opened, into which Curtius precipitated his good steed and himself. Imagine the great, dusky gap, impenetrably deep, and with half-shaped monsters and hideous faces looming upward out of it, to the vast affright of the good citizens who peeped over the brim! There, now, is a subject, hitherto unthought of, for a grim and ghastly story, and, methinks, with a moral as deep as the gulf itself. Within it, beyond a question, there were prophetic visions, — intimations of all the future calamities of Rome, — shades of Goths, and Gauls, and even of the French soldiers of to-day. It was a pity to close it up so soon! I would give much for a peep into such a chasm."

"I fancy," remarked Miriam, "that every person takes a peep into it in moments of gloom and despondency; that is to say, in his moments of deepest insight."

"Where is it, then?" asked Hilda. "I never peeped into it."

"Wait, and it will open for you," replied her friend. "The chasm was merely one of the orifices of that pit of blackness that lies beneath us, everywhere. The firmest substance of human happiness is but a thin crust spread over it, with just reality enough to bear up the illusive stage-scenery amid which we tread. It needs no earthquake to open the chasm. A footstep, a little heavier than ordinary, will serve; and we must step very daintily, not to break through the crust at any moment. By and by, we inevitably sink! It was a foolish piece of heroism in Curtius to precipitate himself there, in advance; for all Rome, you see, has been swallowed up in that gulf, in spite of him. The Palace of the Cæsars has gone down thither, with a hollow, rumbling sound of its fragments! All the temples have tumbled into it; and thousands of statues have been thrown after! All the armies and the triumphs have marched into the great chasm, with their martial music playing, as they stepped over the brink. All the heroes, the statesmen, and the poets! All piled upon poor Curtius, who thought to have saved them all! I am loath to smile at the self-conceit of that gallant horseman, but cannot well avoid it."

"It grieves me to hear you speak thus, Miriam," said Hilda, whose natural and cheerful piety was shocked by her friend's gloomy view of human destinies. "It seems to me that there is no chasm, nor any hideous emptiness under our feet, except what the evil within us digs. If there be such a chasm, let us bridge it over with good thoughts and deeds, and we shall tread safely to the other side. It was the guilt of Rome, no doubt, that caused this gulf to open; and Curtius filled it up with his heroic self-sacrifice and patriotism, which was the best virtue that the old Romans knew. Every wrong thing makes the gulf deeper; every right one helps to fill it up. As the evil of Rome was far more than its good, the whole commonwealth finally sank into it, indeed, but of no original necessity."

ARCH OF TITUS

"Well, Hilda, it came to the same thing at last," answered Miriam, despondingly.

"Doubtless, too," resumed the sculptor (for his imagination was greatly excited by the idea of this wondrous chasm), "all the blood that the Romans shed, whether on battle-fields, or in the Coliseum, or on the cross,—in whatever public or private murder,—ran into this fatal gulf, and formed a mighty subterranean lake of gore, right beneath our feet. The blood from the thirty wounds in Cæsar's breast flowed hitherward, and that pure little rivulet from Virginia's bosom, too! Virginia, beyond all question, was stabbed by her father, precisely where we are standing."

"Then the spot is hallowed forever!" said Hilda.

"Is there such blessed potency in bloodshed?" asked Miriam. "Nay, Hilda, do not protest! I take your meaning rightly."

They again moved forward. And still, from the Forum and the Via Sacra, from beneath the arches of the Temple of Peace on one side, and the acclivity of the Palace of the Cæsars on the other, there arose singing voices of parties that were strolling through the moonlight. Thus, the air was full of kindred melodies that encountered one another, and twined themselves into a broad, vague music, out of which no single strain could be disentangled. These good examples, as well as the harmonious influences of the hour, incited our artist-friends to make proof of their own vocal powers. With what skill and breath they had, they set up a choral strain,—"Hail, Columbia!" we believe,—which those old Roman echoes must have found it exceeding difficult to repeat aright. Even Hilda poured the slender sweetness of her note into her country's song. Miriam was at first silent, being perhaps unfamiliar with the air and burden. But, suddenly, she threw out such a swell and gush of sound, that it seemed to pervade the whole choir of other voices, and then to rise above them all, and become audible in what would else have been the silence of an upper region.   That volume of melodious voice was one of the tokens of a great trouble.   There had long been an impulse upon her — amounting, at last, to a necessity — to shriek aloud; but she had struggled against it, till the thunderous anthem gave her an opportunity to relieve her heart by a great cry.

They passed the solitary Column of Phocas, and looked down into the excavated space, where a confusion of pillars, arches, pavements, and shattered blocks and shafts — the crumbs of various ruin dropped from the devouring maw of Time — stand, or lie, at the base of the Capitoline Hill.   That renowned hillock (for it is little more) now arose abruptly above them. The ponderous masonry, with which the hill-side is built up, is as old as Rome itself, and looks likely to endure while the world retains any substance or permanence.   It once sustained the Capitol, and now bears up the great pile which the mediæval builders raised on the antique foundation, and that still loftier tower, which looks abroad upon a larger page of deeper historic interest than any other scene can show. On the same pedestal of Roman masonry, other structures will doubtless rise, and vanish like ephemeral things.

To a spectator on the spot, it is remarkable that the events of Roman history, and Roman life itself, appear not so distant as the Gothic ages which succeeded them.   We stand in the Forum, or on the height of the Capitol, and seem to see the Roman epoch close at hand. We forget that a chasm extends between it and ourselves, in which lie all those dark, rude, unlettered centuries, around the birth-time of Christianity, as well as the age of chivalry and romance, the feudal system, and the infancy of a better civilization than that of Rome. Or, if we remember these mediæval times, they look further off than the Augustan age. The reason may be, that the old Roman literature survives, and creates for us an intimacy with the classic ages, which we have no means of forming with the subsequent ones.

The Italian climate, moreover, robs age of its reverence and makes it look newer than it is. Not the Coliseum, nor the tombs of the Appian Way, nor the oldest pillar in the Forum, nor any other Roman ruin, be it as dilapidated as it may, ever give the impression of venerable antiquity which we gather, along with the ivy, from the gray walls of an English abbey or castle. And yet every brick or stone, which we pick up among the former, had fallen ages before the foundation of the latter was begun. This is owing to the kindliness with which Nature takes an English ruin to her heart, covering it with ivy, as tenderly as Robin Redbreast covered the dead babes with forest leaves. She strives to make it a part of herself, gradually obliterating the handiwork of man, and supplanting it with her own mosses and trailing verdure, till she has won the whole structure back. But, in Italy, whenever man has once hewn a stone, Nature forthwith relinquishes her right to it, and never lays her finger on it again. Age after age finds it bare and naked, in the barren sunshine, and leaves it so. Besides this natural disadvantage, too, each succeeding century, in Rome, has done its best to ruin the very ruins, so far as their picturesque

effect is concerned, by stealing away the marble and
hewn stone, and leaving only yellow bricks, which
never can look venerable.

The party ascended the winding way that leads from
the Forum to the Piazza of the Campidoglio on the
summit of the Capitoline Hill.   They stood awhile to
contemplate the bronze equestrian statue of Marcus
Aurelius.   The moonlight glistened upon traces of the
gilding which had once covered both rider and steed;
these were almost gone, but the aspect of dignity was
still perfect, clothing the figure as it were with an imperial robe of light.   It is the most majestic representation of the kingly character that ever the world has
seen.   A sight of the old heathen emperor is enough
to create an evanescent sentiment of loyalty even in
a democratic bosom, so august does he look, so fit to
rule, so worthy of man's profoundest homage and
obedience, so inevitably attractive of his love.   He
stretches forth his hand with an air of grand beneficence and unlimited authority, as if uttering a decree
from which no appeal was permissible, but in which
the obedient subject would find his highest interests
consulted; a command that was in itself a benediction.

"The sculptor of this statue knew what a king
should be," observed Kenyon, "and knew, likewise,
the heart of mankind, and how it craves a true ruler,
under whatever title, as a child its father."

"Oh, if there were but one such man as this!" exclaimed Miriam.   "One such man in an age, and one
in all the world; then how speedily would the strife,
wickedness, and sorrow of us poor creatures be relieved.   We would come to him with our griefs, whatever they might be, — even a poor, frail woman bur-

MARCUS AURELIUS

dened with her heavy heart, — and lay them at his feet, and never need to take them up again. The rightful king would see to all."

"What an idea of the regal office and duty!" said Kenyon, with a smile. "It is a woman's idea of the whole matter to perfection. It is Hilda's, too, no doubt?"

"No," answered the quiet Hilda; "I should never look for such assistance from an earthly king."

"Hilda, my religious Hilda," whispered Miriam, suddenly drawing the girl close to her, "do you know how it is with me? I would give all I have or hope — my life, oh how freely — for one instant of your trust in God! You little guess my need of it. You really think, then, that He sees and cares for us?"

"Miriam, you frighten me."

"Hush, hush! do not let them hear you!" whispered Miriam. "I frighten you, you say; for Heaven's sake, how? Am I strange? is there anything wild in my behavior?"

"Only for that moment," replied Hilda, "because you seemed to doubt God's providence."

"We will talk of that another time," said her friend. "Just now it is very dark to me."

On the left of the Piazza of the Campidoglio, as you face cityward, and at the head of the long and stately flight of steps descending from the Capitoline Hill to the level of lower Rome, there is a narrow lane or passage. Into this the party of our friends now turned. The path ascended a little, and ran along under the walls of a palace, but soon passed through a gateway, and terminated in a small paved court-yard. It was bordered by a low parapet.

The spot, for some reason or other, impressed them

as exceedingly lonely. On one side was the great
height of the palace, with the moonshine falling over
it, and showing all the windows barred and shuttered.
Not a human eye could look down into the little court-
yard, even if the seemingly deserted palace had a
tenant.   On all other sides of its narrow compass
there was nothing but the parapet, which as it now appeared was built right on the edge of a steep precipice.
Gazing from its imminent brow, the party beheld a
crowded confusion of roofs spreading over the whole
space between them and the line of hills that lay beyond the Tiber.   A long, misty wreath, just dense
enough to catch a little of the moonshine, floated
above the houses, midway towards the hilly line, and
showed the course of the unseen river.   Far away on
the right, the moon gleamed on the dome of St.
Peter's as well as on many lesser and nearer domes.

"What a beautiful view of the city!" exclaimed
Hilda; "and I never saw Rome from this point before."

"It ought to afford a good prospect," said the sculptor; "for it was from this point — at least we are at
liberty to think so, if we choose — that many a famous
Roman caught his last glimpse of his native city, and
of all other earthly things.   This is one of the sides
of the Tarpeian Rock.   Look over the parapet, and
see what a sheer tumble there might still be for a
traitor, in spite of the thirty feet of soil that have accumulated at the foot of the precipice."

They all bent over, and saw that the cliff fell per-
pendicularly downward to about the depth, or rather
more, at which the tall palace rose in height above their
heads.   Not that it was still the natural, shaggy front
of the original precipice; for it appeared to be cased

in ancient stone-work, through which the primeval rock showed its face here and there grimly and doubtfully. Mosses grew on the slight projections, and little shrubs sprouted out of the crevices, but could not much soften the stern aspect of the cliff. Brightly as the Italian moonlight fell a-down the height, it scarcely showed what portion of it was man's work, and what was nature's, but left it all in very much the same kind of ambiguity and half-knowledge in which antiquarians generally leave the identity of Roman remains.

The roofs of some poor-looking houses, which had been built against the base and sides of the cliff, rose nearly midway to the top; but from an angle of the parapet there was a precipitous plunge straight downward into a stone-paved court.

"I prefer this to any other site as having been veritably the Traitor's Leap," said Kenyon, "because it was so convenient to the Capitol. It was an admirable idea of those stern old fellows to fling their political criminals down from the very summit on which stood the Senate House and Jove's Temple, emblems of the institutions which they sought to violate. It symbolizes how sudden was the fall in those days from the utmost height of ambition to its profoundest ruin."

"Come, come; it is midnight," cried another artist, "too late to be moralizing here. We are literally dreaming on the edge of a precipice. Let us go home."

"It is time, indeed," said Hilda.

The sculptor was not without hopes that he might be favored with the sweet charge of escorting Hilda to the foot of her tower. Accordingly, when the party prepared to turn back, he offered her his arm. Hilda at first accepted it ; but when they had partly threaded the passage between the little court-yard and the Piazza del Campidoglio, she discovered that Miriam had remained behind.

" I must go back," said she, withdrawing her arm from Kenyon's ; " but pray do not come with me. Several times this evening I have had a fancy that Miriam had something on her mind, some sorrow or perplexity, which, perhaps, it would relieve her to tell me about. No, no ; do not turn back ! Donatello will be a sufficient guardian for Miriam and me."

The sculptor was a good deal mortified, and perhaps a little angry : but he knew Hilda's mood of gentle decision and independence too well not to obey her. He therefore suffered the fearless maiden to return alone.

Meanwhile Miriam had not noticed the departure of the rest of the company ; she remained on the edge of the precipice and Donatello along with her.

" It would be a fatal fall, still," she said to herself, looking over the parapet, and shuddering as her eye measured the depth. " Yes ; surely yes ! Even without the weight of an overburdened heart, a human body would fall heavily enough upon those stones to shake all its joints asunder. How soon it would be over ! "

Donatello, of whose presence she was possibly not aware, now pressed closer to her side ; and he, too, like Miriam, bent over the low parapet and trembled violently. Yet he seemed to feel that perilous fascination which haunts the brow of precipices, tempting the unwary one to fling himself over for the very horror of the thing, for, after drawing hastily back, he again looked down, thrusting himself out farther than before. He then stood silent a brief space, struggling, perhaps, to make himself conscious of the historic associations of the scene.

"What are you thinking of, Donatello?" asked Miriam.

"Who are they," said he, looking earnestly in her face, "who have been flung over here in days gone by?"

"Men that cumbered the world," she replied. "Men whose lives were the bane of their fellow-creatures. Men who poisoned the air, which is the common breath of all, for their own selfish purposes. There was short work with such men in old Roman times. Just in the moment of their triumph, a hand, as of an avenging giant, clutched them, and dashed the wretches down this precipice."

"Was it well done?" asked the young man.

"It was well done," answered Miriam; "innocent persons were saved by the destruction of a guilty one, who deserved his doom."

While this brief conversation passed, Donatello had once or twice glanced aside with a watchful air, just as a hound may often be seen to take sidelong note of some suspicious object, while he gives his more direct attention to something nearer at hand. Miriam seemed now first to become aware of the silence that had followed upon the cheerful talk and laughter of a few moments before.

Looking round, she perceived that all her company of merry friends had retired, and Hilda, too, in whose soft and quiet presence she had always an indescribable feeling of security. All gone; and only herself and Donatello left hanging over the brow of the ominous precipice.

Not so, however; not entirely alone! In the basement wall of the palace, shaded from the moon, there was a deep, empty niche, that had probably once contained a statue; not empty, either; for a figure now came forth from it and approached Miriam. She must have had cause to dread some unspeakable evil from this strange persecutor, and to know that this was the very crisis of her calamity; for, as he drew near, such a cold, sick despair crept over her, that it impeded her breath, and benumbed her natural promptitude of thought. Miriam seemed dreamily to remember falling on her knees; but, in her whole recollection of that wild moment, she beheld herself as in a dim show, and could not well distinguish what was done and suffered; no, not even whether she were really an actor and sufferer in the scene.

Hilda, meanwhile, had separated herself from the sculptor, and turned back to rejoin her friend. At a distance, she still heard the mirth of her late companions, who were going down the cityward descent of the Capitoline Hill; they had set up a new stave of melody, in which her own soft voice, as well as the powerful sweetness of Miriam's, was sadly missed.

The door of the little court-yard had swung upon its hinges, and partly closed itself. Hilda (whose native gentleness pervaded all her movements) was quietly opening it, when she was startled, midway, by the noise of a struggle within, beginning and ending all in one breathless instant. Along with it, or closely succeeding it, was a loud, fearful cry, which quivered upward through the air, and sank quivering downward to the earth. Then, a silence! Poor Hilda had looked into the court-yard, and saw the whole quick passage of a deed, which took but that little time to grave itself in the eternal adamant.

CHAPTER XIX.

THE door of the court-yard swung slowly, and closed itself of its own accord. Miriam and Donatello were now alone there. She clasped her hands, and looked wildly at the young man, whose form seemed to have dilated, and whose eyes blazed with the fierce energy that had suddenly inspired him. It had kindled him into a man; it had developed within him an intelligence which was no native characteristic of the Donatello whom we have heretofore known. But that simple and joyous creature was gone forever.

"What have you done?" said Miriam, in a horror-stricken whisper.

The glow of rage was still lurid on Donatello's face, and now flashed out again from his eyes.

"I did what ought to be done to a traitor!" he replied. "I did what your eyes bade me do, when I asked them with mine, as I held the wretch over the precipice!"

These last words struck Miriam like a bullet. Could it be so? Had her eyes provoked or assented to this deed? She had not known it. But, alas! looking back into the frenzy and turmoil of the scene just acted, she could not deny — she was not sure whether it might be so, or no — that a wild joy had flamed up in her heart, when she beheld her persecutor in his mortal peril. Was it horror? — or ecstasy? — or both in one? Be the emotion what it might, it had blazed up more madly, when Donatello flung his victim off the cliff, and more and more, while his shriek went quivering downward. With the dead thump upon the stones below, had come an unutterable horror.

"And my eyes bade you do it!" repeated she.

They both leaned over the parapet, and gazed downward as earnestly as if some inestimable treasure had fallen over, and were yet recoverable. On the pavement, below, was a dark mass, lying in a heap, with little or nothing human in its appearance, except that the hands were stretched out, as if they might have clutched, for a moment, at the small square stones. But there was no motion in them now. Miriam watched the heap of mortality while she could count a hundred, which she took pains to do. No stir; not a finger moved!

"You have killed him, Donatello! He is quite dead!" said she. "Stone dead! Would I were so, too!"

"Did you not mean that he should die?" sternly asked Donatello, still in the glow of that intelligence which passion had developed in him. "There was short time to weigh the matter; but he had his trial in that breath or two while I held him over the cliff, and his sentence in that one glance, when your eyes responded to mine! Say that I have slain him against your will, — say that he died without your whole consent, — and, in another breath, you shall see me lying beside him."

"Oh, never!" cried Miriam. "My one, own friend! Never, never, never!"

She turned to him, — the guilty, blood-stained,

lonely woman, — she turned to her fellow - criminal, the youth, so lately innocent, whom she had drawn into her doom. She pressed him close, close to her bosom, with a clinging embrace that brought their two hearts together, till the horror and agony of each was combined into one emotion, and that a kind of rapture.

"Yes, Donatello, you speak the truth!" said she; "my heart consented to what you did. We two slew yonder wretch. The deed knots us together, for time and eternity, like the coil of a serpent!"

They threw one other glance at the heap of death below, to assure themselves that it was there; so like a dream was the whole thing. Then they turned from that fatal precipice, and came out of the court-yard, arm in arm, heart in heart. Instinctively, they were heedful not to sever themselves so much as a pace or two from one another, for fear of the terror and deadly chill that would thenceforth wait for them in solitude. Their deed — the crime which Donatello wrought, and Miriam accepted on the instant — had wreathed itself, as she said, like a serpent, in inextricable links about both their souls, and drew them into one, by its terrible contractile power. It was closer than a marriage-bond. So intimate, in those first moments, was the union, that it seemed as if their new sympathy annihilated all other ties, and that they were released from the chain of humanity; a new sphere, a special law, had been created for them alone. The world could not come near them; they were safe!

When they reached the flight of steps leading downward from the Capitol, there was a far - off noise of singing and laughter. Swift, indeed, had been the rush of the crisis that was come and gone! This was

still the merriment of the party that had so recently
been their companions. They recognized the voices
which, a little while ago, had accorded and sung in
cadence with their own. But they were familiar voices
no more; they sounded strangely, and, as it were, out
of the depths of space; so remote was all that per-
tained to the past life of these guilty ones, in the moral
seclusion that had suddenly extended itself around
them. But how close, and ever closer, did the breath
of the immeasurable waste, that lay between them and
all brotherhood or sisterhood, now press them one
within the other!

"O friend!" cried Miriam, so putting her soul into
the word that it took a heavy richness of meaning,
and seemed never to have been spoken before, — "O
friend, are you conscious, as I am, of this companionship that knits our heart-strings together?"

"I feel it, Miriam," said Donatello. "We draw
one breath; we live one life!"

"Only yesterday," continued Miriam; "nay, only
a short half-hour ago, I shivered in an icy solitude.
No friendship, no sisterhood, could come near enough
to keep the warmth within my heart. In an instant,
all is changed! There can be no more loneliness!"

"None, Miriam!" said Donatello.

"None, my beautiful one!" responded Miriam, gazing in his face, which had taken a higher, almost an
heroic aspect, from the strength of passion. "None,
my innocent one! Surely, it is no crime that we have
committed. One wretched and worthless life has been
sacrificed to cement two other lives for evermore."

"For evermore, Miriam!" said Donatello; "cemented with his blood!"

The young man started at the word which he had

himself spoken; it may be that it brought home, to
the simplicity of his imagination, what he had not before dreamed of, — the ever-increasing loathsomeness
of a union that consists in guilt. Cemented with
blood, which would corrupt and grow more noisome
forever and forever, but bind them none the less
strictly for that.

"Forget it! Cast it all behind you!" said Miriam,
detecting, by her sympathy, the pang that was in his
heart. "The deed has done its office, and has no existence any more."

They flung the past behind them, as she counselled,
or else distilled from it a fiery intoxication, which sufficed to carry them triumphantly through those first
moments of their doom. For, guilt has its moment of
rapture too. The foremost result of a broken law is
ever an ecstatic sense of freedom. And thus there
exhaled upward (out of their dark sympathy, at the
base of which lay a human corpse) a bliss, or an insanity, which the unhappy pair imagined to be well
worth the sleepy innocence that was forever lost to
them.

As their spirits rose to the solemn madness of the
occasion, they went onward, — not stealthily, not fearfully, — but with a stately gait and aspect. Passion
lent them (as it does to meaner shapes) its brief nobility of carriage. They trod through the streets of
Rome, as if they, too, were among the majestic and
guilty shadows, that, from ages long gone by, have
haunted the blood-stained city. And, at Miriam's
suggestion, they turned aside, for the sake of treading
loftily past the old site of Pompey's Forum.

"For there was a great deed done here!" she said,
— "a deed of blood like ours! Who knows, but we

may meet the high and ever-sad fraternity of Cæsar's murderers, and exchange a salutation?"

"Are they our brethren, now?" asked Donatello.

"Yes; all of them," said Miriam; "and many another, whom the world little dreams of, has been made our brother or our sister, by what we have done within this hour!"

And, at the thought, she shivered. Where, then, was the seclusion, the remoteness, the strange, lonesome Paradise, into which she and her one companion had been transported by their crime? Was there, indeed, no such refuge, but only a crowded thoroughfare and jostling throng of criminals? And was it true, that whatever hand had a blood-stain on it, — or had poured out poison, — or strangled a babe at its birth, — or clutched a grandsire's throat, he sleeping, and robbed him of his few last breaths, — had now the right to offer itself in fellowship with their two hands? Too certainly, that right existed. It is a terrible thought, that an individual wrong-doing melts into the great mass of human crime, and makes us, — who dreamed only of our own little separate sin, — makes us guilty of the whole. And thus Miriam and her lover were not an insulated pair, but members of an innumerable confraternity of guilty ones, all shuddering at each other.

"But not now; not yet," she murmured to herself. "To-night, at least, there shall be no remorse!"

Wandering without a purpose, it so chanced that they turned into a street, at one extremity of which stood Hilda's tower. There was a light in her high chamber; a light, too, at the Virgin's shrine; and the glimmer of these two was the loftiest light beneath the stars. Miriam drew Donatello's arm, to make him stop, and while they stood at some distance looking at Hilda's window, they beheld her approach and throw it open. She leaned far forth, and extended her clasped hands towards the sky.

"The good, pure, child! She is praying, Donatello," said Miriam, with a kind of simple joy at witnessing the devoutness of her friend. Then her own sin rushed upon her, and she shouted, with the rich strength of her voice, "Pray for us, Hilda; we need it!"

Whether Hilda heard and recognized the voice we cannot tell. The window was immediately closed, and her form disappeared from behind the snowy curtain. Miriam felt this to be a token that the cry of her condemned spirit was shut out of heaven.

VOL. VI.

CHAPTER XX.

THE BURIAL CHANT.

THE Church of the Capuchins (where, as the reader may remember, some of our acquaintances had made an engagement to meet) stands a little aside from the Piazza Barberini. Thither, at the hour agreed upon, on the morning after the scenes last described, Miriam and Donatello directed their steps. At no time are people so sedulously careful to keep their trifling appointments, attend to their ordinary occupations, and thus put a commonplace aspect on life, as when conscious of some secret that if suspected would make them look monstrous in the general eye.

Yet how tame and wearisome is the impression of all ordinary things in the contrast with such a fact! How sick and tremulous, the next morning, is the spirit that has dared so much only the night before! How icy cold is the heart, when the fervor, the wild ecstasy of passion, has faded away, and sunk down among the dead ashes of the fire that blazed so fiercely, and was fed by the very substance of its life! How faintly does the criminal stagger onward, lacking the impulse of that strong madness that hurried him into guilt, and treacherously deserts him in the midst of it!

When Miriam and Donatello drew near the church, they found only Kenyon awaiting them on the steps. Hilda had likewise promised to be of the party, but had not yet appeared. Meeting the sculptor, Miriam put a force upon herself and succeeded in creating an artificial flow of spirits, which, to any but the nicest observation, was quite as effective as a natural one. She spoke sympathizingly to the sculptor on the subject of Hilda's absence, and somewhat annoyed him by alluding in Donatello's hearing to an attachment which had never been openly avowed, though perhaps plainly enough betrayed. He fancied that Miriam did not quite recognize the limits of the strictest delicacy; he even went so far as to generalize, and conclude within himself, that this deficiency is a more general failing in woman than in man, the highest refinement being a masculine attribute.

But the idea was unjust to the sex at large, and especially so to this poor Miriam, who was hardly responsible for her frantic efforts to be gay. Possibly, moreover, the nice action of the mind is set ajar by any violent shock, as of great misfortune or great crime, so that the finer perceptions may be blurred thenceforth, and the effect be traceable in all the minutest conduct of life.

"Did you see anything of the dear child after you left us?" asked Miriam, still keeping Hilda as her topic of conversation. "I missed her sadly on my way homeward; for nothing insures me such delightful and innocent dreams (I have experienced it twenty times) as a talk late in the evening with Hilda."

"So I should imagine," said the sculptor, gravely; "but it is an advantage that I have little or no opportunity of enjoying. I know not what became of Hilda after my parting from you. She was not especially my companion in any part of our walk. The last I saw of her she was hastening back to rejoin you in the court-yard of the Palazzo Caffarelli."

" Impossible! " cried Miriam, starting.

" Then did you not see her again? " inquired Ken•yon, in some alarm.

" Not there," answered Miriam, quietly; " indeed, I followed pretty closely on the heels of the rest of the party.   But do not be alarmed on Hilda's account; the Virgin is bound to watch over the good child, for the sake of the piety with which she keeps the lamp alight at her shrine.   And, besides, I have always felt that Hilda is just as safe in these evil streets of Rome as her white doves when they fly downwards from the tower-top, and run to and fro among the horses' feet. There is certainly a providence on purpose for Hilda, if for no other human creature."

" I religiously believe it," rejoined the sculptor; " and yet my mind would be the easier, if I knew that she had returned safely to her tower."

" Then make yourself quite easy," answered Miriam. " I saw her (and it is the last sweet sight that I remember) leaning from her window midway between earth and sky! "

Kenyon now looked at Donatello.

" You seem out of spirits, my dear friend," he observed.   " This languid Roman atmosphere is not the airy wine that you were accustomed to breathe at home.   I have not forgotten your hospitable invitation to meet you this summer at your castle among the Apennines.   It is my fixed purpose to come, I assure you.   We shall both be the better for some deep draughts of the mountain-breezes."

" It may be," said Donatello, with unwonted sombreness; " the old house seemed joyous when I was a child. But as I remember it now it was a grim place, too."

The sculptor looked more attentively at the young

man, and was surprised and alarmed to observe how entirely the fine, fresh glow of animal spirits had departed out of his face. Hitherto, moreover, even while he was standing perfectly still, there had been a kind of possible gambol indicated in his aspect. It was quite gone now. All his youthful gayety, and with it his simplicity of manner, was eclipsed, if not utterly extinct.

"You are surely ill, my dear fellow," exclaimed Kenyon.

"Am I? Perhaps so," said Donatello indifferently; "I never have been ill, and know not what it may be."

"Do not make the poor lad fancy-sick," whispered Miriam, pulling the sculptor's sleeve. "He is of a nature to lie down and die at once, if he finds himself drawing such melancholy breaths as we ordinary people are enforced to burden our lungs withal. But we must get him away from this old, dreamy, and dreary Rome, where nobody but himself ever thought of being gay. Its influences are too heavy to sustain the life of such a creature."

The above conversation had passed chiefly on the steps of the Cappuccini; and, having said so much, Miriam lifted the leathern curtain that hangs before all church-doors in Italy.

"Hilda has forgotten her appointment," she observed, "or else her maiden slumbers are very sound this morning. We will wait for her no longer."

They entered the nave. The interior of the church was of moderate compass, but of good architecture, with a vaulted roof over the nave, and a row of dusky chapels on either side of it instead of the customary side-aisles. Each chapel had its saintly shrine, hung

round with offerings; its picture above the altar, although closely veiled, if by any painter of renown;
and its hallowed tapers, burning continually, to set
alight the devotion of the worshippers. The pavement of the nave was chiefly of marble, and looked
old and broken, and was shabbily patched here and
there with tiles of brick; it was inlaid, moreover,
with tombstones of the mediæval taste, on which were
quaintly sculptured borders, figures, and portraits in
bas-relief, and Latin epitaphs, now grown illegible by
the tread of footsteps over them. The church apper-
tains to a convent of Capuchin monks; and, as usually
happens when a reverend brotherhood have such an
edifice in charge, the floor seemed never to have been
scrubbed or swept, and had as little the aspect of sanctity as a kennel; whereas, in all churches of nunneries,
the maiden sisterhood invariably show the purity of
their own hearts by the virgin cleanliness and visible
consecration of the walls and pavement.

As our friends entered the church, their eyes rested
at once on a remarkable object in the centre of the
nave. It was either the actual body, or, as might
rather have been supposed at first glance, the cunningly wrought waxen face and suitably draped figure
of a dead monk. This image of wax or clay-cold reality, whichever it might be, lay on a slightly elevated
bier, with three tall candles burning on each side,
another tall candle at the head, and another at the
foot. There was music, too, in harmony with so funereal a spectacle. From beneath the pavement of the
church came the deep, lugubrious strain of a *De Pro-
fundis*, which sounded like an utterance of the tomb
itself; so dismally did it rumble through the burial-
vaults, and ooze up among the flat gravestones and sad
epitaphs, filling the church as with a gloomy mist.

"I must look more closely at that dead monk before we leave the church," remarked the sculptor. "In the study of my art, I have gained many a hint from the dead, which the living could never have given me."

"I can well imagine it," answered Miriam. "One clay image is readily copied from another. But let us first see Guido's picture. The light is favorable now."

Accordingly, they turned into the first chapel on the right hand, as you enter the nave ; and there they beheld, — not the picture, indeed, — but a closely drawn curtain. The churchmen of Italy make no scruple of sacrificing the very purpose for which a work of sacred art has been created ; that of opening the way for religious sentiment through the quick medium of sight, by bringing angels, saints, and martyrs down visibly upon earth ; of sacrificing this high purpose, and, for aught they know, the welfare of many souls along with it, to the hope of a paltry fee. Every work by an artist of celebrity is hidden behind a veil, and seldom revealed, except to Protestants, who scorn it as an object of devotion, and value it only for its artistic merit.

The sacristan was quickly found, however, and lost no time in disclosing the youthful Archangel, setting his divine foot on the head of his fallen adversary. It was an image of that greatest of future events, which we hope for so ardently, — at least, while we are young, — but find so very long in coming, — the triumph of goodness over the evil principle.

"Where can Hilda be ? " exclaimed Kenyon. " It is not her custom ever to fail in an engagement ; and the present one was made entirely on her account. Except herself, you know, we were all agreed in our recollection of the picture."

"But we were wrong, and Hilda right, as you perceive," said Miriam, directing his attention to the point on which their dispute of the night before had arisen. "It is not easy to detect her astray as regards any picture on which those clear, soft eyes of hers have ever rested."

"And she has studied and admired few pictures so much as this," observed the sculptor. "No wonder; for there is hardly another so beautiful in the world. What an expression of heavenly severity in the Archangel's face! There is a degree of pain, trouble, and disgust at being brought in contact with sin, even for the purpose of quelling and punishing it; and yet a celestial tranquillity pervades his whole being."

"I have never been able," said Miriam, "to admire this picture nearly so much as Hilda does, in its moral and intellectual aspect. If it cost her more trouble to be good, if her soul were less white and pure, she would be a more competent critic of this picture, and would estimate it not half so high. I see its defects to-day more clearly than ever before."

"What are some of them?" asked Kenyon.

"That Archangel, now," Miriam continued; "how fair he looks, with his unruffled wings, with his unhacked sword, and clad in his bright armor, and that exquisitely fitting sky-blue tunic, cut in the latest Paradisiacal mode! What a dainty air of the first celestial society! With what half-scornful delicacy he sets his prettily sandalled foot on the head of his prostrate foe! But, is it thus that virtue looks the moment after its death-struggle with evil? No, no; I could have told Guido better. A full third of the Archangel's feathers should have been torn from his wings; the rest all ruffled, till they looked like Satan's own! His sword should be streaming with blood, and perhaps broken half-way to the hilt; his armor crushed, his robes rent, his breast gory; a bleeding gash on his brow, cutting right across the stern scowl of battle! He should press his foot hard down upon the old serpent, as if his very soul depended upon it, feeling him squirm mightily, and doubting whether the fight were half over yet, and how the victory might turn! And, with all this fierceness, this grimness, this unutterable horror, there should still be something high, tender, and holy in Michael's eyes, and around his mouth. But the battle never was such child's play as Guido's dapper Archangel seems to have found it."

"For Heaven's sake, Miriam," cried Kenyon, astonished at the wild energy of her talk; "paint the picture of man's struggle against sin according to your own idea! I think it will be a masterpiece."

"The picture would have its share of truth, I assure you," she answered; "but I am sadly afraid the victory would fall on the wrong side. Just fancy a smoke-blackened, fiery-eyed demon, bestriding that nice young angel, clutching his white throat with one of his hinder claws; and giving a triumphant whisk of his scaly tail, with a poisonous dart at the end of it! That is what they risk, poor souls, who do battle with Michael's enemy."

It now, perhaps, struck Miriam that her mental disquietude was impelling her to an undue vivacity; for she paused, and turned away from the picture, without saying a word more about it. All this while, moreover, Donatello had been very ill at ease, casting awestricken and inquiring glances at the dead monk; as if he could look nowhere but at that ghastly object, merely because it shocked him. Death has probably a peculiar horror and ugliness, when forced upon the contemplation of a person so naturally joyous as Donatello, who lived with completeness in the present moment, and was able to form but vague images of the future.

" What is the matter, Donatello ? " whispered Miriam, soothingly. " You are quite in a tremble, my poor friend ! What is it ? "

" This awful chant from beneath the church," answered Donatello ; " it oppresses me ; the air is so heavy with it that I can scarcely draw my breath. And yonder dead monk ! I feel as if he were lying right across my heart."

" Take courage ! " whispered she again ; " come, we will approach close to the dead monk. The only way, in such cases, is to stare the ugly horror right in the face ; never a sidelong glance, nor half-look, for those are what show a frightful thing in its frightfullest aspect. Lean on me, dearest friend ! My heart is very strong for both of us. Be brave ; and all is well."

Donatello hung back for a moment, but then pressed close to Miriam's side, and suffered her to lead him up to the bier. The sculptor followed. A number of persons, chiefly women, with several children among them, were standing about the corpse ; and as our three friends drew nigh, a mother knelt down, and caused her little boy to kneel, both kissing the beads and crucifix that hung from the monk's girdle. Possibly he had died in the odor of sanctity ; or, at all events, death and his brown frock and cowl made a sacred image of this reverend father.

CHAPTER XXI.

THE dead monk was clad, as when alive, in the brown woollen frock of the Capuchins, with the hood drawn over his head, but so as to leave the features and a portion of the beard uncovered. His rosary and cross hung at his side; his hands were folded over his breast; his feet (he was of a barefooted order in his lifetime, and continued so in death) protruded from beneath his habit, stiff and stark, with a more waxen look than even his face. They were tied together at the ankles with a black ribbon.

The countenance, as we have already said, was fully displayed. It had a purplish hue upon it, unlike the paleness of an ordinary corpse, but as little resembling the flush of natural life. The eyelids were but partially drawn down, and showed the eyeballs beneath; as if the deceased friar were stealing a glimpse at the by-standers, to watch whether they were duly impressed with the solemnity of his obsequies. The shaggy eyebrows gave sternness to the look.

Miriam passed between two of the lighted candles, and stood close beside the bier.

"My God!" murmured she. "What is this?"

She grasped Donatello's hand, and, at the same instant, felt him give a convulsive shudder, which she knew to have been caused by a sudden and terrible throb of the heart. His hand, by an instantaneous change, became like ice within hers, which likewise grew so icy, that their insensible fingers might have rattled, one against the other. No wonder that their blood curdled ; no wonder that their hearts leaped and paused ! The dead face of the monk, gazing at them beneath its half-closed eyelids, was the same visage that had glared upon their naked souls, the past midnight, as Donatello flung him over the precipice.

The sculptor was standing at the foot of the bier, and had not yet seen the monk's features.

"Those naked feet!" said he. "I know not why, but they affect me strangely. They have walked to and fro over the hard pavements of Rome, and through a hundred other rough ways of this life, where the monk went begging for his brotherhood ; along the cloisters and dreary corridors of his convent, too, from his youth upward ! It is a suggestive idea, to track those worn feet backward through all the paths they have trodden, ever since they were the tender and rosy little feet of a baby, and (cold as they now are) were kept warm in his mother's hand."

As his companions, whom the sculptor supposed to be close by him, made no response to his fanciful musing, he looked up, and saw them at the head of the bier. He advanced thither himself.

"Ha !" exclaimed he.

He cast a horror-stricken and bewildered glance at Miriam, but withdrew it immediately. Not that he had any definite suspicion, or, it may be, even a remote idea, that she could be held responsible, in the least degree, for this man's sudden death. In truth, it seemed too wild a thought to connect, in reality, Miriam's persecutor of many past months and the vagabond of the preceding night, with the dead Cap-

uchin of to-day. It resembled one of those unaccountable changes and interminglings of identity,
which so often occur among the personages of a
dream. But Kenyon, as befitted the professor of
an imaginative art, was endowed with an exceedingly
quick sensibility, which was apt to give him intimations of the true state of matters that lay beyond his
actual vision. There was a whisper in his ear; it
said, "Hush!" Without asking himself wherefore,
he resolved to be silent as regarded the mysterious
discovery which he had made, and to leave any remark or exclamation to be voluntarily offered by Miriam. If she never spoke, then let the riddle be un-
solved.

And now occurred a circumstance that would seem
too fantastic to be told, if it had not actually happened, precisely as we set it down. As the three
friends stood by the bier, they saw that a little stream
of blood had begun to ooze from the dead monk's
nostrils; it crept slowly towards the thicket of his
beard, where, in the course of a moment or two, it hid
itself.

"How strange!" ejaculated Kenyon. "The monk
died of apoplexy, I suppose, or by some sudden accident, and the blood has not yet congealed."

"Do you consider that a sufficient explanation?"
asked Miriam, with a smile from which the sculptor
involuntarily turned away his eyes. "Does it satisfy
you?"

"And why not?" he inquired.

"Of course, you know the old superstition about
this phenomenon of blood flowing from a dead body,"
she rejoined. "How can we tell but that the murderer of this monk (or, possibly, it may be only that

privileged murderer, his physician) may have just entered the church?"

"I cannot jest about it," said Kenyon. "It is an ugly sight!"

"True, true; horrible to see, or dream of!" she replied, with one of those long, tremulous sighs, which so often betray a sick heart by escaping unexpectedly. "We will not look at it any more. Come away, Donatello. Let us escape from this dismal church. The sunshine will do you good."

When had ever a woman such a trial to sustain as this! By no possible supposition could Miriam explain the identity of the dead Capuchin, quietly and decorously laid out in the nave of his convent church, with that of her murdered persecutor, flung heedlessly at the foot of the precipice. The effect upon her imagination was as if a strange and unknown corpse had miraculously, while she was gazing at it, assumed the likeness of that face, so terrible henceforth in her remembrance. It was a symbol, perhaps, of the deadly iteration with which she was doomed to behold the image of her crime reflected back upon her in a thousand ways, and converting the great, calm face of Nature, in the whole, and in its innumerable details, into a manifold reminiscence of that one dead visage.

No sooner had Miriam turned away from the bier, and gone a few steps, than she fancied the likeness altogether an illusion, which would vanish at a closer and colder view. She must look at it again, therefore, and at once; or else the grave would close over the face, and leave the awful fantasy that had connected itself therewith fixed ineffaceably in her brain.

"Wait for me, one moment!" she said to her companions. "Only a moment!"

So she went back, and gazed once more at the corpse. Yes; these were the features that Miriam had known so well; this was the visage that she remembered from a far longer date than the most intimate of her friends suspected; this form of clay had held the evil spirit which blasted her sweet youth, and compelled her, as it were, to stain her womanhood with crime. But, whether it were the majesty of death, or something originally noble and lofty in the character of the dead, which the soul had stamped upon the features, as it left them; so it was that Miriam now quailed and shook, not for the vulgar horror of the spectacle, but for the severe, reproachful glance that seemed to come from between those half-closed lids. True, there had been nothing, in his lifetime, viler than this man. She knew it; there was no other fact within her consciousness that she felt to be so certain; and yet, because her persecutor found himself safe and irrefutable in death, he frowned upon his victim, and threw back the blame on her!

"Is it thou, indeed?" she murmured, under her breath. "Then thou hast no right to scowl upon me so! But art thou real, or a vision?"

She bent down over the dead monk, till one of her rich curls brushed against his forehead. She touched one of his folded hands with her finger.

"It is he," said Miriam. "There is the scar, that I know so well, on his brow. And it is no vision; he is palpable to my touch! I will question the fact no longer, but deal with it as I best can."

It was wonderful to see how the crisis developed in Miriam its own proper strength, and the faculty of sustaining the demands which it made upon her fortitude. She ceased to tremble; the beautiful woman gazed sternly at her dead enemy, endeavoring to meet and quell the look of accusation that he threw from between his half-closed eyelids.

"No; thou shalt not scowl me down!" said she. "Neither now, nor when we stand together at the judgment-seat. I fear not to meet thee there. Farewell, till that next encounter!"

Haughtily waving her hand, Miriam rejoined her friends, who were awaiting her at the door of the church. As they went out, the sacristan stopped them, and proposed to show the cemetery of the convent, where the deceased members of the fraternity are laid to rest in sacred earth, brought long ago from Jerusalem.

"And will yonder monk be buried there?" she asked.

"Brother Antonio?" exclaimed the sacristan. "Surely, our good brother will be put to bed there! His grave is already dug, and the last occupant has made room for him. Will you look at it, signorina?"

"I will!" said Miriam.

"Then excuse me," observed Kenyon; "for I shall leave you. One dead monk has more than sufficed me; and I am not bold enough to face the whole mortality of the convent."

It was easy to see, by Donatello's looks, that he, as well as the sculptor, would gladly have escaped a visit to the famous cemetery of the Cappuccini. But Miriam's nerves were strained to such a pitch, that she anticipated a certain solace and absolute relief in passing from one ghastly spectacle to another of long-accumulated ugliness; and there was, besides, a singular sense of duty which impelled her to look at the final resting-place of the being whose fate had been so

disastrously involved with her own. She therefore
followed the sacristan's guidance, and drew her companion along with her, whispering encouragement as
they went.

The cemetery is beneath the church, but entirely
above ground, and lighted by a row of iron-grated
windows without glass. A corridor runs along beside these windows, and gives access to three or four
vaulted recesses, or chapels, of considerable breadth
and height, the floor of which consists of the consecrated earth of Jerusalem. It is smoothed decorously
over the deceased brethren of the convent, and is kept
quite free from grass or weeds, such as would grow
even in these gloomy recesses, if pains were not bestowed to root them up. But, as the cemetery is small,
and it is a precious privilege to sleep in holy ground,
the brotherhood are immemorially accustomed, when
one of their number dies, to take the longest-buried
skeleton out of the oldest grave, and lay the new slum-
berer there instead. Thus, each of the good friars, in
his turn, enjoys the luxury of a consecrated bed, attended with the slight drawback of being forced to get
up long before daybreak, as it were, and make room
for another lodger.

The arrangement of the unearthed skeletons is what
makes the special interest of the cemetery. The arched
and vaulted walls of the burial recesses are supported
by massive pillars and pilasters made of thigh-bones
and skulls; the whole material of the structure appears to be of a similar kind; and the knobs and
embossed ornaments of this strange architecture are
represented by the joints of the spine, and the more
delicate tracery by the smaller bones of the human
frame. The summits of the arches are adorned with

entire skeletons, looking as if they were wrought most skilfully in bas-relief. There is no possibility of describing how ugly and grotesque is the effect, combined with a certain artistic merit, nor how much perverted ingenuity has been shown in this queer way, nor what a multitude of dead monks, through how many hundred years, must have contributed their bony framework to build up these great arches of mortality. On some of the skulls there are inscriptions, purporting that such a monk, who formerly made use of that particular headpiece, died on such a day and year; but vastly the greater number are piled up indistinguishably into the architectural design, like the many deaths that make up the one glory of a victory.

In the side walls of the vaults are niches where skeleton monks sit or stand, clad in the brown habits that they wore in life, and labelled with their names and the dates of their decease. Their skulls (some quite bare, and others still covered with yellow skin, and hair that has known the earth-damps) look out from beneath their hoods, grinning hideously repulsive. One reverend father has his mouth wide open, as if he had died in the midst of a howl of terror and remorse, which perhaps is even now screeching through eternity. As a general thing, however, these frocked and hooded skeletons seem to take a more cheerful view of their position, and try with ghastly smiles to turn it into a jest. But the cemetery of the Capuchins is no place to nourish celestial hopes: the soul sinks forlorn and wretched under all this burden of dusty death; the holy earth from Jerusalem, so imbued is it with mortality, has grown as barren of the flowers of Paradise as it is of earthly weeds and grass. Thank Heaven for its blue sky; it needs a long, up-

ward gaze to give us back our faith. Not here can
we feel ourselves immortal, where the very altars in
these chapels of horrible consecration are heaps of human bones.

Yet let us give the cemetery the praise that it de-
serves. There is no disagreeable scent, such as might
have been expected from the decay of so many holy
persons, in whatever odor of sanctity they may have
taken their departure. The same number of living
monks would not smell half so unexceptionably.

Miriam went gloomily along the corridor, from one
vaulted Golgotha to another, until in the farthest recess she beheld an open grave.

"Is that for him who lies yonder in the nave?" she
asked.

"Yes, signorina, this is to be the resting-place of
Brother Antonio, who came to his death last night,"
answered the sacristan; "and in yonder niche, you
see, sits a brother who was buried thirty years ago,
and has risen to give him place."

"It is not a satisfactory idea," observed Miriam,
"that you poor friars cannot call even your graves
permanently your own. You must lie down in them,
methinks, with a nervous anticipation of being disturbed, like weary men who know that they shall be
summoned out of bed at midnight. Is it not possible
(if money were to be paid for the privilege) to leave
Brother Antonio — if that be his name — in the occupancy of that narrow grave till the last trumpet
sounds?"

"By no means, signorina; neither is it needful or
desirable," answered the sacristan. "A quarter of a
century's sleep in the sweet earth of Jerusalem is
better than a thousand years in any other soil. Our

brethren find good rest there. No ghost was ever
known to steal out of this blessed cemetery."

"That is well," responded Miriam; "may he whom
you now lay to sleep prove no exception to the rule!"

As they left the cemetery she put money into the
sacristan's hand to an amount that made his eyes open
wide and glisten, and requested that it might be expended in masses for the repose of Father Antonio's
soul.

CHAPTER XXII.

THE MEDICI GARDENS.

" DONATELLO," said Miriam, anxiously, as they came through the Piazza Barberini, "what can I do for you, my beloved friend? You are shaking as with the cold fit of the Roman fever."

" Yes," said Donatello; " my heart shivers."

As soon as she could collect her thoughts, Miriam led the young man to the gardens of the Villa Medici, hoping that the quiet shade and sunshine of that delightful retreat would a little revive his spirits. The grounds are there laid out in the old fashion of straight paths, with borders of box, which form hedges of great height and density, and are shorn and trimmed to the evenness of a wall of stone, at the top and sides. There are green alleys, with long vistas overshadowed by ilex-trees; and at each intersection of the paths, the visitor finds seats of lichen-covered stone to repose upon, and marble statues that look forlornly at him, regretful of their lost noses. In the more open portions of the garden, before the sculptured front of the villa, you see fountains and flower-beds, and, in their season, a profusion of roses, from which the genial sun of Italy distils a fragrance, to be scattered abroad by the no less genial breeze.

But Donatello drew no delight from these things. He walked onward in silent apathy, and looked at Miriam with strangely half-awakened and bewildered eyes, when she sought to bring his mind into sympathy with hers, and so relieve his heart of the burden that lay lumpishly upon it.

She made him sit down on a stone bench, where two embowered alleys crossed each other; so that they could discern the approach of any casual intruder a long way down the path.

"My sweet friend," she said, taking one of his passive hands in both of hers, "what can I say to comfort you?"

"Nothing!" replied Donatello, with sombre reserve. "Nothing will ever comfort me."

"I accept my own misery," continued Miriam, "my own guilt, if guilt it be; and, whether guilt or misery, I shall know how to deal with it. But you, dearest friend, that were the rarest creature in all this world, and seemed a being to whom sorrow could not cling, — you, whom I half fancied to belong to a race that had vanished forever, you only surviving, to show mankind how genial and how joyous life used to be, in some long-gone age, — what had you to do with grief or crime?"

"They came to me as to other men," said Donatello, broodingly. "Doubtless I was born to them."

"No, no; they came with me," replied Miriam. "Mine is the responsibility! Alas! wherefore was I born? Why did we ever meet? Why did I not drive you from me, knowing — for my heart foreboded it — that the cloud in which I walked would likewise envelop you!"

Donatello stirred uneasily, with the irritable impatience that is often combined with a mood of leaden despondency. A brown lizard with two tails — a monster often engendered by the Roman sunshine —

ran across his foot, and made him start. Then he sat silent awhile, and so did Miriam, trying to dissolve her whole heart into sympathy, and lavish it all upon him, were it only for a moment's cordial.

The young man lifted his hand to his breast, and, unintentionally, as Miriam's hand was within his, he lifted that along with it.

"I have a great weight here!" said he.

The fancy struck Miriam (but she drove it resolutely down) that Donatello almost imperceptibly shuddered, while, in pressing his own hand against his heart, he pressed hers there too.

"Rest your heart on me, dearest one!" she resumed. "Let me bear all its weight; I am well able to bear it; for I am a woman, and I love you! I love you, Donatello! Is there no comfort for you in this avowal? Look at me! Heretofore, you have found me pleasant to your sight. Gaze into my eyes! Gaze into my soul! Search as deeply as you may, you can never see half the tenderness and devotion that I henceforth cherish for you. All that I ask is your acceptance of the utter self-sacrifice (but it shall be no sacrifice, to my great love) with which I seek to remedy the evil you have incurred for my sake!"

All this fervor on Miriam's part; on Donatello's, a heavy silence.

"Oh, speak to me!" she exclaimed. "Only promise me to be, by and by, a little happy!"

"Happy?" murmured Donatello. "Ah, never again! never again!"

"Never? Ah, that is a terrible word to say to me!" answered Miriam. "A terrible word to let fall upon a woman's heart, when she loves you, and is conscious of having caused your misery! If you love me, Dona-

tello, speak it not again.   And surely you did love
me?"

"I did," replied Donatello, gloomily and absently.

Miriam released the young man's hand, but suffered
one of her own to lie close to his, and waited a moment
to see whether he would make any effort to retain it.
There was much depending upon that simple experi-
ment.

With a deep sigh — as when, sometimes, a slum-
berer turns over in a troubled dream — Donatello
changed his position, and clasped both his hands over
his forehead.   The genial warmth of a Roman April
kindling into May was in the atmosphere around
them; but when Miriam saw that involuntary movement and heard that sigh of relief (for so she interpreted it), a shiver ran through her frame, as if the
iciest wind of the Apennines were blowing over her.

"He has done himself a greater wrong than I
dreamed of," thought she, with unutterable compas-
sion.   "Alas! it was a sad mistake!   He might have
had a kind of bliss in the consequences of this deed,
had he been impelled to it by a love vital enough to
survive the frenzy of that terrible moment, — mighty
enough to make its own law, and justify itself against
the natural remorse.   But to have perpetrated a dreadful murder (and such was his crime, unless love, an-
nihilating moral distinctions, made it otherwise) on no
better warrant than a boy's idle fantasy!   I pity him
from the very depths of my soul!   As for myself, I
am past my own or other's pity."

She arose from the young man's side, and stood before him with a sad, commiserating aspect; it was the
look of a ruined soul, bewailing, in him, a grief less
than what her profounder sympathies imposed upon
herself.

" Donatello, we must part," she said, with melancholy firmness. " Yes ; leave me ! Go back to your old tower, which overlooks the green valley you have told me of among the Apennines. Then, all that has passed will be recognized as but an ugly dream. For, in dreams, the conscience sleeps, and we often stain ourselves with guilt of which we should be incapable in our waking moments. The deed you seemed to do, last night, was no more than such a dream ; there was as little substance in what you fancied yourself doing. Go ; and forget it all ! "

" Ah, that terrible face ! " said Donatello, pressing his hands over his eyes. " Do you call that unreal ? "

" Yes ; for you beheld it with dreaming eyes," replied Miriam. " It was unreal ; and, that you may feel it so, it is requisite that you see this face of mine no more. Once, you may have thought it beautiful ; now, it has lost its charm. Yet it would still retain a miserable potency to bring back the past illusion, and, in its train, the remorse and anguish that would darken all your life. Leave me, therefore, and forget me."

" Forget you, Miriam ! " said Donatello, roused somewhat from his apathy of despair. " If I could remember you, and behold you, apart from that frightful visage which stares at me over your shoulder, that were a consolation, at least, if not a joy."

" But since that visage haunts you along with mine," rejoined Miriam, glancing behind her, " we needs must part. Farewell, then ! But if ever — in distress, peril, shame, poverty, or whatever anguish is most poignant, whatever burden heaviest — you should require a life to be given wholly, only to make your own a little easier, then summon me ! As the case now stands between us, you have bought me dear, and find me of little worth. Fling me away, therefore! May you never need me more! But, if otherwise, a wish — almost an unuttered wish — will bring me to you!"

She stood a moment, expecting a reply. But Donatello's eyes had again fallen on the ground, and he had not, in his bewildered mind and overburdened heart, a word to respond.

"That hour I speak of may never come," said Miriam. "So farewell, — farewell forever."

"Farewell," said Donatello.

His voice hardly made its way through the environment of unaccustomed thoughts and emotions which had settled over him like a dense and dark cloud. Not improbably, he beheld Miriam through so dim a medium that she looked visionary; heard her speak only in a thin, faint echo.

She turned from the young man, and, much as her heart yearned towards him, she would not profane that heavy parting by an embrace, or even a pressure of the hand. So soon after the semblance of such mighty love, and after it had been the impulse to so terrible a deed, they parted, in all outward show, as coldly as people part whose whole mutual intercourse has been encircled within a single hour.

And Donatello, when Miriam had departed, stretched himself at full length on the stone bench, and drew his hat over his eyes, as the idle and light-hearted youths of dreamy Italy are accustomed to do, when they lie down in the first convenient shade, and snatch a noonday slumber. A stupor was upon him, which he mistook for such drowsiness as he had known in his innocent past life. But, by and by, he raised himself slowly and left the garden. Sometimes poor Donatello started, as if he heard a shriek ; sometimes he shrank back, as if a face, fearful to behold, were thrust close to his own. In this dismal mood, bewildered with the novelty of sin and grief, he had little left of that singular resemblance, on account of which, and for their sport, his three friends had fantastically recognized him as the veritable Faun of Praxiteles.

CHAPTER XXIII.

MIRIAM AND HILDA.

On leaving the Medici Gardens Miriam felt herself
astray in the world ; and having no special reason to
seek one place more than another, she suffered chance
to direct her steps as it would. Thus it happened,
that, involving herself in the crookedness of Rome,
she saw Hilda's tower rising before her, and was put
in mind to climb to the young girl's eyry, and ask
why she had broken her engagement at the church of
the Capuchins. People often do the idlest acts of
their lifetime in their heaviest and most anxious moments ; so that it would have been no wonder had
Miriam been impelled only by so slight a motive of
curiosity as we have indicated. But she remembered,
too, and with a quaking heart, what the sculptor had
mentioned of Hilda's retracing her steps towards the
court-yard of the Palazzo Caffarelli in quest of Miriam
herself. Had she been compelled to choose between
infamy in the eyes of the whole world, or in Hilda's
eyes alone, she would unhesitatingly have accepted the
former, on condition of remaining spotless in the estimation of her white-souled friend. This possibility,
therefore, that Hilda had witnessed the scene of the
past night, was unquestionably the cause that drew
Miriam to the tower, and made her linger and falter
as she approached it.

As she drew near, there were tokens to which her

disturbed mind gave a sinister interpretation. Some of her friend's airy family, the doves, with their heads imbedded disconsolately in their bosoms, were huddled in a corner of the piazza ; others had alighted on the heads, wings, shoulders, and trumpets of the marble angels which adorned the façade of the neighboring church ; two or three had betaken themselves to the Virgin's shrine ; and as many as could find room were sitting on Hilda's window-sill. But all of them, so Miriam fancied, had a look of weary expectation and disappointment, — no flights, no flutterings, no cooing murmur ; something that ought to have made their day glad and bright was evidently left out of this day's history. And, furthermore, Hilda's white window-curtain was closely drawn, with only that one little aperture at the side, which Miriam remembered noticing the night before.

"Be quiet," said Miriam to her own heart, pressing her hand hard upon it. "Why shouldst thou throb now? Hast thou not endured more terrible things than this?"

Whatever were her apprehensions, she would not turn back. It might be — and the solace would be worth a world — that Hilda, knowing nothing of the past night's calamity, would greet her friend with a sunny smile, and so restore a portion of the vital warmth, for lack of which her soul was frozen. But could Miriam, guilty as she was, permit Hilda to kiss her cheek, to clasp her hand, and thus be no longer so unspotted from the world as heretofore?

"I will never permit her sweet touch again," said Miriam, toiling up the staircase, "if I can find strength of heart to forbid it. But, oh! it would be so soothing in this wintry fever-fit of my heart. There can be no harm to my white Hilda in one parting kiss. That shall be all!"

But, on reaching the upper landing-place, Miriam paused, and stirred not again till she had brought herself to an immovable resolve.

"My lips, my hand, shall never meet Hilda's more," said she.

Meanwhile, Hilda sat listlessly in her painting-room. Had you looked into the little adjoining chamber, you might have seen the slight imprint of her figure on the bed, but would also have detected at once that the white counterpane had not been turned down. The pillow was more disturbed; she had turned her face upon it, the poor child, and bedewed it with some of those tears (among the most chill and forlorn that gush from human sorrow) which the innocent heart pours forth at its first actual discovery that sin is in the world. The young and pure are not apt to find out that miserable truth until it is brought home to them by the guiltiness of some trusted friend. They may have heard much of the evil of the world, and seem to know it, but only as an impalpable theory. In due time, some mortal, whom they reverence too highly, is commissioned by Providence to teach them this direful lesson; he perpetrates a sin; and Adam falls anew, and Paradise, heretofore in unfaded bloom, is lost again, and closed forever, with the fiery swords gleaming at its gates.

The chair in which Hilda sat was near the portrait of Beatrice Cenci, which had not yet been taken from the easel. It is a peculiarity of this picture, that its profoundest expression eludes a straightforward glance, and can only be caught by side glimpses, or when the eye falls casually upon it; even as if the

painted face had a life and consciousness of its own,
and, resolving not to betray its secret of grief or guilt,
permitted the true tokens to come forth only when it
imagined itself unseen. No other such magical effect
has ever been wrought by pencil.

Now, opposite the easel hung a looking-glass, in
which Beatrice's face and Hilda's were both reflected.
In one of her weary, nerveless changes of position,
Hilda happened to throw her eyes on the glass, and
took in both these images at one unpremeditated
glance. She fancied — nor was it without horror —
that Beatrice's expression, seen aside and vanishing
in a moment, had been depicted in her own face likewise, and flitted from it as timorously.

" Am I, too, stained with guilt ? " thought the poor
girl, hiding her face in her hands.

Not so, thank Heaven ! But, as regards Beatrice's
picture, the incident suggests a theory which may account for its unutterable grief and mysterious shadow
of guilt, without detracting from the purity which we
love to attribute to that ill-fated girl. Who, indeed,
can look at that mouth, — with its lips half apart, as
innocent as a baby's that has been crying, — and not
pronounce Beatrice sinless ? It was the intimate consciousness of her father's sin that threw its shadow
over her, and frightened her into a remote and inac-
cessible region, where no sympathy could come. It
was the knowledge of Miriam's guilt that lent the
same expression to Hilda's face.

But Hilda nervously moved her chair, so that the
images in the glass should be no longer visible. She
now watched a speck of sunshine that came through
a shuttered window, and crept from object to object,
indicating each with a touch of its bright finger, and

then letting them all vanish successively. In like manner, her mind, so like sunlight in its natural cheerfulness, went from thought to thought, but found nothing that it could dwell upon for comfort. Never before had this young, energetic, active spirit known what it is to be despondent. It was the unreality of the world that made her so. Her dearest friend, whose heart seemed the most solid and richest of Hilda's possessions, had no existence for her any more; and in that dreary void, out of which Miriam had disappeared, the substance, the truth, the integrity of life, the motives of effort, the joy of success, had departed along with her.

It was long past noon, when a step came up the staircase. It had passed beyond the limits where there was communication with the lower regions of the palace, and was mounting the successive flights which led only to Hilda's precincts. Faint as the tread was, she heard and recognized it. It startled her into sudden life. Her first impulse was to spring to the door of the studio, and fasten it with lock and bolt. But a second thought made her feel that this would be an unworthy cowardice, on her own part, and also that Miriam — only yesterday her closest friend — had a right to be told, face to face, that thenceforth they must be forever strangers.

She heard Miriam pause, outside of the door. We have already seen what was the latter's resolve with respect to any kiss or pressure of the hand between Hilda and herself. We know not what became of the resolution. As Miriam was of a highly impulsive character, it may have vanished at the first sight of Hilda; but, at all events, she appeared to have dressed herself up in a garb of sunshine, and was disclosed, as

the door swung open, in all the glow of her remarkable beauty. The truth was, her heart leaped conclu-
sively towards the only refuge that it had, or hoped.
She forgot, just one instant, all cause for holding herself aloof. Ordinarily there was a certain reserve in
Miriam's demonstrations of affection, in consonance
with the delicacy of her friend. To-day, she opened
her arms to take Hilda in.

"Dearest, darling Hilda!" she exclaimed. "It
gives me new life to see you!"

Hilda was standing in the middle of the room.
When her friend made a step or two from the door,
she put forth her hands with an involuntary repellent
gesture, so expressive, that Miriam at once felt a great
chasm opening itself between them two. They might
gaze at one another from the opposite side, but without the possibility of ever meeting more; or, at least,
since the chasm could never be bridged over, they
must tread the whole round of Eternity to meet on
the other side. There was even a terror in the thought
of their meeting again. It was as if Hilda or Miriam
were dead, and could no longer hold intercourse without violating a spiritual law.

Yet, in the wantonness of her despair, Miriam made
one more step towards the friend whom she had lost.

"Do not come nearer, Miriam!" said Hilda.

Her look and tone were those of sorrowful entreaty,
and yet they expressed a kind of confidence, as if the
girl were conscious of a safeguard that could not be
violated.

"What has happened between us, Hilda?" asked
Miriam. "Are we not friends?"

"No, no!" said Hilda, shuddering.

"At least we have been friends," continued Miriam.

"I loved you dearly! I love you still! You were to me as a younger sister; yes, dearer than sisters of the same blood; for you and I were so lonely, Hilda, that the whole world pressed us together by its solitude and strangeness. Then, will you not touch my hand? Am I not the same as yesterday?"

"Alas! no, Miriam!" said Hilda.

"Yes, the same, — the same for you, Hilda," rejoined her lost friend. "Were you to touch my hand, you would find it as warm to your grasp as ever. If you were sick or suffering, I would watch night and day for you. It is in such simple offices that true affection shows itself; and so I speak of them. Yet now, Hilda, your very look seems to put me beyond the limits of human kind!"

"It is not I, Miriam," said Hilda; "not I that have done this."

"You, and you only, Hilda," replied Miriam, stirred up to make her own cause good by the repellent force which her friend opposed to her. "I am a woman, as I was yesterday; endowed with the same truth of nature, the same warmth of heart, the same genuine and earnest love, which you have always known in me. In any regard that concerns yourself, I am not changed. And believe me, Hilda, when a human being has chosen a friend out of all the world, it is only some faithlessness between themselves, rendering true intercourse impossible, that can justify either friend in severing the bond. Have I deceived you? Then cast me off! Have I wronged you personally? Then forgive me, if you can. But, have I sinned against God and man, and deeply sinned? Then be more my friend than ever, for I need you more."

" Do not bewilder me thus, Miriam ! " exclaimed Hilda, who had not forborne to express, by look and gesture, the anguish which this interview inflicted on her. " If I were one of God's angels, with a nature incapable of stain, and garments that never could be spotted, I would keep ever at your side, and try to lead you upward. But I am a poor, lonely girl, whom God has set here in an evil world, and given her only a white robe, and bid her wear it back to Him, as white as when she put it on. Your powerful magnetism would be too much for me. The pure, white atmosphere, in which I try to discern what things are good and true, would be discolored. And, therefore, Miriam, before it is too late, I mean to put faith in this awful heart-quake, which warns me henceforth to avoid you."

" Ah, this is hard ! Ah, this is terrible ! " murmured Miriam, dropping her forehead in her hands. In a moment or two she looked up again, as pale as death, but with a composed countenance : " I always said, Hilda, that you were merciless ; for I had a perception of it, even while you loved me best. You have no sin, nor any conception of what it is ; and therefore you are so terribly severe ! As an angel, you are not amiss ; but, as a human creature, and a woman among earthly men and women, you need a sin to soften you."

" God forgive me," said Hilda, " if I have said a needlessly cruel word ! "

" Let it pass," answered Miriam ; " I, whose heart it has smitten upon, forgive you. And tell me, before we part forever, what have you seen or known of me, since we last met ? "

" A terrible thing, Miriam," said Hilda, growing paler than before.

"Do you see it written in my face, or painted in my eyes?" inquired Miriam, her trouble seeking relief in a half-frenzied raillery. "I would fain know how it is that Providence, or fate, brings eye-witnesses to watch us, when we fancy ourselves acting in the remotest privacy. Did all Rome see it, then? Or, at least, our merry company of artists? Or is it some blood-stain on me, or death-scent in my garments? They say that monstrous deformities sprout out of fiends, who once were lovely angels. Do you perceive such in me already? Tell me, by our past friendship, Hilda, all you know."

Thus adjured, and frightened by the wild emotion which Miriam could not suppress, Hilda strove to tell what she had witnessed.

"After the rest of the party had passed on, I went back to speak to you," she said; "for there seemed to be a trouble on your mind, and I wished to share it with you, if you could permit me. The door of the little court-yard was partly shut; but I pushed it open, and saw you within, and Donatello, and a third person, whom I had before noticed in the shadow of a niche. He approached you, Miriam. You knelt to him! — I saw Donatello spring upon him! I would have shrieked, but my throat was dry. I would have rushed forward, but my limbs seemed rooted to the earth. It was like a flash of lightning. A look passed from your eyes to Donatello's — a look" —

"Yes, Hilda, yes!" exclaimed Miriam, with intense eagerness. "Do not pause now! That look?"

"It revealed all your heart, Miriam," continued Hilda, covering her eyes as if to shut out the recollection; "a look of hatred, triumph, vengeance, and, as it were, joy at some unhoped-for relief."

" Ah! Donatello was right, then," murmured Miriam, who shook throughout all her frame. " My eyes bade him do it! Go on, Hilda."

" It all passed so quickly, — all like a glare of lightning," said Hilda, " and yet it seemed to me that Donatello had paused, while one might draw a breath. But that look! — Ah, Miriam, spare me. Need I tell more? "

" No more; there needs no more, Hilda," replied Miriam, bowing her head, as if listening to a sentence of condemnation from a supreme tribunal. " It is enough! You have satisfied my mind on a point where it was greatly disturbed. Henceforward, I shall be quiet. Thank you, Hilda."

She was on the point of departing, but turned back again from the threshold.

" This is a terrible secret to be kept in a young girl's bosom," she observed; " what will you do with it, my poor child? "

" Heaven help and guide me," answered Hilda, bursting into tears; " for the burden of it crushes me to the earth! It seems a crime to know of such a thing, and to keep it to myself. It knocks within my heart continually, threatening, imploring, insisting to be let out! Oh, my mother! — my mother! Were she yet living, I would travel over land and sea to tell her this dark secret, as I told all the little troubles of my infancy. But I am alone — alone! Miriam, you were my dearest, only friend. Advise me what to do."

This was a singular appeal, no doubt, from the stainless maiden to the guilty woman, whom she had just banished from her heart forever. But it bore striking testimony to the impression which Miriam's natural uprightness and impulsive generosity had made on the friend who knew her best; and it deeply comforted the poor criminal, by proving to her that the bond between Hilda and herself was vital yet.

As far as she was able, Miriam at once responded to the girl's cry for help.

" If I deemed it good for your peace of mind," she said, " to bear testimony against me for this deed, in the face of all the world, no consideration of myself should weigh with me an instant. But I believe that you would find no relief in such a course. What men call justice lies chiefly in outward formalities, and has never the close application and fitness that would be satisfactory to a soul like yours. I cannot be fairly tried and judged before an earthly tribunal; and of this, Hilda, you would perhaps become fatally conscious when it was too late. Roman justice, above all things, is a byword. What have you to do with it? Leave all such thoughts aside! Yet, Hilda, I would not have you keep my secret imprisoned in your heart if it tries to leap out, and stings you, like a wild, venomous thing, when you thrust it back again. Have you no other friend, now that you have been forced to give me up? "

" No other," answered Hilda, sadly.

" Yes ; Kenyon ! " rejoined Miriam.

" He cannot be my friend," said Hilda, " because — because — I have fancied that he sought to be something more."

" Fear nothing ! " replied Miriam, shaking her head, with a strange smile. " This story will frighten his new-born love out of its little life, if that be what you wish. Tell him the secret, then, and take his wise and honorable counsel as to what should next be done. I know not what else to say."

"I never dreamed," said Hilda, — "how could you think it? — of betraying you to justice. But I see how it is, Miriam. I must keep your secret, and die of it, unless God sends me some relief by methods which are now beyond my power to imagine. It is very dreadful. Ah! now I understand how the sins of generations past have created an atmosphere of sin for those that follow. While there is a single guilty person in the universe, each innocent one must feel his innocence tortured by that guilt. Your deed, Miriam, has darkened the whole sky!"

Poor Hilda turned from her unhappy friend, and, sinking on her knees in a corner of the chamber, could not be prevailed upon to utter another word. And Miriam, with a long regard from the threshold, bade farewell to this doves' nest, this one little nook of pure thoughts and innocent enthusiasms, into which she had brought such trouble. Every crime destroys more Edens than our own!

CHAPTER XXIV.

IT was in June that the sculptor, Kenyon, arrived on horseback at the gate of an ancient country-house (which, from some of its features, might almost be called a castle) situated in a part of Tuscany somewhat remote from the ordinary track of tourists. Thither we must now accompany him, and endeavor to make our story flow onward, like a streamlet, past a gray tower that rises on the hill-side, overlooking a spacious valley, which is set in the grand framework of the Apennines.

The sculptor had left Rome with the retreating tide of foreign residents. For, as summer approaches, the Niobe of Nations is made to bewail anew, and doubtless with sincerity, the loss of that large part of her population, which she derives from other lands, and on whom depends much of whatever remnant of prosperity she still enjoys. Rome, at this season, is pervaded and overhung with atmospheric terrors, and insulated within a charmed and deadly circle. The crowd of wandering tourists betake themselves to Switzerland, to the Rhine, or, from this central home of the world, to their native homes in England or America, which they are apt thenceforward to look upon as provincial, after once having yielded to the spell of the Eternal City. The artist, who contemplates an indefinite succession of winters in this home of art (though his first thought was merely to improve himself by a brief visit), goes forth, in the summer time, to sketch scenery and costume among the Tuscan hills, and pour, if he can, the purple air of Italy over his canvas. He studies the old schools of art in the mountain-towns where they were born, and where they are still to be seen in the faded frescos of Giotto and Cimabue, on the walls of many a church, or in the dark chapels, in which the sacristan draws aside the veil from a treasured picture of Perugino. Thence, the happy painter goes to walk the long, bright galleries of Florence, or to steal glowing colors from the miraculous works, which he finds in a score of Venetian palaces. Such summers as these, spent amid whatever is exquisite in art, or wild and picturesque in nature, may not inadequately repay him for the chill neglect and disappointment through which he has probably languished, in his Roman winter. This sunny, shadowy, breezy, wandering life, in which he seeks for beauty as his treasure, and gathers for his winter's honey what is but a passing fragrance to all other men, is worth living for, come afterwards what may. Even if he die unrecognized, the artist has had his share of enjoyment and success.

Kenyon had seen, at a distance of many miles, the old villa or castle, towards which his journey lay, looking from its height over a broad expanse of valley. As he drew nearer, however, it had been hidden among the inequalities of the hill-side, until the winding road brought him almost to the iron gateway. The sculptor found this substantial barrier fastened with lock and bolt. There was no bell, nor other instrument of sound ; and, after summoning the invisible garrison with his voice, instead of a trumpet, he had leisure to take a glance at the exterior of the fortress.

About thirty yards within the gateway rose a square tower, lofty enough to be a very prominent object in the landscape, and more than sufficiently massive in proportion to its height. Its antiquity was evidently such, that, in a climate of more abundant moisture, the ivy would have mantled it from head to foot in a garment that might, by this time, have been centuries old, though ever new. In the dry Italian air, however, Nature had only so far adopted this old pile of stone-work as to cover almost every hand's-breadth of it with close-clinging lichens and yellow moss; and the immemorial growth of these kindly productions rendered the general hue of the tower soft and venerable, and took away the aspect of nakedness which would have made its age drearier than now.

Up and down the height of the tower were scattered three or four windows, the lower ones grated with iron bars, the upper ones vacant both of window-frames and glass. Besides these larger openings, there were several loopholes and little square apertures, which might be supposed to light the staircase, that doubtless climbed the interior towards the battlemented and machicolated summit. With this last-mentioned warlike garniture upon its stern old head and brow, the tower seemed evidently a stronghold of times long past. Many a cross-bowman had shot his shafts from those windows and loopholes, and from the vantage-height of those gray battlements; many a flight of arrows, too, had hit all round about the embrasures above, or the apertures below, where the helmet of a defender had momentarily glimmered. On festal nights, moreover, a hundred lamps had often gleamed afar over the valley, suspended from the iron hooks that were ranged for the purpose beneath the battlements and every window.

Connected with the tower, and extending behind it, there seemed to be a very spacious residence, chiefly of more modern date. It perhaps owed much of its fresher appearance, however, to a coat of stucco and yellow wash, which is a sort of renovation very much in vogue with the Italians. Kenyon noticed over a doorway, in the portion of the edifice immediately adjacent to the tower, a cross, which, with a bell suspended above the roof, indicated that this was a consecrated precinct, and the chapel of the mansion.

Meanwhile, the hot sun so incommoded the unsheltered traveller, that he shouted forth another impatient summons. Happening, at the same moment, to look upward, he saw a figure leaning from an embrasure of the battlements, and gazing down at him.

" Ho, Signore Count ! " cried the sculptor, waving his straw hat, for he recognized the face, after a moment's doubt. " This is a warm reception, truly ! Pray bid your porter let me in, before the sun shrivels me quite into a cinder."

" I will come myself," responded Donatello, flinging down his voice out of the clouds, as it were ; " old Tomaso and old Stella are both asleep, no doubt, and the rest of the people are in the vineyard. But I have expected you, and you are welcome ! "

The young Count — as perhaps we had better designate him in his ancestral tower — vanished from the battlements ; and Kenyon saw his figure appear successively at each of the windows, as he descended. On every reappearance, he turned his face towards the sculptor and gave a nod and smile ; for a kindly impulse prompted him thus to assure his visitor of a welcome, after keeping him so long at an inhospitable threshold.

Kenyon, however (naturally and professionally expert at reading the expression of the human countenance), had a vague sense that this was not the young friend whom he had known so familiarly in Rome; not the sylvan and untutored youth, whom Miriam, Hilda, and himself had liked, laughed at, and sported with; not the Donatello whose identity they had so playfully mixed up with that of the Faun of Praxiteles.

Finally, when his host had emerged from a side portal of the mansion, and approached the gateway, the traveller still felt that there was something lost, or something gained (he hardly knew which), that set the Donatello of to-day irreconcilably at odds with him of yesterday. His very gait showed it, in a certain gravity, a weight and measure of step, that had nothing in common with the irregular buoyancy which used to distinguish him. His face was paler and thinner, and the lips less full and less apart.

"I have looked for you a long while," said Donatello; and, though his voice sounded differently, and cut out its words more sharply than had been its wont, still there was a smile shining on his face, that, for the moment, quite brought back the Faun. "I shall be more cheerful, perhaps, now that you have come. It is very solitary here."

"I have come slowly along, often lingering, often turning aside," replied Kenyon; "for I found a great deal to interest me in the mediæval sculpture hidden away in the churches hereabouts. An artist, whether painter or sculptor, may be pardoned for loitering through such a region. But what a fine old tower! Its tall front is like a page of black-letter, taken from the history of the Italian republics."

"I know little or nothing of its history," said the Count, glancing upward at the battlements, where he had just been standing. "But I thank my forefathers for building it so high. I like the windy summit better than the world below, and spend much of my time there, nowadays."

"It is a pity you are not a star-gazer," observed Kenyon, also looking up. "It is higher than Galileo's tower, which I saw, a week or two ago, outside of the walls of Florence."

"A star-gazer? I am one," replied Donatello. "I sleep in the tower, and often watch very late on the battlements. There is a dismal old staircase to climb, however, before reaching the top, and a succession of dismal chambers, from story to story. Some of them were prison chambers in times past, as old Tomaso will tell you."

The repugnance intimated in his tone at the idea of this gloomy staircase and these ghostly, dimly lighted rooms, reminded Kenyon of the original Donatello, much more than his present custom of midnight vigils on the battlements.

"I shall be glad to share your watch," said the guest; "especially by moonlight. The prospect of this broad valley must be very fine. But I was not aware, my friend, that these were your country habits. I have fancied you in a sort of Arcadian life, tasting rich figs, and squeezing the juice out of the sunniest grapes, and sleeping soundly all night, after a day of simple pleasures."

"I may have known such a life, when I was younger," answered the Count, gravely. "I am not a boy now. Time flies over us, but leaves its shadow behind."

The sculptor could not but smile at the triteness of the remark, which, nevertheless, had a kind of originality as coming from Donatello. He had thought it out from his own experience, and perhaps considered himself as communicating a new truth to mankind.

They were now advancing up the court-yard; and the long extent of the villa, with its iron-barred lower windows and balconied upper ones, became visible, stretching back towards a grove of trees.

" At some period of your family history," observed Kenyon, " the Counts of Monte Beni must have led a patriarchal life in this vast house. A great-grandsire and all his descendants might find ample verge here, and with space, too, for each separate brood of little ones to play within its own precincts. Is your present household a large one? "

" Only myself," answered Donatello, " and Tomaso, who has been butler since my grandfather's time, and old Stella, who goes sweeping and dusting about the chambers, and Girolamo, the cook, who has but an idle life of it. He shall send you up a chicken forthwith. But, first of all, I must summon one of the contadini from the farm-house yonder, to take your horse to the stable."

Accordingly, the young Count shouted amain, and with such effect, that, after several repetitions of the outcry, an old gray woman protruded her head and a broom-handle from a chamber window; the venerable butler emerged from a recess in the side of the house, where was a well, or reservoir, in which he had been cleansing a small wine-cask; and a sunburnt contadino, in his shirt-sleeves, showed himself on the outskirts of the vineyard, with some kind of a farming tool in his hand. Donatello found employment for all

these retainers in providing accomodation for his guest
and steed, and then ushered the sculptor into the vesti-
bule of the house.

It was a square and lofty entrance-room, which, by
the solidity of its construction, might have been an
Etruscan tomb, being paved and walled with heavy
blocks of stone, and vaulted almost as massively over-
head. On two sides, there were doors, opening into
long suites of anterooms and saloons; on the third
side, a stone staircase, of spacious breadth, ascending,
by dignified degrees and with wide resting-places, to
another floor of similar extent. Through one of the
doors, which was ajar, Kenyon beheld an almost interminable vista of apartments, opening one beyond the
other, and reminding him of the hundred rooms in
Blue Beard's castle, or the countless halls in some
palace of the Arabian Nights.

It must have been a numerous family, indeed, that
could ever have sufficed to people with human life so
large an abode as this, and impart social warmth to
such a wide world within doors. The sculptor confessed to himself, that Donatello could allege reason
enough for growing melancholy, having only his own
personality to vivify it all.

" How a woman's face would brighten it up!" he
ejaculated, not intending to be overheard.

But, glancing at Donatello, he saw a stern and sorrowful look in his eyes, which altered his youthful
face as if it had seen thirty years of trouble; and, at
the same moment, old Stella showed herself through
one of the doorways, as the only representative of her
sex at Monte Beni.

CHAPTER XXV.

SUNSHINE.

" COME," said the Count, " I see you already find the old house dismal. So do I, indeed! And yet it was a cheerful place in my boyhood. But, you see, in my father's days (and the same was true of all my endless line of grandfathers, as I have heard), there used to be uncles, aunts, and all manner of kindred, dwelling together as one family. They were a merry and kindly race of people, for the most part, and kept one another's hearts warm."

" Two hearts might be enough for warmth," observed the sculptor, " even in so large a house as this. One solitary heart, it is true, may be apt to shiver a little. But, I trust, my friend, that the genial blood of your race still flows in many veins besides your own ? "

" I am the last," said Donatello, gloomily. " They have all vanished from me, since my childhood. Old Tomaso will tell you that the air of Monte Beni is not so favorable to length of days as it used to be. But that is not the secret of the quick extinction of my kindred."

" Then you are aware of a more satisfactory reason ? " suggested Kenyon.

" I thought of one, the other night, while I was gazing at the stars," answered Donatello ; " but, pardon me, I do not mean to tell it. One cause, however, of the longer and healthier life of my forefathers was, that they had many pleasant customs, and means of making themselves glad, and their guests and friends along with them. Nowadays we have but one!"

"And what is that?" asked the sculptor.

"You shall see!" said his young host.

By this time, he had ushered the sculptor into one of the numberless saloons; and, calling for refreshment, old Stella placed a cold fowl upon the table, and quickly followed it with a savory omelet, which Girolamo had lost no time in preparing. She also brought some cherries, plums, and apricots, and a plate full of particularly delicate figs, of last year's growth. The butler showing his white head at the door, his master beckoned to him.

"Tomaso, bring some Sunshine!" said he.

The readiest method of obeying this order, one might suppose, would have been, to fling wide the green window-blinds, and let the glow of the summer noon into the carefully shaded room. But, at Monte Beni, with provident caution against the wintry days, when there is little sunshine, and the rainy ones, when there is none, it was the hereditary custom to keep their Sunshine stored away in the cellar. Old Tomaso quickly produced some of it in a small, straw-covered flask, out of which he extracted the cork, and inserted a little cotton wool, to absorb the olive-oil that kept the precious liquid from the air.

"This is a wine," observed the Count, "the secret of making which has been kept in our family for centuries upon centuries; nor would it avail any man to steal the secret, unless he could also steal the vineyard, in which alone the Monte Beni grape can be produced. There is little else left me, save that patch of vines.

Taste some of their juice, and tell me whether it is worthy to be called Sunshine! for that is its name."

"A glorious name, too!" cried the sculptor.

"Taste it," said Donatello, filling his friend's glass, and pouring likewise a little into his own. "But first smell its fragrance; for the wine is very lavish of it, and will scatter it all abroad."

"Ah, how exquisite!" said Kenyon. "No other wine has a bouquet like this. The flavor must be rare, indeed, if it fulfil the promise of this fragrance, which is like the airy sweetness of youthful hopes, that no realities will ever satisfy!"

This invaluable liquor was of a pale golden hue, like other of the rarest Italian wines, and, if carelessly and irreligiously quaffed, might have been mistaken for a very fine sort of champagne. It was not, however, an effervescing wine, although its delicate piquancy produced a somewhat similar effect upon the palate. Sipping, the guest longed to sip again; but the wine demanded so deliberate a pause, in order to detect the hidden peculiarities and subtile exquisiteness of its flavor, that to drink it was really more a moral than a physical enjoyment. There was a deliciousness in it that eluded analysis, and — like whatever else is superlatively good — was perhaps better appreciated in the memory than by present consciousness.

One of its most ethereal charms lay in the transitory life of the wine's richest qualities; for, while it required a certain leisure and delay, yet, if you lingered too long upon the draught, it became disenchanted both of its fragrance and its flavor.

The lustre should not be forgotten, among the other admirable endowments of the Monte Beni wine; for, as it stood in Kenyon's glass, a little circle of light glowed on the table round about it, as if it were really so much golden sunshine.

"I feel myself a better man for that ethereal potation," observed the sculptor. "The finest Orvieto, or that famous wine, the Est Est Est of Montefiascone, is vulgar in comparison. This is surely the wine of the Golden Age, such as Bacchus himself first taught mankind to press from the choicest of his grapes. My dear Count, why is it not illustrious? The pale, liquid gold, in every such flask as that, might be solidified into golden scudi, and would quickly make you a millionnaire!"

Tomaso, the old butler, who was standing by the table, and enjoying the praises of the wine quite as much as if bestowed upon himself, made answer, —

"We have a tradition, signore," said he, "that this rare wine of our vineyard would lose all its wonderful qualities, if any of it were sent to market. The Counts of Monte Beni have never parted with a single flask of it for gold. At their banquets, in the olden time, they have entertained princes, cardinals, and once an emperor, and once a pope, with this delicious wine, and always, even to this day, it has been their custom to let it flow freely, when those whom they love and honor sit at the board. But the grand duke himself could not drink that wine, except it were under this very roof!"

"What you tell me, my good friend," replied Kenyon, "makes me venerate the Sunshine of Monte Beni even more abundantly than before. As I understand you, it is a sort of consecrated juice, and symbolizes the holy virtues of hospitality and social kindness?"

"Why, partly so, Signore," said the old butler, with a shrewd twinkle in his eye; "but, to speak out all the truth, there is another excellent reason why neither a cask nor a flask of our precious vintage should ever be sent to market. The wine, Signore, is so fond of its native home, that a transportation of even a few miles turns it quite sour. And yet it is a wine that keeps well in the cellar, underneath this floor, and gathers fragrance, flavor, and brightness, in its dark dungeon. That very flask of Sunshine, now, has kept itself for you, sir guest (as a maid reserves her sweetness till her lover comes for it), ever since a merry vintage-time, when the Signore Count here was a boy!"

"You must not wait for Tomaso to end his discourse about the wine, before drinking off your glass," observed Donatello. "When once the flask is uncorked, its finest qualities lose little time in making their escape. I doubt whether your last sip will be quite so delicious as you found the first."

And, in truth, the sculptor fancied that the Sunshine became almost imperceptibly clouded, as he approached the bottom of the flask. The effect of the wine, however, was a gentle exhilaration, which did not so speedily pass away.

Being thus refreshed, Kenyon looked around him at the antique saloon in which they sat. It was constructed in a most ponderous style, with a stone floor, on which heavy pilasters were planted against the wall, supporting arches that crossed one another in the vaulted ceiling. The upright walls, as well as the compartments of the roof, were completely covered with frescos, which doubtless had been brilliant when first executed, and perhaps for generations afterwards. The designs were of a festive and joyous character, representing Arcadian scenes, where nymphs, fauns, and satyrs disported themselves among mortal youths and maidens ; and Pan, and the god of wine, and he of sunshine and music, disdained not to brighten some sylvan merry-making with the scarcely veiled glory of their presence. A wreath of dancing figures, in admirable variety of shape and motion, was festooned quite round the cornice of the room.

In its first splendor, the saloon must have presented an aspect both gorgeous and enlivening; for it invested some of the cheerfullest ideas and emotions of which the human mind is susceptible with the external reality of beautiful form, and rich, harmonious glow and variety of color. But the frescos were now very ancient. They had been rubbed and scrubbed by old Stella and many a predecessor, and had been defaced in one spot, and retouched in another, and had peeled from the wall in patches, and had hidden some of their brightest portions under dreary dust, till the joyousness had quite vanished out of them all. It was often difficult to puzzle out the design ; and even where it was more readily intelligible, the figures showed like the ghosts of dead and buried joys, — the closer their resemblance to the happy past, the gloomier now. For it is thus, that with only an inconsiderable change, the gladdest objects and existences become the saddest; hope fading into disappointment; joy darkening into grief, and festal splendor into funereal duskiness ; and all evolving, as their moral, a grim identity between gay things and sorrowful ones. Only give them a little time, and they turn out to be just alike !

" There has been much festivity in this saloon, if I may judge by the character of its frescos," remarked Kenyon, whose spirits were still upheld by the mild potency of the Monte Beni wine. "Your forefathers, my dear Count, must have been joyous fellows, keeping up the vintage merriment throughout the year. It does me good to think of them gladdening the hearts of men and women, with their wine of Sunshine, even in the Iron Age, as Pan and Bacchus, whom we see yonder, did in the Golden one!"

"Yes; there have been merry times in the banquet-hall of Monte Beni, even within my own remembrance," replied Donatello, looking gravely at the painted walls. "It was meant for mirth, as you see; and when I brought my own cheerfulness into the saloon, these frescos looked cheerful too. But, methinks, they have all faded since I saw them last."

"It would be a good idea," said the sculptor, falling into his companion's vein, and helping him out with an illustration which Donatello himself could not have put into shape, "to convert this saloon into a chapel; and when the priest tells his hearers of the instability of earthly joys, and would show how drearily they vanish, he may point to these pictures, that were so joyous and are so dismal. He could not illustrate his theme so aptly in any other way."

"True, indeed," answered the Count, his former simplicity strangely mixing itself up with an experience that had changed him; "and yonder, where the minstrels used to stand, the altar shall be placed. A sinful man might do all the more effective penance in this old banquet-hall."

"But I should regret to have suggested so ungenial a transformation in your hospitable saloon," continued Kenyon, duly noting the change in Donatello's characteristics. "You startle me, my friend, by so ascetic a design! It would hardly have entered your head, when

DINING-ROOM OF AN ITALIAN PALACE

we first met. Pray do not, — if I may take the freedom of a somewhat elder man to advise you," added
he, smiling, — " pray do not, under a notion of improvement, take upon yourself to be sombre, thoughtful, and penitential, like all the rest of us."

Donatello made no answer, but sat awhile, appearing to follow with his eyes one of the figures, which
was repeated many times over in the groups upon the
walls and ceiling. It formed the principal link of an
allegory, by which (as is often the case in such pictorial designs) the whole series of frescos were bound
together, but which it would be impossible, or, at least,
very wearisome, to unravel. The sculptor's eyes took
a similar direction, and soon began to trace through
the vicissitudes, — once gay, now sombre, — in which
the old artist had involved it, the same individual figure. He fancied a resemblance in it to Donatello
himself ; and it put him in mind of one of the purposes with which he had come to Monte Beni.

"My dear Count," said he, "I have a proposal to
make. You must let me employ a little of my leisure
in modelling your bust. You remember what a striking resemblance we all of us — Hilda, Miriam, and I —
found between your features and those of the Faun of
Praxiteles. Then, it seemed an identity ; but now that
I know your face better, the likeness is far less apparent. Your head in marble would be a treasure to me.
Shall I have it ? "

" I have a weakness which I fear I cannot overcome," replied the Count, turning away his face. " It
troubles me to be looked at steadfastly."

" I have observed it since we have been sitting here,
though never before," rejoined the sculptor. " It is
a kind of nervousness, I apprehend, which you caught

in the Roman air, and which grows upon you, in your solitary life. It need be no hindrance to my taking your bust; for I will catch the likeness and expression by side glimpses, which (if portrait-painters and bust-makers did but know it) always bring home richer results than a broad stare."

"You may take me if you have the power," said Donatello; but, even as he spoke, he turned away his face; "and if you can see what makes me shrink from you, you are welcome to put it in the bust. It is not my will, but my necessity, to avoid men's eyes. Only," he added, with a smile which made Kenyon doubt whether he might not as well copy the Faun as model a new bust, — "only, you know, you must not insist on my uncovering these ears of mine!"

"Nay; I never should dream of such a thing," answered the sculptor, laughing, as the young Count shook his clustering curls. "I could not hope to persuade you, remembering how Miriam once failed!"

Nothing is more unaccountable than the spell that often lurks in a spoken word. A thought may be present to the mind, so distinctly that no utterance could make it more so; and two minds may be conscious of the same thought, in which one or both take the profoundest interest; but as long as it remains unspoken, their familiar talk flows quietly over the hidden idea, as a rivulet may sparkle and dimple over something sunken in its bed. But, speak the word; and it is like bringing up a drowned body out of the deepest pool of the rivulet, which has been aware of the horrible secret all along, in spite of its smiling surface.

And even so, when Kenyon chanced to make a distinct reference to Donatello's relations with Miriam (though the subject was already in both their minds), a ghastly emotion rose up out of the depths of the young Count's heart. He trembled either with anger or terror, and glared at the sculptor with wild eyes, like a wolf that meets you in the forest, and hesitates whether to flee or turn to bay. But, as Kenyon still looked calmly at him, his aspect gradually became less disturbed, though far from resuming its former quietude.

"You have spoken her name," said he, at last, in an altered and tremulous tone; "tell me, now, all that you know of her."

"I scarcely think that I have any later intelligence than yourself," answered Kenyon; "Miriam left Rome at about the time of your own departure. Within a day or two after our last meeting at the Church of the Capuchins, I called at her studio and found it vacant. Whither she has gone, I cannot tell."

Donatello asked no further questions.

They rose from table, and strolled together about the premises, whiling away the afternoon with brief intervals of unsatisfactory conversation, and many shadowy silences. The sculptor had a perception of change in his companion, — possibly of growth and development, but certainly of change, — which saddened him, because it took away much of the simple grace that was the best of Donatello's peculiarities.

Kenyon betook himself to repose that night in a grim, old, vaulted apartment, which, in the lapse of five or six centuries, had probably been the birth, bridal, and death chamber of a great many generations of the Monte Beni family. He was aroused, soon after daylight, by the clamor of a tribe of beggars who had taken their stand in a little rustic lane that crept beside that portion of the villa, and were addressing their petitions to the open windows. By and by, they appeared to have received alms, and took their departure.

"Some charitable Christian has sent those vagabonds away," thought the sculptor, as he resumed his interrupted nap; "who could it be? Donatello has his own rooms in the tower; Stella, Tomaso, and the cook are a world's width off; and I fancied myself the only inhabitant in this part of the house."

In the breadth and space which so delightfully characterize an Italian villa, a dozen guests might have had each his suite of apartments without infringing upon one another's ample precincts. But, so far as Kenyon knew, he was the only visitor beneath Donatello's widely extended roof.

CHAPTER XXVI.

THE PEDIGREE OF MONTE BENI.

FROM the old butler, whom he found to be a very gracious and affable personage, Kenyon soon learned many curious particulars about the family history and hereditary peculiarities of the Counts of Monte Beni. There was a pedigree, the later portion of which — that is to say, for a little more than a thousand years — a genealogist would have found delight in tracing out, link by link, and authenticating by records and documentary evidences. It would have been as difficult, however, to follow up the stream of Donatello's ancestry to its dim source, as travellers have found it to reach the mysterious fountains of the Nile. And, far beyond the region of definite and demonstrable fact, a romancer might have strayed into a region of old poetry, where the rich soil, so long uncultivated and untrodden, had lapsed into nearly its primeval state of wilderness. Among those antique paths, now overgrown with tangled and riotous vegetation, the wanderer must needs follow his own guidance, and arrive nowhither at last.

The race of Monte Beni, beyond a doubt, was one of the oldest in Italy, where families appear to survive at least, if not to flourish, on their half-decayed roots, oftener than in England or France. It came down in a broad track from the Middle Ages; but, at epochs anterior to those, it was distinctly visible in the gloom

of the period before chivalry put forth its flower ; and
further still, we are almost afraid to say, it was seen,
though with a fainter and wavering course, in the early
morn of Christendom, when the Roman Empire had
hardly begun to show symptoms of decline. At that
venerable distance, the heralds gave up the lineage in
despair.

But where written record left the genealogy of
Monte Beni, tradition took it up, and carried it without dread or shame beyond the Imperial ages into the
times of the Roman republic; beyond those, again,
into the epoch of kingly rule. Nor even so remotely
among the mossy centuries did it pause, but strayed
onward into that gray antiquity of which there is no
token left, save its cavernous tombs, and a few bronzes,
and some quaintly wrought ornaments of gold, and
gems with mystic figures and inscriptions. There, or
thereabouts, the line was supposed to have had its origin in the sylvan life of Etruria, while Italy was yet
guiltless of Rome.

Of course, as we regret to say, the earlier and very
much the larger portion of this respectable descent —
and the same is true of many briefer pedigrees — must
be looked upon as altogether mythical. Still, it threw
a romantic interest around the unquestionable antiquity of the Monte Beni family, and over that tract
of their own vines and fig-trees, beneath the shade of
which they had unquestionably dwelt for immemorial
ages. And there they had laid the foundations of
their tower, so long ago that one half of its height
was said to be sunken under the surface and to hide
subterranean chambers which once were cheerful with
the olden sunshine.

One story, or myth, that had mixed itself up with

their mouldy genealogy, interested the sculptor by its wild, and perhaps grotesque, yet not unfascinating peculiarity. He caught at it the more eagerly, as it afforded a shadowy and whimsical semblance of explanation for the likeness which he, with Miriam and Hilda, had seen or fancied, between Donatello and the Faun of Praxiteles.

The Monte Beni family, as this legend averred, drew their origin from the Pelasgic race, who peopled Italy in times that may be called prehistoric. It was the same noble breed of men, of Asiatic birth, that settled in Greece; the same happy and poetic kindred who dwelt in Arcadia, and — whether they ever lived such life or not — enriched the world with dreams, at least, and fables, lovely, if unsubstantial, of a Golden Age. In those delicious times, when deities and demigods appeared familiarly on earth, mingling with its inhabitants as friend with friend, — when nymphs, satyrs, and the whole train of classic faith or fable hardly took pains to hide themselves in the primeval woods, — at that auspicious period the lineage of Monte Beni had its rise. Its progenitor was a being not altogether human, yet partaking so largely of the gentlest human qualities, as to be neither awful nor shocking to the imagination. A sylvan creature, native among the woods, had loved a mortal maiden, and — perhaps by kindness, and the subtile courtesies which love might teach to his simplicity, or possibly by a ruder wooing — had won her to his haunts. In due time, he gained her womanly affection; and, making their bridal bower, for aught we know, in the hollow of a great tree, the pair spent a happy wedded life in that ancient neighborhood where now stood Donatello's tower.

From this union sprang a vigorous progeny that took its place unquestioned among human families. In that age, however, and long afterwards, it showed the ineffaceable lineaments of its wild paternity: it was a pleasant and kindly race of men, but capable of savage fierceness, and never quite restrainable within the trammels of social law. They were strong, active, genial, cheerful as the sunshine, passionate as the tornado. Their lives were rendered blissful by an unsought harmony with nature.

But, as centuries passed away, the Faun's wild blood had necessarily been attempered with constant intermixtures from the more ordinary streams of human life. It lost many of its original qualities, and served, for the most part, only to bestow an unconquerable vigor, which kept the family from extinction, and enabled them to make their own part good throughout the perils and rude emergencies of their interminable descent. In the constant wars with which Italy was plagued, by the dissensions of her petty states and republics, there was a demand for native hardihood.

The successive members of the Monte Beni family showed valor and policy enough, at all events, to keep their hereditary possessions out of the clutch of grasping neighbors, and probably differed very little from the other feudal barons with whom they fought and feasted. Such a degree of conformity with the manners of the generations, through which it survived, must have been essential to the prolonged continuance of the race.

It is well known, however, that any hereditary peculiarity — as a supernumerary finger, or an anomalous shape of feature, like the Austrian lip — is wont to

show itself in a family after a very wayward fashion.
It skips at its own pleasure along the line, and, latent
for half a century or so, crops out again in a great-
grandson. And thus, it was said, from a period beyond memory or record, there had ever and anon been
a descendant of the Monte Benis bearing nearly all
the characteristics that were attributed to the original
founder of the race. Some traditions even went so
far as to enumerate the ears, covered with a delicate
fur, and shaped like a pointed leaf, among the proofs
of authentic descent which were seen in these favored
individuals. We appreciate the beauty of such tokens
of a nearer kindred to the great family of nature than
other mortals bear ; but it would be idle to ask credit
for a statement which might be deemed to partake so
largely of the grotesque.

But it was indisputable that, once in a century, or
oftener, a son of Monte Beni gathered into himself
the scattered qualities of his race, and reproduced the
character that had been assigned to it from immemorial times. Beautiful, strong, brave, kindly, sincere,
of honest impulses, and endowed with simple tastes
and the love of homely pleasures, he was believed to
possess gifts by which he could associate himself with
the wild things of the forests, and with the fowls of
the air, and could feel a sympathy even with the trees,
among which it was his joy to dwell. On the other
hand, there were deficiencies both of intellect and
heart, and especially, as it seemed, in the development
of the higher portion of man's nature. These defects
were less perceptible in early youth, but showed themselves more strongly with advancing age, when, as the
animal spirits settled down upon a lower level, the
representative of the Monte Benis was apt to become

sensual, addicted to gross pleasures, heavy, unsympathizing, and insulated within the narrow limits of a
surly selfishness.

A similar change, indeed, is no more than what we
constantly observe to take place in persons who are
not careful to substitute other graces for those which
they inevitably lose along with the quick sensibility
and joyous vivacity of youth. At worst, the reigning
Count of Monte Beni, as his hair grew white, was still
a jolly old fellow over his flask of wine, — the wine
that Bacchus himself was fabled to have taught his
sylvan ancestor how to express, and from what choicest grapes, which would ripen only in a certain divinely favored portion of the Monte Beni vineyard.

The family, be it observed, were both proud and
ashamed of these legends; but whatever part of them
they might consent to incorporate into their ancestral
history, they steadily repudiated all that referred to
their one distinctive feature, the pointed and furry
ears. In a great many years past, no sober credence
had been yielded to the mythical portion of the pedigree. It might, however, be considered as typifying some such assemblage of qualities — in this case,
chiefly remarkable for their simplicity and naturalness
— as, when they reappear in successive generations,
constitute what we call family character. The sculptor found, moreover, on the evidence of some old portraits, that the physical features of the race had long
been similar to what he now saw them in Donatello.
With accumulating years, it is true, the Monte Beni
face had a tendency to look grim and savage; and, in
two or three instances, the family pictures glared at
the spectator in the eyes like some surly animal, that
had lost its good-humor when it outlived its playfulness.

The young Count accorded his guest full liberty to investigate the personal annals of these pictured wor-thies, as well as all the rest of his progenitors ; and ample materials were at hand in many chests of worm-eaten papers and yellow parchments, that had been gathering into larger and dustier piles ever since the dark ages. But, to confess the truth, the information afforded by these musty documents was so much more prosaic than what Kenyon acquired from Tomaso's legends, that even the superior authenticity of the for-mer could not reconcile him to its dulness.

What especially delighted the sculptor was the anal-ogy between Donatello's character, as he himself knew it, and those peculiar traits which the old butler's nar-rative assumed to have been long hereditary in the race. He was amused at finding, too, that not only Tomaso but the peasantry of the estate and neighbor-ing village recognized his friend as a genuine Monte Beni, of the original type. They seemed to cherish a great affection for the young Count, and were full of stories about his sportive childhood ; how he had played among the little rustics, and been at once the wildest and the sweetest of them all ; and how, in his very infancy, he had plunged into the deep pools of the streamlets and never been drowned, and had clambered to the topmost branches of tall trees with-out ever breaking his neck. No such mischance could happen to the sylvan child, because, handling all the elements of nature so fearlessly and freely, nothing had either the power or the will to do him harm.

He grew up, said these humble friends, the play-mate not only of all mortal kind, but of creatures of the woods ; although, when Kenyon pressed them for some particulars of this latter mode of companionship,

VOL. VI.

they could remember little more than a few anecdotes of a pet fox, which used to growl and snap at everybody save Donatello himself.

But they enlarged — and never were weary of the theme — upon the blithesome effects of Donatello's presence in his rosy childhood and budding youth. Their hovels had always glowed like sunshine when he entered them; so that, as the peasants expressed it, their young master had never darkened a doorway in his life. He was the soul of vintage festivals. While he was a mere infant, scarcely able to run alone, it had been the custom to make him tread the wine-press with his tender little feet, if it were only to crush one cluster of the grapes. And the grape-juice that gushed beneath his childish tread, be it ever so small in quantity, sufficed to impart a pleasant flavor to a whole cask of wine. The race of Monte Beni — so these rustic chroniclers assured the sculptor — had possessed the gift from the oldest of old times of expressing good wine from ordinary grapes, and a ravishing liquor from the choice growth of their vineyard.

In a word, as he listened to such tales as these, Kenyon could have imagined that the valleys and hill-sides about him were a veritable Arcadia; and that Donatello was not merely a sylvan faun, but the genial wine-god in his very person. Making many allowances for the poetic fancies of Italian peasants, he set it down for fact, that his friend, in a simple way, and among rustic folks, had been an exceedingly delightful fellow in his younger days.

But the contadini sometimes added, shaking their heads and sighing, that the young Count was sadly changed since he went to Rome. The village girls now missed the merry smile with which he used to greet them.

The sculptor inquired of his good friend Tomaso, whether he, too, had noticed the shadow which was said to have recently fallen over Donatello's life.

" Ah, yes, Signore ! " answered the old butler, " it is even so, since he came back from that wicked and miserable city. The world has grown either too evil, or else too wise and sad, for such men as the old Counts of Monte Beni used to be. His very first taste of it, as you see, has changed and spoilt my poor young lord. There had not been a single count in the family these hundred years or more, who was so true a Monte Beni, of the antique stamp, as this poor signorino ; and now it brings the tears into my eyes to hear him sighing over a cup of Sunshine ! Ah, it is a sad world now ! "

" Then you think there was a merrier world once ? " asked Kenyon.

" Surely, Signore," said Tomaso ; " a merrier world, and merrier Counts of Monte Beni to live in it ! Such tales of them as I have heard, when I was a child on my grandfather's knee ! The good old man remembered a lord of Monte Beni — at least, he had heard of such a one, though I will not make oath upon the holy crucifix that my grandsire lived in his time — who used to go into the woods and call pretty damsels out of the fountains, and out of the trunks of the old trees. That merry lord was known to dance with them a whole long summer afternoon ! When shall we see such frolics in our days ? "

" Not soon, I am afraid," acquiesced the sculptor. " You are right, excellent Tomaso ; the world is sadder now ! "

And, in truth, while our friend smiled at these wild fables, he sighed in the same breath to think how the

once genial earth produces, in every successive generation, fewer flowers than used to gladden the preceding ones.   Not that the modes and seeming possibilities of human enjoyment are rarer in our refined and
softened era, — on the contrary, they never before
were nearly so abundant, — but that mankind are getting so far beyond the childhood of their race that
they scorn to be happy any longer.   A simple and
joyous character can find no place for itself among
the sage and sombre figures that would put his unsophisticated cheerfulness to shame.   The entire system
of man's affairs, as at present established, is built up
purposely to exclude the careless and happy soul.   The
very children would upbraid the wretched individual
who should endeavor to take life and the world as —
what we might naturally suppose them meant for — a
place and opportunity for enjoyment.

It is the iron rule in our day to require an object
and a purpose in life.   It makes us all parts of a com-
plicated scheme of progress, which can only result in
our arrival at a colder and drearier region than we
were born in.   It insists upon everybody's adding
somewhat — a mite, perhaps, but earned by incessant
effort — to an accumulated pile of usefulness, of which
the only use will be, to burden our posterity with even
heavier thoughts and more inordinate labor than our
own.   No life now wanders like an unfettered stream;
there is a mill-wheel for the tiniest rivulet to turn.
We go all wrong, by too strenuous a resolution to go
all right.

Therefore it was — so, at least, the sculptor thought,
although partly suspicious of Donatello's darker misfortune — that the young Count found it impossible
nowadays to be what his forefathers had been.   He

could not live their healthy life of animal spirits, in
their sympathy with nature, and brotherhood with all
that breathed around them. Nature, in beast, fowl,
and tree, and earth, flood, and sky, is what it was of
old; but sin, care, and self-consciousness have set the
human portion of the world askew; and thus the simplest character is ever the soonest to go astray.

"At any rate, Tomaso," said Kenyon, doing his
best to comfort the old man, "let us hope that your
young lord will still enjoy himself at vintage-time.
By the aspect of the vineyard, I judge that this will
be a famous year for the golden wine of Monte Beni.
As long as your grapes produce that admirable liquor,
sad as you think the world, neither the Count nor his
guests will quite forget to smile."

"Ah, Signore," rejoined the butler with a sigh, "but
he scarcely wets his lips with the sunny juice."

"There is yet another hope," observed Kenyon;
"the young Count may fall in love, and bring home a
fair and laughing wife to chase the gloom out of yonder old, frescoed saloon. Do you think he could do a
better thing, my good Tomaso?"

"Maybe not, Signore," said the sage butler, looking earnestly at him; "and, maybe, not a worse!"

The sculptor fancied that the good old man had it
partly in his mind to make some remark, or communi-
cate some fact, which, on second thoughts, he resolved
to keep concealed in his own breast. He now took his
departure cellarward, shaking his white head and mut-
tering to himself, and did not reappear till dinner-
time, when he favored Kenyon, whom he had taken
far into his good graces, with a choicer flask of Sunshine than had yet blessed his palate.

To say the truth, this golden wine was no unnecessary ingredient towards making the life of Monte Beni palatable. It seemed a pity that Donatello did not drink a little more of it, and go jollily to bed at least, even if he should awake with an accession of darker melancholy the next morning.

Nevertheless, there was no lack of outward means for leading an agreeable life in the old villa. Wandering musicians haunted the precincts of Monte Beni, where they seemed to claim a prescriptive right ; they made the lawn and shrubbery tuneful with the sound of fiddle, harp, and flute, and now and then with the tangled squeaking of a bagpipe. Improvvisatori likewise came and told tales or recited verses to the contadini — among whom Kenyon was often an auditor — after their day's work in the vineyard. Jugglers, too, obtained permission to do feats of magic in the hall, where they set even the sage Tomaso, and Stella, Girolamo, and the peasant-girls from the farm-house, all of a broad grin, between merriment and wonder. These good people got food and lodging for their pleasant pains, and some of the small wine of Tuscany, and a reasonable handful of the Grand Duke's copper coin, to keep up the hospitable renown of Monte Beni. But very seldom had they the young Count as a listener or a spectator.

There were sometimes dances by moonlight on the lawn, but never since he came from Rome did Donatello's presence deepen the blushes of the pretty contadinas, or his footstep weary out the most agile partner or competitor, as once it was sure to do.

Paupers — for this kind of vermin infested the house of Monte Beni worse than any other spot in beggar-haunted Italy — stood beneath all the windows, making loud supplication, or even establishing them-

selves on the marble steps of the grand entrance.
They ate and drank, and filled their bags, and pock-
eted the little money that was given them, and went
forth on their devious ways, showering blessings innumerable on the mansion and its lord, and on the souls
of his deceased forefathers, who had always been just
such simpletons as to be compassionate to beggary.
But, in spite of their favorable prayers, — by which
Italian philanthropists set great store, — a cloud
seemed to hang over these once Arcadian precincts,
and to be darkest around the summit of the tower
where Donatello was wont to sit and brood.

CHAPTER XXVII.

AFTER the sculptor's arrival, however, the young Count sometimes came down from his forlorn elevation, and rambled with him among the neighboring woods and hills. He led his friend to many enchanting nooks, with which he himself had been familiar in his childhood. But of late, as he remarked to Kenyon, a sort of strangeness had overgrown them, like clusters of dark shrubbery, so that he hardly recognized the places which he had known and loved so well.

To the sculptor's eye, nevertheless, they were still rich with beauty. They were picturesque in that sweetly impressive way where wildness, in a long lapse of years, has crept over scenes that have been once adorned with the careful art and toil of man; and when man could do no more for them, time and nature came, and wrought hand in hand to bring them to a soft and venerable perfection. There grew the fig-tree that had run wild and taken to wife the vine, which likewise had gone rampant out of all human control ; so that the two wild things had tangled and knotted themselves into a wild marriage-bond, and hung their various progeny — the luscious figs, the grapes, oozy with the Southern juice, and both endowed with a wild flavor that added the final charm — on the same bough together.

In Kenyon's opinion, never was any other nook so

lovely as a certain little dell which he and Donatello visited. It was hollowed in among the hills, and open to a glimpse of the broad, fertile valley. A fountain had its birth here, and fell into a marble basin, which was all covered with moss and shaggy with water-weeds. Over the gush of the small stream, with an urn in her arms, stood a marble nymph, whose nakedness the moss had kindly clothed as with a garment; and the long trails and tresses of the maidenhair had done what they could in the poor thing's behalf, by hanging themselves about her waist. In former days — it might be a remote antiquity — this lady of the fountain had first received the infant tide into her urn and poured it thence into the marble basin. But now the sculptured urn had a great crack from top to bottom; and the discontented nymph was compelled to see the basin fill itself through a channel which she could not control, although with water long ago consecrated to her.

For this reason, or some other, she looked terribly forlorn; and you might have fancied that the whole fountain was but the overflow of her lonely tears.

"This was a place that I used greatly to delight in," remarked Donatello, sighing. "As a child, and as a boy, I have been very happy here."

"And, as a man, I should ask no fitter place to be happy in," answered Kenyon. "But you, my friend, are of such a social nature, that I should hardly have thought these lonely haunts would take your fancy. It is a place for a poet to dream in, and people it with the beings of his imagination."

"I am no poet, that I know of," said Donatello, "but yet, as I tell you, I have been very happy here, in the company of this fountain and this nymph. It is said that a Faun, my oldest forefather, brought home hither to this very spot a human maiden, whom he loved and wedded. This spring of delicious water was their household well."

"It is a most enchanting fable!" exclaimed Kenyon; "that is, if it be not a fact."

"And why not a fact?" said the simple Donatello. "There is, likewise, another sweet old story connected with this spot. But, now that I remember it, it seems to me more sad than sweet, though formerly the sorrow, in which it closes, did not so much impress me. If I had the gift of tale-telling, this one would be sure to interest you mightily."

"Pray tell it," said Kenyon; "no matter whether well or ill. These wild legends have often the most powerful charm when least artfully told."

So the young Count narrated a myth of one of his progenitors, — he might have lived a century ago, or a thousand years, or before the Christian epoch, for anything that Donatello knew to the contrary, — who had made acquaintance with a fair creature belonging to this fountain. Whether woman or sprite was a mystery, as was all else about her, except that her life and soul were somehow interfused throughout the gushing water. She was a fresh, cool, dewy thing, sunny and shadowy, full of pleasant little mischiefs, fitful and changeable with the whim of the moment, but yet as constant as her native stream, which kept the same gush and flow forever, while marble crumbled over and around it. The fountain woman loved the youth, — a knight, as Donatello called him, — for, according to the legend, his race was akin to hers. At least, whether kin or no, there had been friendship and sympathy of old betwixt an ancestor of his, with furry ears, and the long-lived lady of the fountain.

And, after all those ages, she was still as young as a May morning, and as frolicsome as a bird upon a tree, or a breeze that makes merry with the leaves.

She taught him how to call her from her pebbly source, and they spent many a happy hour together, more especially in the fervor of the summer days. For often as he sat waiting for her by the margin of the spring, she would suddenly fall down around him in a shower of sunny rain-drops, with a rainbow glancing through them, and forthwith gather herself up into the likeness of a beautiful girl, laughing — or was it the warble of the rill over the pebbles ? — to see the youth's amazement.

Thus, kind maiden that she was, the hot atmosphere became deliciously cool and fragrant for this favored knight; and, furthermore, when he knelt down to drink out of the spring, nothing was more common than for a pair of rosy lips to come up out of its little depths, and touch his mouth with the thrill of a sweet, cool, dewy kiss !

" It is a delightful story for the hot noon of your Tuscan summer," observed the sculptor, at this point. " But the deportment of the watery lady must have had a most chilling influence in midwinter. Her lover would find it, very literally, a cold reception ! "

" I suppose," said Donatello, rather sulkily, " you are making fun of the story. But I see nothing laughable in the thing itself, nor in what you say about it."

He went on to relate, that for a long while the knight found infinite pleasure and comfort in the friendship of the fountain nymph. In his merriest hours, she gladdened him with her sportive humor. If ever he was annoyed with earthly trouble, she laid her moist hand upon his brow, and charmed the fret and fever quite away.

But one day — one fatal noontide — the young knight came rushing with hasty and irregular steps to the accustomed fountain. He called the nymph; but — no doubt because there was something unusual and frightful in his tone — she did not appear, nor answer him. He flung himself down, and washed his hands and bathed his feverish brow in the cool, pure water. And then, there was a sound of woe; it might have been a woman's voice; it might have been only the sighing of the brook over the pebbles. The water shrank away from the youth's hands, and left his brow as dry and feverish as before. —

Donatello here came to a dead pause.

"Why did the water shrink from this unhappy knight?" inquired the sculptor.

"Because he had tried to wash off a blood-stain!" said the young Count, in a horror-stricken whisper. "The guilty man had polluted the pure water. The nymph might have comforted him in sorrow, but could not cleanse his conscience of a crime."

"And did he never behold her more?" asked Kenyon.

"Never but once," replied his friend. "He never beheld her blessed face but once again, and then there was a blood-stain on the poor nymph's brow; it was the stain his guilt had left in the fountain where he tried to wash it off. He mourned for her his whole life long, and employed the best sculptor of the time to carve this statue of the nymph from his description of her aspect. But, though my ancestor would fain have had the image wear her happiest look, the artist, unlike yourself, was so impressed with the mournfulness of the story, that, in spite of his best efforts, he made her forlorn, and forever weeping, as you see ! "

Kenyon found a certain charm in this simple legend. Whether so intended or not, he understood it as an apologue, typifying the soothing and genial effects of an habitual intercourse with nature, in all ordinary cares and griefs ; while, on the other hand, her mild influences fall short in their effect upon the ruder passions, and are altogether powerless in the dread fever-fit or deadly chill of guilt.

" Do you say," he asked, " that the nymph's face has never since been shown to any mortal ? Methinks you, by your native qualities, are as well entitled to her favor as ever your progenitor could have been. Why have you not summoned her ? "

" I called her often when I was a silly child," answered Donatello ; and he added, in an inward voice, " Thank Heaven, she did not come ! "

" Then you never saw her ? " said the sculptor.

" Never in my life ! " rejoined the Count. " No, my dear friend, I have not seen the nymph ; although here, by her fountain, I used to make many strange acquaintances ; for, from my earliest childhood, I was familiar with whatever creatures haunt the woods. You would have laughed to see the friends I had among them ; yes, among the wild, nimble things, that reckon man their deadliest enemy ! How it was first taught me, I cannot tell ; but there was a charm — a voice, a murmur, a kind of chant — by which I called the woodland inhabitants, the furry people, and the feathered people, in a language that they seemed to understand."

" I have heard of such a gift," responded the sculptor, gravely, " but never before met with a person en

dowed with it. Pray, try the charm; and lest I
should frighten your friends away, I will withdraw
into this thicket, and merely peep at them."

" I doubt," said Donatello, " whether they will remember my voice now. It changes, you know, as the
boy grows towards manhood."

Nevertheless, as the young Count's good-nature and
easy persuadability were among his best characteristics, he set about complying with Kenyon's request.
The latter, in his concealment among the shrubberies,
heard him send forth a sort of modulated breath, wild,
rude, yet harmonious.   It struck the auditor as at
once the strangest and the most natural utterance that
had ever reached his ears.   Any idle boy, it should
seem, singing to himself and setting his wordless song
to no other or more definite tune than the play of his
own pulses, might produce a sound almost identical
with this ; and yet, it was as individual as a murmur
of the breeze. Donatello tried it, over and over again,
with many breaks, at first, and pauses of uncertainty ;
then with more confidence, and a fuller swell, like a
wayfarer groping out of obscurity into the light, and
moving with freer footsteps as it brightens around
him.

Anon, his voice appeared to fill the air, yet not with
an obtrusive clangor. The sound was of a murmurous
character, soft, attractive, persuasive, friendly.   The
sculptor fancied that such might have been the original voice and utterance of the natural man, before
the sophistication of the human intellect formed what
we now call language.   In this broad dialect — broad
as the sympathies of nature — the . human brother
might have spoken to his inarticulate brotherhood that
prowl the woods, or soar upon the wing, and have

been intelligible to such extent as to win their confidence.

The sound had its pathos too. At some of its simple cadences, the tears came quietly into Kenyon's eyes. They welled up slowly from his heart, which was thrilling with an emotion more delightful than he had often felt before, but which he forbore to analyze, lest, if he seized it, it should at once perish in his grasp.

Donatello paused two or three times, and seemed to listen; then, recommencing, he poured his spirit and life more earnestly into the strain. And, finally, — or else the sculptor's hope and imagination deceived him, — soft treads were audible upon the fallen leaves. There was a rustling among the shrubbery; a whir of wings, moreover, that hovered in the air. It may have been all an illusion; but Kenyon fancied that he could distinguish the stealthy, cat-like movement of some small forest citizen, and that he could even see its doubtful shadow, if not really its substance. But, all at once, whatever might be the reason, there ensued a hurried rush and scamper of little feet; and then the sculptor heard a wild, sorrowful cry, and through the crevices of the thicket beheld Donatello fling himself on the ground.

Emerging from his hiding-place, he saw no living thing, save a brown lizard (it was of the tarantula species) rustling away through the sunshine. To all present appearance, this venomous reptile was the only creature that had responded to the young Count's efforts to renew his intercourse with the lower orders of nature.

"What has happened to you?" exclaimed Kenyon, stooping down over his friend, and wondering at the anguish which he betrayed.

"Death, death!" sobbed Donatello. "They know it!"

He grovelled beside the fountain, in a fit of such passionate sobbing and weeping, that it seemed as if his heart had broken, and spilt its wild sorrows upon the ground. His unrestrained grief and childish tears made Kenyon sensible in how small a degree the customs and restraints of society had really acted upon this young man, in spite of the quietude of his ordinary deportment. In response to his friend's efforts to console him, he murmured words hardly more articulate than the strange chant which he had so recently been breathing into the air.

"They know it!" was all that Kenyon could yet distinguish, — "they know it!"

"Who know it?" asked the sculptor. "And what is it they know?"

"They know it!" repeated Donatello, trembling. "They shun me! All nature shrinks from me, and shudders at me! I live in the midst of a curse, that hems me round with a circle of fire! No innocent thing can come near me."

"Be comforted, my dear friend," said Kenyon, kneeling beside him. "You labor under some illusion, but no curse. As for this strange, natural spell, which you have been exercising, and of which I have heard before, though I never believed in, nor expected to witness it, I am satisfied that you still possess it. It was my own half-concealed presence, no doubt, and some involuntary little movement of mine, that scared away your forest friends."

"They are friends of mine no longer," answered Donatello.

"We all of us, as we grow older," rejoined Kenyon,

" lose somewhat of our proximity to nature.   It is the
price we pay for experience."

" A heavy price, then ! " said Donatello, rising from
the ground.   " But we will speak no more of it.   Forget this scene, my dear friend.   In your eyes, it must
look very absurd.   It is a grief, I presume, to all men,
to find the pleasant privileges and properties of early
life departing from them.   That grief has now befallen me.   Well; I shall waste no more tears for such
a cause ! "

Nothing else made Kenyon so sensible of a change
in Donatello, as his newly acquired power of dealing
with his own emotions, and, after a struggle more or
less fierce, thrusting them down into the prison-cells
where he usually kept them confined.   The restraint,
which he now put upon himself, and the mask of dull
composure which he succeeded in clasping over his
still beautiful, and once faun-like face, affected the
sensitive sculptor more sadly than even the unrestrained passion of the preceding scene.   It is a very
miserable epoch, when the evil necessities of life, in
our tortuous world, first get the better of us so far
as to compel us to attempt throwing a cloud over our
transparency.   Simplicity increases in value the longer
we can keep it, and the further we carry it onward
into life ; the loss of a child's simplicity, in the inevitable lapse of years, causes but a natural sigh or two,
because even his mother feared that he could not keep
it always.   But after a young man has brought it
through his childhood, and has still worn it in his
bosom, not as an early dew-drop, but as a diamond
of pure, white, lustre, — it is a pity to lose it, then.
And thus, when Kenyon saw how much his friend had
now to hide, and how well he hid it, he would have

wept, although his tears would have been even idler than those which Donatello had just shed.

They parted on the lawn before the house, the Count to climb his tower, and the sculptor to read an antique edition of Dante, which he had found among some old volumes of Catholic devotion, in a seldom-visited room. Tomaso met him in the entrance-hall, and showed a desire to speak.

"Our poor signorino looks very sad to-day!" he said.

"Even so, good Tomaso," replied the sculptor. "Would that we could raise his spirits a little!"

"There might be means, Signore," answered the old butler, "if one might but be sure that they were the right ones. We men are but rough nurses for a sick body or a sick spirit."

"Women, you would say, my good friend, are better," said the sculptor, struck by an intelligence in the butler's face. "That is possible! But it depends."

"Ah; we will wait a little longer," said Tomaso, with the customary shake of his head.

CHAPTER XXVIII.

THE OWL TOWER.

"WILL you not show me your tower?" said the sculptor one day to his friend.

"It is plainly enough to be seen, methinks," answered the Count, with a kind of sulkiness that often appeared in him, as one of the little symptoms of inward trouble.

"Yes; its exterior is visible far and wide," said Kenyon. "But such a gray, moss-grown tower as this, however valuable as an object of scenery, will certainly be quite as interesting inside as out. It cannot be less than six hundred years old; the foundations and lower story are much older than that, I should judge; and traditions probably cling to the walls within quite as plentifully as the gray and yellow lichens cluster on its face without."

"No doubt," replied Donatello; "but I know little of such things, and never could comprehend the interest which some of you Forestieri take in them. A year or two ago an English signore, with a venerable white beard—they say he was a magician, too—came hither from as far off as Florence, just to see my tower."

"Ah, I have seen him at Florence," observed Kenyon. "He is a necromancer, as you say, and dwells in an old mansion of the Knights Templars, close by the Ponte Vecchio, with a great many ghostly books, pictures, and antiquities, to make the house gloomy, and one bright-eyed little girl, to keep it cheerful! "

" I know him only by his white beard," said Donatello ; " but he could have told you a great deal about the tower, and the sieges which it has stood, and the prisoners who have been confined in it. And he gathered up all the traditions of the Monte Beni family, and, among the rest, the sad one which I told you at the fountain the other day. He had known mighty poets, he said, in his earlier life ; and the most illustrious of them would have rejoiced to preserve such a legend in immortal rhyme, — especially if he could have had some of our wine of Sunshine to help out his inspiration! "

" Any man might be a poet, as well as Byron, with such wine and such a theme," rejoined the sculptor. " But, shall we climb your tower ? The thunder-storm gathering yonder among the hills will be a spectacle worth witnessing."

" Come, then," said the Count, adding, with a sigh, " it has a weary staircase, and dismal chambers, and it is very lonesome at the summit! "

" Like a man's life, when he has climbed to eminence," remarked the sculptor ; " or, let us rather say, with its difficult steps, and the dark prison-cells you speak of, your tower resembles the spiritual experience of many a sinful soul, which, nevertheless, may struggle upward into the pure air and light of Heaven at last! "

Donatello sighed again, and led the way up into the tower.

Mounting the broad staircase that ascended from the entrance-hall, they traversed the great wilderness of a house, through some obscure passages, and came to a low, ancient doorway. It admitted them to a narrow turret - stair which zigzagged upward, lighted in its progress by loopholes and iron-barred windows. Reaching the top of the first flight, the Count threw open a door of worm-eaten oak, and disclosed a chamber that occupied the whole area of the tower. It was most pitiably forlorn of aspect, with a brick-paved floor, bare holes through the massive walls, grated with iron, instead of windows, and for furniture an old stool, which increased the dreariness of the place tenfold, by suggesting an idea of its having once been tenanted.

"This was a prisoner's cell in the old days," said Donatello; " the white-bearded necromancer, of whom I told you, found out that a certain famous monk was confined here, about five hundred years ago. He was a very holy man, and was afterwards burned at the stake in the Grand-ducal Square at Firenze. There have always been stories, Tomaso says, of a hooded monk creeping up and down these stairs, or standing in the doorway of this chamber. It must needs be the ghost of the ancient prisoner. Do you believe in ghosts ? "

" I can hardly tell," replied Kenyon; "on the whole, I think not."

" Neither do I," responded the Count; "for, if spirits ever come back, I should surely have met one within these two months past. Ghosts never rise ! So much I know, and am glad to know it ! "

Following the narrow staircase still higher, they came to another room of similar size and equally forlorn, but inhabited by two personages of a race which from time immemorial have held proprietorship and occupancy in ruined towers. These were a pair of owls, who, being doubtless acquainted with Donatello, showed little sign of alarm at the entrance of visitors. They gave a dismal croak or two, and hopped aside into the darkest corner, since it was not yet their hour to flap duskily abroad.

"They do not desert me, like my other feathered acquaintances," observed the young Count, with a sad smile, alluding to the scene which Kenyon had witnessed at the fountain-side. "When I was a wild, playful boy, the owls did not love me half so well."

He made no further pause here, but led his friend up another flight of steps; while, at every stage, the windows and narrow loopholes afforded Kenyon more extensive eyeshots over hill and valley, and allowed him to taste the cool purity of mid-atmosphere. At length they reached the topmost chamber, directly beneath the roof of the tower.

"This is my own abode," said Donatello; "my own owl's nest."

In fact, the room was fitted up as a bedchamber, though in a style of the utmost simplicity. It likewise served as an oratory; there being a crucifix in one corner, and a multitude of holy emblems, such as Catholics judge it necessary to help their devotion withal. Several ugly little prints, representing the sufferings of the Saviour, and the martyrdoms of saints, hung on the wall; and, behind the crucifix, there was a good copy of Titian's Magdalen of the Pitti Palace, clad only in the flow of her golden ringlets. She had a confident look (but it was Titian's fault, not the penitent woman's), as if expecting to win heaven by the free display of her earthly charms. Inside of a glass case appeared an image of the sacred Bambino, in the guise of a little waxen boy, very

GRAND DUCAL SQUARE, AND PALAZZO VECCHIO, FLORENCE

prettily made, reclining among flowers, like a Cupid, and holding up a heart that resembled a bit of red sealing-wax. A small vase of precious marble was full of holy water.

Beneath the crucifix, on a table, lay a human skull, which looked as if it might have been dug up out of some old grave. But, examining it more closely, Kenyon saw that it was carved in gray alabaster, most skilfully done to the death, with accurate imitation of the teeth, the sutures, the empty eye-caverns, and the fragile little bones of the nose. This hideous emblem rested on a cushion of white marble, so nicely wrought that you seemed to see the impression of the heavy skull in a silken and downy substance.

Donatello dipped his fingers into the holy-water vase, and crossed himself. After doing so he trembled.

"I have no right to make the sacred symbol on a sinful breast!" he said.

"On what mortal breast can it be made, then?" asked the sculptor. "Is there one that hides no sin?"

"But these blessed emblems make you smile, I fear," resumed the Count, looking askance at his friend. "You heretics, I know, attempt to pray without even a crucifix to kneel at."

"I, at least, whom you call a heretic, reverence that holy symbol," answered Kenyon. "What I am most inclined to murmur at is this death's-head. I could laugh, moreover, in its ugly face! It is absurdly monstrous, my dear friend, thus to fling the dead-weight of our mortality upon our immortal hopes. While we live on earth, 't is true, we must needs carry our skeletons about with us; but, for Heaven's sake, do not let us burden our spirits with them, in our fee-

ble efforts to soar upward! Believe me, it will change
the whole aspect of death, if you can once disconnect
it, in your idea, with that corruption from which it
disengages our higher part."

"I do not well understand you," said Donatello;
and he took up the alabaster skull, shuddering, and
evidently feeling it a kind of penance to touch it. "I
only know that this skull has been in my family for
centuries. Old Tomaso has a story that it was copied
by a famous sculptor from the skull of that same unhappy knight who loved the fountain-lady, and lost
her by a blood-stain. He lived and died with a deep
sense of sin upon him, and, on his death-bed, he ordained that this token of him should go down to his
posterity. And my forefathers, being a cheerful race
of men in their natural disposition, found it needful
to have the skull often before their eyes, because they
dearly loved life and its enjoyments, and hated the
very thought of death."

"I am afraid," said Kenyon, "they liked it none
the better, for seeing its face under this abominable
mask."

Without further discussion, the Count led the way
up one more flight of stairs, at the end of which they
emerged upon the summit of the tower. The sculptor
felt as if his being were suddenly magnified a hundred-fold; so wide was the Umbrian valley that suddenly opened before him, set in its grand framework
of nearer and more distant hills. It seemed as if all
Italy lay under his eyes in that one picture. For there
was the broad, sunny smile of God, which we fancy
to be spread over that favored land more abundantly
than on other regions, and, beneath it, glowed a most
rich and varied fertility. The trim vineyards were

there, and the fig-trees, and the mulberries, and the
smoky-hued tracts of the olive-orchards; there, too,
were fields of every kind of grain, among which waved
the Indian corn, putting Kenyon in mind of the fondly
remembered acres of his father's homestead. White
villas, gray convents, church - spires, villages, towns,
each with its battlemented walls and towered gateway, were scattered upon this spacious map; a river
gleamed across it; and lakes opened their blue eyes
in its face, reflecting heaven, lest mortals should forget that better land when they beheld the earth so
beautiful.

What made the valley look still wider was the two
or three varieties of weather that were visible on its
surface, all at the same instant of time. Here lay the
quiet sunshine; there fell the great black patches of
ominous shadow from the clouds; and behind them,
like a giant of league-long strides, came hurrying the
thunder-storm, which had already swept midway across
the plain. In the rear of the approaching tempest,
brightened forth again the sunny splendor, which its
progress had darkened with so terrible a frown.

All round this majestic landscape, the bald-peaked
or forest-crowned mountains descended boldly upon the
plain. On many of their spurs and midway declivities,
and even on their summits, stood cities, some of them
famous of old; for these had been the seats and nurse-
ries of early art, where the flower of beauty sprang out
of a rocky soil, and in a high, keen atmosphere, when
the richest and most sheltered gardens failed to nourish it.

"Thank God for letting me again behold this
scene!" said the sculptor, a devout man in his way,
reverently taking off his hat. "I have viewed it from

many points, and never without as full a sensation of gratitude as my heart seems capable of feeling. How it strengthens the poor human spirit in its reliance on His providence, to ascend but this little way above the common level, and so attain a somewhat wider glimpse of His dealings with mankind! He doeth all things right! His will be done!"

"You discern something that is hidden from me," observed Donatello, gloomily, yet striving with unwonted grasp to catch the analogies which so cheered his friend. "I see sunshine on one spot, and cloud in another, and no reason for it in either case. The sun on you; the cloud on me! What comfort can I draw from this?"

"Nay; I cannot preach," said Kenyon, "with a page of heaven and a page of earth spread wide open before us! Only begin to read it, and you will find it interpreting itself without the aid of words. It is a great mistake to try to put our best thoughts into human language. When we ascend into the higher regions of emotion and spiritual enjoyment, they are only expressible by such grand hieroglyphics as these around us."

They stood awhile, contemplating the scene; but, as inevitably happens after a spiritual flight, it was not long before the sculptor felt his wings flagging in the rarity of the upper atmosphere. He was glad to let himself quietly downward out of the mid-sky, as it were, and alight on the solid platform of the battlemented tower. He looked about him, and beheld growing out of the stone pavement, which formed the roof, a little shrub, with green and glossy leaves. It was the only green thing there; and Heaven knows how its seeds had ever been planted, at that airy

height, or how it had found nourishment for its small
life in the chinks of the stones ; for it had no earth,
and nothing more like soil than the crumbling mortar,
which had been crammed into the crevices in a long-
past age.

Yet the plant seemed fond of its native site ; and
Donatello said it had always grown there, from his
earliest remembrance, and never, he believed, any
smaller or any larger than they saw it now.

"I wonder if the shrub teaches you any good lesson," said he, observing the interest with which Kenyon examined it. "If the wide valley has a great
meaning, the plant ought to have at least a little one ;
and it has been growing on our tower long enough to
have learned how to speak it."

"Oh, certainly!" answered the sculptor; "the shrub
has its moral, or it would have perished long ago.
And, no doubt, it is for your use and edification, since
you have had it before your eyes all your lifetime, and
now are moved to ask what may be its lesson."

"It teaches me nothing," said the simple Donatello,
stooping over the plant, and perplexing himself with a
minute scrutiny. "But here was a worm that would
have killed it ; an ugly creature, which I will fling over
the battlements."

CHAPTER XXIX.

THE sculptor now looked through an embrasure, and threw down a bit of lime, watching its fall, till it struck upon a stone bench at the rocky foundation of the tower, and flew into many fragments.

"Pray pardon me for helping Time to crumble away your ancestral walls," said he. "But I am one of those persons who have a natural tendency to climb heights, and to stand on the verge of them, measuring the depth below. If I were to do just as I like, at this moment, I should fling myself down after that bit of lime. It is a very singular temptation, and all but irresistible; partly, I believe, because it might be so easily done, and partly because such momentous consequences would ensue, without my being compelled to wait a moment for them. Have you never felt this strange impulse of an evil spirit at your back, shoving you towards a precipice?"

"Ah, no!" cried Donatello, shrinking from the battlemented wall with a face of horror. "I cling to life in a way which you cannot conceive; it has been so rich, so warm, so sunny! — and beyond its verge, nothing but the chilly dark! And then a fall from a precipice is such an awful death!"

"Nay; if it be a great height," said Kenyon, "a man would leave his life in the air, and never feel the hard shock at the bottom."

"That is not the way with this kind of death!" exclaimed Donatello, in a low, horror - stricken voice,
which grew higher and more full of emotion as he
proceeded. "Imagine a fellow-creature, — breathing,
now, and looking you in the face, — and now tumbling down, down, down, with a long shriek wavering
after him, all the way! He does not leave his life
in the air! No; but it keeps in him till he thumps
against the stones, a horribly long while; then he
lies there frightfully quiet, a dead heap of bruised
flesh and broken bones! A quiver runs through the
crushed mass; and no more movement after that!
No; not if you would give your soul to make him stir
a finger! Ah, terrible! Yes, yes; I would fain fling
myself down for the very dread of it, that I might endure it once for all, and dream of it no more!"

"How forcibly, how frightfully you conceive this!"
said the sculptor, aghast at the passionate horror which
was betrayed in the Count's words, and still more in
his wild gestures and ghastly look. "Nay, if the
height of your tower affects your imagination thus,
you do wrong to trust yourself here in solitude, and
in the night-time, and at all unguarded hours. You
are not safe in your chamber. It is but a step or
two; and what if a vivid dream should lead you up
hither, at midnight, and act itself out as a reality!"

Donatello had hidden his face in his hands, and was
leaning against the parapet.

"No fear of that!" said he. "Whatever the dream
may be, I am too genuine a coward to act out my own
death in it."

The paroxysm passed away, and the two friends
continued their desultory talk, very much as if no such
interruption had occurred. Nevertheless, it affected the

sculptor with infinite pity to see this young man, who had been born to gladness as an assured heritage, now involved in a misty bewilderment of grievous thoughts, amid which he seemed to go staggering blindfold. Kenyon, not without an unshaped suspicion of the definite fact, knew that his condition must have resulted from the weight and gloom of life, now first, through the agency of a secret trouble, making themselves felt on a character that had heretofore breathed only an atmosphere of joy. The effect of this hard lesson, upon Donatello's intellect and disposition, was very striking. It was perceptible that he had already had glimpses of strange and subtle matters in those dark caverns, into which all men must descend, if they would know anything beneath the surface and illusive pleasures of existence. And when they emerge, though dazzled and blinded by the first glare of daylight, they take truer and sadder views of life forever afterwards.

From some mysterious source, as the sculptor felt assured, a soul had been inspired into the young Count's simplicity, since their intercourse in Rome. He now showed a far deeper sense, and an intelligence that began to deal with high subjects, though in a feeble and childish way. He evinced, too, a more definite and nobler individuality, but developed out of grief and pain, and fearfully conscious of the pangs that had given it birth. Every human life, if it ascends to truth or delves down to reality, must undergo a similar change ; but sometimes, perhaps, the instruction comes without the sorrow ; and oftener the sorrow teaches no lesson that abides with us. In Donatello's case, it was pitiful, and almost ludicrous, to observe the confused struggle that he made ; how completely he was taken by surprise : how ill-prepared he stood, on this old battle-field of the world, to fight with such an inevitable foe as mortal calamity, and sin for its stronger ally.

" And yet," thought Kenyon, " the poor fellow bears himself like a hero, too! If he would only tell me his trouble, or give me an opening to speak frankly about it, I might help him; but he finds it too horrible to be uttered, and fancies himself the only mortal that ever felt the anguish of remorse. Yes; he believes that nobody ever endured his agony before; so that — sharp enough in itself — it has all the additional zest of a torture just invented to plague him individually."

The sculptor endeavored to dismiss the painful subject from his mind; and, leaning against the battlements, he turned his face southward and westward, and gazed across the breadth of the valley. His thoughts flew far beyond even those wide boundaries, taking an air-line from Donatello's tower to another turret that ascended into the sky of the summer afternoon, invisibly to him, above the roofs of distant Rome. Then rose tumultuously into his consciousness that strong love for Hilda, which it was his habit to confine in one of the heart's inner chambers, because he had found no encouragement to bring it forward. But now, he felt a strange pull at his heartstrings. It could not have been more perceptible, if all the way between these battlements and Hilda's dove-cote had stretched an exquisitely sensitive cord, which, at the hither end, was knotted with his aforesaid heartstrings, and, at the remoter one, was grasped by a gentle hand. His breath grew tremulous. He put his hand to his breast; so distinctly did he seem to feel that cord drawn once, and again, and again, as if — though still it was bashfully intimated — there were an impor-

tunate demand for his presence. Oh, for the white
wings of Hilda's doves, that he might have flown
thither, and alighted at the Virgin's shrine!

But lovers, and Kenyon knew it well, project so
lifelike a copy of their mistresses out of their own imaginations, that it can pull at the heartstrings almost
as perceptibly as the genuine original. No airy intimations are to be trusted ; no evidences of responsive affection less positive than whispered and broken
words, or tender pressures of the hand, allowed and
half returned; or glances, that distil many passionate
avowals into one gleam of richly colored light. Even
these should be weighed rigorously, at the instant;
for, in another instant, the imagination seizes on them
as its property, and stamps them with its own arbi-
trary value. But Hilda's maidenly reserve had given
her lover no such tokens, to be interpreted either by
his hopes or fears.

"Yonder, over mountain and valley, lies Rome,"
said the sculptor ; " shall you return thither in the
autumn ? "

"Never ! I hate Rome," answered Donatello ;
"and have good cause."

"And yet it was a pleasant winter that we spent
there," observed Kenyon, " and with pleasant friends
about us. You would meet them again there, — all
of them."

" All ? " asked Donatello.

" All, to the best of my belief," said the sculptor :
" but you need not go to Rome to seek them. If
there were one of those friends whose lifetime was
twisted with your own, I am enough of a fatalist to feel
assured that you will meet that one again, wander
whither you may. Neither can we escape the compan-

ions whom Providence assigns for us, by climbing an old tower like this."

"Yet the stairs are steep and dark," rejoined the Count; "none but yourself would seek me here, or find me, if they sought."

As Donatello did not take advantage of this opening which his friend had kindly afforded him to pour out his hidden troubles, the latter again threw aside the subject, and returned to the enjoyment of the scene before him. The thunder-storm, which he had beheld striding across the valley, had passed to the left of Monte Beni, and was continuing its march towards the hills that formed the boundary on the eastward. Above the whole valley, indeed, the sky was heavy with tumbling vapors, interspersed with which were tracts of blue, vividly brightened by the sun; but, in the east, where the tempest was yet trailing its ragged skirts, lay a dusky region of cloud and sullen mist, in which some of the hills appeared of a dark-purple hue. Others became so indistinct, that the spectator could not tell rocky height from impalpable cloud. Far into this misty cloud-region, however, — within the domain of chaos, as it were, — hill-tops were seen brightening in the sunshine; they looked like fragments of the world, broken adrift and based on nothingness, or like portions of a sphere destined to exist, but not yet finally compacted.

The sculptor, habitually drawing many of the images and illustrations of his thoughts from the plastic art, fancied that the scene represented the process of the Creator, when he held the new, imperfect earth in his hand, and modelled it.

"What a magic is in mist and vapor among the mountains!" he exclaimed. "With their help, one single scene becomes a thousand. The cloud-scenery gives such variety to a hilly landscape that it would be worth while to journalize its aspect from hour to hour. A cloud, however, — as I have myself experienced, — is apt to grow solid and as heavy as a stone the instant that you take in hand to describe it. But, in my own heart, I have found great use in clouds. Such silvery ones as those to the northward, for example, have often suggested sculpturesque groups, figures, and attitudes; they are especially rich in attitudes of living repose, which a sculptor only hits upon by the rarest good fortune. When I go back to my dear native land, the clouds along the horizon will be my only gallery of art!"

"I can see cloud-shapes, too," said Donatello; "yonder is one that shifts strangely; it has been like people whom I knew. And now, if I watch it a little longer, it will take the figure of a monk reclining, with his cowl about his head and drawn partly over his face, and — well! did I not tell you so?"

"I think," remarked Kenyon, "we can hardly be gazing at the same cloud. What I behold is a reclining figure, to be sure, but feminine, and with a despondent air, wonderfully well expressed in the wavering outline from head to foot. It moves my very heart by something indefinable that it suggests."

"I see the figure, and almost the face," said the Count; adding, in a lower voice, "It is Miriam's!"

"No, not Miriam's," answered the sculptor.

While the two gazers thus found their own reminiscences and presentiments floating among the clouds, the day drew to its close, and now showed them the fair spectacle of an Italian sunset. The sky was soft and bright, but not so gorgeous as Kenyon had seen it,

a thousand times, in America; for there the western
sky is wont to be set aflame with breadths and depths
of color with which poets seek in vain to dye their
verses, and which painters never dare to copy. As
beheld from the tower of Monte Beni, the scene was
tenderly magnificent, with mild gradations of hue, and
a lavish outpouring of gold, but rather such gold as
we see on the leaf of a bright flower than the burnished glow of metal from the mine. Or, if metallic, it
looked airy and unsubstantial, like the glorified dreams
of an alchemist. And speedily — more speedily than
in our own clime — came the twilight, and, brightening through its gray transparency, the stars.

A swarm of minute insects that had been hovering
all day round the battlements were now swept away
by the freshness of a rising breeze. The two owls in
the chamber beneath Donatello's uttered their soft
melancholy cry, — which, with national avoidance of
harsh sounds, Italian owls substitute for the hoot of
their kindred in other countries, — and flew darkling
forth among the shrubbery. A convent-bell rang out
near at hand, and was not only echoed among the
hills, but answered by another bell, and still another,
which doubtless had farther and farther responses, at
various distances along the valley; for, like the English drumbeat around the globe, there is a chain of
convent-bells from end to end, and cross-wise, and in
all possible directions over priest-ridden Italy.

"Come," said the sculptor, "the evening air grows
cool. It is time to descend."

"Time for you, my friend," replied the Count; and
he hesitated a little before adding, "I must keep a
vigil here for some hours longer. It is my frequent
custom to keep vigils; and sometimes the thought oc-

curs to me whether it were not better to keep them in yonder convent, the bell of which just now seemed to summon me. Should I do wisely, do you think, to exchange this old tower for a cell?"

"What! Turn monk?" exclaimed his friend. "A horrible idea!"

"True," said Donatello, sighing. "Therefore, if at all, I purpose doing it."

"Then think of it no more, for Heaven's sake!" cried the sculptor. "There are a thousand better and more poignant methods of being miserable than that, if to be miserable is what you wish. Nay; I question whether a monk keeps himself up to the intellectual and spiritual height which misery implies. A monk — I judge from their sensual physiognomies, which meet me at every turn — is inevitably a beast! Their souls, if they have any to begin with, perish out of them, before their sluggish, swinish existence is half done. Better, a million times, to stand star-gazing on these airy battlements, than to smother your new germ of a higher life in a monkish cell!"

"You make me tremble," said Donatello, "by your bold aspersion of men who have devoted themselves to God's service!"

"They serve neither God nor man, and themselves least of all, though their motives be utterly selfish," replied Kenyon. "Avoid the convent, my dear friend, as you would shun the death of the soul! But, for my own part, if I had an insupportable burden, — if, for any cause, I were bent upon sacrificing every earthly hope as a peace-offering towards Heaven, — I would make the wide world my cell, and good deeds to mankind my prayer. Many penitent men have done this, and found peace in it."

" Ah, but you are a heretic! " said the Count.

Yet his face brightened beneath the stars; and, looking at it through the twilight, the sculptor's remembrance went back to that scene in the Capitol, where, both in features and expression, Donatello had seemed identical with the Faun. And still there was a resemblance; for now, when first the idea was suggested of living for the welfare of his fellow-creatures, the original beauty, which sorrow had partly effaced, came back elevated and spiritualized. In the black depths, the Faun had found a soul, and was struggling with it towards the light of heaven.

The illumination, it is true, soon faded out of Donatello's face. The idea of life-long and unselfish effort was too high to be received by him with more than a momentary comprehension. An Italian, indeed, seldom dreams of being philanthropic, except in bestowing alms among the paupers, who appeal to his beneficence at every step; nor does it occur to him that there are fitter modes of propitiating Heaven than by penances, pilgrimages, and offerings at shrines. Perhaps, too, their system has its share of moral advantages; they, at all events, cannot well pride themselves, as our own more energetic benevolence is apt to do, upon sharing in the counsels of Providence and kindly helping out its otherwise impracticable designs.

And now the broad valley twinkled with lights, that glimmered through its duskiness, like the fire-flies in the garden of a Florentine palace. A gleam of lightning from the rear of the tempest showed the circumference of hills, and the great space between, as the last cannon-flash of a retreating army reddens across the field where it has fought. The sculptor was on the point of descending the turret-stair, when, somewhere in the darkness that lay beneath them, a woman's voice was heard, singing a low, sad strain.

" Hark ! " said he, laying his hand on Donatello's arm.

And Donatello had said, " Hark ! " at the same instant.

The song, if song it could be called, that had only a wild rhythm, and flowed forth in the fitful measure of a wind-harp, did not clothe itself in the sharp brilliancy of the Italian tongue. The words, so far as they could be distinguished, were German, and therefore unintelligible to the Count, and hardly less so to the sculptor ; being softened and molten, as it were, into the melancholy richness of the voice that sung them. It was as the murmur of a soul bewildered amid the sinful gloom of earth, and retaining only enough memory of a better state to make sad music of the wail, which would else have been a despairing shriek. Never was there profounder pathos than breathed through that mysterious voice ; it brought the tears into the sculptor's eyes, with remembrances and forebodings of whatever sorrow he had felt or apprehended ; it made Donatello sob, as chiming in with the anguish that he found unutterable, and giving it the expression which he vaguely sought.

But, when the emotion was at its profoundest depth, the voice rose out of it, yet so gradually that a gloom seemed to pervade it, far upward from the abyss, and not entirely to fall away as it ascended into a higher and purer region. At last, the auditors would have fancied that the melody, with its rich sweetness all there, and much of its sorrow gone, was floating around the very summit of the tower.

" Donatello," said the sculptor, when there was

silence again, " had that voice no message for your ear ? "

" I dare not receive it," said Donatello ; " the anguish of which it spoke abides with me : the hope dies away with the breath that brought it hither. It is not good for me to hear that voice."

The sculptor sighed, and left the poor penitent keeping his vigil on the tower.

CHAPTER XXX.

DONATELLO'S BUST.

KENYON, it will be remembered, had asked Donatello's permission to model his bust. The work had now made considerable progress, and necessarily kept the sculptor's thoughts brooding much and often upon his host's personal characteristics. These it was his difficult office to bring out from their depths, and interpret them to all men, showing them what they could not discern for themselves, yet must be compelled to recognize at a glance, on the surface of a block of marble.

He had never undertaken a portrait-bust which gave him so much trouble as Donatello's; not that there was any special difficulty in hitting the likeness, though even in this respect the grace and harmony of the features seemed inconsistent with a prominent expression of individuality; but he was chiefly perplexed how to make this genial and kind type of countenance the index of the mind within. His acuteness and his sympathies, indeed, were both somewhat at fault in their efforts to enlighten him as to the moral phase through which the Count was now passing. If at one sitting he caught a glimpse of what appeared to be a genuine and permanent trait, it would probably be less perceptible on a second occasion, and perhaps have vanished entirely at a third. So evanescent a show of character threw the sculptor into despair; not marble or clay, but cloud and vapor, was the material in which it ought to be represented. Even the ponderous depression which constantly weighed upon Donatello's heart could not compel him into the kind of repose which the plastic art requires.

Hopeless of a good result, Kenyon gave up all preconceptions about the character of his subject, and let his hands work uncontrolled with the clay, somewhat as a spiritual medium, while holding a pen, yields it to an unseen guidance other than that of her own will. Now and then he fancied that this plan was destined to be the successful one. A skill and insight beyond his consciousness seemed occasionally to take up the task. The mystery, the miracle, of imbuing an inanimate substance with thought, feeling, and all the intangible attributes of the soul, appeared on the verge of being wrought. And now, as he flattered himself, the true image of his friend was about to emerge from the facile material, bringing with it more of Donatello's character than the keenest observer could detect at any one moment in the face of the original. Vain expectation! some touch, whereby the artist thought to improve or hasten the result, interfered with the design of his unseen spiritual assistant, and spoilt the whole. There was still the moist, brown clay, indeed, and the features of Donatello, but without any semblance of intelligent and sympathetic life.

"The difficulty will drive me mad, I verily believe!" cried the sculptor, nervously. "Look at the wretched piece of work yourself, my dear friend, and tell me whether you recognize any manner of likeness to your inner man?"

"None," replied Donatello, speaking the simple truth. "It is like looking a stranger in the face."

This frankly unfavorable testimony so wrought with the sensitive artist, that he fell into a passion with the stubborn image, and cared not what might happen to it thenceforward. Wielding that wonderful power which sculptors possess over moist clay, however refractory it may show itself in certain respects, he compressed, elongated, widened, and otherwise altered the features of the bust in mere recklessness, and at every change inquired of the Count whether the expression became anywise more satisfactory.

"Stop!" cried Donatello, at last, catching the sculptor's hand. "Let it remain so!"

By some accidental handling of the clay, entirely independent of his own will, Kenyon had given the countenance a distorted and violent look, combining animal fierceness with intelligent hatred. Had Hilda, or had Miriam, seen the bust, with the expression which it had now assumed, they might have recognized Donatello's face as they beheld it at that terrible moment when he held his victim over the edge of the precipice.

"What have I done?" said the sculptor, shocked at his own casual production. "It were a sin to let the clay which bears your features harden into a look like that. Cain never wore an uglier one."

"For that very reason, let it remain!" answered the Count, who had grown pale as ashes at the aspect of his crime, thus strangely presented to him in another of the many guises under which guilt stares the criminal in the face. "Do not alter it! Chisel it, rather, in eternal marble! I will set it up in my oratory and keep it continually before my eyes. Sadder and more horrible is a face like this, alive with my own crime, than the dead skull which my forefathers handed down to me!"

But, without in the least heeding Donatello's remonstrances, the sculptor again applied his artful fingers to the clay, and compelled the bust to dismiss the expression that had so startled them both.

"Believe me," said he, turning his eyes upon his friend, full of grave and tender sympathy, "you know not what is requisite for your spiritual growth, seeking, as you do, to keep your soul perpetually in the unwholesome region of remorse. It was needful for you to pass through that dark valley, but it is infinitely dangerous to linger there too long; there is poison in the atmosphere, when we sit down and brood in it, instead of girding up our loins to press onward. Not despondency, not slothful anguish, is what you now require, — but effort! Has there been an unalterable evil in your young life? Then crowd it out with good, or it will lie corrupting there forever, and cause your capacity for better things to partake its noisome corruption!"

"You stir up many thoughts," said Donatello, pressing his hand upon his brow, "but the multitude and the whirl of them make me dizzy."

They now left the sculptor's temporary studio, without observing that his last accidental touches, with which he hurriedly effaced the look of deadly rage, had given the bust a higher and sweeter expression than it had hitherto worn. It is to be regretted that Kenyon had not seen it; for only an artist, perhaps, can conceive the irksomeness, the irritation of brain, the depression of spirits, that resulted from his failure to satisfy himself, after so much toil and thought as he had bestowed on Donatello's bust. In case of success, indeed, all this thoughtful toil would have been reckoned, not only as well bestowed, but as among the happiest hours of his life ; whereas, deeming himself to have failed, it was just so much of life that had better never have been lived ; for thus does the good or ill result of his labor throw back sunshine or gloom upon the artist's mind. The sculptor, therefore, would have done well to glance again at his work ; for here were still the features of the antique Faun, but now illuminated with a higher meaning, such as the old marble never bore.

Donatello having quitted him, Kenyon spent the rest of the day strolling about the pleasant precincts of Monte Beni, where the summer was now so far advanced that it began, indeed, to partake of the ripe wealth of autumn. Apricots had long been abundant, and had passed away, and plums and cherries along with them. But now came great, juicy pears, melting and delicious, and peaches of goodly size and tempting aspect, though cold and watery to the palate, compared with the sculptor's rich reminiscences of that fruit in America. The purple figs had already enjoyed their day, and the white ones were luscious now. The contadini (who, by this time, knew Kenyon well) found many clusters of ripe grapes for him, in every little globe of which was included a fragrant draught of the sunny Monte Beni wine.

Unexpectedly, in a nook, close by the farm-house, he happened upon a spot where the vintage had actually commenced. A great heap of early ripened grapes had been gathered, and thrown into a mighty tub. In the middle of it stood a lusty and jolly contadino, nor stood, merely, but stamped with all his might, and danced amain ; while the red juice bathed his feet, and threw its foam midway up his brown and shaggy legs. Here, then, was the very process that shows so picturesquely in Scripture and in poetry, of treading out the wine-press and dyeing the feet and garments with the crimson effusion as with the blood of a battle-field. The memory of the process does not make the Tuscan wine taste more deliciously. The contadini hospitably offered Kenyon a sample of the new liquor, that had already stood fermenting for a day or two. He had tried a similar draught, however, in years past, and was little inclined to make proof of it again ; for he knew that it would be a sour and bitter juice, a wine of woe and tribulation, and that the more a man drinks of such liquor, the sorrier he is likely to be.

The scene reminded the sculptor of our New England vintages, where the big piles of golden and rosy apples lie under the orchard trees, in the mild, autumnal sunshine ; and the creaking cider-mill, set in motion by a circumgyratory horse, is all a-gush with the luscious juice. To speak frankly, the cider-making is the more picturesque sight of the two, and the new, sweet cider an infinitely better drink than the ordinary, unripe Tuscan wine. Such as it is, however, the latter fills thousands upon thousands of small, flat barrels, and, still growing thinner and sharper, loses the little life it had, as wine, and becomes apotheosized as a more praiseworthy vinegar.

Yet all these vineyard scenes, and the processes connected with the culture of the grape, had a flavor of poetry about them. The toil that produces those kindly gifts of nature which are not the substance of life, but its luxury, is unlike other toil. We are inclined to fancy that it does not bend the sturdy frame and stiffen the overwrought muscles, like the labor that is devoted in sad, hard earnest to raise grain for

sour bread.   Certainly, the sunburnt young men and
dark - cheeked, laughing girls, who weeded the rich
acres of Monte Beni, might well enough have passed
for inhabitants of an unsophisticated Arcadia.   Later
in the season, when the true vintage-time should come,
and the wine of Sunshine gush into the vats, it was
hardly too wild a dream that Bacchus himself might
revisit the haunts which he loved of old.   But, alas!
where now would he find the Faun with whom we see
him consorting in so many an antique group?

Donatello's remorseful anguish saddened this primitive and delightful life.   Kenyon had a pain of his
own, moreover, although not all a pain, in the never-
quiet, never - satisfied yearning of his heart towards
Hilda.   He was authorized to use little freedom towards that shy maiden, even in his visions; so that he
almost reproached himself when sometimes his imagination pictured in detail the sweet years that they
might spend together, in a retreat like this.   It had
just that rarest quality of remoteness from the actual
and ordinary world — a remoteness through which all
delights might visit them freely, sifted from all troubles — which lovers so reasonably insist upon, in their
ideal arrangements for a happy union.   It is possible,
indeed, that even Donatello's grief and Kenyon's pale,
sunless affection lent a charm to Monte Beni, which it
would not have retained amid a more abundant joyousness.   The sculptor strayed amid its vineyards and
orchards, its dells and tangled shrubberies, with somewhat the sensations of an adventurer who should find
his way to the site of ancient Eden, and behold its loveliness through the transparency of that gloom which
has been brooding over those haunts of innocence ever
since the fall.   Adam saw it in a brighter sunshine,

but never knew the shade of pensive beauty which Eden won from his expulsion.

It was in the decline of the afternoon that Kenyon returned from his long, musing ramble. Old Tomaso — between whom and himself for some time past there had been a mysterious understanding, — met him in the entrance-hall, and drew him a little aside.

"The signorina would speak with you," he whispered.

"In the chapel?" asked the sculptor.

"No; in the saloon beyond it," answered the butler: "the entrance — you once saw the signorina appear through it — is near the altar, hidden behind the tapestry."

Kenyon lost no time in obeying the summons.

CHAPTER XXXI.

THE MARBLE SALOON.

IN an old Tuscan villa, a chapel ordinarily makes
one among the numerous apartments; though it often
happens that the door is permanently closed, the key
lost, and the place left to itself, in dusty sanctity, like
that chamber in man's heart where he hides his religious awe. This was very much the case with the chapel
of Monte Beni. One rainy day, however, in his wanderings through the great, intricate house, Kenyon had
unexpectedly found his way into it, and been impressed
by its solemn aspect. The arched windows, high upward in the wall, and darkened with dust and cobweb,
threw down a dim light that showed the altar, with a
picture of a martyrdom above, and some tall tapers
ranged before it. They had apparently been lighted,
and burned an hour or two, and been extinguished
perhaps half a century before. The marble vase at
the entrance held some hardened mud at the bottom,
accruing from the dust that had settled in it during
the gradual evaporation of the holy water; and a spi-
der (being an insect that delights in pointing the moral
of desolation and neglect) had taken pains to weave
a prodigiously thick tissue across the circular brim.
An old family banner, tattered by the moths, drooped
from the vaulted roof. In niches there were some mediæval busts of Donatello's forgotten ancestry; and
among them, it might be, the forlorn visage of that

hapless knight between whom and the fountain-nymph
had occurred such tender love-passages.

Throughout all the jovial prosperity of Monte Beni,
this one spot within the domestic walls had kept itself
silent, stern, and sad. When the individual or the
family retired from song and mirth, they here sought
those realities which men do not invite their festive associates to share. And here, on the occasion above referred to, the sculptor had discovered — accidentally,
so far as he was concerned, though with a purpose on
her part — that there was a guest under Donatello's
roof, whose presence the Count did not suspect. An
interview had since taken place, and he was now summoned to another.

He crossed the chapel, in compliance with Tomaso's
instructions, and, passing through the side entrance,
found himself in a saloon, of no great size, but more
magnificent than he had supposed the villa to contain.
As it was vacant, Kenyon had leisure to pace it once
or twice, and examine it with a careless sort of scrutiny, before any person appeared.

This beautiful hall was floored with rich marbles, in
artistically arranged figures and compartments. The
walls, likewise, were almost entirely cased in marble of
various kinds, the prevalent variety being giallo antico,
intermixed with verd-antique, and others equally precious. The splendor of the giallo antico, however, was
what gave character to the saloon; and the large and
deep niches, apparently intended for full-length statues, along the walls, were lined with the same costly
material. Without visiting Italy, one can have no idea
of the beauty and magnificence that are produced by
these fittings-up of polished marble. Without such
experience, indeed, we do not even know what marble

means, in any sense, save as the white limestone of which we carve our mantel-pieces. This rich hall of Monte Beni, moreover, was adorned, at its upper end, with two pillars that seemed to consist of Oriental alabaster; and wherever there was a space vacant of precious and variegated marble, it was frescoed with ornaments in arabesque. Above, there was a coved and vaulted ceiling, glowing with pictured scenes, which affected Kenyon with a vague sense of splendor, without his twisting his neck to gaze at them.

It is one of the special excellences of such a saloon of polished and richly colored marble, that decay can never tarnish it. Until the house crumbles down upon it, it shines indestructibly, and, with a little dusting, looks just as brilliant in its three hundredth year as the day after the final slab of giallo antico was fitted into the wall. To the sculptor, at this first view of it, it seemed a hall where the sun was magically imprisoned, and must always shine. He anticipated Miriam's entrance, arrayed in queenly robes, and beaming with even more than the singular beauty that had heretofore distinguished her.

While this thought was passing through his mind, the pillared door, at the upper end of the saloon, was partly opened, and Miriam appeared. She was very pale, and dressed in deep mourning. As she advanced towards the sculptor, the feebleness of her step was so apparent that he made haste to meet her, apprehending that she might sink down on the marble floor, without the instant support of his arm.

But, with a gleam of her natural self-reliance, she declined his aid, and, after touching her cold hand to his, went and sat down on one of the cushioned divans that were ranged against the wall.

"You are very ill, Miriam!" said Kenyon, much shocked at her appearance. "I had not thought of this."

"No; not so ill as I seem to you," she answered; adding despondently, "yet I am ill enough I believe, to die, unless some change speedily occurs."

"What, then, is your disorder?" asked the sculptor; "and what the remedy?"

"The disorder!" repeated Miriam. "There is none that I know of save too much life and strength, without a purpose for one or the other. It is my too redundant energy that is slowly — or perhaps rapidly — wearing me away, because I can apply it to no use. The object, which I am bound to consider my only one on earth, fails me utterly. The sacrifice which I yearn to make of myself, my hopes, my everything, is coldly put aside. Nothing is left for me but to brood, brood, brood, all day, all night, in unprofitable longings and repinings."

"This is very sad, Miriam," said Kenyon.

"Ay, indeed; I fancy so," she replied, with a short, unnatural laugh.

"With all your activity of mind," resumed he, "so fertile in plans as I have known you, can you imagine no method of bringing your resources into play?"

"My mind is not active any longer," answered Miriam, in a cold, indifferent tone. "It deals with one thought and no more. One recollection paralyzes it. It is not remorse; do not think it! I put myself out of the question, and feel neither regret nor penitence on my own behalf. But what benumbs me, what robs me of all power,'— it is no secret for a woman to tell a man, yet I care not though you know it, — is the certainty that I am, and must ever be, an object of horror in Donatello's sight."

The sculptor — a young man, and cherishing a love which insulated him from the wild experiences which some men gather — was startled to perceive how Miriam's rich, ill-regulated nature impelled her to fling herself, conscience and all, on one passion, the object of which intellectually seemed far beneath her.

"How have you obtained the certainty of which you speak?" asked he, after a pause.

"Oh, by a sure token," said Miriam; "a gesture, merely; a shudder, a cold shiver, that ran through him one sunny morning when his hand happened to touch mine! But it was enough."

"I firmly believe, Miriam," said the sculptor, "that he loves you still."

She started, and a flush of color came tremulously over the paleness of her cheek.

"Yes," repeated Kenyon, "if my interest in Donatello — and in yourself, Miriam — endows me with any true insight, he not only loves you still, but with a force and depth proportioned to the stronger grasp of his faculties, in their new development."

"Do not deceive me," said Miriam, growing pale again.

"Not for the world!" replied Kenyon. "Here is what I take to be the truth. There was an interval, no doubt, when the horror of some calamity, which I need not shape out in my conjectures, threw Donatello into a stupor of misery. Connected with the first shock there was an intolerable pain and shuddering repugnance attaching themselves to all the circumstances and surroundings of the event that so terribly affected him. Was his dearest friend involved within the horror of that moment? He would shrink from her as he shrank most of all from himself. But as his mind roused itself, — as it rose to a higher life than he had hitherto experienced, — whatever had been true and permanent within him revived by the self-same impulse. So has it been with his love."

"But, surely," said Miriam, "he knows that I am here! Why, then, except that I am odious to him, does he not bid me welcome?"

"He is, I believe, aware of your presence here," answered the sculptor. "Your song, a night or two ago, must have revealed it to him, and, in truth, I had fancied that there was already a consciousness of it in his mind. But, the more passionately he longs for your society, the more religiously he deems himself bound to avoid it. The idea of a life-long penance has taken strong possession of Donatello. He gropes blindly about him for some method of sharp self-torture, and finds, of course, no other so efficacious as this."

"But, he loves me," repeated Miriam, in a low voice, to herself. "Yes; he loves me!"

It was strange to observe the womanly softness that came over her, as she admitted that comfort into her bosom. The cold, unnatural indifference of her manner, a kind of frozen passionateness which had shocked and chilled the sculptor, disappeared. She blushed, and turned away her eyes, knowing that there was more surprise and joy in their dewy glances than any man save one ought to detect there.

"In other respects," she inquired at length, "is he much changed?"

"A wonderful process is going forward in Donatello's mind," answered the sculptor. "The germs of faculties that have heretofore slept are fast springing into activity. The world of thought is disclosing itself to his inward sight. He startles me, at times, with his perception of deep truths ; and, quite as often, it must be owned, he compels me to smile by the inter-mixture of his former simplicity with a new intelli-gence. But, he is bewildered with the revelations that each day brings. Out of his bitter agony, a soul and intellect, I could almost say, have been inspired into him."

" Ah, I could help him here ! " cried Miriam, clasp-ing her hands. " And how sweet a toil to bend and adapt my whole nature to do him good ! To instruct, to elevate, to enrich his mind with the wealth that would flow in upon me, had I such a motive for ac-quiring it ! Who else can perform the task ? Who else has the tender sympathy which he requires? Who else, save only me, — a woman, a sharer in the same dread secret, a partaker in one identical guilt, — could meet him on such terms of intimate equality as the case demands ? With this object before me, I might feel a right to live ! Without it, it is a shame for me to have lived so long."

"I fully agree with you," said Kenyon, " that your true place is by his side."

" Surely it is," replied Miriam. " If Donatello is entitled to aught on earth, it is to my complete self-sacrifice for his sake. It does not weaken his claim, methinks, that my only prospect of happiness — a fearful word, however — lies in the good that may ac-crue to him from our intercourse. But he rejects me ! He will not listen to the whisper of his heart, telling him that she, most wretched, who beguiled him into evil, might guide him to a higher innocence than that from which he fell. How is this first, great difficulty to be obviated ?"

" It lies at your own option, Miriam, to do away

the obstacle, at any moment," remarked the sculptor.
" It is but to ascend Donatello's tower, and you will
meet him there, under the eye of God."

" I dare not," answered Miriam. " No ; I dare
not ! "

" Do you fear," asked the sculptor, " the dread eye-
witness whom I have named ? "

" No ; for, as far as I can see into that cloudy and
inscrutable thing, my heart, it has none but pure motives," replied Miriam. " But, my friend, you little
know what a weak or what a strong creature a woman
is ! I fear not Heaven, in this case, at least, but —
shall I confess it ? — I am greatly in dread of Donatello. Once he shuddered at my touch. If he shudder once again, or frown, I die ! "

Kenyon could not but marvel at the subjection into
which this proud and self-dependent woman had wil-
fully flung herself, hanging her life upon the chance
of an angry or favorable regard from a person who, a
little while before, had seemed the plaything of a moment. But, in Miriam's eyes, Donatello was always,
thenceforth, invested with the tragic dignity of their
hour of crime ; and, furthermore, the keen and deep
insight, with which her love endowed her, enabled her
to know him far better than he could be known by
ordinary observation. Beyond all question, since she
loved him so, there was a force in Donatello worthy
of her respect and love.

" You see my weakness," said Miriam, flinging out
her hands, as a person does when a defect is acknowledged, and beyond remedy. " What I need, now, is
an opportunity to show my strength."

" It has occurred to me," Kenyon remarked, " that
the time is come when it may be desirable to remove

Donatello from the complete seclusion in which he buries himself. He has struggled long enough with one idea. He now needs a variety of thought, which cannot be otherwise so readily supplied to him, as through the medium of a variety of scenes. His mind is awakened, now; his heart, though full of pain, is no longer benumbed. They should have food and solace. If he linger here much longer, I fear that he may sink back into a lethargy. The extreme excitability, which circumstances have imparted to his moral system, has its dangers and its advantages; it being one of the dangers, that an obdurate scar may supervene upon its very tenderness. Solitude has done what it could for him; now, for a while, let him be enticed into the outer world."

" What is your plan, then ? " asked Miriam.

" Simply," replied Kenyon, " to persuade Donatello to be my companion in a ramble among these hills and valleys. The little adventures and vicissitudes of travel will do him infinite good. After his recent profound experience, he will re-create the world by the new eyes with which he will regard it. He will escape, I hope, out of a morbid life, and find his way into a healthy one."

" And what is to be my part in this process ? " inquired Miriam, sadly, and not without jealousy. " You are taking him from me, and putting yourself, and all manner of living interests, into the place which I ought to fill ! "

" It would rejoice me, Miriam, to yield the entire responsibility of this office to yourself," answered the sculptor. " I do not pretend to be the guide and counsellor whom Donatello needs ; for, to mention no other obstacle, I am a man, and between man and man there is always an insuperable gulf. They can never quite grasp each other's hands ; and therefore man never derives any intimate help, any heart sustenance, from his brother man, but from woman, — his mother, his sister, or his wife. Be Donatello's friend at need, therefore, and most gladly will I resign him ! "

" It is not kind to taunt me thus," said Miriam. " I have told you that I cannot do what you suggest, because I dare not."

" Well, then," rejoined the sculptor, " see if there is any possibility of adapting yourself to my scheme. The incidents of a journey often fling people together in the oddest and therefore the most natural way. Supposing you were to find yourself on the same route, a reunion with Donatello might ensue, and Providence have a larger hand in it than either of us."

" It is not a hopeful plan," said Miriam, shaking her head, after a moment's thought; "yet I will not reject it without a trial. Only in case it fail, here is a resolution to which I bind myself, come what come may ! You know the bronze statue of Pope Julius in the great square of Perugia? I remember standing in the shadow of that statue one sunny noontime, and being impressed by its paternal aspect, and fancying that a blessing fell upon me from its outstretched hand. Ever since, I have had a superstition, — you will call it foolish, but sad and ill-fated persons always dream such things, — that, if I waited long enough in that same spot, some good event would come to pass. Well, my friend, precisely a fortnight after you begin your tour, — unless we sooner meet, — bring Donatello, at noon, to the base of the statue. You will find me there ! "

Kenyon assented to the proposed arrangement, and,

after some conversation respecting his contemplated line of travel, prepared to take his leave. As he met Miriam's eyes, in bidding farewell, he was surprised at the new, tender gladness that beamed out of them, and at the appearance of health and bloom, which, in this little while, had overspread her face.

" May I tell you, Miriam," said he, smiling, " that you are still as beautiful as ever ? "

" You have a right to notice it," she replied, " for, if it be so, my faded bloom has been revived by the hopes you give me. Do you, then, think me beautiful? I rejoice, most truly. Beauty — if I possess it — shall be one of the instruments by which I will try to educate and elevate him, to whose good I solely dedicate myself."

The sculptor had nearly reached the door, when, hearing her call him, he turned back, and beheld Miriam still standing where he had left her, in the magnificent hall which seemed only a fit setting for her beauty. She beckoned him to return.

" You are a man of refined taste," said she ; " more than that, — a man of delicate sensibility. Now tell me frankly, and on your honor ! Have I not shocked you many times during this interview by my betrayal of woman's cause, my lack of feminine modesty, my reckless, passionate, most indecorous avowal, that I live only in the life of one who, perhaps, scorns and shudders at me ? "

Thus adjured, however difficult the point to which she brought him, the sculptor was not a man to swerve aside from the simple truth.

" Miriam," replied he, " you exaggerate the impression made upon my mind ; but it has been painful, and somewhat of the character which you suppose."

"I knew it," said Miriam, mournfully, and with no resentment. "What remains of my finer nature would have told me so, even if it had not been perceptible in all your manner. Well, my dear friend, when you go back to Rome, tell Hilda what her severity has done! She was all womanhood to me; and when she cast me off, I had no longer any terms to keep with the reserves and decorums of my sex. Hilda has set me free! Pray tell her so, from Miriam, and thank her!"

"I shall tell Hilda nothing that will give her pain," answered Kenyon. "But, Miriam, — though I know not what passed between her and yourself, — I feel, — and let the noble frankness of your disposition forgive me if I say so, — I feel that she was right. You have a thousand admirable qualities. Whatever mass of evil may have fallen into your life, — pardon me, but your own words suggest it, — you are still as capable as ever of many high and heroic virtues. But the white shining purity of Hilda's nature is a thing apart; and she is bound, by the undefiled material of which God moulded her, to keep that severity which I, as well as you, have recognized."

"Oh, you are right!" said Miriam; "I never questioned it; though, as I told you, when she cast me off, it severed some few remaining bonds between me and decorous womanhood. But were there anything to forgive, I do forgive her. May you win her virgin heart; for methinks there can be few men in this evil world who are not more unworthy of her than yourself."

CHAPTER XXXII.

SCENES BY THE WAY.

WHEN it came to the point of quitting the reposeful life of Monte Beni, the sculptor was not without regrets, and would willingly have dreamed a little longer of the sweet paradise on earth that Hilda's presence there might make. Nevertheless, amid all its repose, he had begun to be sensible of a restless melancholy, to which the cultivators of the ideal arts are more liable than sturdier men. On his own part, therefore, and leaving Donatello out of the case, he would have judged it well to go. He made parting visits to the legendary dell, and to other delightful spots with which he had grown familiar; he climbed the tower again, and saw a sunset and a moonrise over the great valley; he drank, on the eve of his departure, one flask, and then another, of the Monte Beni Sunshine, and stored up its flavor in his memory, as the standard of what is exquisite in wine. These things accomplished, Kenyon was ready for the journey.

Donatello had not very easily been stirred out of the peculiar sluggishness, which inthralls and bewitches melancholy people. He had offered merely a passive resistance, however, not an active one, to his friend's schemes; and when the appointed hour came, he yielded to the impulse which Kenyon failed not to apply; and was started upon the journey before he had made up his mind to undertake it. They wan-

dered forth at large, like two knights - errant among
the valleys, and the mountains, and the old mountain-
towns of that picturesque and lovely region.   Save to
keep the appointment with Miriam, a fortnight there-
after, in the great square of Perugia, there was nothing more definite in the sculptor's plan, than that they
should let themselves be blown hither and thither like
winged seeds, that mount upon each wandering breeze.
Yet there was an idea of fatality implied in the simile
of the winged seeds which did not altogether suit Kenyon's fancy; for, if you look closely into the matter,
it will be seen that whatever appears most vagrant,
and utterly purposeless, turns out, in the end, to have
been impelled the most surely on a preordained and
unswerving track.   Chance and change love to deal
with men's settled plans, not with their idle vagaries.
If we desire unexpected and unimaginable events, we
should contrive an iron framework, such as we fancy
may compel the future to take one inevitable shape;
then comes in the unexpected, and shatters our design
in fragments.

The travellers set forth on horseback, and purposed
to perform much of their aimless journeyings under
the moon, and in the cool of the morning or evening
twilight; the midday sun, while summer had hardly
begun to trail its departing skirts over Tuscany, being
still too fervid to allow of noontide exposure.

For a while, they wandered in that same broad
valley which Kenyon had viewed with such delight
from the Monte Beni tower.   The sculptor soon began to enjoy the idle activity of their new life, which
the lapse of a day or two sufficed to establish as a
kind of system; it is so natural for mankind to be no-
madic, that a very little taste of that primitive mode

of existence subverts the settled habits of many preceding years. Kenyon's cares, and whatever gloomy
ideas before possessed him, seemed to be left at Monte
Beni, and were scarcely remembered by the time that
its gray tower grew undistinguishable on the brown
hill-side. His perceptive faculties, which had found
little exercise of late, amid so thoughtful a way of
life, became keen, and kept his eyes busy with a hundred agreeable scenes.

He delighted in the picturesque bits of rustic character and manners, so little of which ever comes upon
the surface of our life at home. There, for example,
were the old women, tending pigs or sheep by the
wayside. As they followed the vagrant steps of their
charge, these venerable ladies kept spinning yarn with
that elsewhere forgotten contrivance, the distaff; and
so wrinkled and stern - looking were they, that you
might have taken them for the Parcæ, spinning the
threads of human destiny. In contrast with their
great-grandmothers were the children, leading goats
of shaggy beard, tied by the horns, and letting them
browse on branch and shrub. It is the fashion of
Italy to add the petty industry of age and childhood
to the hum of human toil. To the eyes of an observer from the Western world, it was a strange spectacle to see sturdy, sunburnt creatures, in petticoats,
but otherwise manlike, toiling side by side with male
laborers, in the rudest work of the fields. These
sturdy women (if as such we must recognize them)
wore the high-crowned, broad-brimmed hat of Tuscan
straw, the customary female head-apparel; and, as
every breeze blew back its breadth of brim, the sunshine constantly added depth to the brown glow of
their cheeks. The elder sisterhood, however, set off

their witch-like ugliness to the worst advantage with
black felt hats, bequeathed them, one would fancy, by
their long-buried husbands.

Another ordinary sight, as sylvan as the above, and
more agreeable, was a girl, bearing on her back a
huge bundle of green twigs and shrubs, or grass, intermixed with scarlet poppies and blue flowers; the
verdant burden being sometimes of such size as to
hide the bearer's figure, and seem a self-moving mass
of fragrant bloom and verdure. Oftener, however,
the bundle reached only half-way down the back of
the rustic nymph, leaving in sight her well-developed
lower limbs, and the crooked knife, hanging behind
her, with which she had been reaping this strange
harvest sheaf. A pre-Raphaelite artist (he, for instance, who painted so marvellously a wind-swept heap
of autumnal leaves) might find an admirable subject
in one of these Tuscan girls, stepping with a free,
erect, and graceful carriage. The miscellaneous herb-
age and tangled twigs and blossoms of her bundle,
crowning her head (while her ruddy, comely face
looks out between the hanging side festoons like a
larger flower), would give the painter boundless scope
for the minute delineation which he loves.

Though mixed up with what was rude and earth-
like, there was still a remote, dream-like, Arcadian
charm, which is scarcely to be found in the daily toil
of other lands. Among the pleasant features of the
wayside were always the vines, clambering on fig-trees,
or other sturdy trunks; they wreathed themselves in
huge and rich festoons, from one tree to another, sus-
pending clusters of ripening grapes in the interval
between. Under such careless mode of culture, the
luxuriant vine is a lovelier spectacle than where it

produces a more precious liquor, and is therefore more artificially restrained and trimmed. Nothing can be more picturesque than an old grape-vine, with almost a trunk of its own, clinging fast around its supporting tree. Nor does the picture lack its moral. You might twist it to more than one grave purpose, as you saw how the knotted, serpentine growth imprisoned within its strong embrace the friend that had supported its tender infancy; and how (as seemingly flexible natures are prone to do) it converted the sturdier tree entirely to its own selfish ends, extending its innumerable arms on every bough, and permitting hardly a leaf to sprout except its own. It occurred to Kenyon, that the enemies of the vine, in his native land, might here have seen an emblem of the remorseless gripe, which the habit of vinous enjoyment lays upon its victim, possessing him wholly, and letting him live no life but such as it bestows.

The scene was not less characteristic when their path led the two wanderers through some small, ancient town. There, besides the peculiarities of present life, they saw tokens of the life that had long ago been lived and flung aside. The little town, such as we see in our mind's eye, would have its gate and its surrounding walls, so ancient and massive that ages had not sufficed to crumble them away; but in the lofty upper portion of the gateway, still standing over the empty arch, where there was no longer a gate to shut, there would be a dove-cote, and peaceful doves for the only warders. Pumpkins lay ripening in the open chambers of the structure. Then, as for the town-wall, on the outside an orchard extends peacefully along its base, full, not of apple-trees, but of those old humorists with gnarled trunks and twisted boughs, the olives. Houses have been built upon the ramparts, or burrowed out of their ponderous foundation. Even the gray, martial towers, crowned with ruined turrets, have been converted into rustic habitations, from the windows of which hang ears of Indian corn. At a door, that has been broken through the massive stone - work, where it was meant to be strongest, some contadini are winnowing grain. Small windows, too, are pierced through the whole line of ancient wall, so that it seems a row of dwellings with one continuous front, built in a strange style of needless strength; but remnants of the old battlements and machicolations are interspersed with the homely chambers and earthen-tiled house-tops; and all along its extent both grape-vines and running flower-shrubs are encouraged to clamber and sport over the roughness of its decay.

Finally the long grass, intermixed with weeds and wild-flowers, waves on the uppermost height of the shattered rampart; and it is exceedingly pleasant in the golden sunshine of the afternoon to behold the warlike precinct so friendly in its old days, and so overgrown with rural peace. In its guard-rooms, its prison-chambers, and scooped out of its ponderous breadth, there are dwellings nowadays where happy human lives are spent. Human parents and broods of children nestle in them, even as the swallows nestle in the little crevices along the broken summit of the wall.

Passing through the gateway of this same little town, challenged only by those watchful sentinels, the pigeons, we find ourselves in a long, narrow street, paved from side to side with flagstones, in the old Roman fashion. Nothing can exceed the grim ugliness of the houses, most of which are three or four stories high,

stone built, gray, dilapidated, or half-covered with
plaster in patches, and contiguous all along from end
to end of the town. Nature, in the shape of tree,
shrub, or grassy sidewalk, is as much shut out from
the one street of the rustic village as from the heart of
any swarming city. The dark and half-ruinous habitations, with their small windows, many of which are
drearily closed with wooden shutters, are but magnified hovels, piled story upon story, and squalid with
the grime that successive ages have left behind them.
It would be a hideous scene to contemplate in a rainy
day, or when no human life pervaded it. In the sum-
mer-noon, however, it possesses vivacity enough to
keep itself cheerful; for all the within-doors of the
village then bubbles over upon the flagstones, or looks
out from the small windows, and from here and there
a balcony. Some of the populace are at the butcher's
shop; others are at the fountain, which gushes into a
marble basin that resembles an antique sarcophagus.
A tailor is sewing before his door with a young priest
seated sociably beside him; a burly friar goes by with
an empty wine-barrel on his head; children are at
play; women, at their own doorsteps, mend clothes,
embroider, weave hats of Tuscan straw, or twirl the
distaff. Many idlers, meanwhile, strolling from one
group to another, let the warm day slide by in the
sweet, interminable task of doing nothing.

From all these people there comes a babblement that
seems quite disproportioned to the number of tongues
that make it. So many words are not uttered in a
New England village throughout the year — except it
be at a political canvass or town-meeting — as are
spoken here, with no especial purpose, in a single day.
Neither so many words, nor so much laughter; for

people talk about nothing as if they were terribly in earnest, and make merry at nothing as if it were the best of all possible jokes. In so long a time as they have existed, and within such narrow precincts, these little walled towns are brought into a closeness of society that makes them but a larger household. All the inhabitants are akin to each, and each to all; they assemble in the street as their common saloon, and thus live and die in a familiarity of intercourse, such as never can be known where a village is open at either end, and all roundabout, and has ample room within itself.

Stuck up beside the door of one house, in this village street, is a withered bough; and on a stone seat, just under the shadow of the bough, sits a party of jolly drinkers, making proof of the new wine, or quaffing the old, as their often-tried and comfortable friend. Kenyon draws bridle here (for the bough, or bush, is a symbol of the wine-shop at this day in Italy, as it was three hundred years ago in England), and calls for a goblet of the deep, mild, purple juice, well diluted with water from the fountain. The Sunshine of Monte Beni would be welcome now. Meanwhile, Donatello has ridden onward, but alights where a shrine, with a burning lamp before it, is built into the wall of an inn-stable. He kneels, and crosses himself, and mutters a brief prayer, without attracting notice from the passers-by, many of whom are parenthetically devout, in a similar fashion. By this time the sculptor has drunk off his wine-and-water, and our two travellers resume their way, emerging from the opposite gate of the village.

Before them, again, lies the broad valley, with a mist so thinly scattered over it as to be perceptible only in the distance, and most so in the nooks of the hills. Now that we have called it mist, it seems a mistake not rather to have called it sunshine; the glory of so much light being mingled with so little gloom, in the airy material of that vapor. Be it mist or sunshine, it adds a touch of ideal beauty to the scene, almost persuading the spectator that this valley and those hills are visionary, because their visible atmosphere is so like the substance of a dream.

Immediately about them, however, there were abundant tokens that the country was not really the paradise it looked to be, at a casual glance. Neither the wretched cottages nor the dreary farm-houses seemed to partake of the prosperity, with which so kindly a climate, and so fertile a portion of Mother Earth's bosom, should have filled them, one and all. But, possibly, the peasant inhabitants do not exist in so grimy a poverty, and in homes so comfortless, as a stranger, with his native ideas of those matters, would be likely to imagine. The Italians appear to possess none of that emulative pride which we see in our New England villages, where every householder, according to his taste and means, endeavors to make his homestead an ornament to the grassy and elm-shadowed wayside. In Italy there are no neat doorsteps and thresholds; no pleasant, vine-sheltered porches; none of those grass-plots or smoothly shorn lawns, which hospitably invite the imagination into the sweet domestic interiors of English life. Everything, however sunny and luxuriant may be the scene around, is especially disheartening in the immediate neighborhood of an Italian home.

An artist, it is true, might often thank his stars for those old houses, so picturesquely time - stained, and

with the plaster falling in blotches from the ancient
brick-work. The prison-like, iron-barred windows,
and the wide-arched, dismal entrance, admitting on one
hand to the stable, on the other to the kitchen, might
impress him as far better worth his pencil than the
newly painted pine boxes, in which — if he be an
American — his countrymen live and thrive. But
there is reason to suspect that a people are waning
to decay and ruin the moment that their life becomes
fascinating either in the poet's imagination or the
painter's eye.

As usual, on Italian waysides, the wanderers passed
great, black crosses, hung with all the instruments of
the sacred agony and passion: there were the crown of
thorns, the hammer and nails, the pincers, the spear,
the sponge; and perched over the whole, the cock that
crowed to St. Peter's remorseful conscience. Thus,
while the fertile scene showed the never-failing beneficence of the Creator towards man in his transitory
state, these symbols reminded each wayfarer of the
Saviour's infinitely greater love for him as an immortal spirit. Beholding these consecrated stations,
the idea seemed to strike Donatello of converting the
otherwise aimless journey into a penitential pilgrimage. At each of them he alighted to kneel and kiss
the cross, and humbly press his forehead against its
foot; and this so invariably, that the sculptor soon
learned to draw bridle of his own accord. It may be,
too, heretic as he was, that Kenyon likewise put up a
prayer, rendered more fervent by the symbols before
his eyes, for the peace of his friend's conscience, and
the pardon of the sin that so oppressed him.

Not only at the crosses did Donatello kneel, but at
each of the many shrines, where the Blessed Virgin in

fresco — faded with sunshine and half washed out with showers — looked benignly at her worshipper; or where she was represented in a wooden image, or a bas-relief of plaster or marble, as accorded with the means of the devout person who built, or restored from a mediæval antiquity, these places of wayside worship. They were everywhere: under arched niches, or in little penthouses with a brick tiled roof, just large enough to shelter them; or perhaps in some bit of old Roman masonry, the founders of which had died before the Advent; or in the wall of a country inn or farm-house; or at the midway point of a bridge; or in the shallow cavity of a natural rock; or high upward in the deep cuts of the road. It appeared to the sculptor that Donatello prayed the more earnestly and the more hopefully at these shrines, because the mild face of the Madonna promised him to intercede as a tender mother betwixt the poor culprit and the awfulness of judgment.

It was beautiful to observe, indeed, how tender was the soul of man and woman towards the Virgin mother, in recognition of the tenderness which, as their faith taught them, she immortally cherishes towards all human souls. In the wire-work screen, before each shrine, hung offerings of roses, or whatever flower was sweetest and most seasonable; some already wilted and withered, some fresh with that very morning's dew-drops. Flowers there were, too, that, being artificial, never bloomed on earth, nor would ever fade. The thought occurred to Kenyon, that flower - pots with living plants might be set within the niches, or even that rose-trees, and all kinds of flowering shrubs, might be reared under the shrines, and taught to twine and wreathe themselves around; so that the Virgin should dwell within a bower of verdure, bloom, and fragrant freshness, symbolizing a homage perpetually new. There are many things in the religious customs of these people that seem good ; many things, at least, that might be both good and beautiful, if the soul of goodness and the sense of beauty were as much alive in the Italians now as they must have been when those customs were first imagined and adopted. But, instead of blossoms on the shrub, or freshly gathered, with the dew-drops on their leaves, their worship, nowadays, is best symbolized by the artificial flower.

The sculptor fancied, moreover (but perhaps it was his heresy that suggested the idea), that it would be of happy influence to place a comfortable and shady seat beneath every wayside shrine. Then the weary and sun-scorched traveller, while resting himself under her protecting shadow, might thank the Virgin for her hospitality. Nor, perchance, were he to regale himself, even in such a consecrated spot, with the fragrance of a pipe, would it rise to heaven more offensively than the smoke of priestly incense. We do ourselves wrong, and too meanly estimate the Holiness above us, when we deem that any act or enjoyment, good in itself, is not good to do religiously.

Whatever may be the iniquities of the papal system, it was a wise and lovely sentiment that set up the frequent shrine and cross along the roadside. No wayfarer, bent on whatever worldly errand, can fail to be reminded, at every mile or two, that this is not the business which most concerns him. The pleasure-seeker is silently admonished to look heavenward for a joy infinitely greater than he now possesses. The wretch in temptation beholds the cross, and is warned that, if he yield, the Saviour's agony for his sake will have been endured in vain. The stubborn criminal, whose heart has long been like a stone, feels it throb anew with dread and hope; and our poor Donatello, as he went kneeling from shrine to cross, and from cross to shrine, doubtless found an efficacy in these symbols that helped him towards a higher penitence.

Whether the young Count of Monte Beni noticed the fact, or no, there was more than one incident of their journey that led Kenyon to believe that they were attended, or closely followed, or preceded, near at hand, by some one who took an interest in their motions. As it were, the step, the sweeping garment, the faintly heard breath, of an invisible companion, was beside them, as they went on their way. It was like a dream that had strayed out of their slumber, and was haunting them in the daytime, when its shadowy substance could have neither density nor outline, in the too obtrusive light. After sunset, it grew a little more distinct.

" On the left of that last shrine," asked the sculptor, as they rode, under the moon, " did you observe the figure of a woman kneeling, with her face hidden in her hands? "

" I never looked that way," replied Donatello. " I was saying my own prayer. It was some penitent, perchance. May the Blessed Virgin be the more gracious to the poor soul, because she is a woman."

CHAPTER XXXIII.

AFTER wide wanderings through the valley, the two travellers directed their course towards its boundary of hills. Here, the natural scenery and men's modifications of it immediately took a different aspect from that of the fertile and smiling plain. Not unfrequently there was a convent on the hill-side ; or, on some insulated promontory, a ruined castle, once the den of a robber chieftain, who was accustomed to dash down from his commanding height upon the road that wound below. For ages back, the old fortress had been flinging down its crumbling ramparts, stone by stone, towards the grimy village at its foot.

Their road wound onward among the hills, which rose steep and lofty from the scanty level space that lay between them. They continually thrust their great bulks before the wayfarers, as if grimly resolute to forbid their passage, or closed abruptly behind them, when they still dared to proceed. A gigantic hill would set its foot right down before them, and only at the last moment would grudgingly withdraw it, just far enough to let them creep towards another obstacle. Adown these rough heights were visible the dry tracks of many a mountain-torrent that had lived a life too fierce and passionate to be a long one. Or, perhaps, a stream was yet hurrying shyly along the edge of a far wider bed of pebbles and shelving rock than it seemed to need, though not too wide for the swollen rage of which this shy rivulet was capable. A stone bridge bestrode it, the ponderous arches of which were upheld and rendered indestructible by the weight of the very stones that threatened to crush them down. Old Roman toil was perceptible in the foundations of that massive bridge ; the first weight that it ever bore was that of an army of the Republic.

Threading these defiles, they would arrive at some immemorial city, crowning the high summit of a hill with its cathedral, its many churches, and public edifices, all of Gothic architecture. With no more level ground than a single piazza, in the midst, the ancient town tumbled its crooked and narrow streets down the mountain-side, through arched passages, and by steps of stone. The aspect of everything was awfully old ; older, indeed, in its effect on the imagination, than Rome itself, because history does not lay its finger on these forgotten edifices and tell us all about their origin. Etruscan princes may have dwelt in them. A thousand years, at all events, would seem but a middle age for these structures. They are built of such huge, square stones, that their appearance of ponderous durability distresses the beholder with the idea that they can never fall,— never crumble away, — never be less fit than now for human habitation. Many of them may once have been palaces, and still retain a squalid grandeur. But, gazing at them, we recognize how undesirable it is to build the tabernacle of our brief life-time out of permanent materials, and with a view to their being occupied by future generations.

All towns should be made capable of purification by fire, or of decay, within each half-century. Otherwise, they become the hereditary haunts of vermin and noi-

someness, besides standing apart from the possibility
of such improvements as are constantly introduced
into the rest of man's contrivances and accommoda-
tions. It is beautiful, no doubt, and exceedingly satisfactory to some of our natural instincts, to imagine our
far posterity dwelling under the same roof-tree as ourselves. Still, when people insist on building indestructible houses, they incur, or their children do, a misfortune analogous to that of the Sibyl, when she obtained
the grievous boon of immortality. So, we may build
almost immortal habitations, it is true; but we cannot
keep them from growing old, musty, unwholesome,
dreary, full of death-scents, ghosts, and murder-stains;
in short, such habitations as one sees everywhere in
Italy, be they hovels or palaces.

"You should go with me to my native country,"
observed the sculptor to Donatello. "In that fortu-
nate land, each generation has only its own sins and
sorrows to bear. Here, it seems as if all the weary
and dreary Past were piled upon the back of the Present. If I were to lose my spirits in this country, —
if I were to suffer any heavy misfortune here, — methinks it would be impossible to stand up against it,
under such adverse influences."

"The sky itself is an old roof, now," answered the
Count; "and, no doubt, the sins of mankind have
made it gloomier than it used to be."

"Oh, my poor Faun," thought Kenyon to himself,
"how art thou changed!"

A city, like this of which we speak, seems a sort of
stony growth out of the hill-side, or a fossilized town;
so ancient and strange it looks, without enough of life
and juiciness in it to be any longer susceptible of decay. An earthquake would afford it the only chance
of being ruined, beyond its present ruin.

Yet, though dead to all the purposes for which we live to-day, the place has its glorious recollections, and not merely rude and warlike ones, but those of brighter and milder triumphs, the fruits of which we still enjoy. Italy can count several of these lifeless towns which, four or five hundred years ago, were each the birthplace of its own school of art; nor have they yet forgotten to be proud of the dark, old pictures, and the faded frescos, the pristine beauty of which was a light and gladness to the world. But now, unless one happens to be a painter, these famous works make us miserably desperate. They are poor, dim ghosts of what, when Giotto or Cimabue first created them, threw a splendor along the stately aisles; so far gone towards nothingness, in our day, that scarcely a hint of design or expression can glimmer through the dusk. Those early artists did well to paint their frescos. Glowing on the church-walls, they might be looked upon as symbols of the living spirit that made Catholicism a true religion, and that glorified it as long as it retained a genuine life; they filled the transepts with a radiant throng of saints and angels, and threw around the high altar a faint reflection — as much as mortals could see, or bear — of a Diviner Presence. But now that the colors are so wretchedly bedimmed, — now that blotches of plastered wall dot the frescos all over, like a mean reality thrusting itself through life's brightest illusions, — the next best artist to Cimabue or Giotto or Ghirlandaio or Pinturicchio will be he that shall reverently cover their ruined masterpieces with whitewash!

Kenyon, however, being an earnest student and critic of Art, lingered long before these pathetic relics; and Donatello, in his present phase of penitence,

thought no time spent amiss while he could be kneeling before an altar.   Whenever they found a cathedral, therefore, or a Gothic church, the two travellers
were of one mind to enter it.   In some of these holy
edifices they saw pictures that time had not dimmed
nor injured in the least, though they perhaps belonged
to as old a school of Art as any that were perishing
around them.   These were the painted windows ; and
as often as he gazed at them the sculptor blessed the
mediæval time, and its gorgeous contrivances of splendor ; for surely the skill of man has never accomplished, nor his mind imagined, any other beauty or
glory worthy to be compared with these.

It is the special excellence of pictured glass, that
the light, which falls merely on the outside of other
pictures, is here interfused throughout the work ; it
illuminates the design, and invests it with a living radiance ; and in requital the unfading colors transmute
the common daylight into a miracle of richness and
glory in its passage through the heavenly substance
of the blessed and angelic shapes which throng the
high-arched window.

" It is a woful thing," cried Kenyon, while one of
these frail yet enduring and fadeless pictures threw its
hues on his face, and on the pavement of the church
around him, — " a sad necessity that any Christian
soul should pass from earth without once seeing an
antique painted window, with the bright Italian sunshine glowing through it !   There is no other such
true symbol of the glories of the better world, where
a celestial radiance will be inherent in all things and
persons, and render each continually transparent to
the sight of all."

" But what a horror it would be," said Donatello,

sadly, " if there were a soul among them through which the light could not be transfused ! "

" Yes ; and perhaps this is to be the punishment of sin," replied the sculptor ; " not that it shall be made evident to the universe, which can profit nothing by such knowledge, but that it shall insulate the sinner from all sweet society by rendering him impermeable to light, and, therefore, unrecognizable in the abode of heavenly simplicity and truth. Then, what remains for him, but the dreariness of infinite and eternal solitude ? "

" That would be a horrible destiny, indeed ! " said Donatello.

His voice as he spoke the words had a hollow and dreary cadence, as if he anticipated some such frozen solitude for himself. A figure in a dark robe was lurking in the obscurity of a side-chapel close by, and made an impulsive movement forward, but hesitated as Donatello spoke again.

" But there might be a more miserable torture than to be solitary forever," said he. " Think of having a single companion in eternity, and instead of finding any consolation, or at all events variety of torture, to see your own weary, weary sin repeated in that inseparable soul."

" I think, my dear Count, you have never read Dante," observed Kenyon. " That idea is somewhat in his style, but I cannot help regretting that it came into your mind just then."

The dark-robed figure had shrunk back, and was quite lost to sight among the shadows of the chapel.

" There was an English poet," resumed Kenyon, turning again towards the window, " who speaks of the ' dim, religious light,' transmitted through painted

glass. I always admired this richly descriptive phrase ;
but, though he was once in Italy, I question whether
Milton ever saw any but the dingy pictures in the dusty
windows of English cathedrals, imperfectly shown by
the gray English daylight. He would else have illuminated that word ' dim ' with some epithet that should
not chase away the dimness, yet should make it glow
like a million of rubies, sapphires, emeralds, and to-
pazes. Is it not so with yonder window ? The pictures are most brilliant in themselves, yet dim with
tenderness and reverence, because God himself is shining through them."

" The pictures fill me with emotion, but not such as
you seem to experience," said Donatello. " I tremble
at those awful saints ; and, most of all, at the figure
above them. He glows with Divine wrath ! "

" My dear friend," said Kenyon, " how strangely
your eyes have transmuted the expression of the figure ! It is divine love, not wrath ! "

" To my eyes," said Donatello, stubbornly, " it is
wrath, not love ! Each must interpret for himself."

The friends left the church, and looking up, from the
exterior, at the window which they had just been contemplating within, nothing was visible but the merest
outline of dusky shapes. Neither the individual likeness of saint, angel, nor Saviour, and far less the combined scheme and purport of the picture, could anywise be made out. That miracle of radiant art, thus
viewed, was nothing better than an incomprehensible
obscurity, without a gleam of beauty to induce the beholder to attempt unravelling it.

" All this," thought the sculptor, " is a most forcible
emblem of the different aspect of religious truth and
sacred story, as viewed from the warm interior of be-

lief, or from its cold and dreary outside. Christian
faith is a grand cathedral, with divinely pictured windows. Standing without, you see no glory, nor can
possibly imagine any; standing within, every ray of
light reveals a harmony of unspeakable splendors."

After Kenyon and Donatello emerged from the
church, however, they had better opportunity for acts
of charity and mercy than for religious contemplation ; being immediately surrounded by a swarm of
beggars, who are the present possessors of Italy, and
share the spoil of the stranger with the fleas and mos-
quitoes, their formidable allies. These pests — the human ones — had hunted the two travellers at every
stage of their journey. From village to village, ragged boys and girls kept almost under the horses' feet ;
hoary grandsires and grandames caught glimpses of
their approach, and hobbled to intercept them at some
point of vantage ; blind men stared them out of countenance with their sightless orbs ; women held up their
unwashed babies ; cripples displayed their wooden legs,
their grievous scars, their dangling, boneless arms, their
broken backs, their burden of a hump, or whatever infirmity or deformity Providence had assigned them for
an inheritance. On the highest mountain summit —
in the most shadowy ravine — there was a beggar waiting for them. In one small village, Kenyon had the
curiosity to count merely how many children were crying, whining, and bellowing all at once for alms. They
proved to be more than forty of as ragged and dirty
little imps as any in the world ; besides whom, all the
wrinkled matrons, and most of the village maids, and
not a few stalwart men, held out their hands grimly,
piteously, or smilingly in the forlorn hope of whatever
trifle of coin might remain in pockets already so fear-

fully taxed. Had they been permitted, they would
gladly have knelt down and worshipped the travellers,
and have cursed them, without rising from their knees,
if the expected boon failed to be awarded.

Yet they were not so miserably poor but that the
grown people kept houses over their heads. In the
way of food, they had, at least, vegetables in their little gardens, pigs and chickens to kill, eggs to fry into
omelets with oil, wine to drink, and many other things
to make life comfortable. As for the children, when
no more small coin appeared to be forthcoming, they
began to laugh and play, and turn heels over head,
showing themselves jolly and vivacious brats, and evidently as well fed as needs be. The truth is, the Italian peasantry look upon strangers as the almoners of
Providence, and therefore feel no more shame in asking and receiving alms, than in availing themselves of
providential bounties in whatever other form.

In accordance with his nature, Donatello was always exceedingly charitable to these ragged battalions,
and appeared to derive a certain consolation from the
prayers which many of them put up in his behalf. In
Italy a copper coin of minute value, will often make
all the difference between a vindictive curse — death
by apoplexy being the favorite one — mumbled in an
old witch's toothless jaws and a prayer from the same
lips, so earnest that it would seem to reward the charitable soul with at least a puff of grateful breath to
help him heavenward. Good wishes being so cheap,
though possibly not very efficacious, and anathemas so
exceedingly bitter, — even if the greater portion of
their poison remain in the mouth that utters them, —
it may be wise to expend some reasonable amount in
the purchase of the former. Donatello invariably did

so ; and as he distributed his alms under the pictured window, of which we have been speaking, no less than seven ancient women lifted their hands and besought blessings on his head.

" Come," said the sculptor, rejoicing at the happier expression which he saw in his friend's face. " I think your steed will not stumble with you to-day. Each of these old dames looks as much like Horace's Atra Cura as can well be conceived ; but, though there are seven of them, they will make your burden on horseback lighter instead of heavier."

" Are we to ride far ? " asked the Count.

" A tolerable journey betwixt now and to-morrow noon," Kenyon replied ; " for, at that hour, I purpose to be standing by the Pope's statue in the great square of Perugia."

CHAPTER XXXIV.

MARKET—DAY IN PERUGIA.

PERUGIA, on its lofty hill-top, was reached by the two travellers before the sun had quite kissed away the early freshness of the morning. Since midnight, there had been a heavy rain, bringing infinite refreshment to the scene of verdure and fertility amid which this ancient civilization stands; insomuch that Kenyon loitered, when they came to the gray city-wall, and was loath to give up the prospect of the sunny wilderness that lay below. It was as green as England, and bright as Italy alone. There was all the wide valley, sweeping down and spreading away on all sides from the weed-grown ramparts, and bounded afar by mountains, which lay asleep in the sun, with thin mists and silvery clouds floating about their heads by way of morning dreams.

"It lacks still two hours of noon," said the sculptor to his friend, as they stood under the arch of the gateway, waiting for their passports to be examined; "will you come with me to see some admirable frescos by Perugino? There is a hall in the Exchange, of no great magnitude, but covered with what must have been — at the time it was painted — such magnificence and beauty as the world had not elsewhere to show."

"It depresses me to look at old frescos," responded the Count; "it is a pain, yet not enough of a pain to answer as a penance."

" Will you look at some pictures by Fra Angelico in the Church of San Domenico?" asked Kenyon; " they are full of religious sincerity. When one studies them faithfully, it is like holding a conversation about heavenly things with a tender and devout-minded man."

" You have shown me some of Fra Angelico's pictures, I remember," answered Donatello; " his angels look as if they had never taken a flight out of heaven; and his saints seem to have been born saints, and always to have lived so. Young maidens, and all innocent persons, I doubt not, may find great delight and profit in looking at such holy pictures. But they are not for me."

" Your criticism, I fancy, has great moral depth," replied Kenyon; " and I see in it the reason why Hilda so highly appreciates Fra Angelico's pictures. Well; we will let all such matters pass for to-day, and stroll about this fine old city till noon."

They wandered to and fro, accordingly, and lost themselves among the strange, precipitate passages, which, in Perugia, are called streets. Some of them are like caverns, being arched all over, and plunging down abruptly towards an unknown darkness; which, when you have fathomed its depths, admits you to a daylight that you scarcely hoped to behold again. Here they met shabby men, and the careworn wives and mothers of the people, some of whom guided children in leading-strings through those dim and antique thoroughfares, where a hundred generations had passed before the little feet of to-day began to tread them. Thence they climbed upward again, and came to the level plateau, on the summit of the hill, where are situated the grand piazza and the principal public edifices.

ANGEL, BY FRA ANGELICO

It happened to be market-day in Perugia. The great square, therefore, presented a far more vivacious spectacle than would have been witnessed in it at any other time of the week, though not so lively as to overcome the gray solemnity of the architectural portion of the scene. In the shadow of the cathedral and other old Gothic structures — seeking shelter from the sunshine that fell across the rest of the piazza — was a crowd of people, engaged as buyers or sellers in the petty traffic of a country-fair. Dealers had erected booths and stalls on the pavement, and overspread them with scanty awnings, beneath which they stood, vociferously crying their merchandise; such as shoes, hats and caps, yarn stockings, cheap jewelry and cutlery, books, chiefly little volumes of a religious character, and a few French novels; toys, tin-ware, old iron, cloth, rosaries of beads, crucifixes, cakes, biscuits, sugar-plums, and innumerable little odds and ends, which we see no object in advertising. Baskets of grapes, figs, and pears stood on the ground. Donkeys, bearing panniers stuffed out with kitchen vegetables, and requiring an ample roadway, roughly shouldered aside the throng.

Crowded as the square was, a juggler found room to spread out a white cloth upon the pavement, and cover it with cups, plates, balls, cards, — the whole material of his magic, in short, — wherewith he proceeded to work miracles under the noonday sun. An organ-grinder at one point, and a clarion and a flute at another, accomplished what they could towards filling the wide space with tuneful noise. Their small uproar, however, was nearly drowned by the multitudinous voices of the people, bargaining, quarrelling, laughing, and babbling copiously at random; for the

briskness of the mountain atmosphere, or some other
cause, made everybody so loquacious, that more words
were wasted in Perugia on this one market-day, than
the noisiest piazza of Rome would utter in a month.

Through all this petty tumult, which kept beguil-
ing one's eyes and upper strata of thought, it was delightful to catch glimpses of the grand old architecture
that stood around the square.   The life of the flitting
moment, existing in the antique shell of an age gone
by, has a fascination which we do not find in either
the past or present, taken by themselves.   It might
seem irreverent to make the gray cathedral and the
tall, time-worn palaces echo back the exuberant vociferation of the market; but they did so, and caused
the sound to assume a kind of poetic rhythm, and
themselves looked only the more majestic for their
condescension.

On one side, there was an immense edifice devoted
to public purposes, with an antique gallery, and a
range of arched and stone-mullioned windows, running along its front; and by way of entrance it had a
central Gothic arch, elaborately wreathed around with
sculptured semicircles, within which the spectator was
aware of a stately and impressive gloom.   Though
merely the municipal council-house and exchange of
a decayed country town, this structure was worthy to
have held in one portion of it the parliament-hall of a
nation, and in the other, the state apartments of its
ruler.   On another side of the square rose the mediæval front of the cathedral, where the imagination of
a Gothic architect had long ago flowered out indestructibly, in the first place, a grand design, and then
covering it with such abundant detail of ornament,
that the magnitude of the work seemed less a miracle

than its minuteness. You would suppose that he must have softened the stone into wax, until his most delicate fancies were modelled in the pliant material, and then had hardened it into stone again. The whole was a vast, black-letter page of the richest and quaintest poetry. In fit keeping with all this old magnificence was a great marble fountain, where again the Gothic imagination showed its overflow and gratuity of device in the manifold sculptures which it lavished as freely as the water did its shifting shapes.

Besides the two venerable structures which we have described, there were lofty palaces, perhaps of as old a date, rising story above story, and adorned with balconies, whence, hundreds of years ago, the princely occupants had been accustomed to gaze down at the sports, business, and popular assemblages of the piazza. And, beyond all question, they thus witnessed the erection of a bronze statue, which, three centuries since, was placed on the pedestal that it still occupies.

" I never come to Perugia," said Kenyon, " without spending as much time as I can spare in studying yonder statue of Pope Julius the Third. Those sculptors of the Middle Age have fitter lessons for the professors of my art than we can find in the Grecian masterpieces. They belong to our Christian civilization ; and, being earnest works, they always express something which we do not get from the antique. Will you look at it ? "

" Willingly," replied the Count, " for I see, even so far off, that the statue is bestowing a benediction, and there is a feeling in my heart that I may be permitted to share it."

Remembering the similar idea which Miriam a short time before had expressed, the sculptor smiled hopefully at the coincidence. They made their way through the throng of the market-place, and approached close to the iron railing that protected the pedestal of the statue.

It was the figure of a pope, arrayed in his pontifical robes, and crowned with the tiara. He sat in a bronze chair, elevated high above the pavement, and seemed to take kindly yet authoritative cognizance of the busy scene which was at that moment passing before his eye. His right hand was raised and spread abroad, as if in the act of shedding forth a benediction, which every man — so broad, so wise, and so serenely affectionate was the bronze pope's regard — might hope to feel quietly descending upon the need, or the distress, that he had closest at his heart. The statue had life and observation in it, as well as patriarchal majesty. An imaginative spectator could not but be impressed with the idea that this benignly awful representative of divine and human authority might rise from his brazen chair, should any great public exigency demand his interposition, and encourage or restrain the people by his gesture, or even by prophetic utterances worthy of so grand a presence.

And, in the long, calm intervals, amid the quiet lapse of ages, the pontiff watched the daily turmoil around his seat, listening with majestic patience to the market cries, and all the petty uproar that awoke the echoes of the stately old piazza. He was the enduring friend of these men, and of their forefathers and children, — the familiar face of generations.

" The pope's blessing, methinks, has fallen upon you," observed the sculptor, looking at his friend.

In truth, Donatello's countenance indicated a healthier spirit than while he was brooding in his melancholy tower. The change of scene, the breaking up of custom, the fresh flow of incidents, the sense of being homeless, and therefore free, had done something for our poor Faun ; these circumstances had at least promoted a reaction, which might else have been slower in its progress. Then, no doubt, the bright day, the gay spectacle of the market-place, and the sympathetic exhilaration of so many people's cheerfulness, had each their suitable effect on a temper naturally prone to be glad. Perhaps, too, he was magnetically conscious of a presence that formerly sufficed to make him happy. Be the cause what it might, Donatello's eyes shone with a serene and hopeful expression while looking upward at the bronze pope, to whose widely diffused blessing, it may be, he attributed all this good influence.

" Yes, my dear friend," said he, in reply to the sculptor's remark, " I feel the blessing upon my spirit."

" It is wonderful," said Kenyon, with a smile, " wonderful and delightful to think how long a good man's beneficence may be potent, even after his death. How great, then, must have been the efficacy of this excellent pontiff's blessing while he was alive ! "

" I have heard," remarked the Count, " that there was a brazen image set up in the wilderness, the sight of which healed the Israelites of their poisonous and rankling wounds. If it be the Blessed Virgin's pleasure, why should not this holy image before us do me equal good ? A wound has long been rankling in my soul, and filling it with poison."

" I did wrong to smile," answered Kenyon. " It is not for me to limit Providence in its operations on man's spirit."

While they stood talking, the clock in the neigh

boring cathedral told the hour, with twelve reverberating strokes, which it flung down upon the crowded market-place, as if warning one and all to take advantage of the bronze pontiff's benediction, or of Heaven's blessing, however proffered, before the opportunity were lost.

"High noon," said the sculptor. "It is Miriam's hour!"

CHAPTER XXXV.

THE BRONZE PONTIFF'S BENEDICTION.

WHEN the last of the twelve strokes had fallen from the cathedral clock, Kenyon threw his eyes over the busy scene of the market-place, expecting to discern Miriam somewhere in the crowd. He looked next towards the cathedral itself, where it was reasonable to imagine that she might have taken shelter, while awaiting her appointed time. Seeing no trace of her in either direction, his eyes came back from their quest somewhat disappointed, and rested on a figure which was leaning, like Donatello and himself, on the iron balustrade that surrounded the statue. Only a moment before, they two had been alone.

It was the figure of a woman, with her head bowed on her hands, as if she deeply felt — what we have been endeavoring to convey into our feeble description — the benign and awe - inspiring influence which the pontiff's statue exercises upon a sensitive spectator. No matter though it were modelled for a Catholic chief priest, the desolate heart, whatever be its religion, recognizes in that image the likeness of a father.

"Miriam," said the sculptor, with a tremor in his voice, "is it yourself?"

"It is I," she replied; "I am faithful to my engagement, though with many fears."

She lifted her head, and revealed to Kenyon — revealed to Donatello likewise — the well-remembered features of Miriam. They were pale and worn, but distinguished even now, though less gorgeously, by a beauty that might be imagined bright enough to glimmer with its own light in a dim cathedral aisle, and had no need to shrink from the severer test of the mid-day sun. But she seemed tremulous, and hardly able to go through with a scene which at a distance she had found courage to undertake.

"You are most welcome, Miriam!" said the sculptor, seeking to afford her the encouragement which he saw she so greatly required. "I have a hopeful trust that the result of this interview will be propitious. Come; let me lead you to Donatello."

"No, Kenyon, no!" whispered Miriam, shrinking back; "unless of his own accord he speaks my name, — unless he bids me stay, — no word shall ever pass between him and me. It is not that I take upon me to be proud at this late hour. Among other feminine qualities, I threw away my pride when Hilda cast me off."

"If not pride, what else restrains you?" Kenyon asked, a little angry at her unseasonable scruples, and also at this half-complaining reference to Hilda's just severity. "After daring so much, it is no time for fear! If we let him part from you without a word, your opportunity of doing him inestimable good is lost forever."

"True; it will be lost forever!" repeated Miriam, sadly. "But, dear friend, will it be my fault? I willingly fling my woman's pride at his feet. But — do you not see? — his heart must be left freely to its own decision whether to recognize me, because on his voluntary choice depends the whole question whether my devotion will do him good or harm. Except he feel an infinite need of me, I am a burden and fatal obstruction to him!"

"Take your own course, then, Miriam," said Kenyon; "and, doubtless, the crisis being what it is, your spirit is better instructed for its emergencies than mine."

While the foregoing words passed between them they had withdrawn a little from the immediate vicinity of the statue, so as to be out of Donatello's hearing. Still, however, they were beneath the pontiff's outstretched hand; and Miriam, with her beauty and her sorrow, looked up into his benignant face, as if she had come thither for his pardon and paternal affection, and despaired of so vast a boon.

Meanwhile, she had not stood thus long in the public square of Perugia, without attracting the observation of many eyes. With their quick sense of beauty, these Italians had recognized her loveliness, and spared not to take their fill of gazing at it; though their native gentleness and courtesy made their homage far less obtrusive than that of Germans, French, or Anglo-Saxons might have been. It is not improbable that Miriam had planned this momentous interview, on so public a spot and at high noon, with an eye to the sort of protection that would be thrown over it by a multitude of eye-witnesses. In circumstances of profound feeling and passion, there is often a sense that too great a seclusion cannot be endured; there is an indefinite dread of being quite alone with the object of our deepest interest. The species of solitude that a crowd harbors within itself is felt to be preferable, in certain conditions of the heart, to the remoteness of a desert or the depths of an untrodden wood. Hatred, love, or whatever kind of too intense emotion, or even indifference, where emotion has once been, instinctively seeks to interpose some barrier between itself and the corresponding passion in another breast. This, we suspect, was what Miriam had thought of, in coming to the thronged piazza ; partly this, and partly, as she said, her superstition that the benign statue held good influences in store.

But Donatello remained leaning against the balustrade. She dared not glance towards him, to see whether he were pale and agitated, or calm as ice. Only, she knew that the moments were fleetly lapsing away, and that his heart must call her soon, or the voice would never reach her. She turned quite away from him and spoke again to the sculptor.

" I have wished to meet you," said she, "for more than one reason. News has come to me respecting a dear friend of ours. Nay, not of mine ! I dare not call her a friend of mine, though once the dearest."

" Do you speak of Hilda?" exclaimed Kenyon, with quick alarm. " Has anything befallen her ? When I last heard of her, she was still in Rome, and well."

"Hilda remains in Rome," replied Miriam, " nor is she ill as regards physical health, though much depressed in spirits. She lives quite alone in her dovecote; not a friend near her, not one in Rome, which, you know, is deserted by all but its native inhabitants. I fear for her health, if she continue long in such solitude, with despondency preying on her mind. I tell you this, knowing the interest which the rare beauty of her character has awakened in you."

"I will go to Rome!" said the sculptor, in great emotion. " Hilda has never allowed me to manifest more than a friendly regard ; but, at least, she cannot prevent my watching over her at a humble distance. I will set out this very hour."

" Do not leave us now ! " whispered Miriam, imploringly, and laying her hand on his arm. " One moment more ! Ah; he has no word for me ! "

" Miriam ! " said Donatello.

Though but a single word, and the first that he had spoken, its tone was a warrant of the sad and tender depth from which it came. It told Miriam things of infinite importance, and, first of all, that he still loved her. The sense of their mutual crime had stunned, but not destroyed, the vitality of his affection ; it was therefore indestructible. That tone, too, bespoke an altered and deepened character ; it told of a vivified intellect, and of spiritual instruction that had come through sorrow and remorse ; so that instead of the wild boy, the thing of sportive, animal nature, the sylvan Faun, here was now the man of feeling and intelligence.

She turned towards him, while his voice still reverberated in the depths of her soul.

" You have called me ! " said she.

" Because my deepest heart has need of you ! " he replied. " Forgive, Miriam, the coldness, the hardness with which I parted from you ! I was bewildered with strange horror and gloom."

" Alas ! and it was I that brought it on you," said she. " What repentance, what self-sacrifice, can atone for that infinite wrong ? There was something so sacred in the innocent and joyous life which you were leading ! A happy person is such an unaccustomed and holy creature in this sad world ! And, encountering so rare a being, and gifted with the power of sympathy with his sunny life, it was my doom, mine, to bring him within the limits of sinful, sorrowful mortality ! Bid me depart, Donatello ! Fling me off !

No good, through my agency, can follow upon such a mighty evil ! "

" Miriam," said he, " our lot lies together. Is it not so ? Tell me, in Heaven's name, if it be otherwise."

Donatello's conscience was evidently perplexed with doubt, whether the communion of a crime, such as they two were jointly stained with, ought not to stifle all the instinctive motions of their hearts, impelling them one towards the other. Miriam, on the other hand, remorsefully questioned with herself whether the misery, already accruing from her influence, should not warn her to withdraw from his path. In this momentous interview, therefore, two souls were groping for each other in the darkness of guilt and sorrow, and hardly were bold enough to grasp the cold hands that they found.

The sculptor stood watching the scene with earnest sympathy.

" It seems irreverent," said he, at length ; " intrusive, if not irreverent, for a third person to thrust himself between the two solely concerned in a crisis like the present. Yet, possibly as a by-stander, though a deeply interested one, I may discern somewhat of truth that is hidden from you both ; nay, at least interpret or suggest some ideas which you might not so readily convey to each other."

" Speak ! " said Miriam.   " We confide in you."

" Speak ! " said Donatello.   " You are true and upright."

" I well know," rejoined Kenyon, " that I shall not succeed in uttering the few, deep words which, in this matter, as in all others, include the absolute truth. But here, Miriam, is one whom a terrible misfortune has begun to educate ; it has taken him, and through

POPE JULIUS III

your agency, out of a wild and happy state, which, within circumscribed limits, gave him joys that he cannot elsewhere find on earth. On his behalf, you have incurred a responsibility which you cannot fling aside. And here, Donatello, is one whom Providence marks out as intimately connected with your destiny. The mysterious process, by which our earthly life instructs us for another state of being, was begun for you by her. She has rich gifts of heart and mind, a suggestive power, a magnetic influence, a sympathetic knowledge, which, wisely and religiously exercised, are what your condition needs. She possesses what you require, and, with utter self-devotion, will use it for your good. The bond betwixt you, therefore, is a true one, and never — except by Heaven's own act — should be rent asunder."

"Ah; he has spoken the truth!" cried Donatello, grasping Miriam's hand.

"The very truth, dear friend," cried Miriam.

"But take heed," resumed the sculptor, anxious not to violate the integrity of his own conscience, — "take heed; for you love one another, and yet your bond is twined with such black threads that you must never look upon it as identical with the ties that unite other loving souls. It is for mutual support; it is for one another's final good; it is for effort, for sacrifice, but not for earthly happiness. If such be your motive, believe me, friends, it were better to relinquish each other's hands at this sad moment. There would be no holy sanction on your wedded life."

"None," said Donatello, shuddering. "We know it well."

"None," repeated Miriam, also shuddering. "United — miserably entangled with me, rather — by a bond

VOL. VI.

of guilt, our union might be for eternity, indeed, and most intimate; but, through all that endless duration, I should be conscious of his horror."

"Not for earthly bliss, therefore," said Kenyon, "but for mutual elevation, and encouragement towards a severe and painful life, you take each other's hands. And if, out of toil, sacrifice, prayer, penitence, and earnest effort towards right things, there comes, at length, a sombre and thoughtful happiness, taste it, and thank Heaven! So that you live not for it, — so that it be a wayside flower, springing along a path that leads to higher ends, — it will be Heaven's gracious gift, and a token that it recognizes your union here below."

"Have you no more to say?" asked Miriam, earnestly. "There is matter of sorrow and lofty consolation strangely mingled in your words."

"Only this, dear Miriam," said the sculptor; "if ever in your lives the highest duty should require from either of you the sacrifice of the other, meet the occasion without shrinking. This is all."

While Kenyon spoke, Donatello had evidently taken in the ideas which he propounded, and had ennobled them by the sincerity of his reception. His aspect unconsciously assumed a dignity, which, elevating his former beauty, accorded with the change that had long been taking place in his interior self. He was a man, revolving grave and deep thoughts in his breast. He still held Miriam's hand; and there they stood, the beautiful man, the beautiful woman, united forever, as they felt, in the presence of these thousand eyewitnesses, who gazed so curiously at the unintelligible scene. Doubtless, the crowd recognized them as lovers, and fancied this a betrothal that was destined to

result in life-long happiness. And, possibly, it might
be so. Who can tell where happiness may come ; or
where, though an expected guest, it may never show
its face ? Perhaps — shy, subtle thing — it had crept
into this sad marriage-bond, when the partners would
have trembled at its presence as a crime.

"Farewell ! " said Kenyon ; " I go to Rome."

"Farewell, true friend ! " said Miriam.

"Farewell ! " said Donatello too. " May you be
happy. You have no guilt to make you shrink from
happiness."

At this moment it so chanced that all the three
friends by one impulse glanced upward at the statue
of Pope Julius ; and there was the majestic figure
stretching out the hand of benediction over them, and
bending down upon this guilty and repentant pair its
visage of grand benignity. There is a singular effect
oftentimes when, out of the midst of engrossing thought
and deep absorption, we suddenly look up, and catch
a glimpse of external objects. We seem at such moments to look farther and deeper into them, than by
any premeditated observation ; it is as if they met our
eyes alive, and with all their hidden meaning on the
surface, but grew again inanimate and inscrutable the
instant that they became aware of our glances. So
now, at that unexpected glimpse, Miriam, Donatello,
and the sculptor, all three imagined that they beheld
the bronze pontiff endowed with spiritual life. A
blessing was felt descending upon them from his outstretched hand ; he approved by look and gesture the
pledge of a deep union that had passed under his au-
spices.

CHAPTER XXXVI.

WHEN we have once known Rome, and left her where she lies, like a long-decaying corpse, retaining a trace of the noble shape it was, but with accumulated dust and a fungous growth overspreading all its more admirable features, — left her in utter weariness, no doubt, of her narrow, crooked, intricate streets, so uncomfortably paved with little squares of lava that to tread over them is a penitential pilgrimage, so indescribably ugly, moreover, so cold, so alley-like, into which the sun never falls, and where a chill wind forces its deadly breath into our lungs, — left her, tired of the sight of those immense seven-storied, yellow-washed hovels, or call them palaces, where all that is dreary in domestic life seems magnified and multiplied, and weary of climbing those staircases, which ascend from a ground-floor of cook-shops, cobblers' stalls, stables, and regiments of cavalry, to a middle region of princes, cardinals, and ambassadors, and an upper tier of artists, just beneath the unattainable sky, — left her, worn out with shivering at the cheerless and smoky fireside by day, and feasting with our own substance the ravenous little populace of a Roman bed at night, — left her, sick at heart of Italian trickery, which has uprooted whatever faith in man's integrity had endured till now, and sick at stomach of sour bread, sour wine, rancid butter, and bad cookery, needlessly bestowed on evil meats, — left her, disgusted with the pretence of holiness and the reality of nastiness, each equally omnipresent, — left her, half lifeless from the languid atmosphere, the vital principle of which has been used up long ago, or corrupted by myriads of slaughters, — left her, crushed down in spirit with the desolation of her ruin, and the hopelessness of her future, — left her, in short, hating her with all our might, and adding our individual curse to the infinite anathema which her old crimes have unmistakably brought down, — when we have left Rome in such mood as this, we are astonished by the discovery, by and by, that our heart-strings have mysteriously attached themselves to the Eternal City, and are drawing us thitherward again, as if it were more familiar, more intimately our home, than even the spot where we were born.

It is with a kindred sentiment, that we now follow the course of our story back through the Flaminian Gate, and, treading our way to the Via Portoghese, climb the staircase to the upper chamber of the tower where we last saw Hilda.

Hilda all along intended to pass the summer in Rome; for she had laid out many high and delightful tasks, which she could the better complete while her favorite haunts were deserted by the multitude that thronged them throughout the winter and early spring. Nor did she dread the summer atmosphere, although generally held to be so pestilential. She had already made trial of it, two years before, and found no worse effect than a kind of dreamy languor, which was dissipated by the first cool breezes that came with autumn. The thickly populated centre of the city, indeed, is never affected by the feverish influence that lies in wait in the Campagna, like a besieging foe, and nightly haunts those beautiful lawns and woodlands, around the suburban villas, just at the season when they most resemble Paradise. What the flaming sword was to the first Eden, such is the malaria to these sweet gardens and groves. We may wander through them, of an afternoon, it is true, but they cannot be made a home and a reality, and to sleep among them is death. They are but illusions, therefore, like the show of gleaming waters and shadowy foliage in a desert.

But Rome, within the walls, at this dreaded season, enjoys its festal days, and makes itself merry with characteristic and hereditary pastimes, for which its broad piazzas afford abundant room. It leads its own life with a freer spirit, now that the artists and foreign visitors are scattered abroad. No bloom, perhaps, would be visible in a cheek that should be unvisited, throughout the summer, by more invigorating winds than any within fifty miles of the city ; no bloom, but yet, if the mind kept its healthy energy, a subdued and colorless well-being. There was consequently little risk in Hilda's purpose to pass the summer days in the galleries of Roman palaces, and her nights in that aerial chamber, whither the heavy breath of the city and its suburbs could not aspire. It would probably harm her no more than it did the white doves, who sought the same high atmosphere at sunset, and, when morning came, flew down into the narrow streets, about their daily business, as Hilda likewise did.

With the Virgin's aid and blessing, which might be hoped for even by a heretic, who so religiously lit the lamp before her shrine, the New England girl would sleep securely in her old Roman tower, and go forth on her pictorial pilgrimages without dread or

peril. In view of such a summer, Hilda had anticipated many months of lonely, but unalloyed enjoyment. Not that she had a churlish disinclination to
society, or needed to be told that we taste one intellectual pleasure twice, and with double the result,
when we taste it with a friend. But, keeping a maiden
heart within her bosom, she rejoiced in the freedom
that enabled her still to choose her own sphere, and
dwell in it, if she pleased, without another inmate.

Her expectation, however, of a delightful summer
was wofully disappointed. Even had she formed no
previous plan of remaining there, it is improbable that
Hilda would have gathered energy to stir from Rome.
A torpor, heretofore unknown to her vivacious though
quiet temperament, had possessed itself of the poor
girl, like a half-dead serpent knotting its cold, inextricable wreaths about her limbs. It was that peculiar
despair, that chill and heavy misery, which only the
innocent can experience, although it possesses many
of the gloomy characteristics that mark a sense of
guilt. It was that heart-sickness, which, it is to be
hoped, we may all of us have been pure enough to
feel, once in our lives, but the capacity for which is
usually exhausted early, and perhaps with a single
agony. It was that dismal certainty of the existence
of evil in the world, which, though we may fancy ourselves fully assured of the sad mystery long before,
never becomes a portion of our practical belief until
it takes substance and reality from the sin of some
guide, whom we have deeply trusted and revered, or
some friend whom we have dearly loved.

When that knowledge comes, it is as if a cloud had
suddenly gathered over the morning light; so dark a
cloud, that there seems to be no longer any sunshine

behind it or above it.   The character of our individual
beloved one having invested itself with all the attributes of right, — that one friend being to us the symbol and representative of whatever is good and true,
— when he falls, the effect is almost as if the sky fell
with him, bringing down in chaotic ruin the columns
that upheld our faith.   We struggle forth again, no
doubt, bruised and bewildered.   We stare wildly about
us, and discover — or, it may be, we never make the
discovery — that it was not actually the sky that has
tumbled down, but merely a frail structure of our own
rearing, which never rose higher than the house-tops,
and has fallen because we founded it on nothing.   But
the crash, and the affright and trouble, are as over-
whelming, for the time, as if the catastrophe involved
the whole moral world.   Remembering these things, let
them suggest one generous motive for walking heed-
fully amid the defilement of earthly ways!   Let us reflect, that the highest path is pointed out by the pure
Ideal of those who look up to us, and who, if we tread
less loftily, may never look so high again.

Hilda's situation was made infinitely more wretched
by the necessity of confining all her trouble within her
own consciousness.   To this innocent girl, holding the
knowledge of Miriam's crime within her tender and
delicate soul, the effect was almost the same as if she
herself had participated in the guilt.   Indeed, partaking the human nature of those who could perpetrate
such deeds, she felt her own spotlessness impugned.

Had there been but a single friend, — or, not a
friend, since friends were no longer to be confided in,
after Miriam had betrayed her trust, — but, had there
been any calm, wise mind, any sympathizing intelligence ; or, if not these, any dull, half-listening ear

into which she might have flung the dreadful secret,
as into an echoless cavern, — what a relief would have
ensued! But this awful loneliness! It enveloped her
whithersoever she went. It was a shadow in the sunshine of festal days; a mist between her eyes and the
pictures at which she strove to look; a chill dungeon,
which kept her in its gray twilight and fed her with
its unwholesome air, fit only for a criminal to breathe
and pine in! She could not escape from it. In the
effort to do so, straying farther into the intricate passages of our nature, she stumbled, ever and again,
over this deadly idea of mortal guilt.

Poor sufferer for another's sin! Poor well-spring
of a virgin's heart, into which a murdered corpse had
casually fallen, and whence it could not be drawn
forth again, but lay there, day after day, night after
night, tainting its sweet atmosphere with the scent of
crime and ugly death!

The strange sorrow that had befallen Hilda did not
fail to impress its mysterious seal upon her face, and
to make itself perceptible to sensitive observers in her
manner and carriage. A young Italian artist, who
frequented the same galleries which Hilda haunted,
grew deeply interested in her expression. One day,
while she stood before Leonardo da Vinci's picture of
Joanna of Aragon, but evidently without seeing it, —
for, though it had attracted her eyes, a fancied resemblance to Miriam had immediately drawn away
her thoughts, — this artist drew a hasty sketch which
he afterwards elaborated into a finished portrait. It
represented Hilda as gazing with sad and earnest horror at a blood-spot which she seemed just then to have
discovered on her white robe. The picture attracted
considerable notice. Copies of an engraving from it

may still be found in the print-shops along the Corso. By many connoisseurs, the idea of the face was supposed to have been suggested by the portrait of Beatrice Cenci; and, in fact, there was a look somewhat similar to poor Beatrice's forlorn gaze out of the dreary isolation and remoteness, in which a terrible doom had involved a tender soul. But the modern artist strenuously upheld the originality of his own picture, as well as the stainless purity of its subject, and chose to call it — and was laughed at for his pains — "Innocence, dying of a blood-stain!"

"Your picture, Signore Panini, does you credit," remarked the picture-dealer, who had bought it of the young man for fifteen scudi, and afterwards sold it for ten times the sum; "but it would be worth a better price if you had given it a more intelligible title. Looking at the face and expression of this fair signorina, we seem to comprehend readily enough, that she is undergoing one or another of those troubles of the heart to which young ladies are but too liable. But what is this blood-stain? And what has innocence to do with it? Has she stabbed her perfidious lover with a bodkin?"

"She! she commit a crime!" cried the young artist. "Can you look at the innocent anguish in her face, and ask that question? No; but, as I read the mystery, a man has been slain in her presence, and the blood, spurting accidentally on her white robe, has made a stain which eats into her life."

"Then, in the name of her patron saint," exclaimed the picture-dealer, "why don't she get the robe made white again at the expense of a few baiocchi to her washer-woman? No, no, my dear Panini. The picture being now my property, I shall call it 'The Sig-

norina's Vengeance.' She has stabbed her lover over-
night, and is repenting it betimes the next morning.
So interpreted, the picture becomes an intelligible and
very natural representation of a not uncommon fact."

Thus coarsely does the world translate all finer
griefs that meet its eye. It is more a coarse world
than an unkind one.

But Hilda sought nothing either from the world's
delicacy or its pity, and never dreamed of its misinter-
pretations. Her doves often flew in through the windows of the tower, winged messengers, bringing her
what sympathy they could, and uttering soft, tender,
and complaining sounds, deep in their bosoms, which
soothed the girl more than a distincter utterance might.
And sometimes Hilda moaned quietly among the doves,
teaching her voice to accord with theirs, and thus finding a temporary relief from the burden of her incom-
municable sorrow, as if a little portion of it, at least,
had been told to these innocent friends, and been understood and pitied.

When she trimmed the lamp before the Virgin's
shrine, Hilda gazed at the sacred image, and, rude as
was the workmanship, beheld, or fancied, expressed
with the quaint, powerful simplicity which sculptors
sometimes had five hundred years ago, a woman's tenderness responding to her gaze. If she knelt, if she
prayed, if her oppressed heart besought the sympathy
of divine womanhood afar in bliss, but not remote, because forever humanized by the memory of mortal
griefs, was Hilda to be blamed? It was not a Catholic kneeling at an idolatrous shrine, but a child lifting
its tear-stained face to seek comfort from a mother.

CHAPTER XXXVII.

HILDA descended, day by day, from her dove-cote, and went to one or another of the great, old palaces, — the Pamfili Doria, the Corsini, the Sciarra, the Borghese, the Colonna, — where the door-keepers knew her well, and offered her a kindly greeting. But they shook their heads and sighed, on observing the languid step with which the poor girl toiled up the grand marble staircases. There was no more of that cheery alacrity with which she used to flit upward, as if her doves had lent her their wings, nor of that glow of happy spirits which had been wont to set the tarnished gilding of the picture-frames and the shabby splendor of the furniture all a-glimmer, as she hastened to her congenial and delightful toil.

An old German artist, whom she often met in the galleries, once laid a paternal hand on Hilda's head, and bade her go back to her own country.

"Go back soon," he said, with kindly freedom and directness, "or you will go never more. And, if you go not, why, at least, do you spend the whole summer-time in Rome ? The air has been breathed too often, in so many thousand years, and is not wholesome for a little foreign flower like you, my child, a delicate wood-anemone from the western forest-land."

"I have no task nor duty anywhere but here," replied Hilda. "The old masters will not set me free !"

" Ah, those old masters ! " cried the veteran artist, shaking his head. " They are a tyrannous race !
You will find them of too mighty a spirit to be dealt
with, for long together, by the slender hand, the fragile mind, and the delicate heart, of a young girl. Remember that Raphael's genius wore out that divinest
painter before half his life was lived. Since you feel
his influence powerfully enough to reproduce his miracles so well, it will assuredly consume you like a
flame."

" That might have been my peril once," answered
Hilda. " It is not so now."

" Yes, fair maiden, you stand in that peril now ! "
insisted the kind old man ; and he added, smiling, yet
in a melancholy vein, and with a German grotesqueness of idea, " Some fine morning, I shall come to the
Pinacotheca of the Vatican, with my palette and my
brushes, and shall look for my little American artist
that sees into the very heart of the grand pictures !
And what shall I behold ? A heap of white ashes on
the marble floor, just in front of the divine Raphael's
picture of the Madonna da Foligno ! Nothing more,
upon my word ! The fire, which the poor child feels
so fervently, will have gone into her innermost, and
burnt her quite up ! "

" It would be a happy martyrdom ! " said Hilda,
faintly smiling. " But I am far from being worthy of
it. What troubles me much, among other troubles, is
quite the reverse of what you think. The old masters
hold me here, it is true, but they no longer warm me
with their influence. It is not flame consuming, but
torpor chilling me, that helps to make me wretched."

" Perchance, then," said the German, looking keenly
at her, " Raphael has a rival in your heart ? He was

your first-love ; but young maidens are not always constant, and one flame is sometimes extinguished by another ! "

Hilda shook her head, and turned away.

She had spoken the truth, however, in alleging that
torpor, rather than fire, was what she had now to
dread.   In those gloomy days that had befallen her, it
was a great additional calamity that she felt conscious
of the present dimness of an insight, which she once
possessed in more than ordinary measure.   She had
lost — and she trembled lest it should have departed
forever — the faculty of appreciating those great works
of art, which heretofore had made so large a portion
of her happiness.   It was no wonder.

A picture, however admirable the painter's art, and
wonderful his power, requires of the spectator a sur-
render of himself, in due proportion with the miracle
which has been wrought.   Let the canvas glow as it
may, you must look with the eye of faith, or its highest excellence escapes you.   There is always the necessity of helping out the painter's art with your own resources of sensibility and imagination.   Not that these
qualities shall really add anything to what the master
has effected ; but they must be put so entirely under
his control, and work along with him to such an extent, that, in a different mood, when you are cold and
critical, instead of sympathetic, you will be apt to
fancy that the loftier merits of the picture were of
your own dreaming, not of his creating.

Like all revelations of the better life, the adequate
perception of a great work of art demands a gifted
simplicity of vision.   In this, and in her self-surrender, and the depth and tenderness of her sympathy,
had lain Hilda's remarkable power as a copyist of the

old masters. And now that her capacity of emotion
was choked up with a horrible experience, it inevitably followed that she should seek in vain, among those
friends so venerated and beloved, for the marvels
which they had heretofore shown her. In spite of a
reverence that lingered longer than her recognition,
their poor worshipper became almost an infidel, and
sometimes doubted whether the pictorial art be not altogether a delusion.

For the first time in her life, Hilda now grew acquainted with that icy demon of weariness, who haunts
great picture galleries. He is a plausible Mephistophe-
les, and possesses the magic that is the destruction of
all other magic. He annihilates color, warmth, and,
more especially, sentiment and passion, at a touch. If
he spare anything, it will be some such matter as an
earthen pipkin, or a bunch of herrings by Teniers; a
brass kettle, in which you can see your face, by Ge-
rard Douw; a furred robe, or the silken texture of a
mantle, or a straw hat, by Van Mieris; or a long-
stalked wine-glass, transparent and full of shifting reflection, or a bit of bread and cheese, or an over-ripe
peach, with a fly upon it, truer than reality itself, by
the school of Dutch conjurers. These men, and a few
Flemings, whispers the wicked demon, were the only
painters. The mighty Italian masters, as you deem
them, were not human, nor addressed their work to
human sympathies, but to a false intellectual taste,
which they themselves were the first to create. Well
might they call their doings " art," for they substituted art instead of nature. Their fashion is past,
and ought, indeed, to have died and been buried along
with them.

Then there is such a terrible lack of variety in their

subjects. The churchmen, their great patrons, suggested most of their themes, and a dead mythology
the rest. A quarter-part, probably, of any large collection of pictures, consists of Virgins and infant
Christs, repeated over and over again in pretty much
an identical spirit, and generally with no more mixture of the Divine than just enough to spoil them as
representations of maternity and childhood, with which
everybody's heart might have something to do. Half
of the other pictures are Magdalens, Flights into
Egypt, Crucifixions, Depositions from the Cross, Pie-
tas, Noli-me-tangeres, or the Sacrifice of Abraham, or
martyrdoms of saints, originally painted as altar-pieces,
or for the shrines of chapels, and wofully lacking the
accompaniments which the artist had in view.

The remainder of the gallery comprises mytholog-
ical subjects, such as nude Venuses, Ledas, Graces,
and, in short, a general apotheosis of nudity, once fresh
and rosy perhaps, but yellow and dingy in our day,
and retaining only a traditionary charm. These im-
pure pictures are from the same illustrious and impious hands that adventured to call before us the august
forms of Apostles and Saints, the Blessed Mother of
the Redeemer, and her Son, at his death, and in his
glory, and even the awfulness of Him, to whom the
martyrs, dead a thousand years ago, have not yet
dared to raise their eyes. They seem to take up one
task or the other — the disrobed woman whom they
call Venus, or the type of highest and tenderest
womanhood in the mother of their Saviour — with
equal readiness, but to achieve the former with far
more satisfactory success. If an artist sometimes produced a picture of the Virgin, possessing warmth
enough to excite devotional feelings, it was probably

the object of his earthly love to whom he thus paid
the stupendous and fearful homage of setting up her
portrait to be worshipped, not figuratively as a mortal,
but by religious souls in their earnest aspirations towards Divinity. And who can trust the religious sentiment of Raphael, or receive any of his Virgins as
heaven-descended likenesses, after seeing, for example,
the Fornarina of the Barberini Palace, and feeling how
sensual the artist must have been to paint such a brazen trollop of his own accord, and lovingly? Would
the Blessed Mary reveal herself to his spiritual vision,
and favor him with sittings alternately with that type
of glowing earthliness, the Fornarina?

But no sooner have we given expression to this irreverent criticism, than a throng of spiritual faces look
reproachfully upon us. We see cherubs by Raphael,
whose baby-innocence could only have been nursed in
paradise; angels by Raphael as innocent as they, but
whose serene intelligence embraces both earthly and
celestial things; madonnas by Raphael, on whose lips
he has impressed a holy and delicate reserve, implying
sanctity on earth, and into whose soft eyes he has
thrown a light which he never could have imagined
except by raising his own eyes with a pure aspiration
heavenward. We remember, too, that divinest countenance in the Transfiguration, and withdraw all that
we have said.

Poor Hilda, however, in her gloomiest moments,
was never guilty of the high treason suggested in the
above remarks against her beloved and honored Raphael. She had a faculty (which, fortunately for
themselves, pure women often have) of ignoring all
moral blotches in a character that won her admira

tion. She purified the objects of her regard by the mere act of turning such spotless eyes upon them.

Hilda's despondency, nevertheless, while it dulled her perceptions in one respect, had deepened them in another; she saw beauty less vividly, but felt truth, or the lack of it, more profoundly. She began to suspect that some, at least, of her venerated painters, had left an inevitable hollowness in their works, because, in the most renowned of them, they essayed to express to the world what they had not in their own souls. They deified their light and wandering affections, and were continually playing off the tremendous jest, alluded to above, of offering the features of some venal beauty to be enshrined in the holiest places. A deficiency of earnestness and absolute truth is generally discoverable in Italian pictures, after the art had become consummate. When you demand what is deepest, these painters have not wherewithal to respond. They substituted a keen intellectual perception, and a marvellous knack of external arrangement, instead of the live sympathy and sentiment which should have been their inspiration. And hence it happens, that shallow and worldly men are among the best critics of their works; a taste for pictorial art is often no more than a polish upon the hard enamel of an artificial character. Hilda had lavished her whole heart upon it, and found (just as if she had lavished it upon a human idol) that the greater part was thrown away.

For some of the earlier painters, however, she still retained much of her former reverence. Fra Angelico, she felt, must have breathed a humble aspiration between every two touches of his brush, in order to have made the finished picture such a visible prayer as we behold it, in the guise of a prim angel, or a

THE TRANSFIGURATION, BY RAPHAEL

saint without the human nature. Through all these
dusky centuries, his works may still help a struggling
heart to pray. Perugino was evidently a devout man;
and the Virgin, therefore, revealed herself to him in
loftier and sweeter faces of celestial womanhood, and
yet with a kind of homeliness in their human mould,
than even the genius of Raphael could imagine. Sodoma, beyond a question, both prayed and wept, while
painting his fresco, at Siena, of Christ bound to a
pillar.

In her present need and hunger for a spiritual revelation, Hilda felt a vast and weary longing to see this
last-mentioned picture once again. It is inexpressibly
touching. So weary is the Saviour, and utterly worn
out with agony, that his lips have fallen apart from
mere exhaustion; his eyes seem to be set; he tries to
lean his head against the pillar, but is kept from sinking down upon the ground only by the cords that
bind him. One of the most striking effects produced
is the sense of loneliness. You behold Christ deserted both in heaven and earth; that despair is in
him which wrung forth the saddest utterance man
ever made, "Why hast Thou forsaken me?" Even
in this extremity, however, he is still divine. The
great and reverent painter has not suffered the Son of
God to be merely an object of pity, though depicting
him in a state so profoundly pitiful. He is rescued
from it, we know not how, — by nothing less than
miracle, — by a celestial majesty and beauty, and
some quality of which these are the outward garniture. He is as much, and as visibly, our Redeemer,
there bound, there fainting, and bleeding from the
scourge, with the cross in view, as if he sat on his
throne of glory in the heavens! Sodoma, in this

matchless picture, has done more towards reconciling the incongruity of Divine Omnipotence and outraged, suffering Humanity, combined in one person, than the theologians ever did.

This hallowed work of genius shows what pictorial art, devoutly exercised, might effect in behalf of religious truth ; involving, as it does, deeper mysteries of revelation, and bringing them closer to man's heart, and making him tenderer to be impressed by them, than the most eloquent words of preacher or prophet.

It is not of pictures like the above that galleries, in Rome or elsewhere, are made up, but of productions immeasurably below them, and requiring to be appreciated by a very different frame of mind. Few amateurs are endowed with a tender susceptibility to the sentiment of a picture ; they are not won from an evil life, nor anywise morally improved by it. The love of art, therefore, differs widely in its influence from the love of nature ; whereas, if art had not strayed away from its legitimate paths and aims, it ought to soften and sweeten the lives of its worshippers, in even a more exquisite degree than the contemplation of natural objects. But, of its own potency, it has no such effect ; and it fails, likewise, in that other test of its moral value which poor Hilda was now involuntarily trying upon it. It cannot comfort the heart in affliction ; it grows dim when the shadow is upon us.

So the melancholy girl wandered through those long galleries, and over the mosaic pavements of vast, solitary saloons, wondering what had become of the splendor that used to beam upon her from the walls. She grew sadly critical, and condemned almost every thing that she was wont to admire. Heretofore, her sympathy went deeply into a picture. yet seemed to leave a depth which it was inadequate to sound; now, on the contrary, her perceptive faculty penetrated the canvas like a steel probe, and found but a crust of paint over an emptiness. Not that she gave up all art as worthless; only it had lost its consecration. One picture in ten thousand, perhaps, ought to live in the applause of mankind, from generation to generation, until the colors fade and blacken out of sight, or the canvas rot entirely away. For the rest, let them be piled in garrets, just as the tolerable poets are shelved, when their little day is over. Is a painter more sacred than a poet?

And as for these galleries of Roman palaces, they were to Hilda, — though she still trod them with the forlorn hope of getting back her sympathies, — they were drearier than the whitewashed walls of a prison corridor. If a magnificent palace were founded, as was generally the case, on hardened guilt and a stony conscience, — if the prince or cardinal who stole the marble of his vast mansion from the Coliseum, or some Roman temple, and perpetrated still deadlier crimes, as probably he did, — there could be no fitter punishment for his ghost than to wander perpetually through these long suites of rooms, over the cold marble or mosaic of the floors, growing chiller at every eternal footstep. Fancy the progenitor of the Dorias thus haunting those heavy halls where his posterity reside! Nor would it assuage his monotonous misery, but increase it manifold, to be compelled to scrutinize those masterpieces of art, which he collected with so much cost and care, and gazing at them unintelligently, still leave a further portion of his vital warmth at every one.

Such, or of a similar kind, is the torment of those

who seek to enjoy pictures in an uncongenial mood. Every haunter of picture galleries, we should imagine, must have experienced it, in greater or less degree; Hilda never till now, but now most bitterly.

And now, for the first time in her lengthened absence, comprising so many years of her young life, she began to be acquainted with the exile's pain. Her pictorial imagination brought up vivid scenes of her native village, with its great, old elm-trees; and the neat, comfortable houses, scattered along the wide, grassy margin of its street, and the white meeting-house, and her mother's very door, and the stream of gold-brown water, which her taste for color had kept flowing, all this while, through her remembrance. Oh, dreary streets, palaces, churches, and imperial sepulchres of hot and dusty Rome, with the muddy Tiber eddying through the midst, instead of the gold-brown rivulet! How she pined under this crumbly magnificence, as if it were piled all upon her human heart! How she yearned for that native homeliness, those familiar sights, those faces which she had known always, those days that never brought any strange event; that life of sober week-days, and a solemn sabbath at the close! The peculiar fragrance of a flower-bed, which Hilda used to cultivate, came freshly to her memory, across the windy sea, and through the long years since the flowers had withered. Her heart grew faint at the hundred reminiscences that were awakened by that remembered smell of dead blossoms; it was like opening a drawer, where many things were laid away, and every one of them scented with lavender and dried rose-leaves.

We ought not to betray Hilda's secret; but it is the truth, that being so sad, and so utterly alone, and in such great need of sympathy, her thoughts sometimes recurred to the sculptor. Had she met him now, her heart, indeed, might not have been won, but her confidence would have flown to him like a bird to its nest. One summer afternoon, especially, Hilda leaned upon the battlements of her tower, and looked over Rome towards the distant mountains, whither Kenyon had told her that he was going.

"Oh, that he were here!" she sighed; "I perish under this terrible secret; and he might help me to endure it. Oh, that he were here!"

That very afternoon, as the reader may remember, Kenyon felt Hilda's hand pulling at the silken cord that was connected with his heartstrings, as he stood looking towards Rome from the battlements of Monte Beni

CHAPTER XXXVIII.

ALTARS AND INCENSE.

ROME has a certain species of consolation readier at hand, for all the necessitous, than any other spot under the sky; and Hilda's despondent state made her peculiarly liable to the peril, if peril it can justly be termed, of seeking, or consenting, to be thus consoled.

Had the Jesuits known the situation of this troubled heart, her inheritance of New England Puritanism would hardly have protected the poor girl from the pious strategy of those good fathers. Knowing, as they do, how to work each proper engine, it would have been ultimately impossible for Hilda to resist the attractions of a faith, which so marvellously adapts itself to every human need. Not, indeed, that it can satisfy the soul's cravings, but, at least, it can sometimes help the soul towards a higher satisfaction than the faith contains within itself. It supplies a multitude of external forms, in which the spiritual may be clothed and manifested; it has many painted windows, as it were, through which the celestial sunshine, else disregarded, may make itself gloriously perceptible in visions of beauty and splendor. There is no one want or weakness of human nature for which Catholicism will own itself without a remedy; cordials, certainly, it possesses in abundance, and sedatives in inexhaustible variety, and what may once have been genuine medicaments, though a little the worse for long keeping.

To do it justice, Catholicism is such a miracle of fitness for its own ends, many of which might seem to be admirable ones, that it is difficult to imagine it a contrivance of mere man. Its mighty machinery was forged and put together, not on middle earth, but either above or below. If there were but angels to work it, instead of the very different class of engineers who now manage its cranks and safety-valves, the system would soon vindicate the dignity and holiness of its origin.

Hilda had heretofore made many pilgrimages among the churches of Rome, for the sake of wondering at their gorgeousness. Without a glimpse at these palaces of worship, it is impossible to imagine the magnificence of the religion that reared them. Many of them shine with burnished gold. They glow with pictures. Their walls, columns, and arches seem a quarry of precious stones, so beautiful and costly are the marbles with which they are inlaid. Their pavements are often a mosaic, of rare workmanship. Around their lofty cornices hover flights of sculptured angels; and within the vault of the ceiling and the swelling interior of the dome, there are frescos of such brilliancy, and wrought with so artful a perspective, that the sky, peopled with sainted forms, appears to be opened, only a little way above the spectator. Then there are chapels, opening from the side-aisles and transepts, decorated by princes for their own burial-places, and as shrines for their especial saints. In these, the splendor of the entire edifice is intensified and gathered to a focus. Unless words were gems, that would flame with many-colored light upon the page, and throw thence a tremulous glimmer into the reader's eyes, it were vain to attempt a description of a princely chapel.

Restless with her trouble, Hilda now entered upon another pilgrimage among these altars and shrines. She climbed the hundred steps of the Ara Cœli ; she trod the broad, silent nave of St. John Lateran ; she stood in the Pantheon, under the round opening in the dome, through which the blue sunny sky still gazes down, as it used to gaze when there were Roman deities in the antique niches. She went into every church that rose before her, but not now to wonder at its magnificence, when she hardly noticed more than if it had been the pine-built interior of a New England meeting-house.

She went — and it was a dangerous errand — to observe how closely and comfortingly the popish faith applied itself to all human occasions. It was impossible to doubt that multitudes of people found their spiritual advantage in it, who would find none at all in our own formless mode of worship; which, besides, so far as the sympathy of prayerful souls is concerned, can be enjoyed only at stated and too unfrequent periods. But here, whenever the hunger for divine nutriment came upon the soul, it could on the instant be appeased. At one or another altar, the incense was forever ascending; the mass always being performed, and carrying upward with it the devotion of such as had not words for their own prayer. And yet, if the worshipper had his individual petition to offer, his own heart-secret to whisper below his breath, there were divine auditors ever ready to receive it from his lips; and what encouraged him still more, these auditors had not always been divine, but kept, within their heavenly memories, the tender humility of a human experience. Now a saint in heaven, but once a man on earth.

Hilda saw peasants, citizens, soldiers, nobles, women with bare heads, ladies in their silks, entering the churches individually, kneeling for moments, or for hours, and directing their inaudible devotions to the shrine of some saint of their own choice. In his hallowed person, they felt themselves possessed of an own friend in heaven. They were too humble to approach the Deity directly. Conscious of their unworthiness, they asked the mediation of their sympathizing patron, who, on the score of his ancient martyrdom, and after many ages of celestial life, might venture to talk with the Divine Presence, almost as friend with friend. Though dumb before its Judge, even despair could speak, and pour out the misery of its soul like water, to an advocate so wise to comprehend the case, and eloquent to plead it, and powerful to win pardon, whatever were the guilt. Hilda witnessed what she deemed to be an example of this species of confidence between a young man and his saint. He stood before a shrine, writhing, wringing his hands, contorting his whole frame in an agony of remorseful recollection, but finally knelt down to weep and pray. If this youth had been a Protestant, he would have kept all that torture pent up in his heart, and let it burn there till it seared him into indifference.

Often and long, Hilda lingered before the shrines and chapels of the Virgin, and departed from them with reluctant steps. Here, perhaps, strange as it may seem, her delicate appreciation of art stood her in good stead, and lost Catholicism a convert. If the painter had represented Mary with a heavenly face, poor Hilda was now in the very mood to worship her, and adopt the faith in which she held so elevated a position. But she saw that it was merely the flattered portrait of an earthly beauty; the wife, at best, of the artist; or, it might be, a peasant-girl of the Campagna, or some Roman princess, to whom he desired to pay his court. For love, or some even less justifiable motive, the old painter had apotheosized these women; he thus gained for them, as far as his skill would go, not only the meed of immortality, but the privilege of presiding over Christian altars, and of being worshipped with far holier fervors than while they dwelt on earth. Hilda's fine sense of the fit and decorous could not be betrayed into kneeling at such a shrine.

She never found just the virgin mother whom she needed. Here, it was an earthly mother, worshipping the earthly baby in her lap, as any and every mother does, from Eve's time downward. In another picture, there was a dim sense, shown in the mother's face, of some divine quality in the child. In a third, the artist seemed to have had a higher perception, and had striven hard to shadow out the Virgin's joy at bringing the Saviour into the world, and her awe and love, inextricably mingled, of the little form which she pressed against her bosom. So far was good. But still, Hilda looked for something more; a face of celestial beauty, but human as well as heavenly, and with the shadow of past grief upon it; bright with immortal youth, yet matronly and motherly; and endowed with a queenly dignity, but infinitely tender, as the highest and deepest attribute of her divinity.

"Ah," thought Hilda to herself, "why should not there be a woman to listen to the prayers of women? a mother in heaven for all motherless girls like me? In all God's thought and care for us, can he have withheld this boon, which our weakness so much needs?"

Oftener than to the other churches, she wandered into St. Peter's. Within its vast limits, she thought, and beneath the sweep of its great dome, there should be space for all forms of Christian truth ; room both for the faithful and the heretic to kneel; due help for every creature's spiritual want.

Hilda had not always been adequately impressed by the grandeur of this mighty cathedral. When she first lifted the heavy leathern curtain, at one of the doors, a shadowy edifice in her imagination had been dazzled out of sight by the reality. Her preconception of St. Peter's was a structure of no definite outline, misty in its architecture, dim and gray and huge, stretching into an interminable perspective, and over-arched by a dome like the cloudy firmament. Beneath that vast breadth and height, as she had fancied them, the personal man might feel his littleness, and the soul triumph in its immensity. So, in her earlier visits, when the compassed splendor of the actual interior glowed before her eyes, she had profanely called it a great prettiness ; a gay piece of cabinet-work, on a Titanic scale ; a jewel-casket, marvellously magnified.

This latter image best pleased her fancy; a casket, all inlaid, in the inside, with precious stones of various hue, so that there should not be a hair's-breadth of the small interior unadorned with its resplendent gem. Then, conceive this minute wonder of a mosaic box, increased to the magnitude of a cathedral, without losing the intense lustre of its littleness, but all its petty glory striving to be sublime. The magic transformation from the minute to the vast has not been so cunningly effected but that the rich adornment still counteracts the impression of space and loftiness. The

spectator is more sensible of its limits than of its extent.

Until after many visits, Hilda continued to mourn
for that dim, illimitable interior, which with her eyes
shut she had seen from childhood, but which vanished
at her first glimpse through the actual door. Her
childish vision seemed preferable to the cathedral
which Michael Angelo, and all the great architects,
had built; because, of the dream edifice, she had said,
" How vast it is! " while of the real St. Peter's she
could only say, " After all, it is not so immense! "
Besides, such as the church is, it can nowhere be made
visible at one glance. It stands in its own way. You
see an aisle, or a transept; you see the nave, or the
tribune; but, on account of its ponderous piers and
other obstructions, it is only by this fragmentary process that you get an idea of the cathedral.

There is no answering such objections. The great
church smiles calmly upon its critics, and, for all response, says, " Look at me! " and if you still murmur
for the loss of your shadowy perspective, there comes
no reply, save, " Look at me! " in endless repetition,
as the one thing to be said. And, after looking many
times, with long intervals between, you discover that
the cathedral has gradually extended itself over the
whole compass of your idea; it covers all the site of
your visionary temple, and has room for its cloudy
pinnacles beneath the dome.

One afternoon, as Hilda entered St. Peter's in sombre mood, its interior beamed upon her with all the
effect of a new creation. It seemed an embodiment
of whatever the imagination could conceive, or the
heart desire, as a magnificent, comprehensive, majestic
symbol of religious faith. All splendor was included

within its verge, and there was space for all. She gazed with delight even at the multiplicity of orna- ment. She was glad at the cherubim that fluttered upon the pilasters, and of the marble doves, hovering unexpectedly, with green olive-branches of precious stones. She could spare nothing, now, of the mani- fold magnificence that had been lavished, in a hun- dred places, richly enough to have made world-famous shrines in any other church, but which here melted away into the vast sunny breadth, and were of no sep- arate account. Yet each contributed its little all to- wards the grandeur of the whole.

She would not have banished one of those grim popes, who sit each over his own tomb, scattering cold benedictions out of their marble hands ; nor a single frozen sister of the Allegoric family, to whom — as, like hired mourners at an English funeral, it costs them no wear and tear of heart — is assigned the office of weeping for the dead. If you choose to see these things, they present themselves ; if you deem them un- suitable and out of place, they vanish, individually, but leave their life upon the walls.

The pavement ! it stretched out illimitably, a plain of many-colored marble, where thousands of worship- pers might kneel together, and shadowless angels tread among them without brushing their heavenly garments against those earthly ones. The roof ! the dome ! Rich, gorgeous, filled with sunshine, cheerfully sub- lime, and fadeless after centuries, those lofty depths seemed to translate the heavens to mortal comprehen- sion, and help the spirit upward to a yet higher and wider sphere. Must not the faith, that built this matchless edifice, and warmed, illuminated, and over- flowed from it, include whatever can satisfy human aspirations at the loftiest, or minister to human necessity at the sorest? If Religion had a material home, was it not here?

As the scene which we but faintly suggest shone calmly before the New England maiden at her entrance, she moved, as if by very instinct, to one of the vases of holy water, upborne against a column by two mighty cherubs. Hilda dipped her fingers, and had almost signed the cross upon her breast, but forbore, and trembled, while shaking the water from her finger-tips. She felt as if her mother's spirit, somewhere within the dome, were looking down upon her child, the daughter of Puritan forefathers, and weeping to behold her ensnared by these gaudy superstitions. So she strayed sadly onward, up the nave, and towards the hundred golden lights that swarm before the high altar. Seeing a woman, a priest, and a soldier kneel to kiss the toe of the brazen St. Peter, who protrudes it beyond his pedestal, for the purpose, polished bright with former salutations, while a child stood on tiptoe to do the same, the glory of the church was darkened before Hilda's eyes. But again she went onward into remoter regions. She turned into the right transept, and thence found her way to a shrine, in the extreme corner of the edifice, which is adorned with a mosaic copy of Guido's beautiful Archangel, treading on the prostrate fiend.

This was one of the few pictures, which, in these dreary days, had not faded nor deteriorated in Hilda's estimation; not that it was better than many in which she no longer took an interest; but the subtile delicacy of the painter's genius was peculiarly adapted to her character. She felt, while gazing at it, that the artist had done a great thing, not merely for the

THE STATUE OF ST. PETER

Church of Rome, but for the cause of Good. The moral of the picture, the immortal youth and loveliness of Virtue, and its irresistible might against ugly Evil, appealed as much to Puritans as Catholics.

Suddenly, and as if it were done in a dream, Hilda found herself kneeling before the shrine, under the ever-burning lamp that throws its rays upon the Archangel's face. She laid her forehead on the marble steps before the altar, and sobbed out a prayer; she hardly knew to whom, whether Michael, the Virgin, or the Father; she hardly knew for what, save only a vague longing, that thus the burden of her spirit might be lightened a little.

In an instant she snatched herself up, as it were, from her knees, all a-throb with the emotions which were struggling to force their way out of her heart by the avenue that had so nearly been opened for them. Yet there was a strange sense of relief won by that momentary, passionate prayer; a strange joy, moreover, whether from what she had done, or for what she had escaped doing, Hilda could not tell. But she felt as one half stifled, who has stolen a breath of air.

Next to the shrine where she had knelt, there is another, adorned with a picture by Guercino, representing a maiden's body in the jaws of the sepulchre, and her lover weeping over it; while her beatified spirit looks down upon the scene, in the society of the Saviour and a throng of saints. Hilda wondered if it were not possible, by some miracle of faith, so to rise above her present despondency that she might look down upon what she was, just as Petronilla in the picture looked at her own corpse. A hope, born of hysteric trouble, fluttered in her heart. A presentiment, or what she fancied such, whispered her, that,

before she had finished the circuit of the cathedral, relief would come.

The unhappy are continually tantalized by similar
delusions of succor near at hand ; at least, the despair
is very dark that has no such will-o'-the-wisp to glimmer in it.

CHAPTER XXXIX.

THE WORLD'S CATHEDRAL.

STILL gliding onward, Hilda now looked up into
the dome, where the sunshine came through the western windows, and threw across long shafts of light.
They rested upon the mosaic figures of two evange-
lists above the cornice. These great beams of radiance, traversing what seemed the empty space, were
made visible in misty glory, by the holy cloud of incense, else unseen, which had risen into the middle
dome. It was to Hilda as if she beheld the worship
of the priest and people ascending heavenward, purified from its alloy of earth, and acquiring celestial
substance in the golden atmosphere to which it as-
pired. She wondered if angels did not sometimes
hover within the dome, and show themselves, in brief
glimpses, floating amid the sunshine and the glorified
vapor, to those who devoutly worshipped on the pavement.

She had now come into the southern transept.
Around this portion of the church are ranged a number of confessionals. They are small tabernacles of
carved wood, with a closet for the priest in the centre;
and, on either side, a space for a penitent to kneel,
and breathe his confession through a perforated au-
ricle into the good father's ear. Observing this arrangement, though already familiar to her, our poor
Hilda was anew impressed with the infinite conven-

ience — if we may use so poor a phrase — of the Catholic religion to its devout believers.

Who, in truth, that considers the matter, can resist a similar impression! In the hottest fever-fit of life, they can always find, ready for their need, a cool, quiet, beautiful place of worship. They may enter its sacred precincts at any hour, leaving the fret and trouble of the world behind them, and purifying themselves with a touch of holy water at the threshold. In the calm interior, fragrant of rich and soothing incense, they may hold converse with some saint, their awful, kindly friend. And, most precious privilege of all, whatever perplexity, sorrow, guilt, may weigh upon their souls, they can fling down the dark burden at the foot of the cross, and go forth — to sin no more, nor be any longer disquieted ; but to live again in the freshness and elasticity of innocence.

" Do not these inestimable advantages," thought Hilda, " or some of them at least, belong to Christianity itself ? Are they not a part of the blessings which the system was meant to bestow upon mankind? Can the faith in which I was born and bred be perfect, if it leave a weak girl like me to wander, desolate, with this great trouble crushing me down ? "

A poignant anguish thrilled within her breast; it was like a thing that had life, and was struggling to get out.

"Oh, help ! Oh, help ! " cried Hilda; " I cannot, cannot bear it ! "

Only by the reverberations that followed — arch echoing the sound to arch, and a pope of bronze repeating it to a pope of marble, as each sat enthroned over his tomb — did Hilda become aware that she had really spoken above her breath. But, in that great

space, there is no need to hush up the heart within
one's own bosom, so carefully as elsewhere; and if the
cry reached any distant auditor, it came broken into
many fragments, and from various quarters of the
church.

Approaching one of the confessionals, she saw a woman kneeling within. Just as Hilda drew near, the
penitent rose, came forth, and kissed the hand of the
priest, who regarded her with a look of paternal benignity, and appeared to be giving her some spiritual
counsel, in a low voice. She then knelt to receive his
blessing, which was fervently bestowed. Hilda was so
struck with the peace and joy in the woman's face,
that, as the latter retired, she could not help speaking
to her.

"You look very happy!" said she. "Is it so sweet,
then, to go to the confessional?"

"Oh, very sweet, my dear signorina!" answered the
woman, with moistened eyes and an affectionate smile;
for she was so thoroughly softened with what she had
been doing, that she felt as if Hilda were her younger
sister. "My heart is at rest now. Thanks be to the
Saviour, and the Blessed Virgin and the saints, and
this good father, there is no more trouble for poor Te-
resa!"

"I am glad for your sake," said Hilda, sighing for
her own. "I am a poor heretic, but a human sister;
and I rejoice for you!"

She went from one to another of the confessionals,
and, looking at each, perceived that they were inscribed
with gilt letters: on one, PRO ITALICA LINGUA; on
another, PRO FLANDRICA LINGUA; on a third, PRO
POLONICA LINGUA; on a fourth, PRO ILLYRICA LIN-
GUA; on a fifth, PRO HISPANICA LINGUA. In this

vast and hospitable cathedral, worthy to be the religious heart of the whole world, there was room for all
nations; there was access to the Divine Grace for
every Christian soul; there was an ear for what the
overburdened heart might have to murmur, speak in
what native tongue it would.

When Hilda had almost completed the circuit of
the transept, she came to a confessional — the central
part was closed, but a mystic rod protruded from it,
indicating the presence of a priest within — on which
was inscribed, PRO ANGLICA LINGUA.

It was the word in season! If she had heard her
mother's voice from within the tabernacle, calling her,
in her own mother-tongue, to come and lay her poor
head in her lap, and sob out all her troubles, Hilda
could not have responded with a more inevitable obedience. She did not think; she only felt. Within
her heart was a great need. Close at hand, within the
veil of the confessional, was the relief. She flung herself down in the penitent's place; and, tremulously,
passionately, with sobs, tears, and the turbulent overflow of emotion too long repressed, she poured out the
dark story which had infused its poison into her innocent life.

Hilda had not seen, nor could she now see the visage of the priest. But, at intervals, in the pauses of
that strange confession, half choked by the struggle of
her feelings toward an outlet, she heard a mild, calm
voice, somewhat mellowed by age. It spoke soothingly; it encouraged her; it led her on by apposite
questions that seemed to be suggested by a great and
tender interest, and acted like magnetism in attracting
the girl's confidence to this unseen friend. The priest's
share in the interview, indeed, resembled that of one

who removes the stones, clustered branches, or whatever entanglements impede the current of a swollen
stream. Hilda could have imagined — so much to the
purpose were his inquiries — that he was already acquainted with some outline of what she strove to tell
him.

Thus assisted, she revealed the whole of her terrible
secret! The whole, except that no name escaped her
lips.

And, ah, what a relief! When the hysteric gasp,
the strife between words and sobs, had subsided, what
a torture had passed away from her soul! It was all
gone; her bosom was as pure now as in her childhood.
She was a girl again; she was Hilda of the dove-cote;
not that doubtful creature whom her own doves had
hardly recognized as their mistress and playmate, by
reason of the death-scent that clung to her garments!

After she had ceased to speak, Hilda heard the priest
bestir himself with an old man's reluctant movement.
He stepped out of the confessional; and as the girl
was still kneeling in the penitential corner, he summoned her forth.

" Stand up, my daughter," said the mild voice of
the confessor ; " what we have further to say must be
spoken face to face."

Hilda did his bidding, and stood before him with a
downcast visage, which flushed and grew pale again.
But it had the wonderful beauty which we may often
observe in those who have recently gone through a
great struggle, and won the peace that lies just on the
other side. We see it in a new mother's face; we see
it in the faces of the dead ; and in Hilda's countenance — which had always a rare natural charm for
her friends — this glory of peace made her as lovely
as an angel.

On her part, Hilda beheld a venerable figure with hair as white as snow, and a face strikingly characterized by benevolence. It bore marks of thought, however, and penetrative insight; although the keen glances of the eyes were now somewhat bedimmed with tears, which the aged shed, or almost shed, on lighter stress of emotion than would elicit them from younger men.

"It has not escaped my observation, daughter," said the priest, "that this is your first acquaintance with the confessional. How is this?"

"Father," replied Hilda, raising her eyes, and again letting them fall, "I am of New England birth, and was bred as what you call a heretic."

"From New England!" exclaimed the priest. "It was my own birthplace, likewise; nor have fifty years of absence made me cease to love it. But, a heretic! And are you reconciled to the Church?"

"Never, father," said Hilda.

"And, that being the case," demanded the old man, "on what ground, my daughter, have you sought to avail yourself of these blessed privileges, confined exclusively to members of the one true Church, of confession and absolution?"

"Absolution, father?" exclaimed Hilda, shrinking back. "Oh no, no! I never dreamed of that! Only our Heavenly Father can forgive my sins; and it is only by sincere repentance of whatever wrong I may have done, and by my own best efforts towards a higher life, that I can hope for his forgiveness! God forbid that I should ask absolution from mortal man!"

"Then, wherefore," rejoined the priest, with somewhat less mildness in his tone, — "wherefore, I ask again, have you taken possession, as I may term it, of this holy ordinance ; being a heretic, and neither seeking to share, nor having faith in, the unspeakable advantages which the Church offers to its penitents?"

"Father," answered Hilda, trying to tell the old man the simple truth, "I am a motherless girl, and a stranger here in Italy. I had only God to take care of me, and be my closest friend ; and the terrible, terrible crime, which I have revealed to you, thrust itself between him and me; so that I groped for him in the darkness, as it were, and found him not, — found nothing but a dreadful solitude, and this crime in the midst of it! I could not bear it. It seemed as if I made the awful guilt my own, by keeping it hidden in my heart. I grew a fearful thing to myself. I was going mad!"

"It was a grievous trial, my poor child!" observed the confessor. "Your relief, I trust, will prove to be greater than you yet know!"

"I feel already how immense it is!" said Hilda, looking gratefully in his face. "Surely, father, it was the hand of Providence that led me hither, and made me feel that this vast temple of Christianity, this great home of religion, must needs contain some cure, some ease, at least, for my unutterable anguish. And it has proved so. I have told the hideous secret; told it under the sacred seal of the confessional ; and now it will burn my poor heart no more!"

"But, daughter," answered the venerable priest, not unmoved by what Hilda said, "you forget! you mistake! — you claim a privilege to which you have not entitled yourself! The seal of the confessional, do you say? God forbid that it should ever be broken where it has been fairly impressed ; but it applies only to matters that have been confided to its keeping in a certain prescribed method, and by persons, moreover, who have faith in the sanctity of the ordinance. I hold myself, and any learned casuist of the Church would hold me, as free to disclose all the particulars of what you term your confession, as if they had come to my knowledge in a secular way."

"This is not right, father!" said Hilda, fixing her eyes on the old man's.

"Do not you see, child," he rejoined, with some little heat, "with all your nicety of conscience, cannot you recognize it as my duty to make the story known to the proper authorities; a great crime against public justice being involved, and further evil consequences likely to ensue?"

"No, father, no!" answered Hilda, courageously, her cheeks flushing and her eyes brightening as she spoke. "Trust a girl's simple heart sooner than any casuist of your Church, however learned he may be. Trust your own heart, too! I came to your confessional, father, as I devoutly believe, by the direct impulse of Heaven, which also brought you hither to-day, in its mercy and love, to relieve me of a torture that I could no longer bear. I trusted in the pledge which your Church has always held sacred between the priest and the human soul, which, through his medium, is struggling towards its Father above. What I have confided to you lies sacredly between God and yourself. Let it rest there, father; for this is right, and if you do otherwise, you will perpetrate a great wrong, both as a priest and a man! And, believe me, no question, no torture, shall ever force my lips to utter what would be necessary, in order to make my confession available towards the punishment of the guilty ones. Leave Providence to deal with them!"

INTERIOR OF ST. PETER'S

"My quiet little countrywoman," said the priest, with half a smile on his kindly old face, "you can pluck up a spirit, I perceive, when you fancy an occasion for one."

"I have spirit only to do what I think right," replied Hilda, simply. "In other respects I am timorous."

"But you confuse yourself between right feelings and very foolish inferences," continued the priest, "as is the wont of women, — so much I have learnt by long experience in the confessional, — be they young or old. However, to set your heart at rest, there is no probable need for me to reveal the matter. What you have told, if I mistake not, and perhaps more, is already known in the quarter which it most concerns."

"Known!" exclaimed Hilda. "Known to the authorities of Rome! And what will be the consequence?"

"Hush," answered the confessor, laying his finger on his lips. "I tell you my supposition — mind, it is no assertion of the fact — in order that you may go the more cheerfully on your way, not deeming yourself burdened with any responsibility as concerns this dark deed. And now, daughter, what have you to give in return for an old man's kindness and sympathy?"

"My grateful remembrance," said Hilda, fervently, "as long as I live!"

"And nothing more?" the priest inquired, with a persuasive smile. "Will you not reward him with a great joy; one of the last joys that he may know on earth, and a fit one to take with him into the better world? In a word, will you not allow me to bring you, as a stray lamb into the true fold? You have experienced some little taste of the relief and comfort which the Church keeps abundantly in store for all its faithful children. Come home, dear child, — poor wanderer, who hast caught a glimpse of the heavenly light, — come home, and be at rest."

"Father," said Hilda, much moved by his kindly earnestness; in which, however, genuine as it was, there might still be a leaven of professional craft, "I dare not come a step farther than Providence shall guide me. Do not let it grieve you, therefore, if I never return to the confessional; never dip my fingers in holy water; never sign my bosom with the cross. I am a daughter of the Puritans. But, in spite of my heresy," she added with a sweet, tearful smile, "you may one day see the poor girl, to whom you have done this great Christian kindness, coming to remind you of it, and thank you for it, in the Better Land."

The old priest shook his head. But, as he stretched out his hands at the same moment, in the act of bene-diction, Hilda knelt down and received the blessing with as devout a simplicity as any Catholic of them all.

CHAPTER XL.

HILDA AND A FRIEND.

WHEN Hilda knelt to receive the priest's benediction, the act was witnessed by a person who stood leaning against the marble balustrade that surrounds the hundred golden lights, before the high altar. He had stood there, indeed, from the moment of the girl's entrance into the confessional. His start of surprise, at first beholding her, and the anxious gloom that afterwards settled on his face, sufficiently betokened that he felt a deep and sad interest in what was going forward.

After Hilda had bidden the priest farewell, she came slowly towards the high altar. The individual, to whom we have alluded, seemed irresolute whether to advance or retire. His hesitation lasted so long, that the maiden, straying through a happy reverie, had crossed the wide extent of the pavement between the confessional and the altar, before he had decided whether to meet her. At last, when within a pace or two, she raised her eyes and recognized Kenyon.

" It is you ! " she exclaimed, with joyful surprise. " I am so happy."

In truth, the sculptor had never before seen, nor hardly imagined, such a figure of peaceful beatitude as Hilda now presented. While coming towards him in the solemn radiance which, at that period of the day, is diffused through the transept, and showered down beneath the dome, she seemed of the same substance as the atmosphere that enveloped her. He could scarcely tell whether she was imbued with sunshine, or whether it was a glow of happiness that shone out of her.

At all events, it was a marvellous change from the sad girl, who had entered the confessional bewildered with anguish, to this bright, yet softened image of religious consolation that emerged from it. It was as if one of the throng of angelic people, who might be hovering in the sunny depths of the dome, had alighted on the pavement. Indeed, this capability of transfiguration, which we often see wrought by inward delight on persons far less capable of it than Hilda, suggests how angels come by their beauty. It grows out of their happiness, and lasts forever only because that is immortal.

She held out her hand, and Kenyon was glad to take it in his own, if only to assure himself that she was made of earthly material.

"Yes, Hilda, I see that you are very happy," he replied, gloomily, and withdrawing his hand after a single pressure. "For me, I never was less so than at this moment."

"Has any misfortune befallen you?" asked Hilda, with earnestness. "Pray tell me, and you shall have my sympathy, though I must still be very happy. Now, I know how it is, that the saints above are touched by the sorrows of distressed people on earth, and yet are never made wretched by them. Not that I profess to be a saint, you know," she added, smiling radiantly. "But the heart grows so large, and so rich, and so variously endowed, when it has a great sense of bliss, that it can give smiles to some, and tears to others, with equal sincerity, and enjoy its own peace throughout all."

"Do not say you are no saint!" answered Kenyon, with a smile, though he felt that the tears stood in his eyes. "You will still be Saint Hilda, whatever church may canonize you."

"Ah! you would not have said so, had you seen me but an hour ago!" murmured she. "I was so wretched, that there seemed a grievous sin in it."

"And what has made you so suddenly happy?" inquired the sculptor. "But first, Hilda, will you not tell me why you were so wretched?"

"Had I met you yesterday, I might have told you that," she replied. "To-day, there is no need."

"Your happiness, then?" said the sculptor, as sadly as before. "Whence comes it?"

"A great burden has been lifted from my heart, — from my conscience, I had almost said," — answered Hilda, without shunning the glance that he fixed upon her. "I am a new creature, since this morning, Heaven be praised for it! It was a blessed hour — a blessed impulse — that brought me to this beautiful and glorious cathedral. I shall hold it in loving remembrance while I live, as the spot where I found infinite peace after infinite trouble."

Her heart seemed so full, that it spilt its new gush of happiness, as it were, like rich and sunny wine out of an over-brimming goblet. Kenyon saw that she was in one of those moods of elevated feeling, when the soul is upheld by a strange tranquillity, which is really more passionate, and less controllable, than emotions far exceeding it in violence. He felt that there would be indelicacy, if he ought not rather to call it impiety, in his stealing upon Hilda, while she was thus beyond her own guardianship, and surprising her out of secrets which she might afterwards bitterly regret betraying to him. Therefore, though yearning to know what had happened, he resolved to forbear further question.

Simple and earnest people, however, being accustomed to speak from their genuine impulses, cannot easily, as craftier men do, avoid the subject which they have at heart. As often as the sculptor unclosed his lips, such words as these were ready to burst out : —

" Hilda, have you flung your angelic purity into that mass of unspeakable corruption, the Roman Church ? "

" What were you saying ? " she asked, as Kenyon forced back an almost uttered exclamation of this kind.

" I was thinking of what you have just remarked about the cathedral," said he, looking up into the mighty hollow of the dome. " It is indeed a magnificent structure, and an adequate expression of the Faith which built it. When I behold it in a proper mood, — that is to say, when I bring my mind into a fair relation with the minds and purposes of its spiritual and material architects, — I see but one or two criticisms to make. One is, that it needs painted windows."

" Oh, no ! " said Hilda. " They would be quite inconsistent with so much richness of color in the interior of the church. Besides, it is a Gothic ornament, and only suited to that style of architecture, which requires a gorgeous dimness."

" Nevertheless," continued the sculptor, " yonder square apertures, filled with ordinary panes of glass, are quite out of keeping with the superabundant splen-

dor of everything about them. They remind me of
that portion of Aladdin's palace which he left unfinished, in order that his royal father-in-law might put
the finishing touch. Daylight, in its natural state,
ought not to be admitted here. It should stream
through a brilliant illusion of saints and hierarchies,
and old scriptural images, and symbolized dogmas,
purple, blue, golden, and a broad flame of scarlet.
Then, it would be just such an illumination as the
Catholic faith allows to its believers. But, give me
— to live and die in — the pure, white light of
heaven ! "

"Why do you look so sorrowfully at me?" asked
Hilda, quietly meeting his disturbed gaze. "What
would you say to me? I love the white light too!"

"I fancied so," answered Kenyon. "Forgive me,
Hilda ; but I must needs speak. You seemed to me a
rare mixture of impressibility, sympathy, sensitiveness
to many influences, with a certain quality of common
sense ;— no, not that, but a higher and finer attribute, for which I find no better word. However tremulously you might vibrate, this quality, I supposed,
would always bring you back to the equipoise. You
were a creature of imagination, and yet as truly a
New England girl as any with whom you grew up in
your native village. If there were one person in the
world whose native rectitude of thought, and something deeper, more reliable, than thought, I would
have trusted against all the arts of a priesthood, —
whose taste alone, so exquisite and sincere that it rose
to be a moral virtue, I would have rested upon as a
sufficient safeguard, — it was yourself ! "

"I am conscious of no such high and delicate qualities as you allow me," answered Hilda. " But what

have I done that a girl of New England birth and culture, with the right sense that her mother taught her,
and the conscience that she developed in her, should
not do?"

"Hilda, I saw you at the confessional!" said
Kenyon.

"Ah, well, my dear friend," replied Hilda casting
down her eyes, and looking somewhat confused, yet
not ashamed, "you must try to forgive me for that, —
if you deem it wrong, — because it has saved my reason, and made me very happy. Had you been here
yesterday, I would have confessed to you."

"Would to Heaven I had!" ejaculated Kenyon.

"I think," Hilda resumed, "I shall never go to the
confessional again; for there can scarcely come such
a sore trial twice in my life. If I had been a wiser
girl, a stronger, and a more sensible, very likely I
might not have gone to the confessional at all. It was
the sin of others that drove me thither; not my own,
though it almost seemed so. Being what I am, I must
either have done what you saw me doing, or have gone
mad. Would that have been better?"

"Then you are not a Catholic?" asked the sculptor,
earnestly.

"Really, I do not quite know what I am," replied
Hilda, encountering his eyes with a frank and simple
gaze. "I have a great deal of faith, and Catholicism
seems to have a great deal of good. Why should not
I be a Catholic, if I find there what I need, and what
I cannot find elsewhere? The more I see of this worship, the more I wonder at the exuberance with which
it adapts itself to all the demands of human infirmity.
If its ministers were but a little more than human,
above all error, pure from all iniquity, what a religion
would it be!"

" I need not fear your conversion to the Catholic faith," remarked Kenyon, " if you are at all aware of the bitter sarcasm implied in your last observation. It is very just. Only the exceeding ingenuity of the system stamps it as the contrivance of man, or some worse author; not an emanation of the broad and simple wisdom from on high."

"It may be so," said Hilda; " but I meant no sarcasm."

Thus conversing, the two friends went together down the grand extent of the nave. Before leaving the church, they turned to admire again its mighty breadth, the remoteness of the glory behind the altar, and the effect of visionary splendor and magnificence imparted by the long bars of smoky sunshine, which travelled so far before arriving at a place of rest.

" Thank Heaven for having brought me hither!" said Hilda, fervently.

Kenyon's mind was deeply disturbed by his idea of her Catholic propensities; and now what he deemed her disproportionate and misapplied veneration for the sublime edifice stung him into irreverence.

" The best thing I know of St. Peter's," observed he, " is its equable temperature. We are now enjoying the coolness of last winter, which, a few months hence, will be the warmth of the present summer. It has no cure, I suspect, in all its length and breadth, for a sick soul, but it would make an admirable atmospheric hospital for sick bodies. What a delightful shelter would it be for the invalids who throng to Rome, where the sirocco steals away their strength, and the tramontana stabs them through and through, like cold steel with a poisoned point! But within these walls, the thermometer never varies. Winter and summer are married at the high altar, and dwell together in perfect harmony."

"Yes," said Hilda; "and I have always felt this soft, unchanging climate of St. Peter's to be another manifestation of its sanctity."

"That is not precisely my idea," replied Kenyon. " But what a delicious life it would be, if a colony of people with delicate lungs — or merely with delicate fancies — could take up their abode in this ever-mild and tranquil air. These architectural tombs of the popes might serve for dwellings, and each brazen sepulchral doorway would become a domestic threshold. Then the lover, if he dared, might say to his mistress, ' Will you share my tomb with me ? ' and, winning her soft consent, he would lead her to the altar, and thence to yonder sepulchre of Pope Gregory, which should be their nuptial home. What a life would be theirs, Hilda, in their marble Eden ! "

"It is not kind, nor like yourself," said Hilda, gently, "to throw ridicule on emotions which are genuine. I revere this glorious church for itself and its purposes ; and love it, moreover, because here I have found sweet peace, after a great anguish."

"Forgive me," answered the sculptor, " and I will do so no more. My heart is not so irreverent as my words."

They went through the piazza of St. Peter's and the adjacent streets, silently at first ; but, before reaching the bridge of St. Angelo, Hilda's flow of spirits began to bubble forth, like the gush of a streamlet that has been shut up by frost, or by a heavy stone over its source. Kenyon had never found her so delightful as now ; so softened out of the chillness of her virgin pride ; so full of fresh thoughts, at which he was often

moved to smile, although, on turning them over a little more, he sometimes discovered that they looked
fanciful only because so absolutely true.

But, indeed, she was not quite in a normal state.
Emerging from gloom into sudden cheerfulness, the
effect upon Hilda was as if she were just now created.
After long torpor, receiving back her intellectual activity, she derived an exquisite pleasure from the use
of her faculties, which were set in motion by causes
that seemed inadequate. She continually brought to
Kenyon's mind the image of a child, making its plaything of every object, but sporting in good faith, and
with a kind of seriousness. Looking up, for example,
at the statue of St. Michael, on the top of Hadrian's
castellated tomb, Hilda fancied an interview between
the Archangel and the old emperor's ghost, who was
naturally displeased at finding his mausoleum, which
he had ordained for the stately and solemn repose of
his ashes, converted to its present purposes.

"But St. Michael, no doubt," she thoughtfully remarked, "would finally convince the Emperor Hadrian that where a warlike despot is sown as the seed,
a fortress and a prison are the only possible crop."

They stopped on the bridge to look into the swift
eddying flow of the yellow Tiber, a mud-puddle in
strenuous motion ; and Hilda wondered whether the
seven - branched golden candlestick, — the holy candlestick of the Jews, — which was lost at the Ponte
Molle, in Constantine's time, had yet been swept as
far down the river as this.

"It probably stuck where it fell," said the sculptor ;
"and, by this time, is imbedded thirty feet deep in
the mud of the Tiber. Nothing will ever bring it to
light again."

"I fancy you are mistaken," replied Hilda, smiling. "There was a meaning and purpose in each of its seven branches, and such a candlestick cannot be lost forever. When it is found again, and seven lights are kindled and burning in it, the whole world will gain the illumination which it needs. Would not this be an admirable idea for a mystic story or parable, or seven-branched allegory, full of poetry, art, philosophy, and religion? It shall be called 'The Recovery of the Sacred Candlestick.' As each branch is lighted, it shall have a differently colored lustre from the other six; and when all the seven are kindled, their radiance shall combine into the intense white light of truth."

"Positively, Hilda, this is a magnificent conception," cried Kenyon. "The more I look at it, the brighter it burns."

"I think so too," said Hilda, enjoying a childlike pleasure in her own idea. "The theme is better suited for verse than prose; and when I go home to America, I will suggest it to one of our poets. Or, seven poets might write the poem together, each lighting a separate branch of the Sacred Candlestick."

"Then you think of going home?" Kenyon asked.

"Only yesterday," she replied, "I longed to flee away. Now, all is changed, and, being happy again, I should feel deep regret at leaving the Pictorial Land. But, I cannot tell. In Rome, there is something dreary and awful, which we can never quite escape. At least, I thought so yesterday."

When they reached the Via Portoghese, and approached Hilda's tower, the doves, who were waiting aloft, flung themselves upon the air, and came floating down about her head. The girl caressed them, and

responded to their cooings with similar sounds from
her own lips, and with words of endearment; and
their joyful flutterings and airy little flights, evidently
impelled by pure exuberance of spirits, seemed to
show that the doves had a real sympathy with their
mistress's state of mind. For peace had descended
upon her like a dove.

Bidding the sculptor farewell, Hilda climbed her
tower, and came forth upon its summit to trim the
Virgin's lamp. The doves, well knowing her custom,
had flown up thither to meet her, and again hovered
about her head; and very lovely was her aspect, in
the evening sunlight, which had little further to do
with the world, just then, save to fling a golden glory
on Hilda's hair, and vanish.

Turning her eyes down into the dusky street which
she had just quitted, Hilda saw the sculptor still
there, and waved her hand to him.

" How sad and dim he looks, down there in that
dreary street ! " she said to herself. " Something
weighs upon his spirits. Would I could comfort
him ! "

" How like a spirit she looks, aloft there, with the
evening glory round her head, and those winged creatures claiming her as akin to them ! " thought Kenyon, on his part. " How far above me ! how unattainable ! Ah, if I could lift myself to her region !
Or, — if it be not a sin to wish it, — would that I
might draw her down to an earthly fireside ! "

What a sweet reverence is that, when a young man
deems his mistress a little more than mortal, and almost chides himself for longing to bring her close to
his heart ! A trifling circumstance, but such as lovers
make much of, gave him hope. One of the doves,

which had been resting on Hilda's shoulder, suddenly flew downward, as if recognizing him as its mistress's dear friend; and, perhaps commissioned with an errand of regard, brushed his upturned face with its wings, and again soared aloft.

The sculptor watched the bird's return, and saw Hilda greet it with a smile.

CHAPTER XLI.

IT being still considerably earlier than the period at
which artists and tourists are accustomed to assemble
in Rome, the sculptor and Hilda found themselves
comparatively alone there. The dense mass of native
Roman life, in the midst of which they were, served
to press them near one another. It was as if they had
been thrown together on a desert island. Or, they
seemed to have wandered, by some strange chance, out
of the common world, and encountered each other in
a depopulated city, where there were streets of lonely
palaces, and unreckonable treasures of beautiful and
admirable things, of which they two became the sole
inheritors.

In such circumstances, Hilda's gentle reserve must
have been stronger than her kindly disposition permitted, if the friendship between Kenyon and herself
had not grown as warm as a maiden's friendship can
ever be, without absolutely and avowedly blooming into
love. On the sculptor's side, the amaranthine flower
was already in full blow. But it is very beautiful,
though the lover's heart may grow chill at the perception, to see how the snow will sometimes linger in a
virgin's breast, even after the spring is well advanced.
In such alpine soils, the summer will not be anticipated ; we seek vainly for passionate flowers, and blossoms of fervid hue and spicy fragrance, finding only

snow-drops and sunless violets, when it is almost the full season for the crimson rose.

With so much tenderness as Hilda had in her nature, it was strange that she so reluctantly admitted the idea of love ; especially, as, in the sculptor, she found both congeniality and variety of taste, and likenesses and differences of character ; these being as essential as those to any poignancy of mutual emotion.

So Hilda, as far as Kenyon could discern, still did not love him, though she admitted him within the quiet circle of her affections as a dear friend and trusty counsellor. If we knew what is best for us, or could be content with what is reasonably good, the sculptor might well have been satisfied, for a season, with this calm intimacy, which so sweetly kept him a stranger in her heart, and a ceremonious guest ; and yet allowed him the free enjoyment of all but its deeper recesses. The flowers that grow outside of those minor sanctities have a wild, hasty charm, which it is well to prove ; there may be sweeter ones within the sacred precinct, but none that will die while you are handling them, and bequeath you a delicious legacy, as these do, in the perception of their evanescence and unreality.

And this may be the reason, after all, why Hilda, like so many other maidens, lingered on the hither side of passion ; her finer instinct and keener sensibility made her enjoy those pale delights in a degree of which men are incapable. She hesitated to grasp a richer happiness, as possessing already such measure of it as her heart could hold, and of a quality most agreeable to her virgin tastes.

Certainly, they both were very happy. Kenyon's genius, unconsciously wrought upon by Hilda's influence, took a more delicate character than heretofore.

He modelled, among other things, a beautiful little statue of maidenhood gathering a snow-drop. It was never put into marble, however, because the sculptor soon recognized it as one of those fragile creations which are true only to the moment that produces them, and are wronged if we try to imprison their airy excellence in a permanent material.

On her part, Hilda returned to her customary occupations with a fresh love for them, and yet with a deeper look into the heart of things ; such as those necessarily acquire who have passed from picture galleries into dungeon gloom, and thence come back to the picture gallery again. It is questionable whether she was ever so perfect a copyist thenceforth. She could not yield herself up to the painter so unreservedly as in times past ; her character had developed a sturdier quality, which made her less pliable to the influence of other minds. She saw into the picture as profoundly as ever, and perhaps more so, but not with the devout sympathy that had formerly given her entire possession of the old master's idea. She had known such a reality, that it taught her to distinguish inevitably the large portion that is unreal, in every work of art. Instructed by sorrow, she felt that there is something beyond almost all which pictorial genius has produced ; and she never forgot those sad wanderings from gallery to gallery, and from church to church, where she had vainly sought a type of the Virgin Mother, or the Saviour, or saint, or martyr, which a soul in extreme need might recognize as the adequate one.

How, indeed, should she have found such ? How could holiness be revealed to the artist of an age when the greatest of them put genius and imagination in the place of spiritual insight, and when, from the pope downward, all Christendom was corrupt?

Meanwhile, months wore away, and Rome received back that large portion of its life-blood which runs in the veins of its foreign and temporary population. English visitors established themselves in the hotels, and in all the sunny suites of apartments, in the streets convenient to the Piazza di Spagna; the English tongue was heard familiarly along the Corso, and English children sported in the Pincian Gardens.

The native Romans, on the other hand, like the butterflies and grasshoppers, resigned themselves to the short, sharp misery which winter brings to a people whose arrangements are made almost exclusively with a view to summer. Keeping no fire within-doors, except possibly a spark or two in the kitchen, they crept out of their cheerless houses into the narrow, sunless, sepulchral streets, bringing their firesides along with them, in the shape of little earthen pots, vases, or pipkins, full of lighted charcoal and warm ashes, over which they held their tingling finger-ends. Even in this half-torpid wretchedness, they still seemed to dread a pestilence in the sunshine, and kept on the shady side of the piazzas, as scrupulously as in summer. Through the open doorways — no need to shut them when the weather within was bleaker than without — a glimpse into the interior of their dwellings showed the uncarpeted brick floors, as dismal as the pavement of a tomb.

They drew their old cloaks about them, nevertheless, and threw the corners over their shoulders, with the dignity of attitude and action that have come down to these modern citizens, as their sole inheritance from the togated nation. Somehow or other, they managed to keep up their poor, frost-bitten hearts against the pitiless atmosphere with a quiet and un-complaining endurance that really seems the most re-spectable point in the present Roman character. For, in New England, or in Russia, or scarcely in a hut of the Esquimaux, there is no such discomfort to be borne as by Romans in wintry weather, when the orange-trees bear icy fruit in the gardens ; and when the rims of all the fountains are shaggy with icicles, and the Fountain of Trevi skimmed almost across with a glassy surface ; and when there is a slide in the piazza of St. Peter's, and a fringe of brown, frozen foam along the eastern shore of the Tiber, and some-times a fall of great snow-flakes into the dreary lanes and alleys of the miserable city. Cold blasts, that bring death with them, now blow upon the shivering invalids, who came hither in the hope of breathing balmy airs.

Wherever we pass our summers, may all our in-clement months, from November to April, henceforth be spent in some country that recognizes winter as an integral portion of its year !

Now, too, there was especial discomfort in the stately picture galleries, where nobody, indeed, — not the princely or priestly founders, nor any who have in-herited their cheerless magnificence, — ever dreamed of such an impossibility as fireside warmth, since those great palaces were built. Hilda, therefore, find-ing her fingers so much benumbed that the spiritual influence could not be transmitted to them, was per-suaded to leave her easel before a picture, on one of these wintry days, and pay a visit to Kenyon's studio. But neither was the studio anything better than a dis-mal den, with its marble shapes shivering around the

walls, cold as the snow-images which the sculptor used
to model in his boyhood, and sadly behold them weep
themselves away at the first thaw.

Kenyon's Roman artisans, all this while, had been
at work on the Cleopatra. The fierce Egyptian queen
had now struggled almost out of the imprisoning stone;
or, rather, the workmen had found her within the mass
of marble, imprisoned there by magic, but still fervid
to the touch with fiery life, the fossil woman of an age
that produced statelier, stronger, and more passionate
creatures than our own. You already felt her compressed heat, and were aware of a tiger-like character
even in her repose. If Octavius should make his appearance, though the marble still held her within its
embrace, it was evident that she would tear herself
forth in a twinkling, either to spring enraged at his
throat, or, sinking into his arms, to make one more
proof of her rich blandishments, or, falling lowly at
his feet, to try the efficacy of a woman's tears.

" I am ashamed to tell you how much I admire this
statue," said Hilda. " No other sculptor could have
done it."

" This is very sweet for me to hear," replied Kenyon; " and since your reserve keeps you from saying
more, I shall imagine you expressing everything that
an artist would wish to hear said about his work."

" You will not easily go beyond my genuine opinion," answered Hilda, with a smile.

" Ah, your kind word makes me very happy," said
the sculptor, " and I need it, just now, on behalf of
my Cleopatra. That inevitable period has come, —
for I have found it inevitable, in regard to all my
works, — when I look at what I fancied to be a statue,
lacking only breath to make it live, and find it a mere

lump of senseless stone, into which I have not really succeeded in moulding the spiritual part of my idea. I should like, now, — only it would be such shameful treatment for a discrowned queen, and my own off-spring too, — I should like to hit poor Cleopatra a bit-ter blow on her Egyptian nose with this mallet."

"That is a blow which all statues seem doomed to receive, sooner or later, though seldom from the hand that sculptured them," said Hilda, laughing. "But you must not let yourself be too much disheartened by the decay of your faith in what you produce. I have heard a poet express similar distaste for his own most exquisite poem, and I am afraid that this final despair, and sense of short-coming, must always be the reward and punishment of those who try to grapple with a great or beautiful idea. It only proves that you have been able to imagine things too high for mortal facul-ties to execute. The idea leaves you an imperfect image of itself, which you at first mistake for the ethereal reality, but soon find that the latter has es-caped out of your closest embrace."

"And the only consolation is," remarked Kenyon, "that the blurred and imperfect image may still make a very respectable appearance in the eyes of those who have not seen the original."

"More than that," rejoined Hilda; "for there is a class of spectators whose sympathy will help them to see the perfect through a mist of imperfection. No-body, I think, ought to read poetry, or look at pic-tures or statues, who cannot find a great deal more in them than the poet or artist has actually expressed. Their highest merit is suggestiveness."

"You, Hilda, are yourself the only critic in whom I have much faith," said Kenyon. "Had you con-demned Cleopatra, nothing should have saved her."

" You invest me with such an awful responsibility," she replied, " that I shall not dare to say a single word about your other works."

" At least," said the sculptor, " tell me whether you recognize this bust ? "

He pointed to a bust of Donatello. It was not the one which Kenyon had begun to model at Monte Beni, but a reminiscence of the Count's face, wrought under the influence of all the sculptor's knowledge of his history, and of his personal and hereditary character. It stood on a wooden pedestal, not nearly finished, but with fine white dust and small chips of marble scattered about it, and itself incrusted all round with the white, shapeless substance of the block. In the midst appeared the features, lacking sharpness, and very much resembling a fossil countenance, — but we have already used this simile, in reference to Cleopatra, — with the accumulations of long-past ages clinging to it.

And yet, strange to say, the face had an expression, and a more recognizable one than Kenyon had succeeded in putting into the clay model at Monte Beni. The reader is probably acquainted with Thorwaldsen's three-fold analogy, — the clay model, the Life; the plaster cast, the Death ; and the sculptured marble, the Resurrection, — and it seemed to be made good by the spirit that was kindling up these imperfect features, like a lambent flame.

" I was not quite sure, at first glance, that I knew the face, " observed Hilda ; " the likeness surely is not a striking one. There is a good deal of external resemblance, still, to the features of the Faun of Praxiteles, between whom and Donatello, you know, we once insisted that there was a perfect twin-brotherhood. But the expression is now so very different ! "

" What do you take it to be?" asked the sculptor.

" I hardly know how to define it," she answered. " But it has an effect as if I could see this countenance gradually brightening while I look at it. It gives the impression of a growing intellectual power and moral sense. Donatello's face used to evince little more than a genial, pleasurable sort of vivacity, and capability of enjoyment. But, here, a soul is being breathed into him; it is the Faun, but advancing towards a state of higher development."

" Hilda, do you see all this?" exclaimed Kenyon, in considerable surprise. " I may have had such an idea in my mind, but was quite unaware that I had succeeded in conveying it into the marble."

" Forgive me," said Hilda, " but I question whether this striking effect has been brought about by any skill or purpose on the sculptor's part. Is it not, perhaps, the chance result of the bust being just so far shaped out, in the marble, as the process of moral growth had advanced in the original? A few more strokes of the chisel might change the whole expression, and so spoil it for what it is now worth."

" I believe you are right," answered Kenyon, thoughtfully examining his work; " and, strangely enough, it was the very expression that I tried unsuccessfully to produce in the clay model. Well; not another chip shall be struck from the marble."

And, accordingly, Donatello's bust (like that rude, rough mass of the head of Brutus, by Michael Angelo, at Florence) has ever since remained in an unfinished state. Most spectators mistake it for an unsuccessful attempt towards copying the features of the Faun of Praxiteles. One observer in a thousand is conscious of something more, and lingers long over this mysteri-

ous face, departing from it reluctantly, and with many
a glance thrown backward. What perplexes him is
the riddle that he sees propounded there ; the riddle
of the soul's growth, taking its first impulse amid remorse and pain, and struggling through the incrusta-
tions of the senses. It was the contemplation of this
imperfect portrait of Donatello that originally interested us in his history, and impelled us to elicit from
Kenyon what he knew of his friend's adventures.

CHAPTER XLII.

REMINISCENCES OF MIRIAM.

WHEN Hilda and himself turned away from the unfinished bust, the sculptor's mind still dwelt upon the reminiscences which it suggested.

"You have not seen Donatello recently," he remarked, "and therefore cannot be aware how sadly he is changed."

"No wonder!" exclaimed Hilda, growing pale.

The terrible scene which she had witnessed, when Donatello's face gleamed out in so fierce a light, came back upon her memory, almost for the first time since she knelt at the confessional. Hilda, as is sometimes the case with persons whose delicate organization requires a peculiar safeguard, had an elastic faculty of throwing off such recollections as would be too painful for endurance. The first shock of Donatello's and Miriam's crime had, indeed, broken through the frail defence of this voluntary forgetfulness; but, once enabled to relieve herself of the ponderous anguish over which she had so long brooded, she had practised a subtile watchfulness in preventing its return.

"No wonder, do you say?" repeated the sculptor, looking at her with interest, but not exactly with surprise; for he had long suspected that Hilda had a painful knowledge of events which he himself little more than surmised. "Then you know! — you have heard! But what can you possibly have heard, and through what channel?"

" Nothing ! " replied Hilda, faintly.   " Not one
word has reached my ears from the lips of any human being.   Let us never speak of it again ! No, no !
never again ! "

"And Miriam ! " said Kenyon, with irrepressible interest.   " Is it also forbidden to speak of her ? "

" Hush ! do not even utter her name ! Try not to
think of it ! " Hilda whispered.   " It may bring terrible consequences ! "

" My dear Hilda ! " exclaimed Kenyon, regarding
her with wonder and deep sympathy.   " My sweet
friend, have you had this secret hidden in your delicate, maidenly heart, through all these many months !
No wonder that your life was withering out of you."

" It was so, indeed ! " said Hilda, shuddering.
" Even now, I sicken at the recollection."

" And how could it have come to your knowledge ? "
continued the sculptor.   " But, no matter ? Do not
torture yourself with referring to the subject.   Only,
if at any time it should be a relief to you, remember
that we can speak freely together, for Miriam has herself suggested a confidence between us."

" Miriam has suggested this ! " exclaimed Hilda.
" Yes, I remember, now, her advising that the secret
should be shared with you.   But I have survived the
death-struggle that it cost me, and need make no further revelations.   And Miriam has spoken to you !
What manner of woman can she be, who, after sharing in such a deed, can make it a topic of conversation
with her friends ? "

" Ah, Hilda," replied Kenyon, " you do not know,
for you could never learn it from your own heart,
which is all purity and rectitude, what a mixture of
good there may be in things evil ; and how the great-

est criminal, if you look at his conduct from his own point of view, or from any side-point, may seem not so unquestionably guilty, after all. So with Miriam; so with Donatello. They are, perhaps, partners in what we must call awful guilt; and yet, I will own to you, — when I think of the original cause, the motives, the feelings, the sudden concurrence of circumstances thrusting them onward, the urgency of the moment, and the sublime unselfishness on either part, — I know not well how to distinguish it from much that the world calls heroism. Might we not render some such verdict as this? — 'Worthy of Death, but not unworthy of Love!'"

"Never!" answered Hilda, looking at the matter through the clear crystal medium of her own integrity. "This thing, as regards its causes, is all a mystery to me, and must remain so. But there is, I believe, only one right and one wrong; and I do not understand, and may God keep me from ever understanding, how two things so totally unlike can be mistaken for one another; nor how two mortal foes, as Right and Wrong surely are, can work together in the same deed. This is my faith; and I should be led astray, if you could persuade me to give it up."

"Alas for poor human nature, then!" said Kenyon, sadly, and yet half smiling at Hilda's unworldly and impracticable theory. "I always felt you, my dear friend, a terribly severe judge, and have been perplexed to conceive how such tender sympathy could coexist with the remorselessness of a steel blade. You need no mercy, and therefore know not how to show any."

"That sounds like a bitter gibe," said Hilda, with the tears springing into her eyes. "But I cannot help it. It does not alter my perception of the truth. If there be any such dreadful mixture of good and evil as you affirm, — and which appears to me almost more shocking than pure evil, — then the good is turned to poison, not the evil to wholesomeness."

The sculptor seemed disposed to say something more, but yielded to the gentle steadfastness with which Hilda declined to listen. She grew very sad ; for a reference to this one dismal topic had set, as it were, a prison-door ajar, and allowed a throng of torturing recollections to escape from their dungeons into the pure air and white radiance of her soul. She bade Kenyon a briefer farewell than ordinary, and went homeward to her tower.

In spite of her efforts to withdraw them to other subjects, her thoughts dwelt upon Miriam ; and, as had not heretofore happened, they brought with them a painful doubt whether a wrong had not been committed on Hilda's part, towards the friend once so beloved. Something that Miriam had said, in their final conversation, recurred to her memory, and seemed now to deserve more weight than Hilda had assigned to it, in her horror at the crime just perpetrated. It was not that the deed looked less wicked and terrible in the retrospect; but she asked herself whether there were not other questions to be considered, aside from that single one of Miriam's guilt or innocence ; as, for example, whether a close bond of friendship, in which we once voluntarily engage, ought to be severed on account of any unworthiness, which we subsequently detect in our friend. For, in these unions of hearts, — call them marriage, or whatever else, — we take each other for better for worse. Availing ourselves of our friend's intimate affection, we pledge our own, as to be relied upon in every emergency. And what sadder, more desperate emergency could there be, than had befallen Miriam ? Who more need the tender succor of the innocent, than wretches stained with guilt ! And must a selfish care for the spotlessness of our own garments keep us from pressing the guilty ones close to our hearts, wherein, for the very reason that we are innocent, lies their securest refuge from further ill ?

It was a sad thing for Hilda to find this moral enigma propounded to her conscience ; and to feel that, whichever way she might settle it, there would be a cry of wrong on the other side. Still, the idea stubbornly came back, that the tie between Miriam and herself had been real, the affection true, and that therefore the implied compact was not to be shaken off.

"Miriam loved me well," thought Hilda, remorsefully, "and I failed her at her sorest need."

Miriam loved her well ; and not less ardent had been the affection which Miriam's warm, tender, and generous characteristics had excited in Hilda's more reserved and quiet nature. It had never been extinguished ; for, in part, the wretchedness which Hilda had since endured was but the struggle and writhing of her sensibility, still yearning towards her friend. And now, at the earliest encouragement, it awoke again, and cried out piteously, complaining of the violence that had been done it.

Recurring to the delinquencies of which she fancied (we say " fancied," because we do not unhesitatingly adopt Hilda's present view, but rather suppose her misled by her feelings) — of which she fancied herself guilty towards her friend, she suddenly remembered a sealed packet that Miriam had confided to her. It

had been put into her hands with earnest injunctions
of secrecy and care, and if unclaimed after a certain
period, was to be delivered according to its address.
Hilda had forgotten it; or, rather, she had kept the
thought of this commission in the background of her
consciousness, with all other thoughts referring to
Miriam.

But now the recollection of this packet, and the evident stress which Miriam laid upon its delivery at the
specified time, impelled Hilda to hurry up the staircase of her tower, dreading lest the period should
already have elapsed.

No; the hour had not gone by, but was on the very
point of passing. Hilda read the brief note of instruction, on a corner of the envelope, and discovered,
that, in case of Miriam's absence from Rome, the
packet was to be taken to its destination that very
day.

" How nearly I had violated my promise ! " said
Hilda. " And, since we are separated forever, it has
the sacredness of an injunction from a dead friend.
There is no time to be lost."

So Hilda set forth in the decline of the afternoon,
and pursued her way towards the quarter of the city
in which stands the Palazzo Cenci. Her habit of self-
reliance was so simply strong, so natural, and now so
well established by long use, that the idea of peril seldom or never occurred to Hilda, in her lonely life.

She differed, in this particular, from the generality
of her sex; although the customs and character of her
native land often produce women who meet the world
with gentle fearlessness, and discover that its terrors
have been absurdly exaggerated by the tradition of
mankind. In ninety-nine cases out of a hundred, the

apprehensiveness of women is quite gratuitous. Even as matters now stand, they are really safer in perilous situations and emergencies than men ; and might be still more so, if they trusted themselves more confidingly to the chivalry of manhood. In all her wanderings about Rome, Hilda had gone and returned as securely as she had been accustomed to tread the familiar street of her New England village, where every face wore a look of recognition. With respect to whatever was evil, foul, and ugly, in this populous and corrupt city, she trod as if invisible, and not only so, but blind. She was altogether unconscious of anything wicked that went along the same pathway, but without jostling or impeding her, any more than gross substance hinders the wanderings of a spirit. Thus it is, that, bad as the world is said to have grown, innocence continues to make a paradise around itself, and keep it still unfallen.

Hilda's present expedition led her into what was — physically, at least — the foulest and ugliest part of Rome. In that vicinity lies the Ghetto, where thousands of Jews are crowded within a narrow compass, and lead a close, unclean, and multitudinous life, resembling that of maggots when they over-populate a decaying cheese.

Hilda passed on the borders of this region, but had no occasion to step within it. Its neighborhood, however, naturally partook of characteristics like its own. There was a confusion of black and hideous houses, piled massively out of the ruins of former ages; rude and destitute of plan, as a pauper would build his hovel, and yet displaying here and there an arched gateway, a cornice, a pillar, or a broken arcade, that might have adorned a palace. Many of the houses, indeed, as they stood, might once have been palaces, and possessed still a squalid kind of grandeur. Dirt was everywhere, strewing the narrow streets, and incrusting the tall shabbiness of the edifices, from the foundations to the roofs; it lay upon the thresholds, and looked out of the windows, and assumed the guise of human life in the children that seemed to be engendered out of it. Their father was the sun, and their mother — a heap of Roman mud.

It is a question of speculative interest, whether the ancient Romans were as unclean a people as we everywhere find those who have succeeded them. There appears to be a kind of malignant spell in the spots that have been inhabited by these masters of the world, or made famous in their history; an inherited and inalienable curse, impelling their successors to fling dirt and defilement upon whatever temple, column, ruined palace, or triumphal arch may be nearest at hand, and on every monument that the old Romans built. It is most probably a classic trait, regularly transmitted downward, and perhaps a little modified by the better civilization of Christianity; so that Cæsar may have trod narrower and filthier ways in his path to the Capitol, than even those of modern Rome.

As the paternal abode of Beatricé, the gloomy old palace of the Cencis had an interest for Hilda, although not sufficiently strong, hitherto, to overcome the disheartening effect of the exterior, and draw her over its threshold. The adjacent piazza, of poor aspect, contained only an old woman selling roasted chestnuts and baked squash-seeds; she looked sharply at Hilda, and inquired whether she had lost her way.

" No," said Hilda; " I seek the Palazzo Cenci."

"Yonder it is, fair signorina," replied the Roman matron. "If you wish that packet delivered, which I see in your hand, my grandson Pietro shall run with it for a baiocco. The Cenci palace is a spot of ill-omen for young maidens."

Hilda thanked the old dame, but alleged the necessity of doing her errand in person. She approached the front of the palace, which, with all its immensity, had but a mean appearance, and seemed an abode which the lovely shade of Beatrice would not be apt to haunt, unless her doom made it inevitable. Some soldiers stood about the portal, and gazed at the brown-haired, fair-cheeked Anglo-Saxon girl, with approving glances, but not indecorously. Hilda began to ascend the staircase, three lofty flights of which were to be surmounted, before reaching the door whither she was bound.

CHAPTER XLIII.

BETWEEN Hilda and the sculptor there had been a kind of half-expressed understanding, that both were to visit the galleries of the Vatican the day subsequent to their meeting at the studio. Kenyon, accordingly, failed not to be there, and wandered through the vast ranges of apartments, but saw nothing of his expected friend. The marble faces, which stand innumerable along the walls, and have kept themselves so calm through the vicissitudes of twenty centuries, had no sympathy for his disappointment; and he, on the other hand, strode past these treasures and marvels of antique art, with the indifference which any preoccupation of the feelings is apt to produce, in reference to objects of sculpture. Being of so cold and pure a substance, and mostly deriving their vitality more from thought than passion, they require to be seen through a perfectly transparent medium.

And, moreover, Kenyon had counted so much upon Hilda's delicate perceptions in enabling him to look at two or three of the statues, about which they had talked together, that the entire purpose of his visit was defeated by her absence. It is a delicious sort of mutual aid, when the united power of two sympathetic, yet dissimilar, intelligences is brought to bear upon a poem by reading it aloud, or upon a picture or statue by viewing it in each other's company. Even if not

a word of criticism be uttered, the insight of either
party is wonderfully deepened, and the comprehension
broadened ; so that the inner mystery of a work of
genius, hidden from one, will often reveal itself to two.
Missing such help, Kenyon saw nothing at the Vatican
which he had not seen a thousand times before, and
more perfectly than now.

In the chill of his disappointment, he suspected that
it was a very cold art to which he had devoted himself. He questioned, at that moment, whether sculpture really ever softens and warms the material which
it handles ; whether carved marble is anything but
limestone, after all ; and whether the Apollo Belvedere itself possesses any merit above its physical
beauty, or is beyond criticism even in that generally
acknowledged excellence. In flitting glances, heretofore, he had seemed to behold this statue, as something ethereal and godlike, but not now.

Nothing pleased him, unless it were the group of
the Laocoön, which, in its immortal agony, impressed
Kenyon as a type of the long, fierce struggle of man,
involved in the knotted entanglements of Error and
Evil, those two snakes, which, if no divine help inter-
vene, will be sure to strangle him and his children in
the end. What he most admired was the strange
calmness diffused through this bitter strife; so that it
resembled the rage of the sea made calm by its immensity, or the tumult of Niagara which ceases to be
tumult because it lasts forever. Thus, in the Laocoön,
the horror of a moment grew to be the fate of interminable ages. Kenyon looked upon the group as the
one triumph of sculpture, creating the repose, which
is essential to it, in the very acme of turbulent effort ;
but, in truth, it was his mood of unwonted despon-

dency that made him so sensitive to the terrible magnificence, as well as to the sad moral, of this work.
Hilda herself could not have helped him to see it with
nearly such intelligence.

A good deal more depressed than the nature of the
disappointment warranted, Kenyon went to his studio,
and took in hand a great lump of clay. He soon
found, however, that his plastic cunning had departed
from him for the time. So he wandered forth again
into the uneasy streets of Rome, and walked up and
down the Corso, where, at that period of the day, a
throng of passers-by and loiterers choked up the narrow sidewalk. A penitent was thus brought in contact with the sculptor.

It was a figure in a white robe, with a kind of fea-
tureless mask over the face, through the apertures of
which the eyes threw an unintelligible light. Such
odd, questionable shapes are often seen gliding through
the streets of Italian cities, and are understood to be
usually persons of rank, who quit their palaces, their
gayeties, their pomp, and pride, and assume the penitential garb for a season, with a view of thus expiat-
ing some crime, or atoning for the aggregate of petty
sins that make up a worldly life. It is their custom
to ask alms, and perhaps to measure the duration of
their penance by the time requisite to accumulate a
sum of money out of the little droppings of individual
charity. The avails are devoted to some beneficent or
religious purpose; so that the benefit accruing to their
own souls is, in a manner, linked with a good done,
or intended, to their fellow-men. These figures have
a ghastly and startling effect, not so much from any
very impressive peculiarity in the garb, as from the
mystery which they bear about with them, and the

THE LAOCOÖN

sense that there is an acknowledged sinfulness as the nucleus of it.

In the present instance, however, the penitent asked no alms of Kenyon; although, for the space of a minute or two, they stood face to face, the hollow eyes of the mask encountering the sculptor's gaze. But, just as the crowd was about to separate them, the former spoke, in a voice not unfamiliar to Kenyon, though rendered remote and strange by the guilty veil through which it penetrated.

" Is all well with you, Signore ? " inquired the penitent, out of the cloud in which he walked.

" All is well," answered Kenyon. " And with you?"

But the masked penitent returned no answer, being borne away by the pressure of the throng.

The sculptor stood watching the figure, and was almost of a mind to hurry after him and follow up the conversation that had been begun; but it occurred to him that there is a sanctity (or, as we might rather term it, an inviolable etiquette) which prohibits the recognition of persons who choose to walk under the veil of penitence.

" How strange ! " thought Kenyon to himself. " It was surely Donatello ! What can bring him to Rome, where his recollections must be so painful, and his presence not without peril ? And Miriam ! Can she have accompanied him ? "

He walked on, thinking of the vast change in Donatello, since those days of gayety and innocence, when the young Italian was new in Rome, and was just beginning to be sensible of a more poignant felicity than he had yet experienced, in the sunny warmth of Miriam's smile. The growth of a soul, which the sculptor half imagined that he had witnessed in his

friend, seemed hardly worth the heavy price that it
had cost, in the sacrifice of those simple enjoyments
that were gone forever. A creature of antique health-
fulness had vanished from the earth; and, in his
stead, there was only one other morbid and remorseful man, among millions that were cast in the same
indistinguishable mould.

The accident of thus meeting Donatello — the glad
Faun of his imagination and memory, now transformed
into a gloomy penitent — contributed to deepen the
cloud that had fallen over Kenyon's spirits. It caused
him to fancy, as we generally do, in the petty troubles
which extend not a hand's-breadth beyond our own
sphere, that the whole world was saddening around
him. It took the sinister aspect of an omen, although
he could not distinctly see what trouble it might fore-
bode.

If it had not been for a peculiar sort of pique, with
which lovers are much conversant, a preposterous
kind of resentment which endeavors to wreak itself on
the beloved object, and on one's own heart, in requital
of mishaps for which neither is in fault, Kenyon
might at once have betaken himself to Hilda's studio, and asked why the appointment was not kept.
But the interview of to-day was to have been so rich
in present joy, and its results so important to his future life, that the bleak failure was too much for his
equanimity. He was angry with poor Hilda, and cen-
sured her without a hearing; angry with himself, too,
and therefore inflicted on this latter criminal the se-
verest penalty in his power; angry with the day that
was passing over him, and would not permit its latter hours to redeem the disappointment of the morning.

To confess the truth, it had been the sculptor's purpose to stake all his hopes on that interview in the galleries of the Vatican. Straying with Hilda through those long vistas of ideal beauty, he meant, at last, to utter himself upon that theme which lovers are fain to discuss in village lanes, in wood-paths, on sea-side sands, in crowded streets; it little matters where, indeed, since roses are sure to blush along the way, and daisies and violets to spring beneath the feet, if the spoken word be graciously received. He was resolved to make proof whether the kindness that Hilda evinced for him was the precious token of an individual preference, or merely the sweet fragrance of her disposition, which other friends might share as largely as himself. He would try if it were possible to take this shy, yet frank, and innocently fearless creature captive, and imprison her in his heart, and make her sensible of a wider freedom there, than in all the world besides.

It was hard, we must allow, to see the shadow of a wintry sunset falling upon a day that was to have been so bright, and to find himself just where yesterday had left him, only with a sense of being drearily balked, and defeated without an opportunity for struggle. So much had been anticipated from these now vanished hours, that it seemed as if no other day could bring back the same golden hopes.

In a case like this, it is doubtful whether Kenyon could have done a much better thing than he actually did, by going to dine at the Café Nuovo, and drinking a flask of Montefiascone; longing, the while, for a beaker or two of Donatello's Sunshine. It would have been just the wine to cure a lover's melancholy, by illuminating his heart with tender light and warmth, and suggestions of undefined hopes, too ethereal for his morbid humor to examine and reject them.

No decided improvement resulting from the draught of Montefiascone, he went to the Teatro Argentino, and sat gloomily to see an Italian comedy, which ought to have cheered him somewhat, being full of glancing merriment, and effective over everybody's risibilities except his own. The sculptor came out, however, before the close of the performance, as disconsolate as he went in.

As he made his way through the complication of narrow streets, which perplex that portion of the city, a carriage passed him. It was driven rapidly, but not too fast for the light of a gas-lamp to flare upon a face within; especially as it was bent forward, appearing to recognize him, while a beckoning hand was protruded from the window. On his part, Kenyon at once knew the face, and hastened to the carriage, which had now stopped.

"Miriam! you in Rome?" he exclaimed. "And your friends know nothing of it?"

"Is all well with you?" she asked.

This inquiry, in the identical words which Donatello had so recently addressed to him, from beneath the penitent's mask, startled the sculptor. Either the previous disquietude of his mind, or some tone in Miriam's voice, or the unaccountableness of beholding her there at all, made it seem ominous.

"All is well, I believe," answered he, doubtfully. "I am aware of no misfortune. Have you any to announce?"

He looked still more earnestly at Miriam, and felt a dreamy uncertainty whether it was really herself to whom he spoke. True; there were those beautiful features, the contour of which he had studied too often, and with a sculptor's accuracy of perception, to be in any doubt that it was Miriam's identical face. But he was conscious of a change, the nature of which he could not satisfactorily define; it might be merely her dress, which, imperfect as the light was, he saw to be richer than the simple garb that she had usually worn. The effect, he fancied, was partly owing to a gem which she had on her bosom; not a diamond, but something that glimmered with a clear, red lustre, like the stars in a southern sky. Somehow or other, this colored light seemed an emanation of herself, as if all that was passionate and glowing, in her native disposition, had crystallized upon her breast, and were just now scintillating more brilliantly than ever, in sympathy with some emotion of her heart.

Of course there could be no real doubt that it was Miriam, his artist friend, with whom and Hilda he had spent so many pleasant and familiar hours, and whom he had last seen at Perugia, bending with Donatello beneath the bronze pope's benediction. It must be that self-same Miriam; but the sensitive sculptor felt a difference of manner, which impressed him more than he conceived it possible to be affected by so external a thing. He remembered the gossip so prevalent in Rome on Miriam's first appearance; how that she was no real artist, but the daughter of an illustrious or golden lineage, who was merely playing at necessity; mingling with human struggle for her pastime; stepping out of her native sphere only for an interlude, just as a princess might alight from her gilded equipage to go on foot through a rustic lane. And now, after a mask in which love and death had performed their several parts, she had resumed her proper character.

" Have you anything to tell me ? " cried he, impatiently ; for nothing causes a more disagreeable vibration of the nerves than this perception of ambiguousness in familiar persons or affairs. " Speak ; for my spirits and patience have been much tried to-day."

Miriam put her finger on her lips, and seemed desirous that Kenyon should know of the presence of a third person. He now saw, indeed, that there was some one beside her in the carriage, hitherto concealed by her attitude ; a man, it appeared, with a sallow Italian face, which the sculptor distinguished but imperfectly, and did not recognize.

" I can tell you nothing," she replied ; and leaning towards him, she whispered, — appearing then more like the Miriam whom he knew than in what had before passed, — " Only, when the lamp goes out do not despair."

The carriage drove on, leaving Kenyon to muse over this unsatisfactory interview, which seemed to have served no better purpose than to fill his mind with more ominous forebodings than before. Why were Donatello and Miriam in Rome, where both, in all likelihood, might have much to dread ? And why had one and the other addressed him with a question that seemed prompted by a knowledge of some calamity, either already fallen on his unconscious head, or impending closely over him ?

" I am sluggish," muttered Kenyon, to himself ; " a weak, nerveless fool, devoid of energy and promptitude ; or neither Donatello nor Miriam could have escaped me thus ! They are aware of some misfortune that concerns me deeply. How soon am I to know it too ? "

There seemed but a single calamity possible to happen within so narrow a sphere as that with which the sculptor was connected; and even to that one mode of evil he could assign no definite shape, but only felt that it must have some reference to Hilda.

Flinging aside the morbid hesitation, and the dally-ings with his own wishes, which he had permitted to influence his mind throughout the day, he now has-tened to the Via Portoghese. Soon the old palace stood before him, with its massive tower rising into the clouded night; obscured from view at its midmost elevation, but revealed again, higher upward, by the Virgin's lamp that twinkled on the summit. Feeble as it was, in the broad, surrounding gloom, that little ray made no inconsiderable illumination among Ken-yon's sombre thoughts; for, remembering Miriam's last words, a fantasy had seized him that he should find the sacred lamp extinguished.

And, even while he stood gazing, as a mariner at the star in which he put his trust, the light quivered, sank, gleamed up again, and finally went out, leaving the battlements of Hilda's tower in utter darkness. For the first time in centuries, the consecrated and legendary flame, before the loftiest shrine in Rome, had ceased to burn.

CHAPTER XLIV.

THE DESERTED SHRINE.

KENYON knew the sanctity which Hilda (faithful Protestant, and daughter of the Puritans, as the girl was) imputed to this shrine. He was aware of the profound feeling of responsibility, as well earthly as religious, with which her conscience had been impressed, when she became the occupant of her aerial chamber, and undertook the task of keeping the consecrated lamp alight. There was an accuracy and a certainty about Hilda's movements, as regarded all matters that lay deep enough to have their roots in right or wrong, which made it as possible and safe to rely upon the timely and careful trimming of this lamp (if she were in life, and able to creep up the steps), as upon the rising of to-morrow's sun, with lustre undiminished from to-day.

The sculptor could scarcely believe his eyes, therefore, when he saw the flame flicker and expire. His sight had surely deceived him. And now, since the light did not reappear, there must be some smoke-wreath or impenetrable mist brooding about the tower's gray old head, and obscuring it from the lower world. But no! For right over the dim battlements, as the wind chased away a mass of clouds, he beheld a star, and, moreover, by an earnest concentration of his sight, was soon able to discern even the darkened shrine itself. There was no obscurity around the tower; no infirmity of his own vision. The flame had exhausted its supply of oil, and become extinct. But where was Hilda?

A man in a cloak happened to be passing; and Kenyon — anxious to distrust the testimony of his senses, if he could get more acceptable evidence on the other side — appealed to him.

"Do me the favor, Signore," said he, "to look at the top of yonder tower, and tell me whether you see the lamp burning at the Virgin's shrine."

"The lamp, Signore?" answered the man, without at first troubling himself to look up. "The lamp that has burned these four hundred years! how is it possible, Signore, that it should not be burning now?"

"But look!" said the sculptor, impatiently.

With good-natured indulgence for what he seemed to consider as the whim of an eccentric Forestiero, the Italian carelessly threw his eyes upwards; but, as soon as he perceived that there was really no light, he lifted his hands with a vivid expression of wonder and alarm.

"The lamp is extinguished!" cried he. "The lamp that has been burning these four hundred years! This surely must portend some great misfortune; and, by my advice, Signore, you will hasten hence, lest the tower tumble on our heads. A priest once told me, that, if the Virgin withdrew her blessing, and the light went out, the old Palazzo del Torre would sink into the earth, with all that dwell in it. There will be a terrible crash before morning!"

The stranger made the best of his way from the doomed premises; while Kenyon — who would willingly have seen the tower crumble down before his eyes, on condition of Hilda's safety — determined, late as it was, to attempt ascertaining if she were in her dove-cote.

Passing through the arched entrance, — which, as is often the case with Roman entrances, was as accessible at midnight as at noon, — he groped his way to the broad staircase, and, lighting his wax taper, went glimmering up the multitude of steps that led to Hilda's door. The hour being so unseasonable, he intended merely to knock, and, as soon as her voice from within should reassure him, to retire, keeping his explanations and apologies for a fitter time. Accordingly, reaching the lofty height where the maiden, as he trusted, lay asleep, with angels watching over her, though the Virgin seemed to have suspended her care, he tapped lightly at the door-panels, — then knocked more forcibly, — then thundered an impatient summons. No answer came; Hilda, evidently, was not there.

After assuring himself that this must be the fact, Kenyon descended the stairs, but made a pause at every successive stage, and knocked at the door of its apartment, regardless whose slumbers he might disturb, in his anxiety to learn where the girl had last been seen. But, at each closed entrance, there came those hollow echoes, which a chamber, or any dwelling, great or small, never sends out, in response to human knuckles or iron hammer, as long as there is life within to keep its heart from getting dreary.

Once, indeed, on the lower landing-place, the sculptor fancied that there was a momentary stir, inside the door, as if somebody were listening at the threshold. He hoped, at least, that the small, iron-barred aperture would be unclosed, through which Roman housekeepers are wont to take careful cognizance of applicants for admission, from a traditionary dread, perhaps, of letting in a robber or assassin. But it remained shut; neither was the sound repeated; and Kenyon concluded that his excited nerves had played a trick upon his senses, as they are apt to do when we most wish for the clear evidence of the latter.

There was nothing to be done, save to go heavily away, and await whatever good or ill to-morrow's day-light might disclose.

Betimes in the morning, therefore, Kenyon went back to the Via Portoghese, before the slant rays of the sun had descended half-way down the gray front of Hilda's tower. As he drew near its base, he saw the doves perched in full session, on the sunny height of the battlements, and a pair of them — who were probably their mistress's especial pets, and the con-fidants of her bosom-secrets, if Hilda had any — came shooting down, and made a feint of alighting on his shoulder. But, though they evidently recognized him, their shyness would not yet allow so decided a demon-stration. Kenyon's eyes followed them as they flew upward, hoping that they might have come as joyful messengers of the girl's safety, and that he should dis-cern her slender form, half hidden by the parapet, trimming the extinguished lamp at the Virgin's shrine, just as other maidens set about the little duties of a household. Or, perhaps, he might see her gentle and sweet face smiling down upon him, midway towards heaven, as if she had flown thither for a day or two, just to visit her kindred, but had been drawn earth-ward again by the spell of unacknowledged love.

But his eyes were blessed by no such fair vision or reality; nor, in truth, were the eager, unquiet flutter-ings of the doves indicative of any joyful intelligence, which they longed to share with Hilda's friend, but of anxious inquiries that they knew not how to utter. They could not tell, any more than he, whither their lost companion had withdrawn herself, but were in the same void despondency with him, feeling their sunny and airy lives darkened and grown imperfect, now that her sweet society was taken out of it.

In the brisk morning air, Kenyon found it much easier to pursue his researches than at the preceding midnight, when, if any slumberers heard the clamor that he made, they had responded only with sullen and drowsy maledictions, and turned to sleep again. It must be a very dear and intimate reality for which people will be content to give up a dream. When the sun was fairly up, however, it was quite another thing. The heterogeneous population, inhabiting the lower floor of the old tower, and the other extensive regions of the palace, were now willing to tell all they knew, and imagine a great deal more. The amiability of these Italians, assisted by their sharp and nimble wits, caused them to overflow with plausible suggestions, and to be very bounteous in their avowals of interest for the lost Hilda. In a less demonstrative people, such expressions would have implied an eagerness to search land and sea, and never rest till she were found. In the mouths that uttered them, they meant good wishes, and were, so far, better than indifference. There was little doubt that many of them felt a genuine kindness for the shy, brown-haired, delicate, young foreign maiden, who had flown from some distant land to alight upon their tower, where she consorted only with the doves. But their energy expended itself in exclamation, and they were content to leave all more active measures to Kenyon, and to the Virgin, whose

affair it was, to see that the faithful votary of her
lamp received no harm.

In a great Parisian domicile, multifarious as its inhabitants might be, the concierge under the archway
would be cognizant of all their incomings and issuings
forth. But, except in rare cases, the general entrance
and main staircase of a Roman house are left as free
as the street, of which they form a sort of by-lane.
The sculptor, therefore, could hope to find information
about Hilda's movements only from casual observers.

On probing the knowledge of these people to the
bottom, there was various testimony as to the period
when the girl had last been seen. Some said that it
was four days since there had been a trace of her; but
an English lady, in the second piano of the palace,
was rather of opinion that she had met her, the morning before, with a drawing-book in her hand. Having
no acquaintance with the young person, she had taken
little notice and might have been mistaken. A count,
on the piano next above, was very certain that he had
lifted his hat to Hilda, under the archway, two afternoons ago. An old woman, who had formerly tended
the shrine, threw some light upon the matter, by testi-
fying that the lamp required to be replenished once,
at least, in three days, though its reservoir of oil was
exceedingly capacious.

On the whole, though there was other evidence
enough to create some perplexity, Kenyon could not
satisfy himself that she had been visible since the
afternoon of the third preceding day, when a fruit-
seller remembered her coming out of the arched passage, with a sealed packet in her hand. As nearly as
he could ascertain, this was within an hour after Hilda
had taken leave of the sculptor, at his own studio,

with the understanding that they were to meet at the
Vatican the next day. Two nights, therefore, had in-
tervened, during which the lost maiden was unac-
counted for.

The door of Hilda's apartments was still locked, as
on the preceding night; but Kenyon sought out the
wife of the person who sublet them, and prevailed on
her to give him admittance by means of the duplicate
key, which the good woman had in her possession.
On entering, the maidenly neatness and simple grace,
recognizable in all the arrangements, made him visibly
sensible that this was the daily haunt of a pure soul,
in whom religion and the love of beauty were at one.

Thence, the sturdy Roman matron led the sculptor
across a narrow passage, and threw open the door of
a small chamber, on the threshold of which he reverently paused. Within, there was a bed, covered with
white drapery, enclosed with snowy curtains, like a
tent, and of barely width enough for a slender figure
to repose upon it. The sight of this cool, airy, and
secluded bower caused the lover's heart to stir as if
enough of Hilda's gentle dreams were lingering there
to make him happy for a single instant. But then
came the closer consciousness of her loss, bringing
along with it a sharp sting of anguish.

"Behold, Signore," said the matron; "here is the
little staircase by which the signorina used to ascend
and trim the Blessed Virgin's lamp. She was worthy
to be a Catholic, such pains the good child bestowed
to keep it burning; and doubtless the Blessed Mary
will intercede for her, in consideration of her pious offices, heretic though she was. What will become of
the old palazzo, now that the lamp is extinguished, the
saints above us only know! Will you mount, Signore,

to the battlements, and see if she have left any trace of herself there?"

The sculptor stepped across the chamber and ascended the little staircase, which gave him access to the breezy summit of the tower. It affected him inexpressibly to see a bouquet of beautiful flowers beneath the shrine, and to recognize in them an offering of his own to Hilda, who had put them in a vase of water, and dedicated them to the Virgin, in a spirit partly fanciful, perhaps, but still partaking of the religious sentiment which so profoundly influenced her character. One rose-bud, indeed, she had selected for herself from the rich mass of flowers; for Kenyon well remembered recognizing it in her bosom when he last saw her at his studio.

"That little part of my great love she took," said he to himself. "The remainder she would have devoted to Heaven; but has left it withering in the sun and wind. Ah! Hilda, Hilda, had you given me a right to watch over you, this evil had not come!"

"Be not downcast, signorino mio," said the Roman matron, in response to the deep sigh which struggled out of Kenyon's breast. "The dear little maiden, as we see, has decked yonder blessed shrine as devoutly as I myself, or any other good Catholic woman, could have done. It is a religious act, and has more than the efficacy of a prayer. The signorina will as surely come back as the sun will fall through the window to-morrow no less than to-day. Her own doves have often been missing for a day or two, but they were sure to come fluttering about her head again, when she least expected them. So will it be with this dove-like child."

"It might be so," thought Kenyon, with yearning

anxiety, " if a pure maiden were as safe as a dove, in this evil world of ours."

As they returned through the studio, with the furniture and arrangements of which the sculptor was familiar, he missed a small ebony writing-desk that he remembered as having always been placed on a table there. He knew that it was Hilda's custom to deposit her letters in this desk, as well as other little objects of which she wished to be specially careful.

" What has become of it ? " he suddenly inquired, laying his hand on the table.

" Become of what, pray ? " exclaimed the woman, a little disturbed. " Does the Signore suspect a robbery, then ? "

" The signorina's writing - desk is gone," replied Kenyon ; " it always stood on this table, and I myself saw it there only a few days ago."

" Ah, well ! " said the woman, recovering her composure, which she seemed partly to have lost. " The signorina has doubtless taken it away with her. The fact is of good omen ; for it proves that she did not go unexpectedly, and is likely to return when it may best suit her convenience."

" This is very singular," observed Kenyon. " Have the rooms been entered by yourself, or any other person, since the signorina's disappearance ? "

" Not by me, Signore, so help me Heaven and the saints ! " said the matron. " And I question whether there are more than two keys in Rome that will suit this strange old lock. Here is one ; and as for the other, the signorina carries it in her pocket."

The sculptor had no reason to doubt the word of this respectable dame. She appeared to be well-meaning and kind-hearted, as Roman matrons gen-

erally are ; except when a fit of passion incites them
to shower horrible curses on an obnoxious individual,
or perhaps to stab him with the steel stiletto that
serves them for a hair-pin.   But Italian asseverations
of any questionable fact, however true they may chance
to be, have no witness of their truth in the faces of
those who utter them.   Their words are spoken with
strange earnestness, and yet do not vouch for themselves as coming from any depth, like roots drawn out
of the substance of the soul, with some of the soil
clinging to them.   There is always a something inscrutable, instead of frankness, in their eyes.   In
short, they lie so much like truth, and speak truth so
much as if they were telling a lie, that their auditor
suspects himself in the wrong, whether he believes or
disbelieves them ; it being the one thing certain, that
falsehood is seldom an intolerable burden to the tenderest of Italian consciences.

" It is very strange what can have become of the
desk ! " repeated Kenyon, looking the woman in the
face.

" Very strange, indeed, Signore," she replied meekly,
without turning away her eyes in the least, but checking his insight of them at about half an inch below
the surface.   " I think the signorina must have taken
it with her."

It seemed idle to linger here any longer.   Kenyon
therefore departed, after making an arrangement with
the woman, by the terms of which she was to allow the
apartments to remain in their present state, on his as-
suming the responsibility for the rent.

He spent the day in making such further search and
investigation as he found practicable ; and, though at
first trammelled by an unwillingness to draw public

attention to Hilda's affairs, the urgency of the circumstances soon compelled him to be thoroughly in earnest. In the course of a week, he tried all conceivable modes of fathoming the mystery, not merely by his personal efforts and those of his brother-artists and friends, but through the police, who readily undertook the task, and expressed strong confidence of success. But the Roman police has very little efficiency, except in the interest of the despotism of which it is a tool. With their cocked hats, shoulder-belts, and swords, they wear a sufficiently imposing aspect, and doubtless keep their eyes open wide enough to track a political offender, but are too often blind to private outrage, be it murder or any lesser crime. Kenyon counted little upon their assistance, and profited by it not at all.

Remembering the mystic words which Miriam had addressed to him, he was anxious to meet her, but knew not whither she had gone, nor how to obtain an interview either with herself or Donatello. The days wore away, and still there were no tidings of the lost one; no lamp rekindled before the Virgin's shrine; no light shining into the lover's heart; no star of Hope — he was ready to say, as he turned his eyes almost reproachfully upward — in heaven itself!

CHAPTER XLV.

THE FLIGHT OF HILDA'S DOVES.

ALONG with the lamp on Hilda's tower, the sculptor now felt that a light had gone out, or, at least, was ominously obscured, to which he owed whatever cheerfulness had heretofore illuminated his cold, artistic life. The idea of this girl had been like a taper of virgin wax, burning with a pure and steady flame, and chasing away the evil spirits out of the magic circle of its beams. It had darted its rays afar, and modified the whole sphere in which Kenyon had his being. Beholding it no more, he at once found himself in darkness and astray.

This was the time, perhaps, when Kenyon first became sensible what a dreary city is Rome, and what a terrible weight is there imposed on human life, when any gloom within the heart corresponds to the spell of ruin, that has been thrown over the site of ancient empire. He wandered, as it were, and stumbled over the fallen columns, and among the tombs, and groped his way into the sepulchral darkness of the catacombs, and found no path emerging from them. The happy may well enough continue to be such, beneath the brilliant sky of Rome. But, if you go thither in melancholy mood, — if you go with a ruin in your heart, or with a vacant site there, where once stood the airy fabric of happiness, now vanished, — all the ponderous gloom of the Roman Past will pile itself upon that spot, and crush you down as with the heaped-up marble and granite, the earth-mounds, and multitudinous bricks of its material decay.

It might be supposed that a melancholy man would here make acquaintance with a grim philosophy. He should learn to bear patiently his individual griefs, that endure only for one little lifetime, when here are the tokens of such infinite misfortune on an imperial scale, and when so many far landmarks of time, all around him, are bringing the remoteness of a thousand years ago into the sphere of yesterday. But it is in vain that you seek this shrub of bitter sweetness among the plants that root themselves on the roughness of massive walls, or trail downward from the capitals of pillars, or spring out of the green turf in the palace of the Cæsars. It does not grow in Rome; not even among the five hundred various weeds which deck the grassy arches of the Coliseum. You look through a vista of century beyond century, — through much shadow, and a little sunshine, — through barbarism and civilization, alternating with one another like actors that have pre-arranged their parts, — through a broad pathway of progressive generations bordered by palaces and temples, and bestridden by old, triumphal arches, until, in the distance, you behold the obelisks, with their unintelligible inscriptions, hinting at a past infinitely more remote than history can define. Your own life is as nothing, when compared with that immeasurable distance ; but still you demand, none the less earnestly, a gleam of sunshine, instead of a speck of shadow, on the step or two that will bring you to your quiet rest.

How exceedingly absurd ! All men, from the date of the earliest obelisk, — and of the whole world, moreover, since that far epoch, and before, — have made a

similar demand, and seldom had their wish. If they
had it, what are they the better now? But, even while
you taunt yourself with this sad lesson, your heart cries
out obstreperously for its small share of earthly happiness, and will not be appeased by the myriads of
dead hopes that lie crushed into the soil of Rome.
How wonderful that this our narrow foothold of the
Present should hold its own so constantly, and, while
every moment changing, should still be like a rock betwixt the encountering tides of the long Past and the
infinite To-come!

Man of marble though he was, the sculptor grieved
for the Irrevocable. Looking back upon Hilda's way
of life, he marvelled at his own blind stupidity, which
had kept him from remonstrating — as a friend, if
with no stronger right — against the risks that she
continually encountered. Being so innocent, she had
no means of estimating those risks, nor even a possibility of suspecting their existence. But he — who had
spent years in Rome, with a man's far wider scope of
observation and experience — knew things that made
him shudder. It seemed to Kenyon, looking through
the darkly colored medium of his fears, that all modes
of crime were crowded into the close intricacy of Roman streets, and that there was no redeeming element,
such as exists in other dissolute and wicked cities.

For here was a priesthood, pampered, sensual, with
red and bloated cheeks, and carnal eyes. With apparently a grosser development of animal life than
most men, they were placed in an unnatural relation
with woman, and thereby lost the healthy, human conscience that pertains to other human beings, who own
the sweet household ties connecting them with wife and
daughter. And here was an indolent nobility, with

no high aims or opportunities, but cultivating a vicious way of life, as if it were an art, and the only one which they cared to learn. Here was a population, high and low, that had no genuine belief in virtue; and if they recognized any act as criminal, they might throw off all care, remorse, and memory of it, by kneeling a little while at the confessional, and rising unburdened, active, elastic, and incited by fresh appetite for the next ensuing sin. Here was a soldiery who felt Rome to be their conquered city, and doubtless considered themselves the legal inheritors of the foul license which Gaul, Goth, and Vandal have here exercised in days gone by.

And what localities for new crime existed in those guilty sites, where the crime of departed ages used to be at home, and had its long, hereditary haunt! What street in Rome, what ancient ruin, what one place where man had standing-room, what fallen stone was there, unstained with one or another kind of guilt! In some of the vicissitudes of the city's pride, or its calamity, the dark tide of human evil had swelled over it, far higher than the Tiber ever rose against the acclivities of the seven hills. To Kenyon's morbid view, there appeared to be a contagious element, rising fog-like from the ancient depravity of Rome, and brooding over the dead and half-rotten city, as nowhere else on earth. It prolonged the tendency to crime, and developed an instantaneous growth of it, whenever an opportunity was found. And where could it be found so readily as here! In those vast palaces, there were a hundred remote nooks where Innocence might shriek in vain. Beneath meaner houses there were unsuspected dungeons that had once been princely chambers, and open to the daylight; but, on account of some wickedness there perpetrated, each passing age had thrown its handful of dust upon the spot, and buried it from sight. Only ruffians knew of its existence, and kept it for murder, and worse crime.

Such was the city through which Hilda, for three years past, had been wandering without a protector or a guide. She had trodden lightly over the crumble of old crimes; she had taken her way amid the grime and corruption which Paganism had left there, and a perverted Christianity had made more noisome; walking saint-like through it all, with white, innocent feet; until, in some dark pitfall that lay right across her path, she had vanished out of sight. It was terrible to imagine what hideous outrage might have thrust her into that abyss!

Then the lover tried to comfort himself with the idea that Hilda's sanctity was a sufficient safeguard. Ah, yes; she was so pure! The angels, that were of the same sisterhood, would never let Hilda come to harm. A miracle would be wrought on her behalf, as naturally as a father would stretch out his hand to save a best-beloved child. Providence would keep a little area and atmosphere about her as safe and wholesome as heaven itself, although the flood of perilous iniquity might hem her round, and its black waves hang curling above her head! But these reflections were of slight avail. No doubt they were the religious truth. Yet the ways of Providence are utterly inscrutable; and many a murder has been done, and many an innocent virgin has lifted her white arms, beseeching its aid in her extremity, and all in vain; so that, though Providence is infinitely good and wise, — and perhaps for that very reason, — it may be half an eternity before the great circle of its scheme shall bring us the superabundant recompense for all these sorrows! But what the lover asked was such prompt consolation as might consist with the brief span of mortal life; the assurance of Hilda's present safety, and her restoration within that very hour.

An imaginative man, he suffered the penalty of his endowment in the hundred-fold variety of gloomily tinted scenes that it presented to him, in which Hilda was always a central figure. The sculptor forgot his marble. Rome ceased to be anything, for him, but a labyrinth of dismal streets, in one or another of which the lost girl had disappeared. He was haunted with the idea, that some circumstance, most important to be known, and, perhaps, easily discoverable, had hitherto been overlooked, and that, if he could lay hold of this one clew, it would guide him directly in the track of Hilda's footsteps. With this purpose in view, he went, every morning, to the Via Portoghese, and made it the starting-point of fresh investigations. After nightfall, too, he invariably returned thither, with a faint hope fluttering at his heart that the lamp might again be shining on the summit of the tower, and would dispel this ugly mystery out of the circle consecrated by its rays. There being no point of which he could take firm hold, his mind was filled with unsubstantial hopes and fears. Once, Kenyon had seemed to cut his life in marble; now he vaguely clutched at it, and found it vapor.

In his unstrung and despondent mood, one trifling circumstance affected him with an idle pang. The doves had at first been faithful to their lost mistress. They failed not to sit in a row upon her window-sill, or to alight on the shrine, or the church-angels, and on the roofs and portals of the neighboring houses, in evident expectation of her reappearance. After the second week, however, they began to take flight, and dropping off by pairs, betook themselves to other dove-cotes. Only a single dove remained, and brooded drearily beneath the shrine. The flock, that had departed, were like the many hopes that had vanished from Kenyon's heart; the one that still lingered, and looked so wretched, — was it a Hope, or already a Despair?

In the street, one day, the sculptor met a priest of mild and venerable aspect; and as his mind dwelt continually upon Hilda, and was especially active in bringing up all incidents that had ever been connected with her, it immediately struck him that this was the very father with whom he had seen her at the confessional. Such trust did Hilda inspire in him, that Kenyon had never asked what was the subject of the communication between herself and this old priest. He had no reason for imagining that it could have any relation with her disappearance, so long subsequently; but, being thus brought face to face with a personage, mysteriously associated, as he now remembered, with her whom he had lost, an impulse ran before his thoughts and led the sculptor to address him.

It might be that the reverend kindliness of the old man's expression took Kenyon's heart by surprise; at all events, he spoke as if there were a recognized acquaintanceship, and an object of mutual interest between them.

"She has gone from me, father," said he.

"Of whom do you speak, my son?" inquired the priest.

"Of that sweet girl," answered Kenyon, "who knelt to you at the confessional. Surely, you remember her, among all the mortals to whose confessions you have listened! For she alone could have had no sins to reveal."

"Yes; I remember," said the priest, with a gleam of recollection in his eyes. "She was made to bear a miraculous testimony to the efficacy of the divine ordinances of the Church, by seizing forcibly upon one of them, and finding immediate relief from it, heretic though she was. It is my purpose to publish a brief narrative of this miracle, for the edification of mankind, in Latin, Italian, and English, from the printing-press of the Propaganda. Poor child! Setting apart her heresy, she was spotless, as you say. And is she dead?"

"Heaven forbid, father!" exclaimed Kenyon, shrinking back. "But she has gone from me, I know not whither. It may be — yes, the idea seizes upon my mind — that what she revealed to you will suggest some clew to the mystery of her disappearance."

"None, my son, none," answered the priest, shaking his head; "nevertheless, I bid you be of good cheer. That young maiden is not doomed to die a heretic. Who knows what the Blessed Virgin may at this moment be doing for her soul! Perhaps, when you next behold her, she will be clad in the shining white robe of the true faith."

This latter suggestion did not convey all the comfort which the old priest possibly intended by it; but he imparted it to the sculptor, along with his blessing, as the two best things that he could bestow, and said nothing further, except to bid him farewell.

When they had parted, however, the idea of Hilda's conversion to Catholicism recurred to her lover's mind, bringing with it certain reflections, that gave a new turn to his surmises about the mystery into which she had vanished. Not that he seriously apprehended —

although the superabundance of her religious sentiment might mislead her for a moment — that the
New England girl would permanently succumb to the
scarlet superstitions which surrounded her in Italy.
But the incident of the confessional — if known, as
probably it was, to the eager propagandists who prowl
about for souls, as cats to catch a mouse — would
surely inspire the most confident expectations of bringing her over to the faith. With so pious an end in
view, would Jesuitical morality be shocked at the
thought of kidnapping the mortal body, for the sake of
the immortal spirit that might otherwise be lost forever? Would not the kind old priest, himself, deem
this to be infinitely the kindest service that he could
perform for the stray lamb, who had so strangely
sought his aid?

If these suppositions were well founded, Hilda was
most likely a prisoner in one of the religious establish-
ments that are so numerous in Rome. The idea, according to the aspect in which it was viewed, brought
now a degree of comfort, and now an additional perplexity. On the one hand, Hilda was safe from any
but spiritual assaults; on the other, where was the
possibility of breaking through all those barred portals, and searching a thousand convent-cells, to set
her free?

Kenyon, however, as it happened, was prevented
from endeavoring to follow out this surmise, which
only the state of hopeless uncertainty, that almost bewildered his reason, could have led him for a moment
to entertain. A communication reached him by an
unknown hand, in consequence of which, and within
an hour after receiving it, he took his way through
one of the gates of Rome.

CHAPTER XLVI.

A WALK ON THE CAMPAGNA.

IT was a bright forenoon of February; a month in which the brief severity of a Roman winter is already past, and when violets and daisies begin to show themselves in spots favored by the sun. The sculptor came out of the city by the gate of San Sebastiano, and walked briskly along the Appian Way.

For the space of a mile or two beyond the gate, this ancient and famous road is as desolate and disagreeable as most of the other Roman avenues. It extends over small, uncomfortable paving-stones, between brick and plastered walls, which are very solidly constructed, and so high as almost to exclude a view of the surrounding country. The houses are of most uninviting aspect, neither picturesque, nor homelike and social; they have seldom or never a door opening on the wayside, but are accessible only from the rear, and frown inhospitably upon the traveller through iron-grated windows. Here and there appears a dreary inn, or a wine-shop, designated by the withered bush beside the entrance, within which you discern a stone-built and sepulchral interior, where guests refresh themselves with sour bread and goats'-milk cheese, washed down with wine of dolorous acerbity.

At frequent intervals along the roadside uprises the ruin of an ancient tomb. As they stand now, these structures are immensely high and broken mounds of conglomerated brick, stone, pebbles, and earth, all molten by time into a mass as solid and indestructible as if each tomb were composed of a single bowlder of granite. When first erected, they were cased externally, no doubt, with slabs of polished marble, artfully wrought bas-reliefs, and all such suitable adornments, and were rendered majestically beautiful by grand architectural designs. This antique splendor has long since been stolen from the dead, to decorate the palaces and churches of the living. Nothing remains to the dishonored sepulchres, except their massiveness.

Even the pyramids form hardly a stranger spectacle, or are more alien from human sympathies, than the tombs of the Appian Way, with their gigantic height, breadth, and solidity, defying time and the elements, and far too mighty to be demolished by an ordinary earthquake. Here you may see a modern dwelling, and a garden with its vines and olive-trees, perched on the lofty dilapidation of a tomb, which forms a precipice of fifty feet in depth on each of the four sides. There is a home on that funereal mound, where generations of children have been born, and successive lives been spent, undisturbed by the ghost of the stern Roman whose ashes were so preposterously burdened. Other sepulchres wear a crown of grass, shrubbery, and forest-trees, which throw out a broad sweep of branches, having had time, twice over, to be a thousand years of age. On one of them stands a tower, which, though immemorially more modern than the tomb, was itself built by immemorial hands, and is now rifted quite from top to bottom by a vast fissure of decay; the tomb-hillock, its foundation, being still as firm as ever, and likely to endure until the last trump shall rend it wide asunder, and summon forth its unknown dead.

Yes ; its unknown dead ! For, except in one or two doubtful instances, these mountainous sepulchral edifices have not availed to keep so much as the bare name of an individual or a family from oblivion.   Ambitious of everlasting remembrance, as they were, the slumberers might just as well have gone quietly to rest, each in his pigeon-hole of a columbarium, or under his little green hillock, in a graveyard, without a headstone to mark the spot.   It is rather satisfactory than otherwise, to think that all these idle pains have turned out so utterly abortive.

About two miles, or more, from the city-gate, and right upon the roadside, Kenyon passed an immense round pile, sepulchral in its original purposes, like those already mentioned.   It was built of great blocks of hewn stone, on a vast, square foundation of rough, agglomerated material, such as composes the mass of all the other ruinous tombs.   But whatever might be the cause, it was in a far better state of preservation than they.   On its broad summit rose the battlements of a mediæval fortress, out of the midst of which (so long since had time begun to crumble the supplemental structure, and cover it with soil, by means of way-side dust) grew trees, bushes, and thick festoons of ivy.   This tomb of a woman had become the citadel and donjon-keep of a castle ; and all the care that Cecilia Metella's husband could bestow, to secure endless peace for her beloved relics, had only sufficed to make that handful of precious ashes the nucleus of battles, long ages after her death.

A little beyond this point, the sculptor turned aside from the Appian Way, and directed his course across

the Campagna, guided by tokens that were obvious
only to himself. On one side of him, but at a distance, the Claudian aqueduct was striding over fields
and water-courses. Before him, many miles away,
with a blue atmosphere between, rose the Alban hills,
brilliantly silvered with snow and sunshine.

He was not without a companion. A buffalo-calf,
that seemed shy and sociable by the self-same impulse, had begun to make acquaintance with him, from
the moment when he left the road. This frolicsome
creature gambolled along, now before, now behind;
standing a moment to gaze at him, with wild, curious
eyes, he leaped aside and shook his shaggy head, as
Kenyon advanced too nigh; then, after loitering in
the rear, he came galloping up, like a charge of cavalry, but halted, all of a sudden, when the sculptor
turned to look, and bolted across the Campagna, at
the slightest signal of nearer approach. The young,
sportive thing, Kenyon half fancied, was serving him
as a guide, like the heifer that led Cadmus to the site
of his destined city; for, in spite of a hundred vagaries, his general course was in the right direction, and
along by several objects which the sculptor had noted
as landmarks of his way.

In this natural intercourse with a rude and healthy
form of animal life, there was something that wonderfully revived Kenyon's spirits. The warm rays of the
sun, too, were wholesome for him in body and soul;
and so was a breeze that bestirred itself occasionally,
as if for the sole purpose of breathing upon his cheek,
and dying softly away, when he would fain have felt a
little more decided kiss. This shy, but loving breeze
reminded him strangely of what Hilda's deportment
had sometimes been towards himself.

The weather had very much to do, no doubt, with
these genial and delightful sensations, that made the
sculptor so happy with mere life, in spite of a head
and heart full of doleful thoughts, anxieties, and fears,
which ought in all reason to have depressed him.   It
was like no weather that exists anywhere, save in Paradise and in Italy; certainly not in America, where it
is always too strenuous on the side either of heat or
cold.   Young as the season was, and wintry as it
would have been under a more rigid sky, it resembled summer rather than what we New-Englanders
recognize in our idea of spring.   But there was an
indescribable something, sweet, fresh, and remotely
affectionate, which the matronly summer loses, and
which thrilled, and, as it were, tickled Kenyon's heart
with a feeling partly of the senses, yet far more a spiritual delight.   In a word, it was as if Hilda's delicate
breath were on his cheek.

After walking at a brisk pace for about half an
hour, he reached a spot where an excavation appeared
to have been begun, at some not very distant period.
There was a hollow space in the earth, looking exceedingly like a deserted cellar, being enclosed within old
subterranean walls, constructed of thin Roman bricks,
and made accessible by a narrow flight of stone steps.
A suburban villa had probably stood over this site, in
the imperial days of Rome, and these might have been
the ruins of a bath-room, or some other apartment
that was required to be wholly or partly under ground.
A spade can scarcely be put into that soil, so rich in
lost and forgotten things, without hitting upon some
discovery which would attract all eyes, in any other
land.   If you dig but a little way, you gather bits of
precious marble, coins, rings, and engraved gems; if

you go deeper, you break into columbaria, or into sculptured and richly frescoed apartments that look like festive halls, but were only sepulchres.

The sculptor descended into the cellar-like cavity, and sat down on a block of stone. His eagerness had brought him thither sooner than the appointed hour. The sunshine fell slantwise into the hollow, and happened to be resting on what Kenyon at first took to be a shapeless fragment of stone, possibly marble, which was partly concealed by the crumbling down of earth.

But his practised eye was soon aware of something artistic in this rude object. To relieve the anxious tedium of his situation, he cleared away some of the soil, which seemed to have fallen very recently, and discovered a headless figure of marble. It was earth-stained, as well it might be, and had a slightly corroded surface, but at once impressed the sculptor as a Greek production, and wonderfully delicate and beautiful. The head was gone; both arms were broken off at the elbow. Protruding from the loose earth, however, Kenyon beheld the fingers of a marble hand; it was still appended to its arm, and a little further search enabled him to find the other. Placing these limbs in what the nice adjustment of the fractures proved to be their true position, the poor, fragmentary woman forthwith showed that she retained her modest instincts to the last. She had perished with them, and snatched them back at the moment of revival. For these long-buried hands immediately disposed themselves in the manner that nature prompts, as the antique artist knew, and as all the world has seen, in the Venus de' Medici.

" What a discovery is here ! " thought Kenyon to himself. " I seek for Hilda, and find a marble wo man ! Is the omen good or ill ? "

In a corner of the excavation lay a small round block of stone, much incrusted with earth that had dried and hardened upon it. So, at least, you would have described this object, until the sculptor lifted it, turned it hither and thither in his hands, brushed off the clinging soil, and finally placed it on the slender neck of the newly discovered statue. The effect was magical. It immediately lighted up and vivified the whole figure, endowing it with personality, soul, and intelligence. The beautiful Idea at once asserted its immortality, and converted that heap of forlorn fragments into a whole, as perfect to the mind, if not to the eye, as when the new marble gleamed with snowy lustre; nor was the impression marred by the earth that still hung upon the exquisitely graceful limbs, and even filled the lovely crevice of the lips. Kenyon cleared it away from between them, and almost deemed himself rewarded with a living smile.

It was either the prototype or a better repetition of the Venus of the Tribune. But those who have been dissatisfied with the small head, the narrow, soulless face, the button-hole eyelids, of that famous statue, and its mouth such as nature never moulded, should see the genial breadth of this far nobler and sweeter countenance. It is one of the few works of antique sculpture in which we recognize womanhood, and that, moreover, without prejudice to its divinity.

Here, then, was a treasure for the sculptor to have found! How happened it to be lying there, beside its grave of twenty centuries? Why were not the tidings of its discovery already noised abroad? The world was richer than yesterday, by something far more precious than gold. Forgotten beauty had come back, as beautiful as ever; a goddess had risen from her long slumber, and was a goddess still. Another cabinet in the Vatican was destined to shine as lustrously as that of the Apollo Belvedere; or, if the aged pope should resign his claim, an emperor would woo this tender marble, and win her as proudly as an imperial bride!

Such were the thoughts with which Kenyon exaggerated to himself the importance of the newly discovered statue, and strove to feel at least a portion of the interest which this event would have inspired in him a little while before. But, in reality, he found it difficult to fix his mind upon the subject. He could hardly, we fear, be reckoned a consummate artist, because there was something dearer to him than his art; and, by the greater strength of a human affection, the divine statue seemed to fall asunder again, and become only a heap of worthless fragments.

While the sculptor sat listlessly gazing at it, there was a sound of small hoofs, clumsily galloping on the Campagna; and, soon, his frisky acquaintance, the buffalo-calf, came and peeped over the edge of the excavation. Almost at the same moment, he heard voices, which approached nearer and nearer; a man's voice, and a feminine one, talking the musical tongue of Italy. Besides the hairy visage of his four-footed friend, Kenyon now saw the figures of a peasant and a contadina, making gestures of salutation to him, on the opposite verge of the hollow space.

CHAPTER XLVII.

THE PEASANT AND CONTADINA.

THEY descended into the excavation : a young peasant, in the short blue jacket, the small-clothes buttoned
at the knee, and buckled shoes, that compose one of
the ugliest dresses ever worn by man, except the wearer's form have a grace which any garb, or the nudity
of an antique statue, would equally set off ; and, hand
in hand with him, a village girl, in one of those brilliant costumes largely kindled up with scarlet, and
decorated with gold embroidery, in which the contadinas array themselves on feast-days. But Kenyon
was not deceived ; he had recognized the voices of his
friends, indeed, even before their disguised figures
came between him and the sunlight. Donatello was
the peasant ; the contadina, with the airy smile, half
mirthful, though it shone out of melancholy eyes, —
was Miriam.

They both greeted the sculptor with a familiar kindness which reminded him of the days when Hilda and
they and he had lived so happily together, before the
mysterious adventure of the catacomb. What a succession of sinister events had followed one spectral figure out of that gloomy labyrinth.

"It is carnival time, you know," said Miriam, as if
in explanation of Donatello's and her own costume.
"Do you remember how merrily we spent the Carnival, last year?"

"It seems many years ago," replied Kenyon. "We are all so changed!"

When individuals approach one another with deep purposes on both sides, they seldom come at once to the matter which they have most at heart. They dread the electric shock of a too sudden contact with it. A natural impulse leads them to steal gradually onward, hiding themselves, as it were, behind a closer, and still a closer topic, until they stand face to face with the true point of interest. Miriam was conscious of this impulse, and partially obeyed it.

"So, your instincts as a sculptor have brought you into the presence of our newly discovered statue," she observed. "Is it not beautiful? A far truer image of immortal womanhood than the poor little damsel at Florence, world-famous though she be."

"Most beautiful," said Kenyon, casting an indifferent glance at the Venus. "The time has been when the sight of this statue would have been enough to make the day memorable."

"And will it not do so, now?" Miriam asked. "I fancied so, indeed, when we discovered it two days ago. It is Donatello's prize. We were sitting here together, planning an interview with you, when his keen eyes detected the fallen goddess, almost entirely buried under that heap of earth, which the clumsy excavators showered down upon her, I suppose. We congratulated ourselves, chiefly for your sake. The eyes of us three are the only ones to which she has yet revealed herself. Does it not frighten you a little, like the apparition of a lovely woman that lived of old, and has long lain in the grave?"

"Ah, Miriam! I cannot respond to you," said the sculptor, with irrepressible impatience. "Imagination and the love of art have both died out of me."

"Miriam," interposed Donatello, with gentle gravity, "why should we keep our friend in suspense? We know what anxiety he feels. Let us give him what intelligence we can."

"You are so direct and immediate, my beloved friend!" answered Miriam with an unquiet smile. "There are several reasons why I should like to play round this matter a little while, and cover it with fanciful thoughts, as we strew a grave with flowers."

"A grave!" exclaimed the sculptor.

"No grave in which your heart need be buried," she replied; "you have no such calamity to dread. But I linger and hesitate, because every word I speak brings me nearer to a crisis from which I shrink. Ah, Donatello! let us live a little longer the life of these last few days! It is so bright, so airy, so childlike, so without either past or future! Here, on the wild Campagna, you seem to have found, both for yourself and me, the life that belonged to you in early youth; the sweet irresponsible life which you inherited from your mythic ancestry, the Fauns of Monte Beni. Our stern and black reality will come upon us speedily enough. But, first, a brief time more of this strange happiness."

"I dare not linger upon it," answered Donatello, with an expression that reminded the sculptor of the gloomiest days of his remorse at Monte Beni. "I dare to be so happy as you have seen me, only because I have felt the time to be so brief."

"One day, then!" pleaded Miriam. "One more day in the wild freedom of this sweet-scented air."

"Well, one more day," said Donatello, smiling; and his smile touched Kenyon with a pathos beyond words, there being gayety and sadness both melted into it; "but here is Hilda's friend, and our own. Comfort him, at least, and set his heart at rest, since you have it partly in your power."

"Ah, surely he might endure his pangs a little longer!" cried Miriam, turning to Kenyon with a tricksy, fitful kind of mirth, that served to hide some solemn necessity, too sad and serious to be looked at in its naked aspect. "You love us both, I think, and will be content to suffer for our sakes, one other day. Do I ask too much?"

"Tell me of Hilda," replied the sculptor; "tell me only that she is safe, and keep back what else you will."

"Hilda is safe," said Miriam. "There is a Providence purposely for Hilda, as I remember to have told you long ago. But a great trouble — an evil deed, let us acknowledge it — has spread out its dark branches so widely, that the shadow falls on innocence as well as guilt. There was one slight link that connected your sweet Hilda with a crime which it was her unhappy fortune to witness, but of which I need not say she was as guiltless as the angels that looked out of heaven, and saw it too. No matter, now, what the consequence has been. You shall have your lost Hilda back, and — who knows? — perhaps tenderer than she was."

"But when will she return?" persisted the sculptor; "tell me the when, and where, and how!"

"A little patience. Do not press me so," said Miriam; and again Kenyon was struck by the spritelike, fitful characteristic of her manner, and a sort of hysteric gayety, which seemed to be a will-o'-the-wisp from a sorrow stagnant at her heart. "You have more time to spare than I. First, listen to something

that I have to tell. We will talk of Hilda by and
by."

Then Miriam spoke of her own life, and told facts
that threw a gleam of light over many things which
had perplexed the sculptor in all his previous knowledge of her. She described herself as springing from
English parentage, on the mother's side, but with a
vein, likewise, of Jewish blood; yet connected, through
her father, with one of those few princely families of
Southern Italy, which still retain great wealth and influence. And she revealed a name, at which her auditor started, and grew pale; for it was one that, only
a few years before, had been familiar to the world in
connection with a mysterious and terrible event. The
reader — if he think it worth while to recall some of
the strange incidents which have been talked of, and
forgotten, within no long time past — will remember
Miriam's name.

"You shudder at me, I perceive," said Miriam, suddenly interrupting her narrative.

"No; you were innocent," replied the sculptor. "I
shudder at the fatality that seems to haunt your footsteps, and throws a shadow of crime about your path,
you being guiltless."

"There was such a fatality," said Miriam; "yes;
the shadow fell upon me, innocent, but I went astray
in it, and wandered — as Hilda could tell you — into
crime."

She went on to say, that, while yet a child, she had
lost her English mother. From a very early period
of her life, there had been a contract of betrothal between herself and a certain marchese, the representative of another branch of her paternal house, — a
family arrangement between two persons of dispro-

portioned ages, and in which feeling went for nothing. Most Italian girls of noble rank would have yielded themselves to such a marriage, as an affair of course. But there was something in Miriam's blood, in her mixed race, in her recollections of her mother, — some characteristic, finally, in her own nature, — which had given her freedom of thought, and force of will, and made this prearranged connection odious to her. More-over, the character of her destined husband would have been a sufficient and insuperable objection; for it be-trayed traits so evil, so treacherous, so vile, and yet so strangely subtle, as could only be accounted for by the insanity which often develops itself in old, close-kept races of men, when long unmixed with newer blood. Reaching the age when the marriage contract should have been fulfilled, Miriam had utterly repudiated it.

Some time afterwards had occurred that terrible event to which Miriam had alluded, when she re-vealed her name; an event, the frightful and mysteri-ous circumstances of which will recur to many minds, but of which few or none can have found for them-selves a satisfactory explanation. It only concerns the present narrative, inasmuch as the suspicion of being at least an accomplice in the crime fell darkly and directly upon Miriam herself.

"But you know that I am innocent!" she cried, in-terrupting herself again, and looking Kenyon in the face.

"I know it by my deepest consciousness," he an-swered; "and I know it by Hilda's trust and entire affection, which you never could have won had you been capable of guilt."

"That is sure ground, indeed, for pronouncing me innocent," said Miriam with the tears gushing into her eyes. "Yet I have since become a horror to your saint-like Hilda, by a crime which she herself saw me help to perpetrate!"

She proceeded with her story. The great influence of her family connections had shielded her from some of the consequences of her imputed guilt. But, in her despair, she had fled from home, and had surrounded her flight with such circumstances as rendered it the most probable conclusion that she had committed suicide. Miriam, however, was not of the feeble nature which takes advantage of that obvious and poor resource in earthly difficulties. She flung herself upon the world, and speedily created a new sphere, in which Hilda's gentle purity, the sculptor's sensibility, clear thought, and genius, and Donatello's genial simplicity, had given her almost her first experience of happiness. Then came that ill-omened adventure of the catacomb. The spectral figure which she encountered there was the evil fate that had haunted her through life.

Looking back upon what had happened, Miriam observed, she now considered him a madman. Insanity must have been mixed up with his original composition, and developed by those very acts of depravity which it suggested, and still more intensified, by the remorse that ultimately followed them. Nothing was stranger in his dark career than the penitence which often seemed to go hand in hand with crime. Since his death, she had ascertained that it finally led him to a convent, where his severe and self-inflicted penance had even acquired him the reputation of unusual sanctity, and had been the cause of his enjoying greater freedom than is commonly allowed to monks.

"Need I tell you more?" asked Miriam, after proceeding thus far. "It is still a dim and dreary mystery, a gloomy twilight into which I guide you; but possibly you may catch a glimpse of much that I myself can explain only by conjecture. At all events, you can comprehend what my situation must have been, after that fatal interview in the catacomb. My persecutor had gone thither for penance, but followed me forth with fresh impulses to crime. He had me in his power. Mad as he was, and wicked as he was, with one word he could have blasted me in the belief of all the world. In your belief too, and Hilda's! Even Donatello would have shrunk from me with horror!"

"Never," said Donatello, "my instinct would have known you innocent."

"Hilda and Donatello and myself, — we three would have acquitted you," said Kenyon, "let the world say what it might. Ah, Miriam, you should have told us this sad story sooner!"

"I thought often of revealing it to you," answered Miriam; "on one occasion, especially, — it was after you had shown me your Cleopatra; it seemed to leap out of my heart, and got as far as my very lips. But finding you cold to accept my confidence, I thrust it back again. Had I obeyed my first impulse, all would have turned out differently."

"And Hilda!" resumed the sculptor. "What can have been her connection with these dark incidents?"

"She will, doubtless, tell you with her own lips," replied Miriam. "Through sources of information which I possess in Rome, I can assure you of her safety. In two days more — by the help of the special Providence that, as I love to tell you, watches over Hilda — she shall rejoin you."

"Still two days more!" murmured the sculptor.

"Ah, you are cruel now! More cruel than you know!" exclaimed Miriam, with another gleam of that fantastic, fitful gayety, which had more than once marked her manner, during this interview. "Spare your poor friends!"

"I know not what you mean, Miriam," said Kenyon.

"No matter," she replied; "you will understand hereafter. But could you think it? Here is Donatello haunted with strange remorse, and an unmitigable resolve to obtain what he deems justice upon himself. He fancies, with a kind of direct simplicity, which I have vainly tried to combat, that, when a wrong has been done, the doer is bound to submit himself to whatsoever tribunal takes cognizance of such things, and abide its judgment. I have assured him that there is no such thing as earthly justice, and especially none here, under the head of Christendom.

"We will not argue the point again," said Donatello, smiling. "I have no head for argument, but only a sense, an impulse, an instinct, I believe, which sometimes leads me right. But why do we talk now of what may make us sorrowful? There are still two days more. Let us be happy!"

It appeared to Kenyon that since he last saw Donatello, some of the sweet and delightful characteristics of the antique Faun had returned to him. There were slight, careless graces, pleasant and simple peculiarities, that had been obliterated by the heavy grief through which he was passing at Monte Beni, and out of which he had hardly emerged, when the sculptor parted with Miriam and him beneath the bronze pontiff's outstretched hand. These happy blossoms had now reappeared. A playfulness came out of his heart,

THE CAMPAGNA, APPIAN WAY, AND CLAUDIAN AQUEDUCT

and glimmered like firelight in his actions, alternating, or even closely intermingled, with profound sympathy and serious thought.

" Is he not beautiful ? " said Miriam, watching the sculptor's eye as it dwelt admiringly on Donatello. " So changed, yet still, in a deeper sense, so much the same ! He has travelled in a circle, as all things heavenly and earthly do, and now comes back to his original self, with an inestimable treasure of improvement won from an experience of pain. How wonderful is this ! I tremble at my own thoughts, yet must needs probe them to their depths. Was the crime — in which he and I were wedded — was it a blessing, in that strange disguise ? Was it a means of education, bringing a simple and imperfect nature to a point of feeling and intelligence which it could have reached under no other discipline ? "

" You stir up deep and perilous matter, Miriam," replied Kenyon. " I dare not follow you into the un- fathomable abysses whither you are tending."

" Yet there is a pleasure in them ! I delight to brood on the verge of this great mystery," returned she. " The story of the fall of man ! Is it not re- peated in our romance of Monte Beni ? And may we follow the analogy yet further ? Was that very sin, — into which Adam precipitated himself and all his race, — was it the destined means by which, over a long pathway of toil and sorrow, we are to attain a higher, brighter, and profounder happiness, than our lost birthright gave ? Will not this idea account for the permitted existence of sin, as no other theory can ? "

" It is too dangerous, Miriam ! I cannot follow you ! " repeated the sculptor. " Mortal man has no right to tread on the ground where you now set your feet."

"Ask Hilda what she thinks of it," said Miriam, with a thoughtful smile. "At least, she might conclude that sin — which man chose instead of good — has been so beneficently handled by omniscience and omnipotence, that, whereas our dark enemy sought to destroy us by it, it has really become an instrument most effective in the education of intellect and soul."

Miriam paused a little longer among these meditations, which the sculptor rightly felt to be so perilous; she then pressed his hand, in token of farewell.

"The day after to-morrow," said she, "an hour before sunset, go to the Corso, and stand in front of the fifth house on your left, beyond the Antonine column. You will learn tidings of a friend."

Kenyon would have besought her for more definite intelligence, but she shook her head, put her finger on her lips, and turned away with an illusive smile. The fancy impressed him, that she, too, like Donatello, had reached a wayside paradise, in their mysterious life-journey, where they both threw down the burden of the before and after, and, except for this interview with himself, were happy in the flitting moment. To-day, Donatello was the sylvan Faun; to-day, Miriam was his fit companion, a Nymph of grove or fountain; to-morrow, — a remorseful man and woman, linked by a marriage-bond of crime, — they would set forth towards an inevitable goal.

CHAPTER XLVIII.

ON the appointed afternoon, Kenyon failed not to
make his appearance in the Corso, and at an hour
much earlier than Miriam had named.

It was carnival time. The merriment of this famous festival was in full progress ; and the stately
avenue of the Corso was peopled with hundreds of fantastic shapes, some of which probably represented the
mirth of ancient times, surviving through all manner
of calamity, ever since the days of the Roman Empire.
For a few afternoons of early spring, this mouldy gayety strays into the sunshine ; all the remainder of the
year, it seems to be shut up in the catacombs or some
other sepulchral storehouse of the past.

Besides these hereditary forms, at which a hundred
generations have laughed, there were others of modern
date, the humorous effluence of the day that was now
passing. It is a day, however, and an age, that appears to be remarkably barren, when compared with
the prolific originality of former times, in productions
of a scenic and ceremonial character, whether grave
or gay. To own the truth, the Carnival is alive, this
present year, only because it has existed through centuries gone by. It is traditionary, not actual. If
decrepit and melancholy Rome smiles, and laughs
broadly, indeed, at carnival time, it is not in the old
simplicity of real mirth, but with a half - conscious

effort, like our self-deceptive pretence of jollity at a threadbare joke. Whatever it may once have been, it is now but a narrow stream of merriment, noisy of set purpose, running along the middle of the Corso, through the solemn heart of the decayed city, without extending its shallow influence on either side. Nor, even within its own limits, does it affect the mass of spectators, but only a comparatively few, in street and balcony, who carry on the warfare of nosegays and counterfeit sugar-plums. The populace look on with staid composure; the nobility and priesthood take little or no part in the matter ; and, but for the hordes of Anglo-Saxons who annually take up the flagging mirth, the Carnival might long ago have been swept away, with the snow-drifts of confetti that whiten all the pavement.

No doubt, however, the worn-out festival is still new to the youthful and light-hearted, who make the worn-out world itself as fresh as Adam found it on his first forenoon in Paradise. It may be only age and care that chill the life out of its grotesque and airy riot, with the impertinence of their cold criticism.

Kenyon, though young, had care enough within his breast to render the Carnival the emptiest of mockeries. Contrasting the stern anxiety of his present mood with the frolic spirit of the preceding year, he fancied that so much trouble had, at all events, brought wisdom in its train. But there is a wisdom that looks grave, and sneers at merriment ; and again a deeper wisdom, that stoops to be gay as often as occasion serves, and oftenest avails itself of shallow and trifling grounds of mirth ; because, if we wait for more substantial ones, we seldom can be gay at all. Therefore, had it been possible, Kenyon would have done well to mask himself in some wild, hairy visage, and plunge into the throng of other maskers, as at the Carnival before. Then, Donatello had danced along the Corso in all the equipment of a Faun, doing the part with wonderful felicity of execution, and revealing furry ears, which looked absolutely real; and Miriam had been, alternately, a lady of the antique régime, in powder and brocade, and the prettiest peasant-girl of the Campagna, in the gayest of costumes; while Hilda, sitting demurely in a balcony, had hit the sculptor with a single rose-bud, — so sweet and fresh a bud that he knew at once whose hand had flung it.

These were all gone; all those dear friends whose sympathetic mirth had made him gay. Kenyon felt as if an interval of many years had passed since the last Carnival. He had grown old, the nimble jollity was tame, and the maskers dull and heavy; the Corso was but a narrow and shabby street of decaying palaces; and even the long, blue streamer of Italian sky, above it, not half so brightly blue as formerly.

Yet, if he could have beheld the scene with his clear, natural eyesight, he might still have found both merriment and splendor in it. Everywhere, and all day long, there had been tokens of the festival, in the baskets brimming over with bouquets, for sale at the street-corners, or borne about on people's heads; while bushels upon bushels of variously colored confetti were displayed, looking just like veritable sugar-plums; so that a stranger would have imagined that the whole commerce and business of stern old Rome lay in flowers and sweets. And, now, in the sunny afternoon, there could hardly be a spectacle more picturesque than the vista of that noble street, stretching into the interminable distance between two rows of lofty edi-

fices, from every window of which, and many a balcony, flaunted gay and gorgeous carpets, bright silks,
scarlet cloths with rich golden fringes, and Gobelin
tapestry, still lustrous with varied hues, though the
product of antique looms. Each separate palace had
put on a gala-dress, and looked festive for the occasion,
whatever sad or guilty secret it might hide within.
Every window, moreover, was alive with the faces of
women, rosy girls, and children, all kindled into brisk
and mirthful expression, by the incidents in the street
below. In the balconies that projected along the palace fronts stood groups of ladies, some beautiful, all
richly dressed, scattering forth their laughter, shrill,
yet sweet, and the musical babble of their voices, to
thicken into an airy tumult over the heads of common
mortals.

All these innumerable eyes looked down into the
street, the whole capacity of which was thronged with
festal figures, in such fantastic variety that it had
taken centuries to contrive them; and through the
midst of the mad, merry stream of human life, rolled
slowly onward a never-ending procession of all the
vehicles in Rome, from the ducal carriage, with the
powdered coachman high in front, and the three golden
lackeys, clinging in the rear, down to the rustic cart
drawn by its single donkey. Among this various
crowd, at windows and in balconies, in cart, cab, barouche, or gorgeous equipage, or bustling to and fro
afoot, there was a sympathy of nonsense; a true and
genial brotherhood and sisterhood, based on the honest
purpose — and a wise one, too — of being foolish, all
together. The sport of mankind, like its deepest earnest, is a battle; so these festive people fought one another with an ammunition of sugar-plums and flowers.

Not that they were veritable sugar-plums, however, but something that resembled them only as the apples of Sodom look like better fruit. They were concocted mostly of lime, with a grain of oat, or some other worthless kernel, in the midst. Besides the hail-storm of confetti, the combatants threw handfuls of flour or lime into the air, where it hung like smoke over a battle-field, or, descending, whitened a black coat or priestly robe, and made the curly locks of youth irreverently hoary.

At the same time with this acrid contest of quick-lime, which caused much effusion of tears from suffering eyes, a gentler warfare of flowers was carried on, principally between knights and ladies. Originally, no doubt, when this pretty custom was first instituted, it may have had a sincere and modest import. Each youth and damsel, gathering bouquets of field-flowers, or the sweetest and fairest that grew in their own gardens, all fresh and virgin blossoms, flung them, with true aim, at the one, or few, whom they regarded with a sentiment of shy partiality at least, if not with love. Often, the lover in the Corso may thus have received from his bright mistress, in her father's princely balcony, the first sweet intimation that his passionate glances had not struck against a heart of marble. What more appropriate mode of suggesting her tender secret could a maiden find than by the soft hit of a rose-bud against a young man's cheek.

This was the pastime and the earnest of a more innocent and homelier age. Nowadays, the nosegays are gathered and tied up by sordid hands, chiefly of the most ordinary flowers, and are sold along the Corso, at mean price, yet more than such venal things are worth. Buying a basketful, you find them miserably wilted, as if they had flown hither and thither through two or three carnival days already; muddy, too, having been fished up from the pavement, where a hundred feet have trampled on them. You may see throngs of men and boys who thrust themselves beneath the horses' hoofs to gather up bouquets that were aimed amiss from balcony and carriage; these they sell again, and yet once more, and ten times over, defiled as they all are with the wicked filth of Rome.

Such are the flowery favors — the fragrant bunches of sentiment — that fly between cavalier and dame, and back again, from one end of the Corso to the other. Perhaps they may symbolize, more aptly than was intended, the poor, battered, wilted hearts of those who fling them; hearts which — crumpled and crushed by former possessors, and stained with various mishap — have been passed from hand to hand along the muddy street-way of life, instead of being treasured in one faithful bosom.

These venal and polluted flowers, therefore, and those deceptive bonbons, are types of the small reality that still subsists in the observance of the Carnival. Yet the government seemed to imagine that there might be excitement enough, — wild mirth, perchance, following its antics beyond law, and frisking from frolic into earnest, — to render it expedient to guard the Corso with an imposing show of military power. Besides the ordinary force of gendarmes, a strong patrol of papal dragoons, in steel helmets and white cloaks, were stationed at all the street-corners. Detachments of French infantry stood by their stacked muskets in the Piazza del Popolo, at one extremity of the course, and before the palace of the Austrian embassy, at the other, and by the column of Antoninus, midway between. Had that chained tiger-cat, the Roman populace, shown only so much as the tip of his claws, the sabres would have been flashing and the bullets whistling, in right earnest, among the combatants who now pelted one another with mock sugarplums and wilted flowers.

But, to do the Roman people justice, they were restrained by a better safeguard than the sabre or the bayonet ; it was their own gentle courtesy, which imparted a sort of sacredness to the hereditary festival. At first sight of a spectacle so fantastic and extravagant, a cool observer might have imagined the whole town gone mad ; but, in the end, he would see that all this apparently unbounded license is kept strictly within a limit of its own ; he would admire a people who can so freely let loose their mirthful propensities, while muzzling those fiercer ones that tend to mischief. Everybody seemed lawless; nobody was rude. If any reveller overstepped the mark, it was sure to be no Roman, but an Englishman or an American ; and even the rougher play of this Gothic race was still softened by the insensible influence of a moral atmosphere more delicate, in some respects, than we breathe at home. Not that, after all, we like the fine Italian spirit better than our own ; popular rudeness is sometimes the symptom of rude moral health. But, where a Carnival is in question, it would probably pass off more decorously, as well as more airily and delightfully, in Rome, than in any Anglo-Saxon city.

When Kenyon emerged from a side-lane into the Corso, the mirth was at its height. Out of the seclusion of his own feelings, he looked forth at the tapestried and damask-curtained palaces, the slow-moving, double line of carriages, and the motley maskers that swarmed on foot, as if he were gazing through the iron lattice of a prison-window. So remote from the scene were his sympathies, that it affected him like a thin dream, through the dim, extravagant material of which he could discern more substantial objects, while too much under its control to start forth broad awake. Just at that moment, too, there came another spectacle, making its way right through the masquerading throng.

It was, first and foremost, a full band of martial music, reverberating, in that narrow and confined, though stately avenue, between the walls of the lofty palaces, and roaring upward to the sky, with melody so powerful that it almost grew to discord. Next came a body of cavalry and mounted gendarmes, with great display of military pomp. They were escorting a long train of equipages, each and all of which shone as gorgeously as Cinderella's coach, with paint and gilding. Like that, too, they were provided with coachmen, of mighty breadth, and enormously tall footmen, in immense, powdered wigs, and all the splendor of gold-laced, three-cornered hats, and embroidered silk coats and breeches. By the old-fashioned magnificence of this procession, it might worthily have included his Holiness in person, with a suite of attendant Cardinals, if those sacred dignitaries would kindly have lent their aid to heighten the frolic of the Carnival. But, for all its show of a martial escort, and its antique splendor of costume, it was but a train of the municipal authorities of Rome, — illusive shadows, every one, and among them a phantom, styled the Roman Senator. — proceeding to the Capitol.

The riotous interchange of nosegays and confetti was partially suspended, while the procession passed

One well - directed shot, however, — it was a double handful of powdered lime, flung by an impious New-Englander, — hit the coachman of the Roman Senator full in the face, and hurt his dignity amazingly. It appeared to be his opinion, that the Republic was again crumbling into ruin, and that the dust of it now filled his nostrils; though, in fact, it would hardly be distinguished from the official powder with which he was already plentifully bestrewn.

While the sculptor, with his dreamy eyes, was taking idle note of this trifling circumstance, two figures passed before him, hand in hand. The countenance of each was covered with an impenetrable black mask; but one seemed a peasant of the Campagna; the other, a contadina in her holiday costume.

CHAPTER XLIX.

THE crowd and confusion, just at that moment, hindered the sculptor from pursuing these figures, — the peasant and contadina, — who, indeed, were but two of a numerous tribe that thronged the Corso, in similar costume. As soon as he could squeeze a passage, Kenyon tried to follow in their footsteps, but quickly lost sight of them, and was thrown off the track by stopping to examine various groups of masqueraders, in which he fancied the objects of his search to be included. He found many a sallow peasant or herdsman of the Campagna, in such a dress as Donatello wore ; many a contadina, too, brown, broad, and sturdy, in her finery of scarlet, and decked out with gold or coral beads, a pair of heavy ear-rings, a curiously wrought cameo or mosaic brooch, and a silver comb or long stiletto among her glossy hair. But those shapes of grace and beauty, which he sought, had vanished.

As soon as the procession of the Senator had passed, the merry-makers resumed their antics with fresh spirit, and the artillery of bouquets and sugar-plums, suspended for a moment, began anew. The sculptor himself, being probably the most anxious and unquiet spectator there, was especially a mark for missiles from all quarters, and for the practical jokes which the license of the Carnival permits. In fact, his sad and contracted brow so ill accorded with the scene, that the revellers might be pardoned for thus using him as the butt of their idle mirth, since he evidently could not otherwise contribute to it.

Fantastic figures, with bulbous heads, the circumference of a bushel, grinned enormously in his face. Harlequins struck him with their wooden swords, and appeared to expect his immediate transformation into some jollier shape. A little, long-tailed, horned fiend sidled up to him, and suddenly blew at him through a tube, enveloping our poor friend in a whole harvest of winged seeds. A biped, with an ass's snout, brayed close to his ear, ending his discordant uproar with a peal of human laughter. Five strapping damsels — so, at least, their petticoats bespoke them, in spite of an awful freedom in the flourish of their legs — joined hands, and danced around him, inviting him by their gestures to perform a hornpipe in the midst. Released from these gay persecutors, a clown in motley rapped him on the back with a blown bladder, in which a handful of dried peas rattled horribly.

Unquestionably, a care-stricken mortal has no business abroad, when the rest of mankind are at high carnival ; they must either pelt him and absolutely martyr him with jests, and finally bury him beneath the aggregate heap ; or else the potency of his darker mood, because the tissue of human life takes a sad dye more readily than a gay one, will quell their holiday humors, like the aspect of a death's-head at a banquet. Only that we know Kenyon's errand, we could hardly forgive him for venturing into the Corso with that troubled face.

Even yet, his merry martyrdom was not half over. There came along a gigantic female figure, seven feet high, at least, and taking up a third of the street's breadth with the preposterously swelling sphere of her crinoline skirts. Singling out the sculptor, she began to make a ponderous assault upon his heart, throwing amorous glances at him out of her great goggle-eyes, offering him a vast bouquet of sunflowers and nettles, and soliciting his pity by all sorts of pathetic and passionate dumb-show. Her suit meeting no favor, the rejected Titaness made a gesture of despair and rage; then suddenly drawing a huge pistol, she took aim right at the obdurate sculptor's breast, and pulled the trigger. The shot took effect, for the abominable plaything went off by a spring, like a boy's popgun, covering Kenyon with a cloud of lime-dust, under shelter of which the revengeful damsel strode away.

Hereupon, a whole host of absurd figures surrounded him pretending to sympathize in his mishap. Clowns and party-colored harlequins; orang-outangs; bear-headed, bull-headed, and dog-headed individuals; faces that would have been human, but for their enormous noses; one terrific creature, with a visage right in the centre of his breast; and all other imaginable kinds of monstrosity and exaggeration. These apparitions appeared to be investigating the case, after the fashion of a coroner's jury, poking their pasteboard countenances close to the sculptor's with an unchangeable grin, that gave still more ludicrous effect to the comic alarm and sorrow of their gestures. Just then, a figure came by, in a gray wig and rusty gown, with an inkhorn at his button-hole, and a pen behind his ear; he announced himself as a notary, and offered to make the last will and testament of the assassinated man. This solemn duty, however, was interrupted by a surgeon, who brandished a lancet, three feet long, and proposed to him to let him take blood.

The affair was so like a feverish dream, that Kenyon resigned himself to let it take its course. Fortunately the humors of the Carnival pass from one absurdity to another, without lingering long enough on any, to wear out even the slightest of them. The passiveness of his demeanor afforded too little scope for such broad merriment as the masqueraders sought. In a few moments they vanished from him, as dreams and spectres do, leaving him at liberty to pursue his quest, with no impediment except the crowd that blocked up the footway.

He had not gone far when the peasant and the contadina met him. They were still hand in hand, and appeared to be straying through the grotesque and animated scene, taking as little part in it as himself. It might be because he recognized them, and knew their solemn secret, that the sculptor fancied a melancholy emotion to be expressed by the very movement and attitudes of these two figures ; and even the grasp of their hands, uniting them so closely, seemed to set them in a sad remoteness from the world at which they gazed.

"I rejoice to meet you," said Kenyon.

But they looked at him through the eye-holes of their black masks, without answering a word.

"Pray give me a little light on the matter which I have so much at heart," said he; "if you know anything of Hilda, for Heaven's sake, speak!"

Still, they were silent; and the sculptor began to imagine that he must have mistaken the identity of these figures, there being such a multitude in similar costume. Yet there was no other Donatello, no other Miriam. He felt, too, that spiritual certainty which impresses us with the presence of our friends, apart from any testimony of the senses.

"You are unkind," resumed he, — "knowing the anxiety which oppresses me, — not to relieve it, if in your power."

The reproach evidently had its effect; for the contadina now spoke, and it was Miriam's voice.

"We gave you all the light we could," said she. "You are yourself unkind, though you little think how much so, to come between us at this hour. There may be a sacred hour, even in carnival time."

In another state of mind, Kenyon could have been amused by the impulsiveness of this response, and a sort of vivacity that he had often noted in Miriam's conversation. But he was conscious of a profound sadness in her tone, overpowering its momentary irritation, and assuring him that a pale, tear-stained face was hidden behind her mask.

"Forgive me!" said he.

Donatello here extended his hand, — not that which was clasping Miriam's, — and she, too, put her free one into the sculptor's left; so that they were a linked circle of three, with many reminiscences and forebodings flashing through their hearts. Kenyon knew intuitively that these once familiar friends were parting with him, now.

"Farewell!" they all three said, in the same breath.

No sooner was the word spoken, than they loosed their hands; and the uproar of the Carnival swept like a tempestuous sea over the spot, which they had included within their small circle of isolated feeling.

By this interview, the sculptor had learned nothing in reference to Hilda; but he understood that he was to adhere to the instructions already received, and await a solution of the mystery in some mode that he could not yet anticipate. Passing his hands over his eyes, and looking about him, — for the event just described had made the scene even more dreamlike than before, — he now found himself approaching that broad piazza bordering on the Corso, which has for its central object the sculptured column of Antoninus. It was not far from this vicinity that Miriam had bid him wait. Struggling onward, as fast as the tide of merry-makers, setting strong against him, would permit, he was now beyond the Palazzo Colonna, and began to count the houses. The fifth was a palace, with a long front upon the Corso, and of stately height, but somewhat grim with age.

Over its arched and pillared entrance there was a balcony, richly hung with tapestry and damask, and tenanted, for the time, by a gentleman of venerable aspect, and a group of ladies. The white hair and whiskers of the former, and the winter-roses in his cheeks, had an English look; the ladies, too, showed a fair-haired Saxon bloom, and seemed to taste the mirth of the Carnival with the freshness of spectators to whom the scene was new. All the party, the old gentleman with grave earnestness, as if he were defending a rampart, and his young companions with exuberance of frolic, showered confetti inexhaustibly upon the passers-by.

In the rear of the balcony, a broad-brimmed, ecclesiastical beaver was visible. An abbate, probably an acquaintance and cicerone of the English family, was sitting there, and enjoying the scene, though partially withdrawn from view, as the decorum for his order dictated.

There seemed no better nor other course for Kenyon, than to keep watch at this appointed spot, waiting for whatever should happen next. Clasping his arm

round a lamp-post, to prevent being carried away by
the turbulent stream of wayfarers, he scrutinized every
face, with the idea that some one of them might meet
his eyes with a glance of intelligence. He looked at
each mask, — harlequin, ape, bulbous-headed monster,
or anything that was absurdest, — not knowing but
that the messenger might come, even in such fantastic
guise. Or, perhaps, one of those quaint figures, in the
stately ruff, the cloak, tunic, and trunk-hose, of three
centuries ago, might bring him tidings of Hilda, out
of that long-past age. At times, his disquietude took
a hopeful aspect; and he fancied that Hilda might
come by, her own sweet self, in some shy disguise
which the instinct of his love would be sure to penetrate. Or, she might be borne past on a triumphal
car, like the one just now approaching, its slow-moving wheels encircled and spoked with foliage, and
drawn by horses, that were harnessed and wreathed
with flowers. Being, at best, so far beyond the bounds
of reasonable conjecture, he might anticipate the wildest event, or find either his hopes or fears disappointed
in what appeared most probable.

The old Englishman and his daughters, in the opposite balcony, must have seen something unutterably
absurd in the sculptor's deportment, poring into this
whirlpool of nonsense so earnestly, in quest of what
was to make his life dark or bright. Earnest people,
who try to get a reality out of human existence, are
necessarily absurd in the view of the revellers and
masqueraders. At all events, after a good deal of
mirth at the expense of his melancholy visage, the
fair occupants of the balcony favored Kenyon with a
salvo of confetti, which came rattling about him like
a hail-storm. Looking up, instinctively, he was sur-

prised to see the abbate in the background lean forward and give a courteous sign of recognition.

It was the same old priest with whom he had seen Hilda, at the confessional; the same with whom he had talked of her disappearance on meeting him in the street.

Yet, whatever might be the reason, Kenyon did not now associate this ecclesiastical personage with the idea of Hilda. His eyes lighted on the old man, just for an instant, and then returned to the eddying throng of the Corso, on his minute scrutiny of which depended, for aught he knew, the sole chance of ever finding any trace of her. There was, about this moment, a bustle on the other side of the street, the cause of which Kenyon did not see, nor exert himself to discover. A small party of soldiers or gendarmes appeared to be concerned in it; they were perhaps arresting some disorderly character, who, under the influence of an extra flask of wine, might have reeled across the mystic limitation of carnival proprieties.

The sculptor heard some people near him talking of the incident.

"That contadina, in a black mask, was a fine figure of a woman."

"She was not amiss," replied a female voice; "but her companion was far the handsomer figure of the two. Could they be really a peasant and a contadina, do you imagine?"

"No, no," said the other. "It is some frolic of the Carnival, carried a little too far."

This conversation might have excited Kenyon's interest; only that, just as the last words were spoken, he was hit by two missiles, both of a kind that were flying abundantly on that gay battle-field. One, we

are ashamed to say, was a cauliflower, which, flung by
a young man from a passing carriage, came with a
prodigious thump against his shoulder ; the other was
a single rose-bud, so fresh that it seemed that moment
gathered.   It flew from the opposite balcony, smote
gently on his lips, and fell into his hand.   He looked
upward, and beheld the face of his lost Hilda !

She was dressed in a white domino, and looked pale
and bewildered, and yet full of tender joy.   Moreover,
there was a gleam of delicate mirthfulness in her eyes,
which the sculptor had seen there only two or three
times, in the course of their acquaintance, but thought
it the most bewitching and fairy-like of all Hilda's expressions.   That soft, mirthful smile caused her to
melt, as it were, into the wild frolic of the Carnival,
and become not so strange and alien to the scene, as
her unexpected apparition must otherwise have made
her.

Meanwhile, the venerable Englishman and his
daughters were staring at poor Hilda in a way that
proved them altogether astonished, as well as inexpressibly shocked, by her sudden intrusion into their
private balcony.   They looked, — as, indeed, English
people of respectability would, if an angel were to
alight in their circle, without due introduction from
somebody whom they knew, in the court above, —
they looked as if an unpardonable liberty had been
taken, and a suitable apology must be made ; after
which, the intruder would be expected to withdraw.

The abbate, however, drew the old gentleman aside,
and whispered a few words that served to mollify
him ; he bestowed on Hilda a sufficiently benignant,
though still a perplexed and questioning regard, and
invited her, in dumb-show, to put herself at her ease.

But, whoever was in fault, our shy and gentle Hilda had dreamed of no intrusion. Whence she had come, or where she had been hidden, during this mysterious interval, we can but imperfectly surmise, and do not mean, at present, to make it a matter of formal explanation with the reader. It is better, perhaps, to fancy that she had been snatched away to a land of picture ; that she had been straying with Claude in the golden light which he used to shed over his landscapes, but which he could never have beheld with his waking eyes till he awoke in the better clime. We will imagine that, for the sake of the true simplicity with which she loved them, Hilda had been permitted, for a season, to converse with the great, departed masters of the pencil, and behold the diviner works which they have painted in heavenly colors. Guido had shown her another portrait of Beatrice Cenci, done from the celestial life, in which that forlorn mystery of the earthly countenance was exchanged for a radiant joy. Perugino had allowed her a glimpse at his easel, on which she discerned what seemed a woman's face, but so divine, by the very depth and softness of its womanhood, that a gush of happy tears blinded the maiden's eyes before she had time to look. Raphael had taken Hilda by the hand, — that fine, forcible hand which Kenyon sculptured, — and drawn aside the curtain of gold-fringed cloud that hung before his latest masterpiece. On earth, Raphael painted the Transfiguration. What higher scene may he have since depicted, not from imagination, but as revealed to his actual sight !

Neither will we retrace the steps by which she returned to the actual world. For the present, be it enough to say that Hilda had been summoned forth from a secret place, and led we know not through what mysterious passages, to a point where the tumult of life burst suddenly upon her ears. She heard the tramp of footsteps, the rattle of wheels, and the mingled hum of a multitude of voices, with strains of music and loud laughter breaking through. Emerging into a great, gloomy hall, a curtain was drawn aside; she found herself gently propelled into an open balcony, whence she looked out upon the festal street, with gay tapestries flaunting over all the palace fronts, the windows thronged with merry faces, and a crowd of maskers rioting upon the pavement below.

Immediately, she seemed to become a portion of the scene. Her pale, large-eyed, fragile beauty, her wondering aspect and bewildered grace, attracted the gaze of many; and there fell around her a shower of bouquets, and bonbons — freshest blossoms and sweetest sugar-plums, sweets to the sweet — such as the revellers of the Carnival reserve as tributes to especial loveliness. Hilda pressed her hand across her brow; she let her eyelids fall, and, lifting them again, looked through the grotesque and gorgeous show, the chaos of mad jollity, in quest of some object by which she might assure herself that the whole spectacle was not an illusion.

Beneath the balcony, she recognized a familiar and fondly remembered face. The spirit of the hour and the scene exercised its influence over her quick and sensitive nature; she caught up one of the rose-buds that had been showered upon her, and aimed it at the sculptor. It hit the mark; he turned his sad eyes upward, and there was Hilda, in whose gentle presence his own secret sorrow and the obtrusive uproar of the Carnival alike died away from his perception.

That night, the lamp beneath the Virgin's shrine burned as brightly as if it had never been extinguished; and though the one faithful dove had gone to her melancholy perch, she greeted Hilda rapturously the next morning, and summoned her less constant companions, whithersoever they had flown, to renew their homage.

CHAPTER L.

MIRIAM, HILDA, KENYON, DONATELLO.

THE gentle reader, we trust, would not thank us for one of those minute elucidations, which are so tedious, and, after all, so unsatisfactory, in clearing up the romantic mysteries of a story. He is too wise to insist upon looking closely at the wrong side of the tapestry, after the right one has been sufficiently displayed to him, woven with the best of the artist's skill, and cunningly arranged with a view to the harmonious exhibition of its colors. If any brilliant, or beautiful, or even tolerable effect have been produced, this pattern of kindly readers will accept it at its worth, without tearing its web apart, with the idle purpose of discovering how the threads have been knit together; for the sagacity by which he is distinguished will long ago have taught him that any narrative of human action and adventure — whether we call it history or romance — is certain to be a fragile handiwork, more easily rent than mended. The actual experience of even the most ordinary life is full of events that never explain themselves, either as regards their origin or their tendency.

It would be easy, from conversations which we have held with the sculptor, to suggest a clew to the mystery of Hilda's disappearance; although, as long as she remained in Italy, there was a remarkable reserve in her communications upon this subject, even to her most intimate friends. Either a pledge of secrecy had been exacted, or a prudential motive warned her not to reveal the stratagems of a religious body, or the secret acts of a despotic government — whichever might be responsible in the present instance — while still within the scope of their jurisdiction. Possibly, she might not herself be fully aware what power had laid its grasp upon her person. What has chiefly perplexed us, however, among Hilda's adventures, is the mode of her release, in which some inscrutable tyranny or other seemed to take part in the frolic of the Carnival. We can only account for it, by supposing that the fitful and fantastic imagination of a woman — sportive, because she must otherwise be desperate — had arranged this incident, and made it the condition of a step which her conscience, or the conscience of another, required her to take.

A few days after Hilda's reappearance, she and the sculptor were straying together through the streets of Rome. Being deep in talk, it so happened that they found themselves near the majestic, pillared portico, and huge, black rotundity of the Pantheon. It stands almost at the central point of the labyrinthine intricacies of the modern city, and often presents itself before the bewildered stranger, when he is in search of other objects. Hilda, looking up, proposed that they should enter.

" I never pass it without going in," she said, " to pay my homage at the tomb of Raphael."

" Nor I," said Kenyon, " without stopping to admire the noblest edifice which the barbarism of the early ages, and the more barbarous pontiffs and princes of later ones, have spared to us."

They went in, accordingly, and stood in the free

space of that great circle, around which are ranged the arched recesses and stately altars, formerly dedicated to heathen gods, but Christianized through twelve centuries gone by. The world has nothing else like the Pantheon. So grand it is, that the pasteboard statues over the lofty cornice do not disturb the effect, any more than the tin crowns and hearts, the dusty artificial flowers, and all manner of trumpery gewgaws, hanging at the saintly shrines. The rust and dinginess that have dimmed the precious marble on the walls; the pavement, with its great squares and rounds of porphyry and granite, cracked crosswise and in a hundred directions, showing how roughly the troublesome ages have trampled here; the gray dome above, with its opening to the sky, as if heaven were looking down into the interior of this place of worship, left unimpeded for prayers to ascend the more freely: all these things make an impression of solemnity, which St. Peter's itself fails to produce.

"I think," said the sculptor, "it is to the aperture in the dome — that great Eye, gazing heavenward — that the Pantheon owes the peculiarity of its effect. It is so heathenish, as it were, — so unlike all the snugness of our modern civilization! Look, too, at the pavement, directly beneath the open space! So much rain has fallen there, in the last two thousand years, that it is green with small, fine moss, such as grows over tombstones in a damp English churchyard."

"I like better," replied Hilda, "to look at the bright, blue sky, roofing the edifice where the builders left it open. It is very delightful, in a breezy day, to see the masses of white cloud float over the opening, and then the sunshine fall through it again, fitfully, as it does now. Would it be any wonder if we were to see angels hovering there, partly in and partly out, with genial, heavenly faces, not intercepting the light, but only transmuting it into beautiful colors? Look at that broad, golden beam — a sloping cataract of sunlight — which comes down from the aperture and rests upon the shrine, at the right hand of the entrance!"

"There is a dusky picture over that altar," observed the sculptor. "Let us go and see if this strong illumination brings out any merit in it."

Approaching the shrine, they found the picture little worth looking at, but could not forbear smiling, to see that a very plump and comfortable tabby-cat — whom we ourselves have often observed haunting the Pantheon — had established herself on the altar, in the genial sunbeam, and was fast asleep among the holy tapers. Their footsteps disturbing her, she awoke, raised herself, and sat blinking in the sun, yet with a certain dignity and self-possession, as if conscious of representing a saint.

"I presume," remarked Kenyon, "that this is the first of the feline race that has ever set herself up as an object of worship, in the Pantheon or elsewhere, since the days of ancient Egypt. See; there is a peasant from the neighboring market, actually kneeling to her! She seems a gracious and benignant saint enough."

"Do not make me laugh," said Hilda, reproachfully, "but help me to drive the creature away. It distresses me to see that poor man, or any human being, directing his prayers so much amiss."

"Then, Hilda," answered the sculptor, more seriously, "the only place in the Pantheon for you and me to kneel is on the pavement beneath the central aperture. If we pray at a saint's shrine, we shall give utterance to earthly wishes; but if we pray face to face with the Deity, we shall feel it impious to petition for aught that is narrow and selfish. Methinks, it is this that makes the Catholics so delight in the worship of saints; they can bring up all their little worldly wants and whims, their individualities and human weaknesses, not as things to be repented of, but to be humored by the canonized humanity to which they pray. Indeed, it is very tempting!"

What Hilda might have answered must be left to conjecture; for as she turned from the shrine, her eyes were attracted to the figure of a female penitent, kneeling on the pavement just beneath the great central eye, in the very spot which Kenyon had designated as the only one whence prayers should ascend. The upturned face was invisible, behind a veil or mask, which formed a part of the garb.

"It cannot be!" whispered Hilda, with emotion. "No; it cannot be!"

"What disturbs you?" asked Kenyon. "Why do you tremble so?"

"If it were possible," she replied, "I should fancy that kneeling figure to be Miriam!"

"As you say, it is impossible," rejoined the sculptor. "We know too well what has befallen both her and Donatello."

"Yes; it is impossible!" repeated Hilda.

Her voice was still tremulous, however, and she seemed unable to withdraw her attention from the kneeling figure. Suddenly, and as if the idea of Miriam had opened the whole volume of Hilda's reminiscences, she put this question to the sculptor: —

"Was Donatello really a Faun?"

"If you had ever studied the pedigree of the far-descended heir of Monte Beni, as I did," answered Kenyon, with an irrepressible smile, "you would have retained few doubts on that point. Faun or not, he had a genial nature, which, had the rest of mankind been in accordance with it, would have made earth a paradise to our poor friend. It seems the moral of his story, that human beings of Donatello's character, compounded especially for happiness, have no longer any business on earth, or elsewhere. Life has grown so sadly serious, that such men must change their nature, or else perish, like the antediluvian creatures, that required, as the condition of their existence, a more summer-like atmosphere than ours."

"I will not accept your moral!" replied the hopeful and happy-natured Hilda.

"Then here is another; take your choice!" said the sculptor, remembering what Miriam had recently suggested, in reference to the same point. "He perpetrated a great crime; and his remorse, gnawing into his soul, has awakened it; developing a thousand high capabilities, moral and intellectual, which we never should have dreamed of asking for, within the scanty compass of the Donatello whom we knew."

"I know not whether this is so," said Hilda. "But what then?"

"Here comes my perplexity," continued Kenyon. "Sin has educated Donatello, and elevated him. Is sin, then, — which we deem such a dreadful blackness in the universe, — is it, like sorrow, merely an element of human education, through which we struggle to a higher and purer state than we could otherwise have attained? Did Adam fall, that we might ultimately rise to a far loftier paradise than his?"

"Oh, hush!" cried Hilda, shrinking from him with an expression of horror which wounded the poor, speculative sculptor to the soul. "This is terrible; and I could weep for you, if you indeed believe it. Do not you perceive what a mockery your creed makes, not only of all religious sentiments, but of moral law? and how it annuls and obliterates whatever precepts of Heaven are written deepest within us? You have shocked me beyond words!"

"Forgive me, Hilda!" exclaimed the sculptor, startled by her agitation; "I never did believe it! But the mind wanders wild and wide; and, so lonely as I live and work, I have neither pole-star above nor light of cottage-windows here below, to bring me home. Were you my guide, my counsellor, my inmost friend, with that white wisdom which clothes you as a celestial garment, all would go well. O Hilda, guide me home!"

"We are both lonely; both far from home!" said Hilda, her eyes filling with tears. "I am a poor, weak girl, and have no such wisdom as you fancy in me."

What further may have passed between these lovers, while standing before the pillared shrine, and the marble Madonna that marks Raphael's tomb, whither they had now wandered, we are unable to record. But when the kneeling figure beneath the open eye of the Pantheon arose, she looked towards the pair, and extended her hands with a gesture of benediction. Then they knew that it was Miriam. They suffered her to glide out of the portal, however, without a greeting; for those extended hands, even while they blessed, seemed to repel, as if Miriam stood on the other side of a fathomless abyss, and warned them from its verge.

So Kenyon won the gentle Hilda's shy affection,

and her consent to be his bride. Another hand must
henceforth trim the lamp before the Virgin's shrine;
for Hilda was coming down from her old tower, to be
herself enshrined and worshipped as a household saint,
in the light of her husband's fireside. And, now that
life had so much human promise in it, they resolved to
go back to their own land; because the years, after
all, have a kind of emptiness, when we spend too many
of them on a foreign shore. We defer the reality of
life, in such cases, until a future moment, when we
shall again breathe our native air; but, by and by,
there are no future moments; or, if we do return, we
find that the native air has lost its invigorating quality, and that life has shifted its reality to the spot
where we have deemed ourselves only temporary residents. Thus, between two countries, we have none at
all, or only that little space of either, in which we
finally lay down our discontented bones. It is wise,
therefore, to come back betimes, or never.

Before they quitted Rome, a bridal gift was laid on
Hilda's table. It was a bracelet, evidently of great
cost, being composed of seven ancient Etruscan gems,
dug out of seven sepulchres, and each one of them the
signet of some princely personage, who had lived an
immemorial time ago. Hilda remembered this precious ornament. It had been Miriam's; and once,
with the exuberance of fancy that distinguished her,
she had amused herself with telling a mythical and
magic legend for each gem, comprising the imaginary
adventures and catastrophe of its former wearer. Thus,
the Etruscan bracelet became the connecting bond of
a series of seven wondrous tales, all of which, as they
were dug out of seven sepulchres, were characterized
by a seven-fold sepulchral gloom; such as Miriam's

imagination, shadowed by her own misfortunes, was
wont to fling over its most sportive flights.

And now, happy as Hilda was, the bracelet brought
the tears into her eyes, as being, in its entire circle,
the symbol of as sad a mystery as any that Miriam
had attached to the separate gems. For, what was
Miriam's life to be? And where was Donatello?
But Hilda had a hopeful soul, and saw sunlight on
the mountain-tops.

CONCLUSION.

THERE comes to the author, from many readers of
the foregoing pages, a demand for further elucidations
respecting the mysteries of the story.

He reluctantly avails himself of the opportunity afforded by a new edition, to explain such incidents and
passages as may have been left too much in the dark ;
reluctantly, he repeats, because the necessity makes
him sensible that he can have succeeded but imperfectly, at best, in throwing about this Romance the
kind of atmosphere essential to the effect at which he
aimed.

He designed the story and the characters to bear, of
course, a certain relation to human nature and human
life, but still to be so artfully and airily removed from
our mundane sphere, that some laws and proprieties
of their own should be implicitly and insensibly acknowledged.

The idea of the modern Faun, for example, loses all
the poetry and beauty which the Author fancied in it,
and becomes nothing better than a grotesque absurdity, if we bring it into the actual light of day. He
had hoped to mystify this anomalous creature between
the Real and the Fantastic, in such a manner that the

reader's sympathies might be excited to a certain pleasurable degree, without impelling him to ask how Cuvier would have classified poor Donatello, or to insist upon being told, in so many words, whether he had furry ears or no. As respects all who ask such questions, the book is, to that extent, a failure.

Nevertheless, the Author fortunately has it in his power to throw light upon several matters in which some of his readers appear to feel an interest. To confess the truth, he was himself troubled with a curiosity similar to that which he has just deprecated on the part of his readers, and once took occasion to cross-examine his friends, Hilda and the sculptor, and to pry into several dark recesses of the story, with which they had heretofore imperfectly acquainted him.

We three had climbed to the top of St. Peter's, and were looking down upon the Rome we were soon to leave, but which (having already sinned sufficiently in that way) it is not my purpose further to describe. It occurred to me, that, being so remote in the upper air, my friends might safely utter, here, the secrets which it would be perilous even to whisper on lower earth.

" Hilda," I began, " can you tell me the contents of that mysterious packet which Miriam intrusted to your charge, and which was addressed to Signore Luca Barboni, at the Palazzo Cenci ? "

" I never had any further knowledge of it," replied Hilda, " nor felt it right to let myself be curious upon the subject."

" As to its precise contents," interposed Kenyon, " it is impossible to speak. But Miriam, isolated as she seemed, had family connections in Rome, one of whom, there is reason to believe, occupied a position in the papal government.

" This Signore Luca Barboni was either the assumed name of the personage in question, or the medium of communication between that individual and Miriam. Now, under such a government as that of Rome, it is obvious that Miriam's privacy and isolated life could only be maintained through the connivance and support of some influential person connected with the administration of affairs.   Free and self-controlled as she appeared, her every movement was watched and investigated far more thoroughly by the priestly rulers than by her dearest friends.

" Miriam, if I mistake not, had a purpose to withdraw herself from this irksome scrutiny, and to seek real obscurity in another land ; and the packet, to be delivered long after her departure, contained a reference to this design, besides certain family documents, which were to be imparted to her relative as from one dead and gone."

"Yes, it is clear as a London fog," I remarked. " On this head no further elucidation can be desired. But when Hilda went quietly to deliver the packet, why did she so mysteriously vanish?"

" You must recollect," replied Kenyon, with a glance of friendly commiseration at my obtuseness, " that Miriam had utterly disappeared, leaving no trace by which her whereabouts could be known.   In the mean time, the municipal authorities had become aware of the murder of the Capuchin ; and from many preceding circumstances, such as his persecution of Miriam, they must have seen an obvious connection between herself and that tragical event.   Furthermore, there is reason to believe that Miriam was suspected of connection with some plot, or political intrigue, of which there may have been tokens in the packet.   And when Hilda appeared, as the bearer of this missive, it was really quite a matter of course, under a despotic government, that she should be detained."

"Ah, quite a matter of course, as you say," answered I. "How excessively stupid in me not to have seen it sooner! But there are other riddles. On the night of the extinction of the lamp, you met Donatello, in a penitent's garb, and afterwards saw and spoke to Miriam, in a coach, with a gem glowing on her bosom. What was the business of these two guilty ones in Rome, and who was Miriam's companion?"

"Who!" repeated Kenyon, "why her official relative, to be sure; and as to their business, Donatello's still gnawing remorse had brought him hitherward, in spite of Miriam's entreaties, and kept him lingering in the neighborhood of Rome, with the ultimate purpose of delivering himself up to justice. Hilda's disappearance, which took place the day before, was known to them through a secret channel, and had brought them into the city, where Miriam, as I surmise, began to make arrangements, even then, for that sad frolic of the Carnival."

"And where was Hilda all that dreary time between?" inquired I.

"Where were you, Hilda?" asked Kenyon, smiling.

Hilda threw her eyes on all sides, and seeing that there was not even a bird of the air to fly away with the secret, nor any human being nearer than the loiterers by the obelisk, in the piazza below, she told us about her mysterious abode.

"I was a prisoner in the Convent of the Sacré Cœur, in the Trinità de' Monte," said she, "but in such kindly custody of pious maidens, and watched over by such a dear old priest, that — had it not been for one or two disturbing recollections, and also because I am a daughter of the Puritans — I could willingly have dwelt there forever.

"My entanglement with Miriam's misfortunes, and the good abbate's mistaken hope of a proselyte, seem to me a sufficient clew to the whole mystery."

"The atmosphere is getting delightfully lucid," observed I, "but there are one or two things that still puzzle me. Could you tell me — and it shall be kept a profound secret, I assure you — what were Miriam's real name and rank, and precisely the nature of the troubles that led to all those direful consequences?"

"Is it possible that you need an answer to those questions?" exclaimed Kenyon, with an aspect of vast surprise. "Have you not even surmised Miriam's name? Think awhile, and you will assuredly remember it. If not, I congratulate you most sincerely; for it indicates that your feelings have never been harrowed by one of the most dreadful and mysterious events that have occurred within the present century!"

"Well," resumed I, after an interval of deep consideration, "I have but few things more to ask. Where, at this moment, is Donatello?"

"The Castle of Saint Angelo," said Kenyon, sadly, turning his face towards that sepulchral fortress, "is no longer a prison; but there are others which have dungeons as deep, and in one of them, I fear, lies our poor Faun."

"And why, then, is Miriam at large?" I asked.

"Call it cruelty if you like, not mercy," answered Kenyon. "But, after all, her crime lay merely in a glance. She did no murder!"

"Only one question more," said I, with intense earnestness. "Did Donatello's ears resemble those of the Faun of Praxiteles?"

"I know, but may not tell," replied Kenyon, smiling mysteriously. "On that point, at all events, there shall be not one word of explanation."

LEAMINGTON, *March* 14. 1860.